Faith, Hope, Love, and Chocolate

by

Cari Schaeffer

Table of Contents

Acknowledgements

I must, first and foremost, thank God for giving me the desire to write and for allowing me to put words on paper. Without Him, I wouldn't be. I dedicate this story to Him because it is for Him that I write.

There are so many that have come along side me on this journey. I sincerely hope I don't forget anyone. If I do, it's because I'm human and will make mistakes.

I want to thank my mother, Margie, for giving me life in the first place. She was nineteen and already a mother when she had me. I'm so grateful to be here. I thank my father for gifting me with his health, brains, and talent with words (according to my mother that is). I never knew you, but I thank you all the same.

I want to thank DeDee Green Clarey, Celeste Benoist, and Gabriel Necochea for reading some very rough drafts of this work and for offering their honest thoughts and opinions about it. Denise Keller and Carolyn Mers edited my book in great detail from cover to cover and I thank them from the bottom of my heart. It wouldn't be what it is without you! I have to thank Gabriel twice because he also helped me with marketing.

Thanks go out to the ladies of my book club, Books, Bites, and Babes, for sharing my passion for great literature, great company, and great food: Denise, Judi, Nancy, Sara, Debbie, Eileen, Mimi, Kim, and Karen. There have been a number of beautiful ladies in our group over the years. I'm sorry that I can't mention you all. Just know you're always in my heart. Thanks for impacting my life in a positive way!

The O'Fallon Writer's Guild deserves gratitude for welcoming an upstart, wannabe writer to your little group. I love the personalities and the promise that our group holds. I especially want to thank Carolyn, Toya, and Sue for their unwavering support of not only my ambitions, but of my project. You rock and you know it.

I truly don't even know where to start when thanking the CIA. No, not the one you're thinking of. I refer to the Christian Independent Authors group. I am so not kidding when I say that this book wouldn't be in your hand right now if it weren't for them. Terri Main, Jan Thompson, and Lynette Bonner are just a very small sampling of the folks there that have made such a tremendous impact on my life, and not just as an aspiring author. To say thank you is too little to express the depth of my gratitude. I also regret that there isn't enough room to name every member; just know that you may not be named, but you are certainly not forgotten.

I want to thank my friend, Steve, for his help in knowing what government agencies to include in the book so that I don't look like a total dork when I write them into the plot. Thanks, Mr. Semi-Anonymous!

Writing this novel has been such an incredible journey. It started with my love of great books. My family attests to the fact that I have been known to read a great novel in a day. I've read many wonderful books and a few not so great books. In fact, after finishing one particular book that in my opinion was not so great, I slammed it shut and determined to write a novel better than that. So I did, I hope. Write on!

Finally, thank you goes to my readers. I'd like to hear from you, too! I love to talk to book clubs and groups to discuss this book. Please feel free to contact me at www.carischaeffer.com and find me on Facebook, as well.

Chapter One

"But Mom, why *not*?!" whines April as she stamps her foot, clenched fists held close to her side. She stands in the doorway of the kitchen as I begin to pull ingredients out of the refrigerator to make dinner. We are having what feels like the millionth conversation about where she can and cannot go at the age of sixteen.

Sighing, I look her calmly in the eyes. I've learned in my parenting experience that if I keep myself calm, it doesn't necessarily calm April down (does anything?), but it keeps our disagreements from becoming the Strauss family version of World War Three.

"April, honey. You are only sixteen-years-old. Sixteen-year-old girls do not belong in a club. I don't care how many of your friends are going, you are not." Good grief. I hate having these conversations.

"Why don't you ever let me go anywhere?!" she whines, stomping out of the room. The stomping continues up the stairs ending with a final slam of her bedroom door.

I groan and cover my eyes with one hand in exasperation, while the other reaches for a handful of dark chocolate M&Ms from the bowl I keep filled in my kitchen. Marilyn Monroe had it wrong; diamonds aren't a girl's best friend, chocolate is. Sarah clucks her tongue.

As usual, she is reading a book. I drop my hand from my eyes and look at her. My middle child has her left leg tucked under her at the kitchen table. Her light brown hair, the same color as mine, is pulled back in a simple pony tail and she's wearing her usual sweat pants/T shirt combo.

Even though she is only twelve, she has an old soul and is thankfully not prone to emotional outbursts. God had been merciful to me; I couldn't handle two of them. She meets my gaze.

"Sorry, Mom. I think April is over reacting. But that's just how she is," she says matter-of-factly and shrugs her shoulders. Her attention returns to her book. As I regard my middle child and munch my M&Ms, I silently pray she'll stay that way. If I survive April's teen years (key word being if), I hope to get a break with Sarah. Only time will tell.

I return to the refrigerator to finish pulling things out to make dinner. Busying myself at the stove, I mull over this most recent conversation with April.

She's only sixteen and so dramatic about everything. April has always erred on the side of drama. When she was a toddler, if another child took a toy she wanted, she would throw herself down and roll around, crying hysterically.

But going to a club? At sixteen? What kind of mother would I be if I allow that? So many things can happen at a club…I shudder considering the possibilities. She could be mugged, drugged, or kidnapped.

What kind of mothers are allowing their sixteen-year-old daughters to go to clubs anyway? April said her friends Heather and Beth were going. I like those girls; they've always been courteous and respectful to me. I always thought their parents were good, honest people, too. I've only met them a few times, but they didn't seem like the kind of parents that would let a sixteen-year-old go to a club. Maybe I should call them…

The humming sound of the garage door opening interrupts my musing. Michael's home. I put the chicken in the oven just as the mud room door opens. The muted thuds of a book bag and sports gear being dropped quickly follow. Andrew, my youngest child, flies into the kitchen looking filthy and disheveled in his soccer practice clothes. He's grinning from ear to ear, cheeks flushed with excitement. His light brown hair is sticking up in all directions, and his mahogany eyes are shining. We share the same physical characteristics and coloring; I imagine I would've looked just like he does if I'd been born a boy.

"Mom! You'll never guess what! Coach said I could be goalie at our next game!" he blurts, his hands jabbing the air as he talks.

"Oh, honey! That's wonderful news. Congratulations! I'm so proud of you." I smile and hug him fiercely. He smells of earth and little boy. "Now go wash up and put your dirty clothes in the laundry. I've got dinner going." He nods quickly, wriggles out of my arms and runs to tell Sarah the news, even though she heard him the first time. She hasn't moved from her perch at the kitchen table.

Smiling, Michael enters the kitchen from the mud room and strides over to give me a kiss. He always looks so dapper in his suit. I do love a sharp dressed man. I'm glad that Michael's job requires him to dress up; otherwise, he'd wear jeans all the time. He pulls that look off well, too.

"How was your day?" I smile up at him and return the kiss. Michael is six feet two inches tall with clean cut dark hair and ocean blue eyes. From the moment I met him, I was attracted. Although I was terrified of any relationship at the time, I could not deny the immediate physical reaction.

"Busy. You smell like chocolate. Been into the bowl already? You'll ruin your dinner, you know." He casts a sideways glance at the ubiquitous bowl of M&Ms, now half empty.

"Yeah, so?" I respond, jutting my chin out in mock defiance. "I'm a grown up. I can ruin my dinner if I want to."

I can't help my chocolate addiction.

"I may need to buy you a three-pound bag after you hear what I have to say," he says quietly.

"A three-pound bag, huh?" This can't be good. "Why's that?" I ask, not sure I want to hear the answer.

He eyes me carefully. "I have to go to Cleveland for another couple of weeks. There have been some issues with one of the drug trials."

My smile disappears. "What? Again?! But you were just there last month!" Panic rises in me. Michael has to travel. Not again.

School has just started, Sarah has basketball, Andrew has soccer, and April is involved with cheerleading and gymnastics. I press my fingertips to my temple as my head swims.

"I'm sorry, honey. But one of the experimental drugs the company developed has some issues. You know how strict the process is and it's already about halfway through the human trials. There's nothing I can do about it. It's not that I want to go, I don't have a choice." He shrugs.

I sigh, release him from my hug, and turn toward the stove. I stir the potatoes a little too roughly and the water splashes onto the stove with a sizzle. "I know," I mumble half heartedly. "But school just started and with all the kids' activities, it's really hard when you're not here." Plus he'll have to travel.

Michael hugs my waist and rests his chin on my shoulder. He tilts his head and kisses my neck in the way that always gives me goose bumps. "I know. I'm sorry, honey. But I really can't help it. Besides, the kids are a bit older and are very capable of helping you out around the house. April is sixteen and has her license. She can drive Sarah or Andrew to practices if you can't. She already takes them to and from school."

I stiffen at the thought of April driving. I still haven't gotten used to that. Michael talked me into letting her get her license. She loves to drive (what sixteen-year-old doesn't?), but being young, enthusiastic, and behind the wheel aren't always a good combination. This reminds me of my conversation with April. I steer the conversation in that direction. It's a safer line of thought for me, too. Much safer than knowing Michael will be travelling. At least I can do something about April.

"Yeah, that sounds soooo easy, doesn't it?" My tone is slightly sarcastic. "The problem is your oldest daughter is upstairs in her room right now bemoaning the fact that her mother never lets her go anywhere."

"What happened this time?" Michael asks with a weary been-there-and-done-that tone.

"Well, apparently, some of her friends are going to a club this Friday night and she wants to go. I told her she's too young and is most certainly not going to a club. You know how well that went over."

He and I agree on most parenting approaches, which makes it easier for all involved. Rarely could our children ever pull the wool over our eyes because we present a fairly united front. That was a lesson we learned early – children are smarter than we give them credit for and they'll play us against each other if given the chance.

The only disparity in our parenting styles is in the minor things, like what constitutes a proper dinner for the kids if I'm not home. I don't feel it's appropriate to have peanut butter and jelly sandwiches followed by ice cream and popcorn with a movie all washed down with soda. Michael doesn't see the harm in it, occasionally. But "occasionally" to him means every time I go out. Fortunately, I don't go out that often. I know I'm hypocritical, what with my M&M addiction.

Michael pinches the bridge of his nose between his brows and closes his eyes. "When does this get easier?" he mumbles.

"I don't know. Maybe when Andrew is twenty-five? But I'm sure something else will pop up then. In the mean time, do you want to go and talk to her?"

"How long has she been in her room? I'd like to know if I should get a trash can lid for a shield or something before I enter the queen's royal chambers," he smirks.

"Well, she went up there just a few minutes before you got home, so I don't know if it's safe just yet. You'll have to call her down for dinner in about fifteen minutes anyway. That is if she'll come down. Perhaps she'll just send for a tray."

Sarah snickers.

I forgot she was there; she's so quiet. That's the thing with having a child like Sarah; I have to watch what I say and where. She could be lurking around the corner reading a book, but her ears are always perked to conversations within ear shot.

Something I've said in the privacy of my home might be repeated with perfect clarity at the most inopportune moments.

Like with my in-laws.

Michael's parents had visited for a week when Sarah was about four-years-old. I made a comment the week before that my husband resembled his mother rather remarkably. More specifically, I said she looks just like him with a tight perm on top and some lipstick. Michael's mother is tall and rather…solidly built. She isn't overweight, but she reminds me of an East German athlete, rather manly in build and with very short hair.

It's the truth, but it isn't flattering and definitely not something I would ever share with her.

That night as we all settled in for dinner, the conversation was going well. We started talking about home fashions which segued into personal fashion. Betty (my mother-in-law) stated she was thinking about changing her hairstyle to something more modern when Sarah blurted out, "But then you won't look just like daddy! Mommy said you look just like daddy with a perm and lipstick."

Oh, dear God. Thanks, child. Thank you very much.

Betty looked at me, blinked and muttered something I don't recall. I couldn't remember how to breathe. My father-in-law Frank cleared his throat and made mention of a recent sports victory to Michael. The conversation effectively ended.

That was an awkward dinner. Truth be told, it was an awkward visit.

My in-laws are gracious people, and they've never brought it up since. Neither have I, but I still blush every time I remember it.

I did have a conversation with Sarah after they left, however, about things that can and cannot be repeated. I also had a conversation with myself about what I should and should not say aloud…ever. Sarah's brain/mouth filter is getting better, but I don't take chances.

Deep embarrassment has a tendency to do that.

"I'm going to change and check on Andrew. He's probably sitting on his bed in his dirty clothes right now forgetting why he's there. Then I'll tell April to wash up and come down," Michael says then smiles and ducks out of the kitchen.

Stealing a quick glance around, I pop a few more M&Ms in my mouth and note the bowl is getting low.

I finish preparing dinner and tell Sarah to set the table. She closes her book and does as she is told.

"Dinner's ready!" I call up the stairs. A muffled acknowledgement from Michael wafts down.

Having traditional family dinners together around the table most nights is important to me because I never had it growing up. My parents were definitely children of the 1960's "free love/no consequence" culture, which meant I was an unfortunate child of the 1970's. With no dad around (he left the house one day and never came back), my mother was reliant on government hand outs and the Salvation Army to feed and clothe me. Mom was always working just to keep us afloat. Growing up, dinner consisted of tuna casserole, Hamburger Helper (sometimes without hamburger), or boxed macaroni and cheese. The latter was more likely because I had to make it and I was very young. Mom worked long hours as a housekeeper at the local hospital. Since she was a high school drop out, it was the best job she could get. She didn't get home until seven or eight at night and was exhausted when she did.

There's an old saying – "What the son wants to forget, the grandson wants to remember." I don't remember where I heard that, but it stuck with me. I grew up in a broken home. I know from personal experience why they are labeled broken; everything and everyone involved is broken when the dad leaves. I swore I wouldn't end up like that when I grew up. I was going to do things differently.

I'd find a way out.

Then I met Paul. A shiver runs down my spine and a familiar pain pierces my heart. I swallow hard and shove the forbidden thought away.

Dinner. My family and dinner are waiting. Focus!

April refuses to come to dinner. Halfway through the meal hunger gets the better of her, and she sulks downstairs and plops into her chair, eyes downcast and arms crossed. Michael and I look at each other knowingly, and he hands me her plate to fill. She takes the plate and eats without a word.

Whatever April may be feeling, she always has a good appetite. She'd never make it on a hunger strike, which isn't bad. She's always been a stick figure, healthy appetite notwithstanding. Her point has been made.

She's still not going to the club on Friday.

Once the dishes are done and the kids in bed, Michael and I head upstairs. I sit down at my vanity to begin my nightly facial cleansing routine while Michael changes.

"How did the talk with April go?" I ask.

He chuckles, joining me in the bathroom. "About as expected. She doesn't think we're being fair. I told her there will be plenty of time for clubs when she's older if she still wants to go. I hope she grows up and doesn't want to go to clubs. Nothing good comes from it." He begins brushing his teeth.

"I swear that girl wears me out. I love her to death, but she's a challenge. I never know what to expect." I rinse off my face and neck and move onto the moisturizer.

"Sure you do. Emotions, that's what," he mouths around his foamy toothbrush.

"When do you have to leave for Cleveland?" I ask, abruptly changing the subject. The question is whinier than I intend.

The subject of his business travel is never pleasant. Even though it's necessary, it's never easy. His job pays well and I'm thankful; it provides for our needs handsomely and allows me the freedom to raise our children.

He holds up one finger, rinses his mouth and throws back a shot of mouthwash. He swishes it back and forth, his gaze lingering on my face. He spits into the sink and dries off his face and hands before answering. "This Monday."

My jaw drops. "Monday? This Monday?! But that's only five days away!" A fresh wave of anxiety tangles with familiar fear. There's no time for me to mentally prepare. It's irrational, I know, but it's real.

Michael is going to miss April's first gymnastics meet as well as Andrew's debut as soccer goalie. This never does get easy, does it?

The fear of losing Michael, especially in a horrible accident, is always at the forefront of my thoughts. I've been through it once. I can't survive it again. The piercing pain swells. You'd think it would diminish after more than twenty years. It hasn't.

The force of it hits me as hard as it did when…the accident happened.

I vividly remember the Highway Patrolman knocking on my door at nine o'clock on a Thursday evening... *"Mrs. Peterson? Mrs. Faith Peterson? I'm Officer Daly with the Colorado State Patrol. May I come in for a few minutes, please? There's been an accident...."*

I brace myself on the bathroom counter and close my eyes, shaking my head.

Get a grip, Faith! It's only to Cleveland and it's a short trip.

What are the chances that I would have to go through another experience like I did with Paul? I know the odds are in my favor, but still... I press my hand to my stomach and suck in a deep breath.

I open my eyes and find Michael leaning against the bathroom door frame, arms crossed, regarding me. He's frowning.

Michael doesn't understand. How can he?

I've never told him about Paul. I've never told anyone about Paul.

"Faith, I know this is difficult for you, but I promise I'll be fine. And so will you. We go through this a lot and it's only for a couple of weeks. I don't know why you get so worked up. I always come home."

His last words stab my heart, causing me to swallow hard. "Well, so far you have." I cross the room and wrap my arms around his waist and bury my face in his chest. He hugs me back, tracing circles on my back with his hand. He tilts my chin up and kisses me tenderly. I return the kiss, my heart still gripped by fear.

God, please don't take him. I can't do that again. Please.

Chapter Two

Monday rolls around fast. I'm not ready. But then again, I'll never be ready for Michael to leave. I help him pack that morning. He would've preferred to pack the day before, but since he doesn't have to be at the airport until ten, I had asked him to wait until morning so I won't have to see visual reminders of his pending departure before absolutely necessary.

It's a small, stupid thing and I know it. I'm thankful he puts up with my quirks. He gets me, even though he doesn't really know me. It's one of the reasons I love him so much.

The kids say their goodbyes before they leave for school. It's uneventful; just the usual hugs and kisses with promises to "be good" elicited from the kids by Michael before they pile into April's Honda Accord and go to school.

I make April promise to text me after she puts her car in park in the parking lot of her school and not a moment before. She sighs impatiently and says, "Don't I always?!"

April grudgingly agrees to be good, too, since (according to her) she is forced to waste away at home on Friday night while all of her friends went out.

Once, April forgot to text me she had arrived safely at school. I was in full panic mode. I called the school and they verified she had indeed arrived.

I had to be sure. I can't take anything for granted.

Not again.

I lectured her at length about it after school and she hasn't missed a text since.

The kids don't have my anxiety. I hide it well. Don't all parents want their kids to be better than they are? Have more than they do? I haven't told them about my past. I don't plan to. It's on a strictly need to know basis. They don't need to know.

I don't talk about it. Ever.

Honk! Honk! The airport shuttle in the driveway announces its arrival. Michael's suitcase is ready at the front door; he always takes a shuttle to the airport. I never drive him there. I can't.

He opens the door and waves to the driver before ducking back inside.

The tears well in my eyes and make me feel so stupid. Here I am, a grown woman of forty-four, married to a wonderful man, a mother of three, and I want to cry because my husband is going on a two- week trip.

To Cleveland, of all places.

It's not like he's going overseas to a war zone for a year. I can't help myself. I am so vulnerable and I hate it. My chin starts to quiver. What am I? Four-years-old?

Michael closes the few feet between us, folding me into his arms. The tears spill over and dribble miserably down my cheeks onto his shirt. I pull my face away.

"I don't want to send you away with a wet shirt." I try to joke, but my chin still quivers and the tears continue to flow. I try to steady my stupid chin by biting down on my lip.

He brushes my tears away. "Everything will be fine, sweetheart. Please, for once, don't worry. I will let you know as soon as I can that I've arrived safely. Besides, you'll be so busy for the next couple of weeks that it will just fly by, I promise. Call your girlfriends and make some plans while I'm gone. I should be able to call you every night." His reassurances can't stop the tears. Finally, he breaks away.

"I've got to get going or I'll miss my flight," he says gently.

I wish he would miss his flight, I think selfishly. I know I'm being silly about this, but I don't have to like it. I try again to get control of myself, at least until he's gone. I don't want to make him feel bad about something so silly.

"Call me as soon as you land. I'll have my cell with me, even in the bathroom." I squeeze him tightly.

"You don't have to go to that extreme, but yes, I will call you as soon as I head toward baggage claim," he chuckles, kissing the tip of my nose. I squeeze him fiercely one last time, nod quickly, and then let him go. My arms ache, as does my heart.

I do my best to arrange my face into a smile and wave as he piles into the shuttle and it drives off. Once the shuttle is out of sight, I make my way back into the house. I say a fervent, silent prayer for the pilot, the plane, the mechanics, and the weather; anything I can think of to pray for Michael to be safe. I won't be able to relax until he calls.

Why do I still pray? Does God hear me? He's got to be busy. I pray out of habit, but why? I don't know. It just comes out at odd times or whenever I'm fearful.

Like now.

Like most days, if I'm being totally honest.

I attended church every Sunday growing up, thanks in large part to my grandparents. They were one of the only stable influences in my life because of my mother's frequent moves, or rather evictions.

When we lived near them, they picked me up without fail every Sunday and took us to the little Sunnyside Community church. When we didn't live near them, they hounded my mother to make sure she sent me to church every week. I remember a school bus that was painted blue with white lettering on the sides picking me up and dropping me off. My mother went on occasion, and even went up to the altar after services and wept.

One Sunday morning, when mom left the pew to go to the altar, I followed behind her. I walked up, knelt at the altar beside her and prayed what the preacher said to pray. I asked Jesus to forgive me of my sins and live in my heart. That day I became a Christian. I was eight years old.

I continued to go to church every Sunday with a renewed passion and belief that life would get better. It did, at least on the inside. My visits to church on Sunday morning were like a breath of fresh air each week, and I dutifully learned my memory verses in Sunday school.

I would wistfully watch the families with mom, dad, and children that sat together as I sat in a pew toward the back of the church. I wanted a daddy at home like the other children had, a daddy that dressed up and went to church every Sunday.

Life at home didn't change much.

I continued to go to church as I got older because it's what I did. My passion waned as time passed. I didn't get into trouble or anything, I just…spread out. I was a teenager and teenagers want to see what else there is.

After Paul's death, my faith and belief in a good God were shattered. How could the God I was raised to believe in allow such a thing to happen?

I did something wrong. I must have, and I needed to be punished. I wasn't good enough or deserving enough.

It was at that moment, for all intents and purposes, I walked away.

But I still pray.

We attend church as a family, albeit infrequently. We attend a large interdenominational church a couple times a year and certainly every Christmas and Easter. I like how big it is. We get lost in the crowd. We don't have to be involved; we just take up space occasionally in a pew and slip right back out again when the service is over.

The door clicks closed behind me. I'm struck at the sudden silence, the absence of him. The pain in my heart throbs, and I can't help remembering how the front door had clicked, too, on that cold January evening after the policeman had left…

"Mrs. Peterson, I'm so very sorry to inform you that there was a terrible accident this evening on Interstate 70. Your husband was involved in a multi-car pile-up. His injuries were such that from all accounts, he died instantly. I hope you can take comfort in knowing he didn't suffer."

As I absorbed the officer's words, my body went numb and I was looking at him through a tunnel.

At some point, there was another patrol car and an ambulance. I didn't know why the ambulance was there. Later, I was told I looked like I was going to pass out. They weren't comfortable leaving me alone.

Alone.

That word took on a wholly different meaning. Unfortunately, I didn't pass out. That would've been merciful.

Instead, I remained (mostly) conscious and vaguely aware of myself and my surroundings.

My memories of that evening are very odd indeed. Some things I remember with the sharpest clarity, others not at all or like it was a dream. Actually, more like my worst nightmare that I never awoke from.

I remember the policeman's exact words when he told me Paul had died, but the rest of the conversation is absent. I remember reading "Bill R., Paramedic" on the name tag of the man that tended to me. I don't know how I got to the sofa I was lying on and I can't remember his face.

Snapping back into the present, I'm sobbing uncontrollably and my breath is coming in short, ragged gasps as I stand in the foyer.

I have to get hold of myself! Michael is fine. He'll call me soon. He will. He'll take off and arrive just fine.

He's fine. I'm fine. Everything is fine. Fine. Fine.

Get busy. Stay busy. Don't think.

The tears flow unchecked. I lurch into the small powder room off the foyer, splash cold water on my face and take slow, deep breaths into the hand towel.

Next comes a flurry of chores: laundry, kitchen, bathrooms, bedrooms, floors, dusting, vacuuming, baseboard scrubbing, silverware polishing. Eventually, the tears cease. With much practice over the years, the ever present anxiety shifts into the background.

I can do this. I can do this.

Several hours later, I plop onto the sofa, exhausted. My stomach is growling fiercely. I glance at the clock. It's nearly one thirty.

Michael is still in the air. My chest squeezes. By my calculations, he should call sometime around five-thirty. The flight from Springfield to Cleveland isn't that long.

Dragging myself off the sofa, I shuffle into the kitchen. I make my lunch and pour a tall glass of iced tea. I perch on a stool at the breakfast bar and scroll aimlessly through my cell phone checking email as I force down a few bites.

I have to stay distracted.

Stay busy. Stay busy.

When I'm almost done, the house phone rings. The caller ID identifies it as Brenda. She's one of my best friends and has been since we moved to Springfield eight years ago. She was one of the first people I met. I was in the elementary school office registering April for second grade (yeesh – has it been that long?) and Brenda was there picking up her sick daughter, who was also in second grade. We hit it off immediately.

Brenda is slightly shorter than me, slender, with bobbed blond hair (and dark roots on very, very rare occasions; nobody knows her true hair color and she likes it that way) and brown eyes. She's so bubbly that I can't imagine anyone not liking Brenda, unless you hate fashion. She's married and has three children the same age as mine. It's like we planned our families together. We obviously didn't; it just worked out that way. It's a perk that her property line, and therefore her backyard fence, butts up against mine. She's always there when I need her.

Brenda doesn't have to work, but to support her shopping habit she works part time at a local upscale boutique called The Place. Strange name, I always thought. Maybe a play on words, like "The Place to Be?" I don't know.

I answer the phone, trying to sound upbeat.

"Hi, Brenda, what's up?"

"I just got off work and wanted to know if you'd like to go get some coffee or something."

I hear traffic noise in the background; she must be walking to her car. "Sure. I could use a diversion right now."

"Is everything okay or are you just busy with stuff?"

"Michael left for Cleveland this morning. He'll be gone for two weeks."

"Oh! I'm sorry. But it's only two weeks, not two months. That's good, right?" Brenda always finds the silver lining. I appreciate that most of the time. She comes across as superficial to those who don't know her.

"Yeah, it is. I still don't like it, though," I say glumly.

"You'll get through it, Faith. You always do!" she replies cheerfully. "Do you want to meet me at Starbucks in, say, twenty minutes?"

"Sure. I'll see you then." We say our goodbyes and hang up.

I haven't even applied make-up yet, so I head to the bathroom and give myself the once over. With the exception of my puffy eyes, the reflection is decent. For forty-four, I look pretty good; just a few crow's feet forming around my eyes, but my wavy light brown hair is still thick and without a trace of grey. My skin is clear and surprisingly smooth. After all I have been through, I should look sixty.

Stay busy. Stay busy.

I do need cosmetic help before going out in public. Starbucks is only ten minutes from my house, but twenty minutes from Brenda's work, so I have a few minutes to spare. I quickly apply some make-up and run my hands through my hair.

I give myself a nod of approval and head to the closet to change into a pair of white Capri's and a maroon short-sleeved, scoop neck shirt. For early September, it's still warm. A pair of gold hoop earrings and white flats completes my outfit, and I head for the door, grabbing my purse on the way out.

I arrive at Starbucks and see Brenda's white BMW SUV pulling into the parking lot at the same time. I thought I saw her driving a blue BMW last time...

It must be that time again; Brenda gets a new BMW every couple of years. It's one of the perks of having a husband who owns a few dealerships. That she needs a job to support her shopping habit boggles the mind. She parks next to my minivan, waving exuberantly.

"Hi, Faith! It's so good to see you!" she squeals as she reaches out to hug me, grinning so wide her usually reluctant dimples are showing. You'd think we hadn't seen each other in years rather than weeks.

Brenda is wearing the latest fashion and accessories, of course. From the top of her perfectly colored and coiffed blond bob, not a single hair out of place, to her color coordinated shoes and matching purse, she's dressed like something out of a fashion magazine. I wear nice clothes, too, but prefer to be comfortable and don't care about the brand names. Truthfully, I don't even know the brand names.

I hug her back and smile. Pulling apart, she looks me up and down. Brenda always judges other people's outfits. She intends to come across as helpful, but is often misconstrued as judgmental. Her comments aren't always well received. She's oblivious.

"You know, we have a really nice gold belt that would finish that outfit perfectly. Want me to pick it up for you? You would look simply darling in it!" she squeals.

"No, thank you. I appreciate that you always think of me, though."

Brenda's face falls briefly in disappointment.

We head into Starbucks and get in line. It's blissfully short because it's two o'clock in the afternoon. I order a decaf Americano and Brenda orders something much more fancy with a lot of syllables. She claims a table while I wait for our drinks.

Once we're settled with drinks in hand, I ask how she's been doing.

"Well," she starts, giving me a knowing look. "You just won't believe what happened at the boutique today! It's a madhouse!" She flutters her hands in the air. "You remember Maryann, the store manager? She made a huge mistake on an order that came in today. Apparently, she was supposed to order twenty-six Fendi bags for the season, but she messed up and ordered twenty-six hundred bags instead!" Brenda's jaw drops and she rolls her eyes.

"You should have seen it when the delivery arrived. Maryann was expecting a couple of boxes, but no! Pallets started showing up at the back door. I swear, I thought Maryann was going to throw up when she saw it and realized what she'd done."

"Wow. That's awful. What did she do?"

"Well, she tried to refuse the delivery, but the guy refused her refusal. He told her it wasn't his problem; he was just the delivery guy. So she got on the phone and called the factory. I didn't hear everything that was said, but by the end she was crying. Apparently, they won't take them back because it was Maryann's mistake, not theirs. I think she might lose her job over it." Brenda sits back and sips her coffee, allowing the disaster to soak into my consciousness.

"That's terrible," I reply. "I'd be devastated. How much do those bags cost anyway?" I honestly have no idea.

Brenda blinks, perplexed. "They're like $350 a purse!" Brenda cries, dumbfounded at my ignorance. My fashion ambivalence has always baffled her. She can't comprehend how any woman cannot know, much less care about, fashion the way she does.

"Oh. Wow. That is awful. So what happens now?"

"I don't know. My shift was over, and I left before there was anymore fall out. I'm sure I'll know more when I work on Thursday," she replies with a shrug. Then she looks at me and her eyes narrow, "So, tell me. What are you going to do the next couple of weeks? Do we need to schedule a dessert dinner?"

Dessert dinners are events that we schedule as often as possible. It started out as a supper club, but we quickly realized that the meal was simply a prelude for the dessert, which we devoured with gusto and great conversation. It became a tradition to have at an assortment of desserts, one of which must always include chocolate.

"Funny you should mention that. Michael suggested I get together with you guys before he left this morning." I swirl my coffee. "I don't know. Maybe. I would love to, but the kids just got back in school and they're all involved in sports. It's crazy. With Michael not here, I don't know that I can do it right now."

"But I think you're going to need it, so make time for it. We can even do it at your house, if you'd like. I can get Mariah to watch the kids at my house with April plus the husbands can have a play date there, too." She smiles triumphantly. She has a point. Mariah is Brenda's oldest daughter, April's best friend. Fortunately, all of our spouses and kids get along.

Maybe Michael and Brenda are right. It may be good for me. The company of my girlfriends is always a balm for my soul. I nod my head and smile.

"Let's do it."

Brenda claps her hands together and bounces in her seat like a child on Christmas morning.

"I'll call the girls tonight! What day do you want to do it?" she asks excitedly. There's no need to say who the girls are; we're a pretty tight knit group. The girls consist of Brenda, Lilly, Michelle, and me. We're all middle aged women with kids, husbands, and issues. Yikes, middle aged. Wow. When did that creep up on me?

"Let's shoot for Thursday," I offer. "It's the only day of the week, other than tonight, that the kids don't have any sports. April does have cheerleading practice, but she'll be done by four-thirty."

"Sounds wonderful! Friday is one of those crazy teacher institute days or some such nonsense, so the kids don't even have school the next day. Perfect! I can hardly wait. Should I call or email everybody, so we can all talk together and plan it? Maybe play some games or..." Brenda continues to bounce.

"Whoa. Slow down, Brenda!" I put my hands up. "I just want to spend the evening with my girlfriends. Don't plan anything elaborate."

"Faith," she rolls her eyes and pats my hand. "It's going to be fine. Trust me! Thursday will be so much fun!"

We finish our drinks and part ways. It's close to three o'clock and the kids will be home from school soon. It was nice to spend some time with Brenda. I am more relaxed, but still anxious for my cell to ring. I know it's too early, but still.

Brenda's right. Thursday will be fun. It's only four days away. I will focus on that and get through this week, at least.

God, I have to get through this.

Chapter Three

Dinner is simple. I make a ham, cheese, and potato casserole. One pot meals are my go-to options for busy nights. Plus I forgot to take anything else out that would thaw in time.

As it nears four-thirty, then five o'clock, the tension builds like a pressure cooker inside of me. I hold my cell phone tightly in my grip under the table all through dinner while having conversations with the kids about their day. I check my cell at least three times to be sure it's turned on, the ringer is up, and I have good reception. Of course I have good reception, but I check anyway.

At five-forty, I'm about to burst.

The battery is (still) charged, the ringer is (still) on, there are (still) three bars for good reception.

No phone call.

The dishes are cleared, loaded in the dishwasher, homework is being done, and all is well with the kids.

No phone call.

I grab a fistful of M&Ms and munch on them while I pace back and forth in the kitchen.

I can't take it anymore.

"I'm going for a run. You okay?" I ask April as she looks up from her books.

"Sure," she says, sounding surprised. Normally I run in the mornings, but I have to do something right now. I will scream if I have to sit still.

Stay busy. Stay busy.

"Thanks, hon. I'll have my cell phone on me if you need anything. I won't be gone too long, and I'll take my usual route."

Taking the stairs two at a time, I quickly change into my running clothes. It's still warm out, so I opt for shorts. I rapidly descend the steps and Andrew looks up.

"Where you going, Mom?" he asks innocently.

"Out for a run, sweetie. I'll be back soon. April and Sarah are here. I won't be gone very long. Keep working on your homework." I give him a quick squeeze and kiss the top of his head. His little hands pat my back as he hugs me.

"Be careful," he says.

Such a sweet boy.

"I will, baby." I glance at my cell once more. It's almost six o'clock.

Panic bubbles up in me.

Darting out the door, I start running before I hit the end of the driveway, skipping my usual walking warm up. I run faster than usual. I can't help it.

Thump, thump, thump.

My footfalls hit the pavement in a soothing rhythmic motion.

I took up running about a year after Paul's death. I got up one day and just started to run. I never liked running before, but it felt good to move, even when nothing else in my life did. I had spent the first six months after his death like a zombie. I barely ate or showered, didn't leave our apartment unless I had to, and life just stopped. I shut everyone out of my life including my mother, whom I haven't spoken to since. His family faded away, as well. That didn't surprise me.

After my zombie stage, I opted for a fresh start, so I packed up my meager belongings and headed for Illinois. I picked it out by randomly jabbing my finger on a map. I never looked back. I took the small life insurance policy that Paul had and paid for my college.

Running is tangible. It became part of my life, part of my routine. It's therapeutic. Some people turn to pills or alcohol or food. I turned to running.

I can choose to think or not think while I'm running. Either way, I'm moving.

As I turn left at the next stop sign and start running up a small hill, my mind unwittingly wanders back to why I took up running.

Back to Paul.

I was totally blindsided when Paul died. But then again, I was totally blindsided with Paul. We were high school sweethearts; we started dating in our junior year. We shared a couple of classes, and he ended up being my lab partner in biology. I was awed at his interest in me; Paul was a star on the football team and came from one of the wealthiest families in Fort Collins.

I came from one of the poorest families. We lived in an old apartment on a not-so-nice side of town.

Plus Paul Peterson was drop dead gorgeous. He had jet black hair and crystal blue eyes, was tall, and his skin was the color of honey. He was the total package and he wanted to date me, Faith Elizabeth Adsila. A nobody from nowhere.

I remember the shock and rush I felt when Paul first asked me out. I almost ruined it because I couldn't believe he was asking me. I stood there, blinking rapidly with my mouth agape like a fly trap. I stuttered something incoherent before finally blurting out "Yes!"

I was such an idiot.

I also remember feeling tingly all over the first time he kissed me. I had never been kissed before.

Paul never cared that my family didn't have money or social standing. He loved me for me. I, of course, fell head over heels madly in love with him. I saw him as my knight in shining armor that would rescue me from my life as it was and whisk me away to a better life where the story would actually end with "…and they lived happily ever after."

It didn't end that way.

Fairy tales are just that: fairy tales and nothing more.

Reaching the top of the hill, my thighs are screaming. The cell phone remains silent.

Run, run, run, *run*!

Paul proposed to me the year after we graduated. To say his parents were livid would be an understatement. They never thought I was good enough for their son and barely tolerated us

28

dating, thinking he would eventually move on when he went away to college. I, of course, stayed at home working at the local drug store. I couldn't afford to go to college.

Paul attended classes at Colorado State University and had come home for Christmas. He showed up at my door with a bouquet of red and white roses and a little black jewelry box.

It was the best moment of my life.

We got married when we were both twenty. Even though Paul was still in college, he didn't want to wait two more years for us to be together as husband and wife. It was a ridiculously small affair, which suited me just fine. His parents refused to help pay for the wedding and my family had no money, so it was only immediate family and friends.

To my surprise, his parents did attend the wedding. They were resigned and cordial, but distant.

Paul graduated with honors and went on to study law immediately afterward. We had decided to wait to start a family until after he finished law school and had himself more established. I still hold some regret about that particular decision.

I've run about fifteen blocks now and am sucking wind. Slowing my pace just enough to round a corner, I keep the brutal pace going on the straight away.

I'm not done yet.

My marriage to Paul was a dream come true. It was the honeymoon that didn't end after the honeymoon. Paul was a wonderful friend, a great lover, and the heart of my life and the life of my heart. Life was perfect with a capital P. I adored him and he adored me.

Panic and pain fight for reign over my mind and heart. I've come to the part I hate the most.

The part that destroyed me.

Paul was coming back from the University after a late afternoon class. He was supposed to be home by seven. It was already eight and I hadn't heard from him. I thought maybe the class ran late or he had hit some traffic. His class had never run late before, but stranger things could happen.

Oh, God.

I had put his dinner in the microwave to heat up when he came home.

Oh, dear God. No.

I flipped through the channels and watched, but didn't hear, what was on the TV screen as I continued to wait.

No, no, no, no.

There was a knock on the door. I couldn't fathom why Paul felt he had to knock on the door to his own home. Silly man! I placed my hand on the door knob, twisted it, and opened the door to a new chapter of my life as I never imagined or wanted it to be.

I became a widow at twenty-two. Two days before our second wedding anniversary.

Mentally unwilling but physically unable to continue, I stop running and bend over to rest my hands on my quivering knees, gasping for breath. My struggle to breathe isn't only because I've been running flat out for almost thirty-five minutes straight.

Slowly standing upright, I pull my cell phone from my pocket. I groan, realizing it's almost six thirty. I thrust it back in my pocket and place my hands on my head and walk in small circles, trying to slow my breathing.

My mind screams, Run, run, run! Stay busy! Stay busy!

My body is on the verge of collapse.

Dear God, why hasn't Michael called yet?!

Mercifully, at that moment, my phone rings. I snatch it from my pocket and answer it before the ring tone is done with its first cycle.

"Hello?!" I pant, my voice quaking and panicky.

"Hi, honey. It's me. I'm here and picking up my luggage now." Michael's voice is velvet in my ears. Relief washes through me and I immediately relax and start walking slowly toward home.

"Oh, sweetie! I'm so glad...you finally called! I thought...you'd call about...an hour ago! What happened?! Did anything...go wrong?" I gasp out my questions in rapid fire, still not fully recovered.

"Everything is fine," he reassures me. "We just had to circle around the airport awhile before it was our turn to land. I called as soon as I could. Are you okay? You sound out of breath."

"I'm better now…that you've called. I went for…a run. I'm headed home," my breathing starts to even out. "How was your flight?"

"Pretty boring. At least I got to fly business class. I need the leg room, and if I have to be stuck on a plane, I appreciate being able to stretch out." I can hear the grin in his voice coupled with lots of background traffic noise.

It occurs to me he might be driving while talking. Not good.

"Are you driving right now?" My voice is high pitched.

"No, honey," he replies, exasperated. "I'm walking to the rental car kiosk. You know I don't do that."

"Sorry. I just wanted to make sure. You know how I worry."

"Yes, I know. But please try not to. Everything is fine, sweetheart. Look, I have to go. I'm at the kiosk and I need to pick up my rental car."

I'm almost home. There's still plenty of daylight and even though the sun is low in the sky, it's still above the tree tops and I spot our home. It's a beautiful Colonial with a large manicured lawn accented by simple landscaping. Gardening has never been my thing. I like rocks; they look good year round.

"Okay, sweetie. Just text me when you get to the hotel and then I promise to leave you alone until tomorrow." I grip the cell phone with both hands. He laughs and promises. We say our goodbyes and hang up.

Yelling coming from the living room greets me when I walk in. April and Andrew are arguing about what channel to watch, even though there is more than one TV in this house. Lovely. My shoulders slump. I take a deep breath and enter the melee. It's been such a long day already.

****

Climbing the stairs slowly for bed later that evening, I am utterly exhausted. The kids are bathed and tucked away, lunches made and waiting in the fridge, homework completed and packed into book bags ready on the bench in the mud room.

I can barely keep my eyes open long enough to wash my face. Suddenly, my eyes flash open and I'm wide awake.

I haven't received a text from Michael saying he arrived at the hotel.

Oh, no! No, no, no, no!!

Fresh panic hits and I scramble through the house, looking for my cell phone. It's sitting on the counter in the kitchen where I left it after my run. There's a text waiting for me. I look at the time. It says seven-twenty. It's now almost ten o'clock.

It's from Michael.

"At the hotel. All is well. Love you and talk to you tomorrow."

I breathe a sigh of relief as I climb the stairs, returning to our bedroom. I must've been busy dealing with the kids when it came through and didn't hear it. I tap a quick response telling him so and put the cell on my nightstand, slumping onto the bed in relief.

I have GOT to stop this! It's been twenty two years, for crying out loud.

The problem is I don't know how to stop. I started out in life feeling abandoned. I was only four and a half when my father left. I vaguely remember him, but I do remember wondering why he left and didn't come back. I wondered if there was something wrong with me that made him leave.

I wasn't good enough to deserve a daddy like all the other little girls. I realize now it's an irrational conclusion, but it's what I thought.

Childhood experiences shape adult behaviors, however irrational they may be.

Then I met and married Paul. He left me, too. He didn't choose to leave, but nonetheless, he's still gone. I was abandoned once again. I didn't even get to say goodbye.

I shake my head. I am not rehashing this again. Not tonight. I'm spent.

In the deepest crevices of my soul, the fear of losing it all again lingers. The thought creeps in that if I reach too far, too high, it will be ripped out from beneath me because I don't deserve it in the first place.

32

I'm not good enough.

Trudging into the bathroom, I brush my teeth, change, and go to bed. Sighing deeply, I close my eyes.

God, please don't take it all away. Not again. I'm begging you.

Chapter Four

Tuesday and Wednesday are spent taking the kids to their various practices, making dinner, chatting with the kids, and doing our evening routine.

Plus running. Always running.

I am mindful of the time each day; Michael usually calls close to eight. He keeps his promise and calls me each night, even if it's only for a few brief minutes. His trip is fairly routine and he expects to be home on time.

Two more days down. Only eleven more to go.

Thursday rolls around quickly. Michael was right about one thing, I am (almost) too busy to mull over his absence.

Almost, but not quite. Eventually I have to turn the lights off, the sounds of the day go quiet, and I'm at the mercy of my own thoughts. That's not good.

I busy myself as much as possible all day, organizing the financial files in our home office even going so far as to create new file folders to replace the ones that show even a hint of wear and tear.

My friends are coming over tonight, so I place a few candles artfully around the living and dining rooms. Candles always add a nice soft touch.

Brenda did email everyone; Michelle has another killer dessert recipe she's been dying to try. I know everything will be delicious; her food always is.

Lilly is coming, as well. She'll bring the wine plus a chocolate hazelnut torte. That usually means some excellent selections from her husband's wine collection.

Her husband, Tony, set aside some space in the corner of their basement and had a wine room, as he likes to call it, professionally installed. Even though only one person can stand upright in it at any given time, it holds about a hundred bottles of wine and is very tastefully done. He's quite proud. He and Lilly really enjoy taking trips that center around wine regions and he stocks up wherever they go.

Lilly is more subdued and reserved than the rest of us. That isn't to say she's shy. I have seen her give quite the tongue lashing to a customer service representative that didn't provide very good customer service. Mind you, it took a rather impressive accumulation of infractions, but when Lilly has had enough, she isn't slow in saying so. Her words are few, but profound. I've never heard Lilly say something she didn't mean. That's quite a statement to be made about any woman.

Lilly's husband is a pediatric dentist, and not surprisingly, she and their two boys have the most beautiful teeth. There's no fear of the dentist from our kids – all of them see him twice a year. They affectionately call him Dr. Tony and look forward to their appointments.

The clock reads two-fifteen. I have time for a run.

I hurry up the stairs, change, pull my hair back in a pony tail, and head out the door. It's a beautiful, crisp day with the last remnants of summer warmth lingering in the air. I take my time stretching and then start speed walking for a few blocks before breaking out into my jog, taking the same route each time. I like routine and besides, everybody knows where I run so if anything were to happen, they'd know where to find me. My cell phone stays with me at all times. Just in case.

I have no fear of being attacked by a stranger; our neighborhood is enviably safe. It's an upscale area with a very low crime rate.

When I return from my run, it's nearly three-fifteen. I climb into my minivan and go pick up Sarah and Andrew because April has cheer practice. On the way home, Sarah is quieter than usual, which is saying something.

"Sarah, honey, is something bothering you?" I peer over at her.

"No," she says, staring out the passenger window. I'm not convinced.

"You're quiet this afternoon. Are you sure there's nothing bothering you?"

"Yes," she says in a monotone.

"If you want to talk about something, just let me know."

"Okay."

I can't force her to tell me anything. Never could. But she'll tell me more in her own time, when she's ready. Or not. It's just her way. There's a tug on my heart that I don't understand.

When we get home, Sarah goes to her room mumbling that she's going to do homework. I watch her climb the stairs. There's obviously something bothering her, and being a twelve-year-old girl, there is any number of things that it could be. I just have to trust that she'll talk when the time's right.

Andrew is already headed toward the television and cartoons. Normally, I wouldn't allow it, but today I just let it be. I head to the kitchen and start dinner, grabbing a handful of M&Ms between tasks.

April bounds in the door at four-thirty, drops her book bag dramatically on the floor and stares excitedly at me with her shaking hands balled into fists next to her face, wearing a huge grin.

"You'll never guess what!" she exclaims.

I can't imagine. "What?"

"Tom Parker asked me to the winter formal!" She starts screaming, jumping up and down, and clapping her hands together. She reminds me of Brenda. I wonder if her daughter and mine were switched at birth.

From what I hear, Tom Parker is The Thing at high school these days, and April has had a crush on him for over a year. That's a long time for her. He is the star wrestler and very hot according to April and her friends.

I smile and try to share in her joy. I am glad she's gotten over the club thing. If she's happy, then I'm happy. She may be emotional, but at least her bursts in either direction are short lived.

"That's wonderful, sweetie. I'm so happy for you!" She rushes over and wraps her arms around me, still bouncing up and

36

down, and squeezes me tight. She pulls back just as quickly and yells, "I have to call Mariah!"

She continues to squeal as she snatches her cell phone from her purse and runs from the kitchen.

After dinner, I remind Andrew to put his toys away and get ready to go to Brenda's house. He wants to keep playing and balks, but eventually complies.

I busy myself making cookies for tonight. Once they're out of the oven and cooling, I set them aside. All I have to do is plate them before my friends arrive.

April is driving herself and her siblings over shortly. She spent the better part of forty-five minutes talking (no, squealing) to Mariah, but they'll still have plenty to say when they're together.

I start laying out the small dessert plates, forks, and napkins as well as the wine and water glasses. I assemble ice water with fresh lemon in my crystal pitcher, and then light the candles that I placed around earlier. It's nearly six o'clock. There's very little for me to do; my cookies are plated, and everything else is taken care of.

The doorbell rings. It's Lilly. She looks chic in her fitted gray sweater dress accented with black shoes and a black beaded necklace clasped at her throat with a beautiful silver pin attached to the left side of her dress just below the collar bone. Her naturally light blond hair and blue eyes stand in stark contrast to her darker wardrobe choice.

Even at thirty-eight years old, she looks stunning. She's slightly plump, but in a voluptuous rather than frumpy sort of way. There is some slight graying at her temples, but it's hardly noticeable unless the sun hits it just right. It's one of the perks of being a natural shade of blond that most other women pay the big bucks for. She can thank her Swedish heritage for that.

"Hi, Faith!" she smiles warmly and hands me the little maroon wine tote that contains both a bottle of red and white wine. "Here's the wine I promised. Tony picked them out himself." He always picks out excellent wines. I give the man credit where credit is due. A large round covered dish is snuggled in the crook of her other arm. She leans in to give me a hug and I return the embrace.

As Lilly steps in, Brenda's BMW pulls into our driveway. Even though she lives right behind me, she drives around the block to my house. She always wears heels; they'd get stuck in the grass. Brenda isn't what anyone would call an outdoor girl. Roughing it for her would be shopping at JC Penney. She waves frantically from the driver's seat before she even puts the vehicle in park.

Did I mention Brenda is bubbly?

She exits her vehicle and walks briskly to the front door, chatting all the way as her designer heels click on the concrete. As usual, she's dressed to the nines without a hair out of place. She squeezes me briefly, but exuberantly.

"I'm so glad Thursday finally came!" she cries. "It felt like it would never get here! Hi Lilly! It's good to see you, too! You look fabulous. Are those new shoes?" She releases me, hugs Lilly with equal enthusiasm and we all enter the house together. Lilly drops her purse on the bench in the foyer and piles her shoes on the floor nearby. She pads into the kitchen, placing the white wine in the fridge to chill. Brenda follows suit with her purse and designer shoes.

The foyer becomes chaotic all of a sudden; April, Sarah, and Andrew all come down the stairs at the same time, pulling on shoes to go to Brenda's house. April and Sarah are having a conversation about the hotness of Tom Parker and his friend Alan. Sarah's mood has brightened. April is still in a very excited state; her voice is high pitched and shrill.

Andrew wants to know if he can bring over his action figures to play with Lilly's son Shane, who's eleven but still interested in them. I say yes, as long as he remembers to bring them all home. He excitedly runs for the basement to grab his case of them almost tripping across the floor as he goes. I shake my head; his mind gets ahead of his body and the combination just doesn't work.

The kids are finally ready. As they head out, I squeeze April's arm and turn her toward me. "Be sure to text me and let me know you got there as soon as you arrive."

"Mom! It's only one block away!" she cries, stomping her foot.

"I know, April. But still, you never know. Promise you'll text me."

"Fine," she breathes, muttering something about not being a baby.

The kids are bustled out the door with a final "Behave!" warning before I turn my attention to my guests. Brenda and Lilly are in the kitchen discussing the finer points of Coco Chanel versus Valentino Garavani shoes. Brenda likes the edgier styles from Valentino whereas Lilly prefers the understated elegance of Chanel. "...you don't have to be flashy to be fashionable," Lilly was saying.

Ugh. So not my topic of choice.

The doorbell rings again. It's Michelle. She's always about ten to fifteen minutes late to any event, even if it's her own. We have all learned to accept that about her. If we ever really need to be somewhere on time, we tell her we need to leave at five-forty-five when we really need to go at six. She shows up at six and we get to our destination on time.

It works like a charm.

Michelle is forty-four and tall with dark, glossy chestnut brown hair that has beautiful natural curls. She wears it in a very flattering shoulder length layered look. Her curls are the bouncy round kind that usually comes from a long time in the salon chair with a skilled hand and a hot curling iron. I've always envied it. Her green eyes haven't faded with age, but her skin is showing some wear and tear from her escapades with sunbathing throughout her life. She claims she doesn't feel right without some color on her skin.

Michelle is more like me in terms of fashion; she looks put together but prefers to wear nice clothes that don't cost what a small family's weekly grocery budget would be. It's not that she can't afford it, of course, but she isn't interested in the accumulation of things. Tonight she's wearing jeans with a turquoise blouse that sets off her tan skin perfectly.

"Hi, Faith! Could you give me a hand with these? Thanks." She thrusts one of the two insulated rectangular containers with straps into my hands. Michelle is straight forward with a no nonsense attitude. It makes her a good business woman.

"Sure. Do you need more help? Lilly and Brenda are already here."

She waves me off. "Don't be silly! This is it."

As she enters and heads toward the kitchen, I can hear the Bose stereo playing light jazz music. Hugs and greetings are exchanged all around as we unwrap dishes and platters and place them on the dining room table.

Everything looks scrumptious and decadent. There's a round of oooohs and aaaaahs as the desserts are unwrapped. The *piece de resistance* is a two pound bag of dark chocolate M&Ms Michelle pulls from her enormous purse.

Holy cow.

"I bought these to munch on after we eat!" She grins and winks at me. She knows my weakness for dark chocolate M&Ms.

"I may have to curse you all later for this when my pants don't fit. But thanks all the same," I laugh. She laughs with me and tosses the bag in my direction. I refill my almost empty bowl of M&Ms and secure the remaining amount, placing it in the cupboard.

My cell chimes on the counter next to me and I glance at it. April has just arrived and is fine. The word fine is in all caps. I know I exasperate her, but I can't help it. They're my babies. I respond briefly and set it aside.

"I can hardly wait to dig in, ladies. I've been saving my Weight Watchers points all week," Brenda beams.

"Good," Lilly pipes in. "Pile it on because that torte took me all afternoon."

"Who's hungry?" Michelle says, rubbing her hands together. We all dig in and fill our plates and glasses, too. The wines Lilly brought match beautifully with our rich desserts.

After polishing off half the desserts, we refill our glasses and head into the living room. The candles are burned down halfway, and we're all quite stuffed and relaxed.

I had never had an affinity for diets, per se. I don't obsess over the numbers on the scale or how I compare to the airbrushed little things in the fashion magazines. My issues are much deeper than that. That's probably why even though I run; I still carry ten to fifteen extra pounds around my hips and backside.

My chocolate addiction doesn't help. I am pear shaped and would have preferred to be apple shaped, if given the choice. At least the apples can suck in their problem areas. Mine just spread out.

"So, what are the boys doing tonight?" Michelle jokes with Brenda. "You are the one who sacrificed your house to the Tasmanian devils for us to have some alone time." The home that hosts the kids and husbands usually ends up a little messy, but nothing has been broken…yet.

"Oh, hardy har har!" Brenda grins and laughs. "They're fine. It's all good. Did Richard say he could make it or not? The last I heard it wasn't likely." She gestures toward Michelle with her glass.

Michelle's husband, Richard, is an economics professor at the University of Illinois and often works long hours or has to teach an evening course. He's average height, slightly balding and sports quite the paunch. He has an engaging, albeit intellectual, personality. At his academic level I shouldn't expect a jokester, I suppose.

"No, he couldn't make it tonight. He's working on a grant or something and the deadline is fast approaching. You know how passionate he is about his work," she sighs. "I guess it's just Tony and Scott tonight to try and keep the peace." Scott is Brenda's husband.

"God help them," Lilly chuckles. "Are you sure the two of them are enough to keep the kids under control?"

"Oh, they're fine." Brenda replies. "Our kids are older now and I think Scott mentioned something about a movie he was going to pop in anyway. The girls always just sit up in Mariah's room and do each other's hair and nails. Once the movie is over, the boys will play in the basement. But I didn't come to talk about the kids tonight. What's everybody been up to? I feel like we haven't been together in ages!"

We haven't had a dessert dinner in months. We try to get together as a group at least monthly, but sometimes our schedules don't mesh. Especially in late summer; that's family vacation time. So in Brenda time, that would equate to ages.

"Well," Michelle starts. "The third daycare center is finally up and running. I think this will be my last one. I can't take the headaches anymore. What with site location, licensing, remodeling, and staffing – I just don't know that it's worth it."

Michelle owns a chain of upscale childcare centers (right now it's only a chain of three) called Early Childhood Academy. The motto is "Training the leaders of tomorrow, today." The centers cater to those wealthy parents that are already looking at Ivy League universities for their preschoolers and want to jump start their education. The ratio of adult to child is very low, so the tuition rivals that of some state colleges. The kids have frequent educational field trips, eat organic food prepared on site by a chef and even learn a foreign language. Michelle cites research that says children learn foreign languages better and become easily fluent if taught before the age of five.

"I had a French tutor lined up, but she said she had a better offer suddenly come up on the East Coast, she was sorry, and poof she's gone. Just left me high and dry!" She laments, sipping her wine. "I couldn't believe it. I'm considering legal action because technically she had already signed a letter of intent. I turned away other candidates because she was so well qualified. Can you imagine the gall?"

"What are you going to do now?" I ask. I can't imagine what she would have to pay someone to teach preschoolers French.

"Well, I still have the other candidates' information from my original search. I just have to go down the list and start the interview process all over again." She shakes her head. "How about you guys? What are you up to? Hopefully, not looking for a French tutor because I'll fight you for it!" She balls her fist and shakes it jokingly.

Brenda regales us with the story of the Fendi bag order fiasco. Apparently, the store manager MaryAnn did lose her job. The owner was furious with her because she made such a huge error and the owner is going to have to pay thousands of dollars for handbags that she most likely won't be able to sell quickly enough, if ever. The job was offered to Brenda, but she refused. The owner brought someone in from outside the store to fill the position. Brenda only has the job to support her shopping habit. She doesn't want to make a career of it.

Honestly, I don't think she wants that level of responsibility. I can see her making the very same mistake. Brenda is detail oriented with her wardrobe and social life, but not much else.

"The new manager is a guy named Nate. He just moved to the area." Brenda finishes her story.

The conversation continues on casually; Lilly is trying to finalize the art program she runs at her children's school. It's a volunteer position, but Lilly takes any endeavor she tackles seriously. Although the school year has already begun, she doesn't have all of the details worked out and projects lined up beyond November. Apparently, she is trying to line up local artists that utilize different mediums to come and give the children hands on demonstrations for the use of each type of medium.

My eyes flicker to the clock above the mantle. It's almost nine o'clock.

Nine o'clock. Michael hasn't called.

The knot in my stomach forms. I've been having such a good time with my friends, it slipped my mind.

Oh, no.

I'm sure he's okay. He has to be. That doesn't stop the irrational, nagging fear from gripping my thoughts. Did I watch the weather report for Cleveland this morning? Was it supposed to rain there today? Slick roads are not good, especially in an unfamiliar city…

It's quiet. My friends are staring at me.

"Huh? What? Did I miss something?" I say sheepishly, looking around. I hadn't been paying attention, so I didn't know where the conversation had gone.

"Faith, Lilly just asked if you were okay. Are you?" Michelle asks, concern coloring her voice.

"I'm fine." I work to keep my face from betraying my inner turmoil. I look down at my half empty glass and swirl it around, buying time to bottle my emotions.

Please, God, let the phone ring.

"No, you're not." Lilly says matter-of-factly, her blue eyes piercing me. "What's wrong?"

I take a deep breath and glance briefly at Lilly. I would swear her gaze goes right through my façade and into my soul. Everyone is still waiting for a response.

"I just noticed the time and realized Michael hasn't called me yet," I say softly.

"Oh, is that all? Gosh, I thought I had said something to offend you. Lord, Faith! I'm sure he's fine. Maybe he had a late dinner." Brenda says dismissively, relief in her voice.

Her flippancy isn't meant to be harmful; she has no idea. Nobody does.

Nobody knows about Paul. It's too painful to think about, much less talk about. They have no clue why I panic so much when Michael leaves. As much as I love my friends, I'm not comfortable exposing everything about myself. Even Michael only knows the surface of my insecurities, not how deep they run.

Or why I have them.

"What about that bothers you so much?" Michelle asks quietly after flicking a stern look at Brenda. She eyes me with sincere curiosity. Michelle is such a fiercely independent woman that I'm sure this attitude of mine baffles her.

"Oh, you know me – Miss Worry Wart!" I smile dismissively and work to keep the tone of my voice light. "I just like to know that he's safe. He's been calling me every night at about eight."

Just then, my cell phone rings in the kitchen and startles all of us.

"That's probably him right now." Michelle reassures me as I hurry into the kitchen to catch it before it goes to voicemail.

"Hello?!" I breathe excitedly into the phone. I picked it up so quickly I didn't even bother to see who it was.

"Hi, sweetheart. It's me. Sorry I'm so late calling. The restaurant had horribly slow service this time." His voice immediately calms me. "How was your day?"

"Fine. It's better now that I hear your voice." I relax against the countertop. "The girls are over right now and we're just sitting around talking."

"I'm glad to hear you took me up on my suggestion."

"Yeah. Me, too. Actually Brenda suggested it. Sometimes I wonder if you're all ganging up on me. How's everything going in Cleveland?"

"Right on schedule. I really don't know why I had to come. They just needed someone to crack the whip, I guess."

"I'm sorry you had to go then, too, especially if it wasn't really necessary."

"I agree, but it's not my decision. I just do as I'm told. Listen, honey, I'm pretty beat. The girls are waiting for you and I know you don't want to be rude. Remember I love you and I'll see you soon."

"Thanks for calling. It really makes my day."

"I know, Faith. I understand. I love you and I'll talk to you tomorrow. Enjoy yourself."

"I will."

We say our goodbyes and I hang up. I return to the living room.

"Feel better?" asks Michelle. Her tone isn't sarcastic, just concerned. She knows I worry and never makes me feel bad. Nodding, I try to take the attention away from me by asking, "So, anyone need their glass refilled?"

Michelle pipes up. "I'll have water. I had my two glasses of wine and that's my limit. Lilly, those wines were delish as was your torte. Pass my compliments on to Tony. He certainly made an excellent choice." She rises from the oversized leather chair in the corner of the room.

"Thanks and I will," says Lilly.

"I think I'll have just a teensy bit more of whatever is left," Brenda chimes in.

We all end up in the kitchen. The conversation, thankfully, turns to other topics. The next time I look at the clock, it's almost eleven.

"Oh! The time has just flown by. I have you all to thank for that; it's been wonderful, but I think it's time we wrap this party up. I know the kids don't have school tomorrow, but I'm afraid I'll turn into a pumpkin if I don't get to bed soon." My last words are muffled by a yawn.

"I agree," sighs Michelle. "I love all of you, but I'm just beat after the day I've had." She moves into the dining room and starts clearing away the remnants.

"Anyone want anything else?" she gestures to the leftovers. The food was beautiful as well as exceptionally tasty quite a few hours ago, but each item has been gouged, cut and scooped to death. We all shake our heads.

Michelle shrugs and begins covering the remains with lids and foil. Everyone chips in to clean up. We've performed this routine at each other's homes so often that it's become automatic.

Once the clean up is done, we say our lengthy goodbyes and work our way to the door.

"As soon as I get home, I'll have April round up your kids and head home," says Brenda.

"Sounds good and thanks. Please be sure they help pick up if there's anything left to do at your house. I don't want them leaving a mess."

"Nonsense!" she says, smiling impishly. "It's not a big deal. Besides, next time we'll have the kids over to your house, and we'll be even."

"You're too funny, Brenda." I give her a quick squeeze. She returns my embrace and then ducks out and disappears into the night. Once the last car pulls out of the driveway, I step inside and close the door behind me, still smiling.

I really am blessed to have such friends. I need to focus on that. Maybe if I'd had friends like that twenty years ago, my own personal pit of hell would've been easier.

Okay, well - maybe not easier, but perhaps at least shorter.

Thanks for my friends, God. Please don't take them away.

Chapter Five

The remaining days before Michael returns go by in a blur of daily activity and nightly emotional battles waiting for his call. He never misses a single night. April doesn't place in her gymnastics competition, which sets her into a crying fit for the rest of the evening. She doesn't even talk to Michael when he calls.

But she still eats dinner.

Andrew blocks multiple attempts at scoring while he plays the goalie position in soccer and his team wins by one goal. He proudly shows the bruises he gets on his chest as a result of his efforts for days afterward to anyone who will look. He hopes they will last until daddy gets home.

They don't.

Sarah never reveals why she's been so morose. I hope it isn't anything serious. There's still that tug on my heart.

Most nights I collapse into a fitful sleep after tossing and turning and trying to read myself into rest. Reading to fall asleep doesn't work for me – I end up getting so involved in the characters that I don't want to put the book down. It's a good distraction, but not when my goal is sleep.

My anxiety builds to a crescendo the night before his flight home. I am beside myself for fear of the what if factor. Try as I might, I can't escape its grip.

Monday arrives and my first thought upon waking is, Today is the day. Michael will be home today. Everything will be okay.

Once again I pray for the pilot, the mechanics, and the weather.

I drag myself out of bed and head downstairs after waking Andrew and Sarah. I brew coffee and cook breakfast. Michael's plane is due to land just after noon.

Sarah is the first one down. She gives me a light squeeze and asks, "Excited about Dad coming home today?" My old soul of a daughter knows I struggle when Michael is gone, even if she doesn't understand why.

"Of course. You know how much I miss him. We all do." I smile and hand her a plate of eggs and sausage.

"Mmmm." She takes her plate to the breakfast bar.

April is the next one to appear.

"Mom! Will you please tell Andrew to hurry up? I need to get into the bathroom or we're going to be late!" she says, her tone exasperated. Her hair is flattened on one side and she has a new pimple outbreak burgeoning on her forehead. She's still in her pajamas.

"Yes. Come get your breakfast and I'll go see what I can do," I sigh, handing breakfast to her on my way to the stairs.

I climb the stairs and knock on the door to the bathroom the kids share. "Andrew? What's taking so long, honey?"

"I'm doing my hair. I'll be out in a little while."

Andrew? Doing his hair? What on earth could a nine year old do to his hair?

"Honey, what exactly are you doing to your hair?" I try the door knob, but it's locked. "Andrew, unlock the door."

A responding sigh comes from the other side. Within seconds, the door knob jiggles and the lock disengages.

I open the door to find Andrew standing in front of the vanity staring at me, an expectant smile on his face. There's a large tube of gel on the counter with more gel on the counter than in the tube. I see the imprint left behind of little swiping fingers where Andrew had scooped some of it off of the counter. A fairly large portion actually made it into his hair because it looks completely wet, but is standing straight up. Well, not straight up. I think that's the look he was going for. I bite on my lower lip, struggling to stifle a giggle.

"Honey, how much of your sister's gel did you use?" I ask him gently.

"Not much, only about half."

Lord, April's not going to be happy.

"Sweetheart, why did you use your sister's gel?"

"I wanted to look cool. Jeremy Benson always looks cool and he uses gel in his hair."

"Well, sweetie, I don't think Jeremy Benson uses quite this much gel. Can I help you…comb it…a bit?" I offer, reaching for his comb.

He considers it for a moment and nods. He turns toward the mirror and allows me to work through his quickly stiffening spikes. I'm not hopeful about the outcome. After combing as much of the gel out as possible, I try to style it the way he describes to me as I work.

"Okay, Andrew. That definitely looks cool. Now go get dressed and come downstairs for breakfast." I kiss his cheek and send him off to his room.

Quickly cleaning up the mess, I go downstairs to intercept April as she is about to come up. I grasp her shoulders and look her squarely in the eyes.

"Andrew wanted to style his hair and got into your gel," I say quickly. Her mouth pops open and she glares at the ceiling before meeting my gaze. She starts to say something, but I interrupt her. "Don't say a word to him about his hair, do you hear me? I'll buy you some more gel, okay? Not a word."

"But...!" she starts.

I hold my index finger up. "April. Not. A. Word."

Her mouth forms a thin line as she crosses her arms and stomps up the stairs. I hear a door slam.

Here we go again.

I return to the kitchen and put Andrew's now cold breakfast in the microwave.

Andrew's footfalls are on the stairs and I quickly turn to Sarah. "Sarah, please be nice to Andrew about his hair, okay?" I say softly.

She looks up surprised, eyebrows raised in a wordless question. At that moment, Andrew comes around the corner beaming. Sarah's expression turns to one of shocked amusement and she presses her lips tightly together and ducks her head, pretending to read her open math book.

"How do I look, Mom?" says Andrew proudly. He's tried to dress himself up. The sleeves on his shirt are rolled up tightly and it's buttoned all the way to his neck. His hair still looks wet, even with my efforts to remove as much gel as possible. The gel is veritable cement, causing his hair to quiver with every movement.

"You look handsome. But can I unbutton the top button of your shirt? It will be more comfortable."

He nods and walks over to me, chin up. I complete the task and hand him his breakfast. He takes it and joins Sarah at the breakfast bar. Sarah still has her lips pressed tightly together, but a giggle bursts through her lips. I shoot her a stern glance. She quiets down. Andrew doesn't notice.

After the kids have left for school, I busy myself clearing breakfast before changing my clothes to go for a run.

Only four hours until Michael gets home!

I'm excited, but fearful. Always fearful.

As I run, I don't allow my mind to dwell on the typical train of thought I have when I'm stressed.

I will not do this today. I will not do this today.

I force myself to focus on putting one foot in front of another, keeping my eyes straight ahead.

Turning into my driveway afterwards, I am out of breath, my muscles are quivering, and I'm sucking wind. My head is clearer and I savor it. I turn my face upwards toward the morning sun, close my eyes, and feel the warmth against my skin even as the air has a bite to it, causing me to shiver. It's only the endorphins that are giving me this feeling, but I don't care.

I'll take it.

I open my eyes and glance at my cell. It's ten o'clock. Michael is in the air at this very moment. Fear grips me. I close my eyes again and focus on breathing.

In...out...in...out.

One last deep breath in before the air escapes my lungs with a whoosh and I duck inside.

I leave my running shoes by the door and head upstairs to shower, peeling off my sticky clothes and throwing them in the hamper on my way into the bathroom. I turn the water on and step inside, letting the warmth of the water run down my back.

As the water heats up in the shower, I contemplate my situation.

I am so sick of feeling like this all the time. I am paralyzed.

Michael has suggested numerous times over the years that I get professional help and I've always shied away from it. He's never really pressed the issue.

Professional help.

Just that phrase alone has always sounded so....I don't know...psycho? It's not like I'm crazy, I'm just...stuck. Everybody has hang ups and issues, right? Maybe they didn't have a life altering catastrophe like I did, but I didn't go crazy.

I eventually got on with my life. I got married and had children. I take care of my family. I'm normal and I'm ...stuck. There's no other word for it.

Besides, what would my friends say if I told them I was seeing a counselor? Or a psychotherapist?

There's that word 'psycho' again.

Whatever I call it, they would have questions they wouldn't ask and answers I couldn't give.

Sighing heavily, I turn off the water, wrap my head in a towel and dry off even as I continue to ponder. I move over to the vanity and begin the morning ritual.

So what if my friends had questions about seeing a therapist? If I had a friend in the same situation, I would suggest they get help, too, wouldn't I?

I don't know. Maybe. It's always easy to give advice, but not so easy to take it.

Thinking about each of my friends, I want to believe they'd support me. In my heart of hearts I want to believe they will, but still...

They don't know the true mess I am. They don't know where I've come from. I'm sure they've all had wonderful lives. I'm the oddball of the group.

So many secrets we women share and yet there are so many more we never do.

I push this train of thought to the back of my mind and realize it's now ten forty-five. It's almost time to go to the airport. It will take almost forty-five minutes to get there, plus I have to find parking. I can't take him to the airport, but I have no problem picking him up because he's coming home rather than leaving me.

I hurry to my closet and look for something to wear. My stomach grumbles. Oh! I forgot to eat breakfast. I really am out of sorts; I love breakfast. Either I eat with the kids or I eat after my run, but I always eat. I pull on my robe and cinch it around my waist while hurrying downstairs.

After washing down some scrambled eggs with water, I grab a small handful of M&Ms and hurry back upstairs to get dressed.

I turn on the flat screen we have mounted in our bedroom. I briefly scan the national news channel to see if there are any plane crashes to report.

I'm not crazy, just cautious.

There's no breaking news in that category, so I finish selecting an outfit. I choose one Michael loves: a sapphire blue lightweight cashmere sweater with three quarter length sleeves and a square neck line paired with a black pin-striped pencil skirt that flatters my pear shape. Michael has always complimented me on my legs and the pencil skirt stops a few inches above my knee. It's a bit chilly, so I wear black tights and low pumps. I finish the look with a silver necklace and matching earrings.

Stepping back to regard myself in the mirror, I automatically smooth the skirt.

Not bad.

The familiar rim of fear in my eyes reflects back to me.

Ignoring that, I glance at the clock on the bedside table. It's after eleven.

Perfect time to go. No more time to think.

Quickly checking the news again (just in case), I click the television off, hurry downstairs, grab my purse and leave.

Traffic isn't bad and I arrive in plenty of time. Entering the terminal, I check one of the overhead monitors for his flight status. It's due to arrive on time, so I turn toward baggage claim. It really stinks that since the attacks of 9/11, we can't meet our loved ones at the gate anymore.

I pace the baggage claim area wringing my purse strap in my fingers, trying not to look as nervous as I feel. My anxiety ticks upward in time with the clock.

After an eternity of waiting, his flight's arrival is announced and the horn sounds obnoxiously over the carousel where his flight's baggage will circulate. Hovering at the entrance for the passengers to arrive, I peer anxiously at the empty space willing Michael into view.

A few passengers begin to stroll through and I anxiously search the faces looking for the only one that matters. The stream of passengers is achingly endless. Finally, he comes around the corner.

A rush of pure relief floods through me. I run toward him as best I can while wearing a pencil skirt and pumps and throw myself into his arms. He catches me and hugs me tightly as I bury my face into his chest, inhaling his distinctive smell. It's musky and sweet and pure Michael.

Nobody else matters; Michael is home and he's safe.

"That's what I love to come home to," Michael murmurs in my ear, a smile in his voice.

Looking up, I'm grinning so hard that my face hurts.

"I just love that you come home," my voice quivers.

He bends down to kiss me. I'm vaguely aware of people pushing past us.

I don't care.

"Let's go get my luggage and go home. I've really missed you," he whispers into my ear. His hands move lower on my back as he squeezes me tightly before letting me go. A thrill goes through me.

The fear and anxiety are all but lost with the relief I feel now mingled with a strong physical hunger for him. Two weeks is a long time after all…

Thank you, God, for letting Michael come home to me.

Chapter Six

Life goes back to normal, if there such a thing for me, once Michael returns. We spend the afternoon getting to know one another in the Biblical sense. The kids are thrilled to see him when they get home from school.

We actually get dressed minutes before they burst through the door with book bags in hand. Their voices are a cacophony of excitement; all three eagerly, and simultaneously, fill him in on everything he missed while he was gone. Michael soaks it all in, enjoying every minute.

I steal myself into the kitchen to start dinner and realize I've once again forgotten to take anything out.

I pop my head around the corner, cup my hands around my mouth to be sure I can be heard and say, "Hey kids! How about we all go out for dinner to celebrate dad coming home?"

There's another round of raucous noise as they proclaim, "Yes, yes, yes!"

Even Sarah seems more animated than usual. April darts upstairs yelling that she has to do something with her hair if she's going out. Andrew runs up to me, hugs my waist, and asks if we can go to Chuck E. Cheese's for dinner.

"No, honey. That's more for a kid's party than a daddy celebration." I kiss his cheek and send him on his way to clean his face and hands before we go. His hair has wilted from its earlier glory and now looks like it just needs to be washed.

"Where are we going?" Sarah asks from her perch on the arm of her father's recliner. She has her arm wrapped around his shoulders and his arms are wrapped around her waist.

I'm thankful my children have the father I never did.

"I don't know. Any suggestions? It's your celebration, after all." I glance at Michael.

"How about that steak house downtown? The food is good and the prices are reasonable," he suggests.

"Sounds good. I'm so hungry I could eat a cow!" I exclaim. My stomach feels like it's stuck to my spine. I've eaten only two eggs all day.

The M&Ms don't count. They never do.

"Worked up an appetite today, did you?" he murmurs suggestively with a wink directed at me. I suppress a grin as the heat rises in my cheeks.

"Yes! I love that place!" Sarah exclaims obliviously as she jumps up. She runs upstairs to tell April.

I jokingly slap Michael on his leg before settling myself onto his lap. "Don't make those comments around the kids. They're getting older, you know."

He wraps his arms around me and chuckles. "I know, but I love it when you blush like that." He nuzzles my neck. I shiver and push him away playfully.

"Come on, I really am starving." I grasp his hand and pull him upstairs. The bed is still messed up from our afternoon activity. I pick up our clothing that was strewn over the floor and throw it into the growing pile in the laundry hamper, making a mental note to do laundry soon.

We freshen up and head downstairs. Andrew is watching television. April and Sarah are sitting on the sofa talking about boys, April more so than Sarah. I notice Sarah chimes in more often these days with these discussions. Tom Parker's name come up frequently; April is still going on about the upcoming winter formal. She and Sarah are discussing dress options.

"Ready to go, kids? Turn the television off," Michael says cheerfully clapping his hands together. All three scramble up and move toward the garage door, slipping on shoes as they go. Once we're all piled into the van, the chatter picks up in the back.

The restaurant isn't packed because it's Monday, so we're seated immediately. Conversation is light and the meal is good. The sun has set as the bill arrives. It's a quiet ride home and I glance back over my shoulder at my children. Andrew buckled in, fast asleep with his head lolled back and mouth open wide. Sarah reading a book, of course, while April stares blankly out the window with ear buds in place, her lips quivering to music only she can hear while she sways back and forth.

I look over at Michael's handsome face, aglow in the dashboard light. He has one hand on the steering wheel and the other on the arm rest near me. I reach over and intertwine my fingers with his, squeezing.

He glances over, smiles, and squeezes in return.

God, can't it just stay like this forever?

There's peace in this moment. I ache for time to freeze right here, right now. I gaze out the window and watch the shifting, blurring scenes of houses streaming past me in rapid succession.

Michael made it home safely from his trip. I love him and he loves me. Our children are happy and healthy. We have a beautiful home to go to. What more could I want in life than this?

Peace. Real, fear-free peace that will never go away. A guarantee that everything won't be snatched away in an instant.

My constant, familiar companion Fear claws at the edges of my mind.

Just for this moment, I want to stay in this place of peace.

****

Michael has the next day off from work because of his trip to Cleveland, which was an apparent success. After the kids are gone, we spend most of the morning in bed before I help him unpack and do laundry. He checks his emails and voicemails. He's a hard worker and can never truly just be off.

He joins me on my morning run, which he loves to do when he is free. These runs are much more enjoyable and can't be considered exercise because we talk so much that we end up walking most of it.

Michael is more than just my husband; he's also my best friend.

"Can I ask you a question?" he says quietly, as we begin ascending a hill in a slow jog.

"Sure."

"Why do you get so worked up about me flying or April driving?"

I almost trip over my own feet.

"I don't know." My eyes bore into the pavement.

"There has to be something that triggers it, Faith," he says gently. I can feel his gaze on me.

I don't know what to say, so I keep jogging and scowling at the pavement.

"Honey, I just want to understand you more." He nudges me with his elbow.

The floor could drop out from under me at any moment. It did once before, and I'm scared to death that it will again. I don't deserve you.

A lump builds in my throat. All I can do is nod.

Change the subject.

"Hey, I bet I can beat you home!" I blurt, taking off in a flat out run.

Running is good, running lets me escape.

Michael sighs heavily as I pull away. He quickly outruns me, but I knew he would. I don't really care who beats whom; I just don't want to talk.

We still have ten blocks to go. My diversion works. When we reach the house, we are both gasping.

Michael lets the subject drop, and for that, I am grateful.

I check my cell when we get inside and there are three text messages waiting for me. One each from Brenda, Lilly, and Michelle.

All three ask if Michael made it all right. Of course, Brenda says she didn't want to interrupt our hellos right after Michael got back. Her message ends with "wink, wink, nudge, nudge".

So typical of Brenda.

I reply to all three with one message, "He got home fine and all is well. Will talk soon."

That night as we're lying in bed, Michael again brings up the topic I least want to discuss.

"Faith, I really want to know why you get so upset when I travel. I want to help. But you have to open up to me."

I immediately stiffen. I so don't want to do this.

Not now, not ever.

"What do you mean?" I ask, feigning ignorance. It's a long shot, but I'll try anything to avoid this.

He sighs heavily, rolls onto his side and props himself onto his elbow facing me. There's a look of exasperation on his face that I can just make out through the moonlight streaming in the window. "You know what I mean, Faith. Why do you get so upset when I leave and stay that way while I'm gone?" he persists.

I stare back at him and blink. There are no words.

"Because I'm scared something will happen to you," my voice is barely audible. At its core it's the truth and it's all I can admit.

His face softens, but he persists. "But why do you get so upset? It's like...it…consumes you or something. I don't understand. It doesn't make any sense. You get yourself all worked up over nothing. "

It's not nothing. It's everything!

"I don't know," I say softly, avoiding his eyes. He cups my face with his hand and forces me to look at him.

I don't want to do this!

My anxiety builds. I freeze under his scrutiny even as my eyes fill with tears. His eyes search my face. I don't know what he sees there, but his face hardens and then suddenly softens. He kisses me and looks deeply in my eyes, his eyebrows knitting together.

"I love you. I am always going to be here. Do you hear me? Why won't you tell me?" he whispers earnestly, inches from my face.

The tears spill over, dribble down my cheeks and land in his palm which still cups my face. I can't answer him. I love him so much, but there's a wall that won't budge. Words won't come. I want to say yes and say no all at the same time.

Closing my eyes, all I can do is sob.

Michael pulls me close to him and rocks me gently back and forth, smoothing my hair, whispering to me all the time that everything is okay.

I wish I could believe him. From all outward appearances, everything is okay. But inside, I'm an absolute mess.

"Maybe you should get some help, honey," he whispers after a few minutes, his arms still wrapped around me. "I want to help you, but I don't know what to do. I don't want you to be so…" he searches for the right word. "…upset. I feel helpless."

"Do you think I'm crazy?" I whisper anxiously.

"No!" he answers quickly, his arms tightening around me. "You're definitely not crazy. But this fear you have is…not normal, honey. I just think perhaps it would help you to talk to someone about it, even if it's not me. Someone who can help you get through it and get…over it, you know?"

"Maybe. I don't know. I don't know that I can talk to a total stranger."

I can't talk about it at all.

"Maybe that's what you need. A stranger to talk to. You certainly won't talk to me." There's an edge to his voice that I don't like. "Besides, that's what counselors are for, aren't they? To help people get through things they can't get through by themselves?"

"I'll think about it. I'm so sorry that I'm like this."

"It's okay, honey." He kisses my forehead and adjusts his position so that my back is to his front, keeping his arms wrapped around me. "I just love you and want you to get better. Maybe seeing a counselor will help."

"Maybe." I kiss his hand.

"Will you at least consider it?"

There's a long pause. "Yes, I'll consider it." I will consider it. I just don't know if I'll do it.

"Good." He kisses me on the cheek and then squeezes me tightly before relaxing.

I lie awake long after Michael's breathing has become deep and steady, my mind racing.

Maybe he's right. Maybe I should talk to a professional. I can keep it a secret from my friends; they don't have to know. But how do I do this? I can't open up to my own husband. How will I be able to open up to some random stranger sitting at a desk?

I picture myself lying on a leather couch in an office while a white haired man that resembles Einstein with his glasses perched on the end of his very long, narrow nose sits at my head in a matching leather chair. He has a notepad open with a fountain pen poised for action and his legs are crossed. The conversation starts with, "So, tell me about your mother..."

I mentally cringe. I don't think I can do it. I promised Michael I would at least consider it. Eventually my mind chews the flavor out of the situation and becomes exhausted. No sense in trying to stay awake when this will all be waiting for me tomorrow. There's always something waiting for me tomorrow.

Oh, God. What next...

Chapter Seven

"Have you given any thought to what we talked about the other night? About getting some help?" Michael asks softly after breakfast three days later.

The butter knife I was using to make a sandwich drops. I hoped he had forgotten about it.

Retrieving the knife, I eye him sharply and resume making the sandwich, flicking a glance behind him to see if the kids are around. They're not.

Crap. I was hoping for an excuse not to have to talk about this.

"Yes," I respond meekly. "I'm still thinking about it. Do you think we can afford it?"

It's a lame diversionary tactic; since I handle the finances, I know we can afford it. Having danced around this issue for so many years, I don't know any other way to deal with it but to deflect attention from it.

"You're stalling, Faith. I know you are. You know we can afford it. This needs to stop and you need to get help." His tone is sharper than usual.

I look at him, hurt. He moves close to me; his eyes are gentle, but his jaw is set.

"Honey, I'm not trying to be mean. I'm just…I want you to get the help you need. I've hoped for years it would get better, that you would get better. But you're not. You need help." He says each word slowly and carefully, reaching out to pull me close.

I shake my head and pull back. He looks surprised. I don't usually resist his embrace. I crave it more than anything sometimes.

"I know I need help. There. I said it. Are you happy? I know I need help, but I don't know that I want to go talk to some stranger."

His words hurt because they're right on target. Deep down, I know he's right.

I don't want him to be right. I don't want to do this.

He gazes at me intently for a moment before pulling me to him again, this time without my resistance.

"I'm sorry, Michael. I don't know what's wrong with me. I just…don't know," I say into his chest.

He sighs and continues to hold me. "I know. Do you want me to call and make an appointment for you? Would that make it easier?" He won't give up easily this time.

My face crumples. I don't want to do this!

I pull back and look up. I had planned a sharp retort, but the words just die on my tongue when I see the sincere love in his eyes.

My resolve melts.

"Michael, I will get help, I promise. But I'll make my own appointment after I research what services are around here, okay?"

He pulls back and places his hands on his hips. "Okay. But I'm giving you one week to make the appointment, or I'm doing it for you, all right? One week, no more."

"Oh, so now you're giving me a deadline? Really?" I can't believe what I'm hearing. I usually get my way.

He eyes me sternly. "Yup. One week."

He's actually giving me a deadline to seek counseling? Am I really that bad?

Wrong question. Can he really tell I'm that bad?

"Fine. Whatever. One week." I turn away and jab the finished sandwich a little roughly into the plastic baggie, causing the bread to rip. Perfect. I finish assembling the remaining lunches and place them on the end of the breakfast bar for the kids to grab as they go.

Michael remains silent, and I refuse to meet his gaze. Finally, he sighs and walks out of the kitchen. I stare balefully at his retreating form.

April bounds down the stairs with Sarah in tow and yells down through the basement door for Andrew to come up so she can leave. He comes up a few minutes later and it's a whirlwind while they put on their shoes, pack their lunches into their backpacks and scramble out the door. Michael reappears and gives each of them a hug and kiss, as do I. Then they're gone and it's silent again.

Michael is the first to break it.

"Faith, I love you. I hope you know that. But we have to move forward, and in order to do that, you need to get help."

His words put my teeth on edge. I really wish he'd quit saying that. I know I need help, but he doesn't have to keep repeating it. I reach for his hand and pull myself to him.

"I know. I know. I said I'll take care of it. Just don't pressure me. I love you, too." I turn my face up and kiss him. We pull apart and he reaches for his brief case.

"I have to get to work or I'll be late for the morning meeting."

"I know. Have a good day and…drive carefully, please." It's a habit.

He looks at me with an amused and slightly exasperated expression. "I will, Faith. I always do. Get help." He grins. I throw the dish towel at him. He ducks into the garage and is gone.

As I load the breakfast dishes into the dishwasher, my thoughts are consumed with the looming deadline to find a counselor. I don't even know where to start.

Do I look in the yellow pages? Google counseling services? I can't ask my friends for a referral. I don't want them to know.

Besides, I doubt my friends have ever needed counseling. That makes the point moot.

My cell phone beeps with a text. I quickly dry my hands and retrieve it. It's from Lilly; she wants to know if we can meet up for lunch sometime next week. I text that I can and for her to let me know when she wants to meet. I hit send and grip the cell in my hand. I'm anxiously waiting for April's text that she arrived safely at school.

My thoughts return to the counseling dilemma.

I have to keep this from my children, too. They will talk about anything that happens. I can just imagine how the information would get jumbled up in translation from child to child to parent. For all I know, they'd have me being committed to an institution by the time it completed the circuit.

The door bell chimes and I jerk.

That's weird. Who could that be at nine in the morning?

I am still in my bathrobe, too. Good grief. I hurry to the door, peering into the peephole. It's a woman I've never seen before. She has a foil covered object nestled in her hands.

A warm smile greets me as I open the door. She's about the same height as me and very trim. She's dressed in a modest blue button down shirt with stylish jeans and tennis shoes. Her glossy black hair is pulled back in a pony tail and her smile reveals perfectly white, straight teeth. Her dark eyes are framed by enviably thick lashes set against slightly olive toned skin. She could be Italian, I think.

"Hi! I'm Julie Jackson. My husband and I just moved in next door." She gestures toward the house on my right with her head as her arms are occupied. The house had been on the market for about five months. I never knew the previous occupants, but I heard through the neighborhood grapevine there was a divorce.

"I hope I'm not intruding. I just wanted to stop by and say hello and introduce myself. I brought you a coffee cake." She holds up the foil-covered pan.

Being caught off guard, I blink at her stupidly before recovering and smiling. "Oh! Where are my manners! I'm sorry." I pull the door wide open and move to the side to allow her to enter, cinching the waist of my robe. "Please, come in. Excuse the mess, the kids left for school this morning, and I was just cleaning up. I haven't even showered yet, obviously." I run my hands through my hair, trying to smooth it.

"Thank you." She enters, still holding the pan in her hands. "Where would you like me to put this?" she asks sweetly, still smiling.

"Sorry! I'll take that. Come into the kitchen." I relieve her of her burden, which is still warm, and lead the way. "Would you like some coffee? I was just going to make some." I sniff the pan; it smells of brown sugar and cinnamon. "It smells wonderful. It would go well with a fresh cup."

"Are you sure you don't mind? I stopped by unannounced and I don't want to interrupt your day."

"Nonsense, there's nothing that can't wait."

"That would be wonderful," she nods and looks around appreciatively. "You have a very lovely home."

She takes a seat at one of the bar stools at the breakfast bar.

"Thank you. When did you move in? I'm sorry I haven't noticed any moving trucks or anything." I am so wrapped up in my own life that I have tunnel vision.

The coffee just starts percolating when my cell beeps. It's a text from April. The kids are safely at school. Michael's text follows suit. I sigh in relief, tap a quick response to both and set the phone aside.

Julie continues our conversation. "We moved in about two weeks ago. I'm almost done unpacking. Our garage is full of empty boxes. The moving company told us to call them when we're ready to have them picked up. I hope it'll be soon. My husband is tired of parking his car outside," she chuckles.

"Your name is Julie, right? Sorry, I'm not good with names." I grin sheepishly.

"That's okay. I'm the same way. I don't think I got your name, though."

I press my hand against my forehead. "Oh. You're right! I really have forgotten my manners, haven't I? I'm Faith." I extend my hand and she takes it.

"Nice to meet you, Faith." She inclines her head and continues smiling. I don't think she's stopped smiling since I opened the door. Her face has the appearance of one that is used to smiling.

I cut the cake into squares, placing our portions on plates.

"How do you like your coffee?" I ask, reaching for mugs.

"Cream and sugar, please."

I pull the cream from the fridge and bring the sugar bowl over. I pour the coffee and hand her one of the steaming mugs.

She wraps both hands around the mug and inhales deeply. "Thank you! This smells wonderful. Coffee is my vice, I have to admit. If I could drink it all day, I would."

"Please, help yourself to the cake. I can't wait to taste it. It really does smell wonderful." I push a plate and fork in her direction. I wait for her to take a piece and then do likewise. It's delicious; the top is crunchy and tastes of cinnamon, nutmeg, and brown sugar.

"That's very sweet of you to say. I love to bake."

Through the course of our conversation, I learn that her husband's name is Ben and he's a minister at a small church in the area. Ben and Julie are both thirty two years old and have no children. They moved here from Indiana to accept the ministerial position. Not having any children seems odd, considering they've been married for ten years. It's a touchy subject, so I don't linger on it and neither does she.

I share similar things about myself; I tell her about Michael and his job and our kids. It's the usual getting-to-know-you chatter when women meet.

Julie is very nice; neither overly enthusiastic nor subdued. She seems genuinely interested in what I have to say.

Finally, our mugs and plates are empty and she rises from her stool. "Thank you for inviting me in, Faith. I really should be going; I know you have things to do. It's been nice to get to know you, and I hope we can become great friends." She smiles warmly and extends her hand.

"You're welcome and thank you so much for the delicious coffee cake." I shake her hand and walk her to the door.

I really like her. That was a nice way to get my day going.

As I load the plates and mugs in the dishwasher, I feel…relaxed. It's unfamiliar.

Once I replace the foil on the coffee cake and put it in the fridge, I head upstairs to shower and get dressed, the relaxed feeling lingering.

When the clock nears one-thirty, I stroll to the end of the driveway to check the mail. Sifting through the mail, one envelope jumps out at me. It's very peculiar. I shuffle back toward the house and into the office just off the entryway, still eyeing the strange envelope.

The envelope itself is unremarkable except that it's yellow, scuffed, and there are multiple layers of forwarding address stamps on top of each other on the front. I can't make out the addresses before my current address, but the return address says "Department of Corrections. Denver, CO."

I freeze and my heart stops cold.

Oh, God. Don't do this to me.

Chapter Eight

What could this possibly be? I haven't had mail from Colorado in years. There's been no need of anything to come from Colorado for an eternity.

This can't be good. This has to do with…Paul.

I can't do this. I can't do this.

My heart pounds and a lump forms in my throat so large I would swear I swallowed a golf ball. My hand balls into a fist, crinkling the envelope. I will it to either reveal itself to me in full or go away.

I start shaking. I can't open it. I can't.

Dread overrides curiosity. Hands still shaking, I throw the offensive envelope in a desk drawer and slam it shut. Whirling around, the rest of the mail is splayed on the floor. I must have dropped it.

Run, run, run, run. *Run!*

Hurriedly gathering up the mail, I drop the stack on the little table by the door in the entryway. Quickly glancing at the clock to gauge how much time I have before the kids come home, I bound up the stairs two at a time to change.

Just like the night Michael left for Cleveland, I bolt out the door and am running full speed before I hit the end of the driveway. I peripherally notice Julie in her driveway, pausing with a box in her arms to look in my direction. Her presence barely registers.

Run!!

I clear my mind and focus on running: the pounding of my shoes hitting the dark pavement, the feel of the air as it hits my face and arms, my clenched fists and bent elbows moving in rhythm to my feet, the rapid intake of cold air as I breathe in coupled with the sharp contrast of the warmth that escapes my mouth as I exhale.

My run is punctuated with thoughts of what the envelope might contain. Try as I might, I can't block it out. My frustration grows.

Maybe knowing is better than not knowing.

No! Run faster!

My muscles and lungs scream. I don't care. I need to keep running. Running farther, faster.

Running away.

I'm jolted by the thought. Is that what I'm doing? Running away?

The errant thought won't leave. Am I trying to run away? From the past, from the hurt, from the fear? Fine; then run away it is! But I never actually run away. I always come home. I keep living.

I kept living after Paul died. The sun rose and the sun set every day. My heart throbbed every day. I never understood how a shattered heart can keep beating, but mine did.

I lurched through the days, the months, the years. I started and finished college, working the whole time.

I get up every single day. I take care of my family. I do what I'm supposed to do. Isn't that enough? Isn't it??

"Isn't that ENOUGH??!!" I scream at the top of my lungs.

I skitter to a stop, realizing I screamed that out loud. My hands are balled into fists at my sides, my face skyward. I'm quivering from head to toe and gasping for air. Grimacing, I glance furtively around looking for any witnesses to my outburst. There are none. I have come to the part of my circuit that is populated with more trees than houses.

"Dear God," I groan, collapsing my face into my hands. I fall to my knees on the pavement.

My outburst puts some things into perspective.

I am a mess. A complete and total mess.

Michael is right. I need help. This isn't getting better; it's festering inside, like a long ignored scratch that's become infected. I've tried to bury it, hoping it would get better. It hasn't.

It won't. Every fiber of my being is infected.

My shoulders slump in defeat.

God, help me.

A sob breaks through. Then another. Dropping onto my bottom, crouching, I weep bitterly.

The distant sound of thunder rumbles and menacing clouds form. The sky is very dark with an angry purple hue on the horizon. I still have about eight blocks to go. I don't care if I get wet; I'm already drenched with sweat. I put my head on my knees. Minutes tick by. I don't know how many. Thunder rumbles and my shadow gradually blends in with the creeping darkness of the oncoming storm.

Finally, I get up and begin walking. The rain starts when I'm about four blocks from home. I know it's going to rain violently when the first drops to hit the pavement are the size of a quarter. Even though it's early afternoon, it looks like dusk.

I am soaked to the bone when I get home and my teeth are chattering. The temperature has dropped noticeably, and the heat I generated from my run has worn off.

I peel off my wet clothes in the mud room, bag them in a small plastic bag and run naked upstairs dumping my wet clothes into the laundry hamper.

The hot shower feels good. I wish it could penetrate my soul; I'm raw and exposed.

I can't run from this anymore. It's too exhausting.

After drying off and pulling on my robe, I plop down on my vanity chair to dry my hair. My thoughts race in time to my pulse.

I am scared.

This is a new kind of fear. It's laced with terror rather than anxiety.

A phrase my grandma always said comes to mind, "Stirring up garbage makes it stink."

"Well, grandma – get ready for a stench that will knock your socks off," I mutter, contemplating myself in the mirror. My eyes are large and round. The expression is disturbing; it reminds me of a cornered cat. I work quickly to rearrange my features; the kids will be home soon and I don't want them to see me like this.

I get dressed quickly, pulling on a pair of black yoga pants and a long sleeved thermal shirt. It's raining buckets outside and the chill hasn't left me. We'll have to make fajitas for dinner rather than grill the steaks.

On my way into the kitchen, I pass the office and cast a sideways glance at the desk. I'm not going to think about this right now.

Soon, the kids are home and the afternoon bustle keeps my mind occupied. When Michael arrives and enters the kitchen to kiss me on the cheek, he looks into my eyes and his brows furrow.

"What's wrong?" he says simply.

"What do you mean?" I reply, trying to smooth my facial expression.

"You look…off somehow. Is everything okay?"

"Sure. Just fine." My voice sounds too high pitched, even to me.

"Uh huh. And I'm the Easter Bunny. What's wrong?" he persists.

I turn my face away and stir peppers and onions. "It's nothing, really. Just a long day, that's all."

He considers me for a moment, and then nods his head. "Fine." He turns on his heel and heads upstairs without another word.

I briefly watch him go before turning my attention back to dinner.

The evening drags on for me. I choke down some bites at dinner. I don't have an appetite. I try to act engaged, asking each of the children about their day. My mind is filled with the possible contents of the envelope.

I don't have to open it. I could just mark it as the wrong address and drop it back in the mail tomorrow. That's a good plan. A very good plan; I don't care what it says or who it's from. I don't.

I can't.

I can feel Michael's eyes on me throughout dinner. I avoid his gaze.

The remains of Julie's coffee cake are devoured for dessert. All three kids ask if our new neighbors have any children. They're disappointed to find out they don't.

It's late in the evening and I linger over loading the dishwasher longer than necessary. Michael pads down the stairs after tucking Andrew in and enters the kitchen, leaning against the door frame with his arms crossed, his eyes burning into me. I ignore him and scrub a glass.

"Faith?" he says a bit sternly. "Will you tell me what's going on?"

I place the rinsed glass in the dishwasher and grab a dinner plate, scrub it, rinse it and place it in the dishwasher, as well.

I glance over at Michael. He's still waiting.

I don't know how to make this go away. What can I say that will make him stop asking me? What will he believe?

Do I really want to lie to him?

If it ends this probing, then yes. I don't want to talk about this. Michael knows nothing about Paul, and he doesn't ever need to. It's buried. He's buried. That stupid envelope should never have shown up.

"Honey, look. It was just a…bad day. I got…overly worked up about you travelling and talked myself into nonsense. Okay? I'm okay." I walk past him and head into the living room, plopping onto the sofa and turning the television on.

He sighs, walks over slowly and turns the television off, taking a stand in front of me.

"Faith, I don't believe you. Something happened today. You are really not yourself, and I can tell when you're trying to fake it."

Feeling trapped, I shoot back at him. "Michael, I am not faking anything! Why would you accuse me like that? Can't I just have a bad day without you grilling me about it? I don't want to talk about it!" I leap up, rush past him, and run upstairs into our room, stopping just short of slamming the door behind me.

The tears start to flow. I angrily wipe them away with my fists. I hope he doesn't follow me. There's nowhere else I can run. Not hearing any footsteps behind me, I turn swiftly and impulsively lock the door.

Washing my face is pointless. I'm sobbing when I crawl into bed and pull the covers over my head.

I don't know when I stopped sobbing or if I stopped sobbing. I don't know when I fell asleep or if I actually slept. My mind fills with vivid images intermingled with violent tossing and turning, throwing the blanket off, and getting tangled in the sheets.

Coffins and prison bars are prominent features as is a shadowy figure in old fashioned black and white striped prison garb.

The eyes look eerily familiar.

Gasping (in the dream? in reality?), I realize the eyes belong to my face and I'm the one who's the prisoner.

Rolling over violently, I cry out. My hands search the bed for a comforting presence. There's only cold, empty space.

At some point, Paul's mangled face looms large before me, and I throw a pillow at it to make the image go away.

A thud answers me. Something hit the floor.

I jerk awake and bolt upright, gasping for air.

Did I imagine the thud? Is someone here? My eyes are wide as they scan the darkness looking for something or someone to identify.

Nothing.

Working to control my racing heart and slow my breathing, I roll over, get up and turn on the bathroom light. Once again scanning the room, the pillow I threw is lying in a heap against my dresser. The bed is a crumpled mess. On the floor next to the thrown pillow is our framed wedding picture.

Mystery solved. The frame is heavy and silver, which would account for the thud I heard.

Worrying the glass may have broken; I hurry over, dropping to my knees beside it. Gingerly examining the glass and, seeing no cracks or obvious missing pieces, I run my fingertips lightly over it. It's intact. My fingers linger on Michael's smiling face looking back at me.

His eyes are so full of love.

Fresh tears fill my eyes.

I want to be better. I do. I just don't know how. I can't tell Michael or anyone about Paul. There's too much hurt. I just want it to go away. This has to stop.

Why won't it just go *away*?

Glancing at the clock, it glares that it's after two. Where's Michael? Realization strikes me; I never unlocked the door. Feeling guilty, I pull myself up, unlock the door, and go downstairs. The couch is empty.

The guest bedroom door is closed. Quietly turning the handle, I peek inside. Sure enough, there's a large form asleep in the bed. I hear Michael's soft, steady breathing. A flash of anger rises in me that he can sleep so peacefully and so soundly while I've been suffering. The anger is almost immediately replaced with guilt and pain. He doesn't know why I suffer.

Plus I'm the one that locked the stupid door.

He did ask.

Yes, but I don't want to talk about it! I answer myself huffily, stiffening.

I linger at the door, unsure what to do next. Should I wake him and ask him to come to bed? Will he even come? He's probably mad at me. Should I join him in the bed? Go to bed again without him? I won't get any sleep anyway, especially without him there.

I'm lost.

My heart aches. I want to feel his arms around me. I take a few steps into the room and hover there, unsure. The tears dribble down my cheeks while I stand there stupidly.

Suddenly, Michael stirs in the bed and glances my way. "Faith?" His voice is thick with sleep. "Honey, come to bed." He lifts the blanket open next to him, gesturing for me to join him.

My shoulders drop and I pad over without answering, exhausted. I don't care where I sleep right now, as long as it's next to him. His warmth is inviting as are his arms which wrap around me. Before I've even settled in completely, his breathing tells me he's already in a deep slumber. Maybe he never really woke up in the first place. Sighing, I close my eyes and join him.

I don't know how to make this right. I don't know what to do. God, I need help.

Chapter Nine

The next morning, the sun beams full in the room. I blink and sit up, confused. Glancing around, I realize I'm in the guest bedroom. Last night floods my mind and I groan. The bedside clock says ten-thirty.

"Ten thirty?! Holy crap!" I say groggily.

It takes me a minute to think about what day it is. It's Friday. The kids have school and Michael should be at work.

What happened? Why am I still in bed?

I bolt out of the bed and dart into the living room, which is just off the hallway from the guest room. Everything is quiet.

Ducking into the kitchen, I find Michael sitting at the kitchen table with his laptop, a coffee mug next to him. There's a faint smell of toast in the air. He's dressed in a pair of faded blue jeans and a gray T-shirt. His fingers click away on the keys, but fall silent when he spies me.

"Morning. Did you sleep well?" he stands, strides over and gives me a cautious hug.

"Eventually, yes. But I slept too long. Where are the kids? Why aren't you at work? It is Friday, right?" I'm still groggy and confused.

He chuckles and releases me. "Yes, it's Friday. The kids are at school. I called in and explained that I needed to take a personal day. I'm just taking care of a few things while I'm here. It's not a big deal. I figured you needed some extra rest, so I let you sleep. From the looks of our bed upstairs, you really needed it. It looks like there was a pro wrestling match with no winners."

Ignoring his last comment, I blush. "Uh, okay. Thank you. Are you sure it's okay to take the day off?"

"Yeah, it's fine. There's really nothing going on that I can't do on line or on Monday. How are you this morning?" he asks cautiously.

"How we are this morning is more important. I'm sorry, Michael."

Michael sighs, looks like he's about to say something before thinking better of it, then shakes his head and hugs me again. "We're okay, honey."

Trying to explain the mess of our bed, I say, "I slept horribly because you weren't there."

Michael is quiet for a moment, sipping his coffee. "I doubt that's completely true, but you're still not going to talk about it, are you? Whatever it is." The edge in his voice is back.

My heart is pierced; I didn't want to get back to this. I hate the distance between us. I have to make it better. Pulling myself close to him, I kiss him on the cheek. "Any coffee left?"

"You'll need to make some fresh. I just drank the last of it. I didn't know how much longer you'd sleep."

"Okay. Do you want some more, too?" I ask, filling the reservoir of the coffee maker with water.

"No. I'm well caffeinated at this point. Thanks, anyway." His fingers click on the keyboard. I finish measuring ground coffee into the paper liner and hit the button to brew.

Michael stops typing and looks at me. "Oh! That reminds me. I met our new neighbor...Jane? Julie?"

"Julie," I confirm.

"Yes, Julie. She stopped by about an hour ago and wanted to say hi. She seems really nice. She would've called first, but she didn't have our number. I gave it to her. I hope you don't mind."

"No, that's okay."

"Good. Anyway, I thanked her for the coffee cake and told her the kids really enjoyed it, too. Did you know her husband is a minister?"

I nod.

"Did you also know that he's a licensed counselor?" he continues, his eyes on me.

I stare at him blankly. "No."

"Well, he is. I was just talking to…Julie…and she mentioned that her husband does counseling at his church."

"How did you get on that topic?" Comprehension is dawning on my groggy mind. I don't like where this is going.

"It was just one of those things, really. She was introducing herself to me and telling me about her husband." He pauses to take a sip from his mug, still eyeing me, as I digest the direction he's headed. "It just sort of came up."

"Oh."

Michael gazes at me quietly for a moment. "Faith, maybe this is just what you need. It might be perfect. He's a licensed counselor and he's also a minister. I think that's important."

"But he's also our neighbor, Michael. Don't you think that would be…I don't know…weird for me to talk to him?"

He shakes his head. "No, I don't think it's weird at all. It's perfect and great timing, too. Why don't you at least give him a call?" He pulls a business card out of his pocket, rises, walks over and pushes it toward me on the counter.

My mouth falls open. "You got his card?!"

"Actually, Julie offered it to me. I probably would've asked for it anyway, even if she hadn't offered, once I found out what he did. This will save you some research time, don't you think?"

I'm stunned and angry. "What? Did you tell her your wife may be crazy or something just because I…we…had a bad night?!" Although yesterday was an eye opening experience about how messed up I am, it doesn't mean Michael has the right to broadcast it.

He holds his hands up in defense. "Whoa, whoa. Back up the truck, Faith. I didn't say anything of the sort. She handed me the card because she said maybe we would like to visit the church." He shakes his head. "Faith, please let's not get into a fight about…what? I don't even have a clue, really."

I take a deep breath, trying to calm myself. Where is all this rage coming from? Michael hasn't done anything wrong and yet I'm attacking him. Again.

I shake my head and rub my face. "You're right. I'm sorry, Michael. I just need coffee." I turn my back to him and watch the coffee brew.

Michael sighs. He returns to his seat and the tapping of the keyboard resumes.

I focus my gaze on the drips of coffee that ripple in the carafe.

Maybe God did hear my prayer for help. Maybe Julie's husband could be a good start. I spy the business card sitting on the edge of the counter.

Finally, I snatch it up and look at it.

The card is simple; it has "Ben Jackson" on the front with some alphabet soup titles after his name followed by "Licensed Individual and Family Counselor", a phone number, and the name of the church on it. The Christian fish symbol is in the corner.

Well, it doesn't look particularly scary.

"Maybe I'll call him," I say quietly, and then glance over at Michael. The bewildered and guardedly anxious look on his face pulls at my heart. "I think you may be right."

He stands up and closes his laptop. He walks over to the sink and puts his mug in it before turning to me. "Look, honey. I know I am being harsh on you, but I just want you to be…better. Okay?" He rubs my arms.

"I know. I want to…be better, too. I'm just scared."

He blinks in surprise. "Scared? Scared of what?"

I shrug my shoulders. "I don't know. Just scared. I can't explain it." My voice becomes a whisper. He puts his finger under my chin and pulls my face up.

"Well, maybe talking is what you need to do. I would love for you to talk to me so I know what's going on." His brows furrow and his jaw clenches.

My heart aches. I keep hurting him and he doesn't even know why. This is my pain, not his. Mine alone.

Michael is still staring at me, waiting.

"I'm so sorry," I whisper. "Please forgive me, Michael. I just don't know what else to say. I will make an appointment."

Michael's face softens. "Good. Come sit down. I'll get your coffee." I had forgotten about the coffee. He leads me into the living room and sits me down on the sofa before disappearing into the kitchen.

Michael reappears with a steaming mug in his hand and clouded concern on his face.

"Here, honey." He hands me the mug and sits next to me. He keeps his eyes cast down. "Faith, I'm sorry you don't...trust me enough to tell me what's wrong."

I gasp in shock. "You think I don't trust you? Why would you think that?"

His eyes whip up. "What else could it be? We've been married for seventeen years, Faith. You've always had this...fear. I don't know why. I didn't cause it, did I? I don't think so, but where does it come from? Why can't I help you?"

I put the mug on the coffee table, groan, and cover my face. "Michael, please. I so don't want to do this."

"See! That's what I mean. Whenever I even ask you about it, you shut me down." He sighs impatiently. "Faith, if you don't get help soon, like make the appointment today, I...don't know what to do. I really don't. But this can't go on."

I drop my hands and stare at him. "Michael, what are you saying? That you'd leave me?" my voice quivers. I couldn't take that. I really couldn't.

He hesitates for a moment and leans back on the sofa. Fear, my old faithful companion, squeezes my heart so hard I can barely breathe. I start to gasp. "Michael, what are you saying?"

"Faith, I am not going to leave you. Please don't jump to that conclusion. It's just that, I don't know. We have to do something. You need help and you won't let me help you. Something obviously happened yesterday. But here I am, clueless as always about what's going on or what to do. Do you have any idea how frustrating that is?"

My thoughts turn to the cursed envelope in the desk and I start crying. Michael puts his arms around me. "Faith, this is what I'm talking about. You're my wife and I love you. I see you're obviously hurting and you won't even tell me why."

"I can't," I whisper.

He pulls me away from him to look me in the face. "What do you mean you can't? Just tell me." His frustration is evident.

"Michael, please. I'm begging you. Don't. Just don't." The tears flow freely.

Michael swears under his breath and closes his eyes. "Okay, Faith. I'm sorry, but I'm going to be firm. You make that appointment today. This is affecting our relationship and it's not healthy. I slept in the guest room last night because of something I don't even know, Faith. If you don't feel like you can make the appointment, I will do it for you."

He's right. I can't argue with him. This is affecting my marriage. I have to do it. I nod in defeat.

"Do you want to make the call or should I?" he says quietly.

"Can I at least wake up first? Eat and maybe shower?" I beg.

His expression softens. "Of course, Faith. Don't make me out to be an ogre, but you didn't answer my question."

"I'll make the appointment," I answer glumly, "after I shower."

"All right." He kisses my forehead and gets up. "I'll go make your breakfast." He starts to walk away, then hesitates before returning to kneel at my side. He brushes his fingers across my cheeks. "I love you, Faith. I really do. Never doubt that."

"I don't want to lose you."

"Ah, Faith. You are not going to lose me." Then he kisses me hard and rises to head into the kitchen.

How does he know?

Ignoring the coffee, I decide I'd rather go shower.

As I enter our bedroom and survey the damage in the light of day, I'm aghast. Michael is right; the bed looks like it was torn apart by madmen. The comforter is strewn over the headboard, the top sheet is practically tied in a knot, pillows are everywhere and even the fitted bottom sheet is pulled up at all four corners.

I hope the kids didn't see it.

Groaning, I lumber into the bathroom, strip and shower.

Wanting to eliminate all evidence from this horrible night afterwards, I make the bed with fresh sheets, making sure the comforter is smoothed perfectly without even the hint of a wrinkle. Satisfied with my work, I pad downstairs, retrieve my coffee mug and find Michael at the kitchen table sipping coffee and reading what looks like some reports from work. My plate of scrambled eggs is waiting for me.

"Thank you." I take my seat. Even if my appetite hasn't returned, I had better choke the food down.

He shrugs. "No problem. It's practically lunch, so I know you have to be hungry."

"Yeah, a little," I lie, forcing myself to take another bite. My appetite awakens as I eat. After scraping the plate clean, I rise to place it in the sink. When I turn around, Michael is leaning against the counter behind me, holding the phone up in my direction.

"You weren't joking, were you?" I retort.

"Hey, you ate, you showered, you need to make a call," he replies firmly.

"Technically, I haven't had my coffee yet."

"Well, that's your own fault, and it wasn't part of the bargain. In my own defense, I did give you coffee." His mouth twitches, and before I can get too worked up, I realize he's teasing me.

I grunt in exasperation and snatch the phone from his hand. "Where's that business card?" I put my hand out, palm up, waiting expectantly.

Without missing a beat, he slowly lifts his other hand where the card is wedged between two fingers. I snatch it quickly. Placing it on the counter, I turn my back and will my heart to stop hammering in my chest as I dial.

"First Christian Church, this is Mrs. Benson. Can I help you?" A matronly sounding woman with a marked Southern drawl answers. Her voice reminds me of my grandmother. It's comforting.

Clearing my throat, I struggle to make my voice sound stronger than I feel. "Hello. My name is Faith Strauss, and I would like to make an appointment to see Ben Jackson for counseling, please."

"Okay, hon. Is it for family or individual counseling, sug?" she drawls.

Her accent and choice of words make me smile. She sounds exactly like my grandmother; she used to call people sug, too. It's a shortened version of the word sugar meant as a Southern term of endearment.

Perhaps this is a good sign, after all.

"Individual, please."

"Okay, hon. When would you like to come in?"

"Um…next week if possible. During the day is best." I pull the calendar off the wall and grab a pen.

"Okay, sug. Pastor Ben is open on…how about Wednesday at ten-thirty in the morning, hon?"

"That will be fine." I scribble the appointment on the calendar.

"Okay, hon. We'll see ya then. Bye now."

"Oh, wait! Do I need to bring anything with me?" I ask quickly before she can hang up.

"No, sug. Just bring yerself," she answers warmly.

"Okay, thanks so much." As I put the phone down, I look at Michael. He has an expectant expression on his face.

"Well?" he asks.

"I have an appointment on Wednesday morning." I point to the calendar where I've scribbled the appointment.

He breathes out a sigh. "Good." He pauses. "I'm proud of you, Faith."

"Hmph. I made the appointment. That's all."

"It's a start. That's all I ask."

I nod. The silence and the distance between us are more than I can stand. I glance over at him. His expression tells me he feels the same way. Closing the short distance between us, I wrap my arms around him and he embraces me.

"I am sorry about last night, Michael. Sorry about…everything. I don't like being separated from you," I murmur.

"Me, either. I was surprised that you actually locked me out, though."

"Lord." I groan. "I'm sorry. It was childish of me, I know. I didn't mean to leave it locked. I just forgot. Forgive me?"

"Of course, I forgive you. But what the heck happened in that bed, Faith? I couldn't believe my eyes when I walked in this morning to take a shower," he chuckles. "I'd have understood if perhaps we had made that mess," he says suggestively.

My cheeks burn. "It was just bad dreams, Michael. I already changed the sheets and made the bed. I'm really sorry."

He squeezes me, burying his face in my hair. "Want to go mess it up again?"

I snort a laugh and turn my face up. My favorite broad smile appears and his eyes are smoldering sapphire embers.

"What do you say?" He tucks a piece of my hair behind my ear. I shake my head; I hate having my hair tucked behind my ear. Michael chuckles. He really can switch from fourth gear to reverse in the span of a heartbeat.

I'm envious.

I smile back and kiss him sincerely. I intend to pull back, but he stops me with his hand behind my head and deepens the kiss. I recognize the urgency in his touch and I respond. We stand there kissing for a few moments when my cell jingles loudly in my purse. I start to pull back and answer it, but Michael's hand, still behind my head, prevents me from pulling away. It continues to ring loudly even as his kiss becomes more insistent.

"Honey," I murmur when he releases my lips for a moment to kiss my neck. "I need to check that. It might…be the kids." My breath is quickening as I respond to his touch.

"Mmm hmm," he murmurs in response, not really hearing me. His mouth moves to my jaw and then my neck as his hands move lower and lower down my back. He squeezes me tightly to him.

"Honey, please." I gasp. "The….kids."

Michael sighs in exasperation, and without releasing me from his grasp, moves us as one the few steps to the counter where he quickly retrieves the intrusive cell from my purse to glance at it.

"It's just Brenda," he says huskily. "Call her back later." He drops the phone back into my purse. It immediately stops chirping and goes to voicemail.

"Okay," I manage to sigh. As if I really have a choice at this point; my body is responding more than my brain.

He begins rapidly walking me backward out of the kitchen and up the stairs, even as his mouth continues to work on me. I might've tripped had it not been for his steadying arms wrapped tightly around me. The rest of the day before the kids come home from school is spent blissfully closing the distance between us in more ways than one.

After seventeen years, the sex just gets better and better. I think that's what comes from having your hearts knitted together in the total commitment of marriage first instead of just your bodies.

I could never do casual hook ups. That must be awful to give away something so precious as though it were nothing. The very thought makes me shudder. I had only been with two men in my life, both after marriage.

I can't imagine anything better than that.

I am thankful, God. Can I please keep him?

Chapter Ten

"I'm glad I took the day off. It's been a good one," Michael murmurs, coming up behind me and wrapping his arms around my waist. I'm in front of the mirror trying to smooth my tousled hair into a pony tail. He smiles at my reflection. I finish securing my pony tail and twist myself around to face him, wrapping my arms around his neck.

"I agree. I'm just sorry how it happened." I intend it as a joke.

Michael winces ever so slightly. "Honey, that's not funny. I'm still worried about you." His arms tense. "I'm still in the dark."

The joke's on me and I'm instantly remorseful. I have to remedy this before the distance between us returns. "I'm sorry, honey. I was just trying to joke with you. I love you." I kiss him quickly.

"I know. I love you, too." He looks as if he wants to say more, but decides against it. A dark cloud descends over his face and I can feel the distance starting to creep back. As proof, he pulls away and leaves the room without another word.

My now empty arms drop to my sides and I throw my head back and groan.

God, what is wrong with me?! Why is this happening?

I can't have this. I simply can't. I run out after him.

"Michael! Wait, please." He's halfway down the stairs and turns around to face me.

"Honey, I'm really sorry. You are right. I need counseling and I'm going to get it. Will you please just be patient with me? You…I can't do it without you."

Michael ascends back up the stairs to me. "All right. As long as you do whatever needs to be done to get better."

I nod my head. He reaches for my hand and grips it firmly. It feels too formal and I instinctively lunge for the comfort of his arms. He drops my hand and reaches for the banister while taking a quick steadying step backward as we almost topple down the stairs. "Whoa, Faith. Don't throw us down the stairs!" he huffs, his other arm tightening around me.

"Sorry," I mumble into his chest. It seems I'm forever saying that.

"Faith, it's going to be okay. We're going to be okay."

I nod my head quickly, relaxing my grip on him.

Michael glances at his watch. "The kids should be home any minute now. You all right?"

"Yes. I'll be…better." I almost said fine, but thought better of it. "I need to start a load of laundry, too. It's really piling up." Michael continues down the stairs as I go back up for the laundry.

I have to get better. I don't know where else to go or what else to do.

I enter the kitchen once I've started the laundry, my mouth feels like it's coated in plastic wrap it's so dry. I fill a glass with water, gulp it down, refill it and finish that glass, too before grabbing a handful of M&Ms and popping them in my mouth.

The bowl is now empty.

Remembering that Brenda had called earlier, I retrieve my cell. There's no voicemail, just a text.

"Call me when you have a chance. B"

That's it. It's typical Brenda. She probably just wants to chat about the latest fashion *faux pas* she witnessed in the shop. I don't really have the mental energy for such a conversation, so I decide to call her back later.

Munching the last of the M&Ms, I hear April's car pull up. Putting the day's events out of my mind, I prepare myself for the onslaught.

****

86

The evening is as relaxed as it can be. The kids are done with school for the week which means no homework, dinner is good and so is the conversation. Michael sits next to me at the table, his body in constant contact with mine, either his leg or his hand touching mine.

It's a comforting posture; it's his way of letting me know that he is here. I'm grateful.

April made plans to go out with her friends. I feel a pang of anxiety and glance at Michael. He takes charge of the conversation, squeezing my hand.

"Who's all going, April and where exactly are you going?"

"It's just to Beth's house then we're going to the movies. There's a seven-thirty show we want to catch." She spears a large piece of her pork chop and crams it into her mouth.

"And…who's going?" Michael persists.

April sighs heavily and rolls her eyes. "Gosh, dad! Let me think." She starts naming names, counting them off on her hand until she reaches six. I recognize all the names; two boys and four girls.

"Who's driving and which theater are you going to?" Michael continues.

She sighs again, flicks a glance at me and swallows her mouthful before answering. "We're all meeting at Beth's house and then her dad is driving us to the AMC Parkway. Their minivan can seat seven people, so I'll be leaving my car at her house."

She looks at me and says, "Mom, I'm only driving to Beth's house, okay? I promise." She crosses her chest with her fingers.

I smile at her and nod. "Good, April. I like that."

"What time are you meeting at Beth's house?" queries Michael.

"I wanted to go right after dinner, if that's okay. We're just gonna hang out until it's time to go."

"That's fine. Text us when you get to Beth's house," Michael states, squeezing my hand.

"Of course. Don't I always?" she responds with a dramatic wave of her hand, staring at me.

Michael smiles at his eldest daughter. "Yes, honey. You do. We appreciate that."

"What are we going to do since April gets to go out tonight?" Andrew whines, his jaw jutting out.

"It's not a contest but what do you want to do, Andrew?" Michael asks.

Andrew's brow furrows in concentration. He looks just like Michael when he does that. "I want to go to Chuck E. Cheese's!" he cries.

There's a collective chuckle.

"We can't do that, Andrew. We've already eaten dinner," snorts Sarah, shaking her head.

His face crumples. "We can still go and play the games," he retorts, jabbing his broccoli with a fork.

"I'm sorry, buddy. No can do tonight. How about let's rent a movie and you can pick it out," Michael offers.

"I think that sounds like fun, Andrew. What do you think?" I ask cheerfully. "You can help me make popcorn."

His face instantly brightens and he nods his head enthusiastically, popping the broccoli into his mouth.

"Mom? Can I invite Shelley over? I don't really want to watch a movie tonight," Sarah asks.

"Sure, honey. Go ahead and give her a call after dinner."

"Cool." Sarah returns her attention to her plate.

The evening finishes without incident. April texts me when she arrives at Beth's house, Shelley is able to come over and spend the night. She and Sarah take over the basement for their sleepover, much to Andrew's consternation.

He quickly becomes engrossed in the fantasy action movie he picked out, however, and munches happily on his popcorn while lying on the floor as the first super power action scene lights up the screen. Michael and I hold hands on the sofa, my leg draped over his casually as we watch the movie with our son.

I don't really care for these kinds of movies; they're always so fantastically ridiculous. I mean, who really shoots lightning bolts out of their hands while wearing a purple leotard? But I plod through because it makes them happy.

Midway through the movie, April texts to ask if she can spend the night at Beth's house. After showing the text to Michael, he shrugs then nods. We know Beth's parents well enough. I reply that it's fine.

After the movie comes to its predictable ending (the superhero gets the girl and saves the world from pending destruction, also of a fantastical nature), Michael squeezes my knee and announces it's time for Andrew to get ready for bed.

Andrew fusses, but he's yawning. He never wants to actually admit to being tired, even when his head is droopy. He slowly pulls himself up from the floor and drags his feet across the floor to the sofa to give us each a hug, being an affectionate little guy.

"Don't forget to put your popcorn bowl in the sink, sweetie." I squeeze him and kiss his cheek.

"Okay, Mom. I will," he mumbles, his mouth stretching into a big "O" as he yawns hard. He picks up his bowl and trudges to the kitchen. It plunks into the sink.

"Go brush your teeth and I'll be up to tuck you in, okay, bud?" Michael calls after him as he makes his slow ascent up the stairs. Andrew mumbles his acknowledgement.

"You ready for bed, too, honey?" Michael turns his gaze on me. "You look like you're about to fall over."

"Yeah. I'll go check on the girls first. They're pretty quiet down there." I kiss him on the cheek as I rise and take the empty popcorn bowl from his lap, nest the empty glasses into each other and head into the kitchen to rinse them before adding all of the dishes from the sink to the dishwasher and starting the cycle.

Descending the basement stairs, I peer around the corner. The girls have their sleeping bags set up on the floor and they're huddled together painting their nails. While Shelley is in shorts and a tank top to sleep in, Sarah's wearing a high necked long sleeved shirt with her shorts.

"Oh!" I'm startled as their faces turn toward me. They're both covered in green goo from hairline to chin. "Uh, what's that on your faces, girls?"

"It's a mask. It's supposed to make our skin radiant," Sarah replies matter-of-factly before turning back to her nails.

Shelley tries to smile, but the face mask begins to crack, so she aborts the effort.

"Okay. Just be sure not to leave it on too long and don't make a mess, okay? Aren't you hot in that shirt, Sarah?" I ask her casually.

Shelley flicks a quick glance at Sarah before looking down at her nails again. Sarah keeps her eyes focused on her nails. "No, I'm fine," she replies.

"All right. Well, we're going to bed. Don't stay up too late. Love you, Sarah."

"Me, too. We won't be up too late. Night. "

I head upstairs to change and wash my face.

Michael's already lying down. He looks up when I come in. "Andrew's already asleep. The girls okay?"

"Yeah, they're fine." I chuckle. "They're being very girly; they have green face masks on and are painting their nails." I can hardly believe Sarah's already at that stage.

Wow, time sure flies.

"Green face masks? What…like Batman and Robin?" he asks, clearly confused.

I shake my head and smile. "No, silly. You know, creamy masks that you rub on your face to make your skin look good?" I swirl my fingers on my own face to demonstrate.

"Oh! Okay. Whatever."

I finish my nightly routine and climb into bed, Michael automatically drawing me close to him. He squeezes me and kisses my cheek.

"It's good to be back in my own bed," he murmurs quietly.

I blink in the darkness. "Yeah. I prefer you right here."

He takes a deep breath and lets it out slowly as his body relaxes. "I'm not going anywhere, Faith. I promise."

"Thank you."

"Mmmm," he replies. He squeezes me one final time and falls silent. Within minutes, his breathing slows and deepens. I've always been envious of how he's always able to fall asleep easily. Not so for me. My mind has to wind down before it can shut off, sort of like a computer.

As I lay in the quiet darkness listening to the sound of Michael breathing, my thoughts drift over recent events, briefly focusing on the events from yesterday that triggered everything that happened today; my breakdown while running after getting that stupid envelope. I never did drop it back off at the post office.

Rats! Oh, well. It can wait for another day, or a week.

I push the envelope, and its contents, from my mind.

I shiver thinking about last night and my fights with Michael today. I hated it and yet couldn't seem to stop myself from attacking him. He got too personal and I felt cornered, trapped.

Now I have a counseling appointment next week with a man I've never met and who is the husband of my next door neighbor that I just met. Sounds like a good reality television series plot line. Except it isn't television.

But it is reality. My reality.

Facing the pain I've only managed to keep at bay is going to be painful. I've often thought of Paul, but never talked about him with anyone.

I remember the headline.

"Young college student killed in drunk driving accident yesterday. Paul David Peterson, twenty two, is survived by a wife and parents…"

But how is talking about it supposed to make it better? I can't even talk to Michael about it and he's my husband.

Stuffing it away hasn't helped, either. My marriage is suffering.

I sigh and squeeze Michael's arm that's wrapped around me. I'm so thankful he's here. He promised he would be here, too.

I begin my descent into slumber and my mind drifts. Not having slept well last night, I'm being pulled under more quickly than usual.

What would my life have been like if Paul had lived? How many children would we have had together? Would they be like April, Sarah, and Andrew? Would they have been the same ages? What would they have looked like? Who would Michael have married instead of me?

My mind goes blank. I can't imagine him with anyone else.

Alternate possibilities, alternate futures. Heart ache and hope, all wrapped up in one life.

Imaginings. Just imaginings.

I inhale deeply, sinking into unconsciousness. I've twisted and twirled the day's events into every imaginable shape in my mind.

God, make me better. I know I'm not good enough. Please help me anyway.

Chapter Eleven

Monday arrives and I have to strengthen myself mentally to face the week. I have to get through it. Sipping my morning coffee, I call Lilly and set up a lunch date with her on Thursday, and then call Brenda and make a lunch date with her for Friday.

Even though I know that Wednesday's therapy session is a good thing, anxiety rears its ugly head each day anticipating it.

Julie's visit on Saturday afternoon certainly helped.

She had stopped by to see how I was doing. She came bearing brownies this time…with nuts.

Chocolate and nuts? My favorite. I'm the only one in the house that likes brownies with nuts, by the way, so they were all mine. Cha-ching!!

When I opened the door, the look on her face was genuinely joyful.

"Hi! I just wanted to drop off some brownies I made. Is this a bad time?" she asked, searching my face.

Blinking in surprise, I returned her smile. She's just so…genuine, I couldn't help myself.

"No! Now's just fine. Would you like to come in?" I stepped back and opened the door wide to allow her passage.

"Are you sure?" she asked hesitantly.

"Yes, yes. Come in, Julie, please. The entry price to my home is baked goods. You've discovered my secret."

She smiled and crossed the threshold into my home, standing awkwardly just inside.

"Please, Julie. Come into the kitchen with me. These smell heavenly." I leaned in to inhale the rich chocolaty aroma of the foil covered dish still clutched in her hands.

"Oh, this? They're just regular old brownies; nothing special. I hope you like them." Her smile returned and she offered me the dish. I took it from her and she followed me into the kitchen.

"I have a bit of a…chocolate obsession. Mostly with M&Ms, but any chocolate will do, really," I admitted sheepishly, gesturing to the always half empty bowl on the counter.

"I love chocolate, too. Almost as much as coffee," she confessed.

"Well…I can make some if you'd like. I think we're making this into a habit, having one of your treats with a cup of coffee."

"Oh, sure. That would be great. But are you sure I'm not intruding?" she implored.

"Absolutely not. Michael took Sarah and Andrew to the park and April is at her friend's house. So I'm just here by myself with the laundry."

"That would be lovely. Thank you, Faith."

As I measured coffee grounds into the paper liner, Julie sliced the still warm brownies and slid a neat square onto the plates I pulled from the cupboard.

"I met your husband yesterday morning. He seems like a very nice man. I think he and Ben would hit it off."

I smiled at her and remained silent, watching the coffee brew. I chanced a glance at her, expecting to see the gleam in her eye of someone looking for a juicy bit of gossip.

There wasn't even the hint of it.

I remembered that she had given her husband's business card to Michael. Surely her husband had already told her I made an appointment to see him.

I better nip this in the bud. "Yeah. I…uh…appreciate that you gave your husband's card to Michael. I called and made an appointment." Stealing a glance at her again, I tried to gauge her response as I busied myself prepping sugar and cream.

"Oh." She sounded genuinely surprised. "I see. Ben is really good at what he does." Then, as if she read my mind she added, "I didn't give his card to your husband because I thought you guys needed counseling. I hope you don't misunderstand. I just gave that to him because I wanted to invite you guys to church and, as I said, I think Ben and Michael would hit it off as friends. You didn't need to tell me you made an appointment."

She smoothed out her napkin as she tried to smooth out this awkward situation. "Please don't worry, Faith. Ben shares nothing outside the office. I don't even know who his patients are. He takes the confidentiality thing seriously, as do I."

I gave her a thin lipped smile and handed her a steaming mug of coffee.

She was content to drop the subject and I was grateful. She has such a calming air about her. It makes me want to talk.

"Listen, Julie. I…I've been going through a lot lately. Michael has been asking me to…get some help." I took a deep breath and sipped my coffee before continuing. Julie waited patiently. "Things are just sort of…coming to a head."

"Faith, you don't have to tell me anything, really. I just want you to know that I'm here if there's anything I can do for you, okay?" She reached across and squeezed my hand.

"Thanks, Julie. It's just such a coincidence that you happened to move in next door and your husband happens to be a counselor." I rolled my eyes, expecting her to blow it off.

"No, I don't think it's coincidental at all," she responded seriously. "God works things out in such a way that He provides just what you need right when you need it. This job Ben got was a long shot and the house next door was also a long shot, but here we are!" She shrugged her shoulders and smiled. Then she looked me directly in the eye and said, "Maybe you've been praying for help, Faith."

My mouth dropped open in utter shock and a cold chill ran through me.

How on earth could she know that?

My expression must've been something to see because her eyes opened wide and her smile disappeared.

"Faith? Are you okay?" she asked anxiously. "Did I say something wrong?"

I shook my head, blinked rapidly and finally blurted, "Uh. Yeah. I mean no. I'm fine." I took a deep breath and tried to relax. "I…I just…I'm shocked that you would say that. About me praying for help." It was my turn to look her in the eye. "How could you know that?"

She placed her hand over her heart and relaxed. The easy smile returned.

"I didn't. I don't. I'm just saying that I believe God hears us when we pray. You mentioned the coincidence of us moving here and Ben being a counselor and it just makes sense to me. I don't believe in coincidences. Things always happen for a reason." She shrugged.

I took an unsteady sip of my coffee. "Wow," was all I could come up with.

"So, you have been praying for help?" she asked.

"Yes, I have. For quite awhile, actually."

She grinned widely. "Then I'm glad we're here." With that, she let the subject drop.

******

As I recall that afternoon, I consider her statement and my situation. I have certainly prayed for help a lot. I've never done the whole on-the-knees kind of praying or spent hours with an open Bible on my lap as I imagine good Christians are supposed to do, so I thought my little not-quite-prayers throughout the day didn't count. I don't think I ever believed they went farther than my own skull.

I'm still not convinced they do.

If what Julie said is true, I wonder why it's taken this long for help to come. Why didn't God help sooner? Why now?

Snapping myself out of my musings, it's nearly nine o'clock. I need to run. Rinsing my now empty coffee mug and placing it in the sink, I jog upstairs to change.

This morning's run is pleasant, the air is crisp and the sky is clear. Autumn has definitely arrived. My breath huffs out in steamy puffs.

I force my mind not to dwell on unpleasant things; I'll save that for Wednesday. Instead, I use the time to enjoy the view and the weather.

When I walk up my driveway after my run, Julie is in her front yard surrounded by various sized moving boxes. Some are flattened and others are stacked waiting to be flattened. Smiling, I call out a greeting to her.

She cups her hand around her mouth and yells across her lawn. "Good morning, Faith! How're you doing?"

"I'm fine! Just out for my morning run!"

"It's a great day for it!" she replies, bending over to pick up another box. "I'm getting my exercise with these boxes!"

"Sure looks that way! Have a good one, Julie!"

"You, too!" She rips the tape from the bottom of the box and stomps on it, causing it to collapse into a disc.

The shrill ring of the telephone demands my attention as soon as I walk in the door. The caller ID identifies it as Michael's work number.

"Hi, sweetie! How's your day going?" I answer eagerly.

"It's going well. Listen, I just wanted to call and let you know that I have to work late tonight. I'll be home around eight or so."

"Oh. Okay. Anything wrong?"

"Not really. Just some stuff that I need to take care of that can't wait. Gene left the company abruptly and Joel, Larry, and I ended up having to take on his workload. Just glancing at it, there's a lot to do," he sighs.

"What a bummer. That really stinks. Is it going to affect your schedule beyond today then, too? I mean, if it's that much work..."

Papers shuffle in the background. "I don't know, maybe. We'll see and I'll let you know as soon as I get a better grip on it. I gotta go, Faith. Just wanted to call and let you know. I love you."

"I love you, too. Be careful and I'll see you when you get home. Do you want me to save your dinner?"

"Sure. Just put it in the fridge and I'll eat when I get home. If it's going to be later than eight, I'll call you back."

"Okay. Thanks, Michael. Bye."

"Bye."

I'm disappointed and sorry that he may have to work late for more than one night. Oh, well. There's nothing I can do. I try to remember who Gene was, but I can't place him.

My stomach grumbles on cue; it's eleven-forty-five. Heading into the kitchen to make lunch, I grab a handful of M&Ms just to curb my hunger. Honest.

Afterwards, my cell phone beeps. It's a text from Brenda. "Where do you want to go Friday? B"

I think for a moment, then type, "How about that new bistro downtown?"

She responds almost immediately. "Sure! Noon?"

"Sounds good. See you then. F"

I mark the information on the wall calendar in the kitchen, and finish perusing the calendar for today. April has cheerleading practice, so I have to pick up Andrew and Sarah.

Andrew is waiting for me at the school entrance when I arrive. I wave my arm out the window to get his attention. He walks briskly toward the van, his backpack bobbing up and down.

"Hi, Andrew! Sorry I'm late. Take your backpack off and put your seatbelt on. We need to get Sarah."

"I know, Mom!" he huffs as he dumps his backpack on the floor next to his seat then rolls his eyes.

"How was your day?" I glance at him in the rearview mirror, making sure his seat belt is buckled. There's a reassuring click.

Just as I begin to pull out, there's a screeching sound.

Automatically, I tense and stomp my foot on the brake, looking around frantically. A number of people are running toward the corner crosswalk. My heart skips a beat.

Dear God, has a child been hit?

"Stay here, Andrew." He nods, looking in the direction where a small crowd has gathered. "I'll be right back." I put the van in park, turn it off, unbuckle myself, and get out, joining the other jogging adults.

Mentally preparing for the worst, I can just make out neon yellow material between the legs of those huddled in the center of the crosswalk.

It's the jacket worn by the crossing guard, Mary, who is lying on the ground.

I sigh in relief, then immediately feel guilty. Poor Mary, it seems like she was always being hit by a car, at least as far as I can remember. She's a rather large and stocky older German woman and had somehow miraculously never broken anything.

Yet.

I hope her record remains clean after this incident.

An onlooker asks, "Has anyone called 911?" followed by an immediate response that they have been.

Mary begins to sit up with accompanying grunts that befit her excessively large frame, despite protests from those gathered.

"No, no! I'm fine!" she says gruffly in her thick German accent. "Get me *up*!"

Mr. Hover, the balding school principal, lumbers over. He's clearly out of shape and out of breath; his face is beet red and beaded with sweat.

"Mary! Are you okay? What happened?" he booms between gasps. "Who did this?"

There's a slim, pimply faced teenage boy standing off to the side. He is standing in front of his vehicle and fumbling nervously with his cell phone, shifting from foot to foot. Clearly anxious, he looks sheepishly at Mary then Mr. Hover before ducking his head and staring at the ground.

Mr. Hover points at him. "You! Did you do this?"

"Y..yes, sir," the boy stammers. "It was an accident. I swear! I didn't see her until she was right there!"

"How can you not see her, she's wearing bright yellow?!" Mr. Hover lumbers toward the boy, who takes a fearful step backwards.

"Oh, Bob! Leave dat boy alone. He barely tapped me," Mary growls, brushing herself off and rubbing her immensely massive left thigh.

How the boy missed her is a mystery indeed.

The small crowd thins, but a few still hover near Mary. In the distance a siren wails, getting louder as it draws closer.

Mary rolls her eyes and throws her hands up in the air. "Oh! And here comes dat ambulance." She shakes her head, muttering something in German. "I said I didn't want it!"

Glancing at my watch, I'm now very late for picking Sarah up. I dial her cell phone.

"Sarah! I'm so sorry I'm late. I'm still at Andrew's school. Mary got hit again. I'll be there soon." I don't need to explain who Mary is or what happened. Sarah went to this elementary school, too, and knows all about Mary.

"Okay. Is Mary all right? I'm just doing my homework," she responds calmly.

Where does Sarah get her calmness from? "Mary is fine. Sorry and I'll be there as soon as I can, okay?

"Okay."

I head back to the van. There's nothing I can do for Mary anyway. Thankfully, she's okay. Maybe she should retire...

I feel sorry for that boy, though.

I pull away after the ambulance comes to a stop near where Mary is now standing, hands on her ample hips, feet wide apart, looking like a linebacker about to take on a worthy opponent. Judging by the expression on her face, she's clearly displeased. I leave the scene in my rearview mirror.

Sarah's waiting on the steps, just as she said. There are still a number of students and faculty milling around. I honk at her to get her attention. She looks up briefly, packs her bag, and walks over.

"Hi! How was your day?" I ask enthusiastically.

"Fine," she says flatly. "I got most of my homework done."

"Good. You won't have too much to do at home, then?"

"No." She buckles herself in. She's more subdued than usual.

"Sarah, is everything all right?"

She turns her face away from me. "Fine."

Unsure of the truthfulness of her statement, I feel a tug on my heart, so I try again.

"Are you sure? You don't sound fine."

"Mom, I'm fine," she insists.

"Okay, honey." Sarah will let me know if something is really wrong. I've never had to worry about her.

She scurries up the stairs as soon as we get home and I quickly text April to remind her to text me when she's on her way.

I get a rapid response. "I will, Mom!"

I wince. I can't help it.

Spaghetti and meatballs, Andrew's favorite, are on the menu. He has his action figures splayed on the living room floor and is making spitting noises as he jerks them through imaginary battle motions.

"Andrew! You have homework to do," I say sternly.

The spitting noises stop momentarily and he sighs. "I know, mom. I'll do it after dinner!" he whines.

The spitting resumes.

Sure he will. After much cajoling and nagging from me, that is.

I call Sarah down to set the table. Her lips are in a thin, tight line and her brows are furrowed as she walks into the kitchen. She's clearly upset.

"Sarah, honey. Are you sure you're okay?"

Rather than meet my eyes, she nods and opens the cupboard, pulling out dinner plates.

"Only set the table for three tonight."

"Dad's not going to be here?" she asks, puzzled. On the nights April has cheerleading or gymnastics, she's the only one missing.

"He has to work late tonight and maybe for the rest of the week, too."

"Oh." She puts one plate back in the cupboard.

When dinner is ready, I set aside servings for Michael and April and place them in the refrigerator.

Dinner is quiet with the exception of Andrew. He rattles on about his day, not forgetting any detail he believes to be pertinent like how many pebbles his friend Corey stuffed up his nose on the playground before he had to go to the nurse's office.

He didn't come back to class afterwards.

"Andrew, you don't stuff pebbles up your nose, do you?" I try to hide my amusement.

"Nah. Corey does that kind of stuff," he replies without looking up, jabbing a meatball with his fork. The lower half of his face is covered in sauce. "I only counted. He got eight this time!"

This time?

I laugh and Sarah snorts.

"When you're done eating, wash up and get started on your homework."

His shoulders slump and he grunts, "Okaaay."

My cell phone beeps and I rise to retrieve it. It's from April; she is leaving practice now. I glance at the time; she should be home in twenty minutes if traffic is good.

My mental countdown begins.

I glance over at Andrew. He's done eating, but is dawdling over his plate obviously trying to avoid homework. I pop a few M&Ms into my mouth and return to the table.

"Andrew, honey. You're done eating. It's time to start your homework."

He makes a face and pushes himself away from the table.

"Take your plate and cup to the sink, then wash your face and hands and bring your book bag over here." I gesture to the seat next to me.

He slumps over momentarily, gets up, and trudges into the kitchen with his dishes. Once he returns, he grabs his book bag from the bench by the garage door, drags it across the floor, and plops it on the table next to me, then slumps into the seat. The space on the table where he ate is splattered with sauce and crumbs around the outline of where his plate once sat.

"I'll load the dishwasher, Mom," says Sarah, glancing at Andrew, as she gathers dishes from the table.

"Thanks, honey." I smile at her. "Do you have very much homework to finish up?"

"No. Just some English."

"All right. I appreciate it." I turn my attention back to Andrew.

Homework in third grade isn't difficult, but it seems that way to Andrew. He likes to read, but only comic books and graphic novels, anything more studious doesn't hold his attention.

I hope this gets better. I can't imagine trying to convince him to do his homework every night for the next nine years.

Just as I've got Andrew settled with pencil in hand and working on his first worksheet, the garage door opens. Moments later, April bursts into the house.

"Hi, Mom!" she says enthusiastically, peering around the corner while dumping her book bag and gym bag in the mudroom. Her cheeks are flushed and her hairline is damp.

"How was practice?"

"Good. Hard today, though. We had a lot of new cheers to learn. More high kicks and stuff," she shrugs, striding past me into the kitchen. She yanks the refrigerator door open and pulls out one of the containers I packed earlier.

"Mine?" she asks, holding one up toward me.

"Yes. The other one is for your father. He has to work late tonight."

"Oh, okay." She pulls the corner of the lid up and pops it into the microwave, pushing buttons to heat it.

"Do you have any homework?"

"No, not tonight. I had two tests today, so no homework."

"That's good. Andrew is finishing up." I regard my youngest, lost in fierce concentration. His face is screwed up, tongue sticking out. He's halfway through with his first sheet.

She glances at him and shrugs her shoulders before turning her attention back to dinner. The microwave beeps. She pulls the container out, grabs a fork from the drawer, and plops down at the table to eat.

"I'm going to shower after I'm done; I feel stinky." April wrinkles her nose. "Then I need to call Mariah, so I'll be upstairs."

"Okay. You look like you feel stinky," I joke. I like to joke with April when she's in the mood.

It doesn't happen often enough.

She laughs and continues eating. Once done, she dumps her dishes in the sink without rinsing them and dashes upstairs. Sarah frowns at her retreating form; she had just finished emptying the sink of dirty dishes.

After Andrew finishes his homework, he eagerly scampers back to the super hero battle scene on the living room floor after packing his backpack in preparation for the next day. I wander into the kitchen, grab a handful of M&Ms, pad into the living room and plop onto the sofa to munch absently, watching Andrew's elaborate battle scene unfold.

The garage door opens again. Relief floods through me. It's Michael. It's almost six-forty-five.

He's home early!

I throw back the few remaining M&Ms and hurry to meet him.

As I enter the mudroom, he's just opening the door. He looks beat. I close the space between us and hug him fiercely.

"I'm so glad you're home, honey! You look tired." I smile and kiss him.

"Yeah. What a mess." He shakes his head and gives me a quick squeeze before releasing me to enter the kitchen. He inhales deeply. "Mmmmm. Smells good in here. Lasagna?"

"No, spaghetti and meatballs. Sit down." I retrieve his dinner from the refrigerator and place it in the microwave.

"Hi, Dad!" Andrew yells from the living room.

"Hi, bud!" Michael slumps in the nearest chair at the table and rubs his eyes. "I can't believe what a mess Gene left. I don't understand what he was doing. This…this is a train wreck." He shakes his head and yawns. "I don't know, Faith. I may be working late for the next couple of weeks at this pace, even with the extra help."

My heart sinks. "Really? It's that bad?" I comfort myself in the knowledge that at least he's doing the work here, not somewhere else.

"Yes. It's that bad," he replies. "Some of the projects may have to be scrapped all together, which isn't going to make anyone happy. One drug in particular was only a few months away from the end of phase three, which is the most expensive. So, as you can imagine, there are some pretty angry folks at work." He yawns again, clasps his hands behind his head and leans back, closing his eyes.

"Why don't you go in the living room and sit down. You look like you're ready to drop. I'll bring your dinner out there."

He opens his eyes and smiles lazily. "No, I better eat in here. I'll fall asleep if I get too comfortable." He yawns again.

"I'm so sorry about this."

"It's okay. At least it's not always like this. I have Joel and Larry helping out. That's why I actually got home earlier than I originally thought. We were all pretty well wiped out, so we called it a night. Plus I'm starving."

I bring his plate and a glass of iced tea over.

He inhales deeply again and smiles appreciatively. "Faith, you are the best cook, hands down." He grabs the garlic bread and takes a huge bite. I sit across from him, put my elbow on the table and rest my chin in my hand.

"Thanks."

He winks at me without slowing down. He spears a meatball and puts the whole thing in his mouth. His plate is already a third gone.

"You can go straight to bed when you're done, if you'd like. You look really tired." I want to spend some time with him, but he may fall asleep on his plate.

"I just might. Where are the girls?"

"Upstairs in their rooms."

"Are they grounded or something? Both girls in their rooms? That's odd," he replies between bites.

"No, they just wanted to be in their rooms, I guess. April said she had a rough practice at cheerleading; she had to learn lots of new cheers. So she showered right after she ate and said she needed to call Mariah. Sarah didn't want to hear Andrew doing his spitting noises, so she went upstairs, too."

"Okay." He spears another meatball. "How was your day?"

"It was good. Uneventful. I got a good run in."

"That's good." His plate is almost empty, as is his glass.

I get up and refill the glass. When I return, his plate is practically licked clean. I place the glass in front of him. He picks it up and drains half of it.

"Thank you."

"Did you get enough to eat?"

"Yes, I'm fine, sweetheart. You always give me plenty." He grins, patting his stomach.

"Do you want a brownie? There's still some left over that Julie dropped off on Saturday."

"Sure. Even with nuts, I can choke it down." He wrinkles his nose and smiles.

I slice a large square, place it on a plate and heat it up in the microwave. Michael devours it. His blinks are becoming slower and longer.

"Honey, why don't you just go upstairs and go to bed. You'll feel much better in the morning."

He rubs his face and replies wearily, "I think I'd better." He yawns very widely. "You don't mind?"

"No. You're exhausted. Go to bed." I stroke his face.

He gets up from the table with a groan and yawns again. I better follow him upstairs to be sure he actually makes it. He might fall asleep on the stairs.

As we pass the living room, Andrew looks up. "Hi, Dad! You look awful." The boy doesn't mince words.

Michael chuckles. "Yeah, I'm sure I do. I'm just really tired. Going to bed now. Come here and give me a hug."

Andrew runs over and grabs Michael around the waist and squeezes. "Dad! Check out the battle! Hulk is gonna smash Spiderman!"

"Sure. Just for a minute, though." He takes Andrew's eager hand and allows himself to be led over to what looks like a messy mixture of legos, super heroes, and miscellaneous toys to me. "What's going on over here?" Michael asks as he points to one particular heap.

As exhausted as he is, Michael always finds the time to be dad. I really wish I'd had a dad like that. I watch as Andrew enthusiastically points out and describes the various battle scenes he's created. Michael offers observations and questions, as needed. When they're done, Michael turns and smiles at me and we head upstairs.

Michael pops his head first into April's door and then into Sarah's, saying hello to each. A blast of music wafts into the hallway when he opens April's door and she's talking over it animatedly, presumably to Mariah. She stops when Michael opens the door. He has a brief conversation with her, and then closes the door again.

Sarah is on her bed, lying on her stomach and reading a book when Michael opens her door. She regards him first, closes the book, and gets up to give him a hug.

"You look terrible, Dad. You okay?" she asks.

He laughs. "So I've been told. Just a long day, pumpkin." He kisses the top of her head. "I'm going to bed."

"Gee, Dad. Going to bed before us? That's just weird," she smiles wryly. "You must be getting old."

"Hardy har har," he jokes back.

"Sleep good." She squeezes him once more, and then returns to her bed and her book.

"You, too, pumpkin." Michael closes her door and drags his feet as he enters our bedroom.

"Do you want to shower first?"

He shakes his head, loosening his tie. "No. I don't think I could stay awake long enough. I just want to go to bed."

I pull the covers back and rearrange the pillows for him to climb in. He sits on the edge of the bed with a huff and pulls his shoes and socks off. Once he strips down to his boxers, he crawls under the covers with a satisfied sigh. His eyes close before his head hits the pillow.

I kiss him and he kisses me back weakly. "Sleep good, sweetie. I'll try not to wake you when I come up."

"'Kay." Within a few seconds, I hear a soft snore. He's already asleep.

After the kids are all in bed for the night, I crawl in next to him, trying not to disturb him and snuggle close. He doesn't move.

My mind drifts. Wednesday is almost here. Day after tomorrow. It's coming quickly and I wonder how it's going to go.

God, I hope it goes easy. I need this, but I don't know how. Will you help me? I'll do anything. Please?

Chapter Twelve

Tuesday passes quickly. It has a lot to do with that anxious butterflies-in-the-stomach feeling I always get before I have to do something unpleasant. I keep myself busy; my morning run is faster than usual and my already clean house gets a second scrubbing.

Michael works until late in the evening again and collapses in bed right after eating. I want to talk to him about Wednesday, but he's got so much going on with work that I don't. This is something I have to do on my own.

In order to burn off extra energy, I make bread. Kneading the dough proves therapeutic; I work it until my wrists ache.

Wednesday morning, I open my eyes and roll over to look at the clock. It's a full thirty minutes before the alarm is supposed to go off. I better just get this over with.

I groan and get up. Michael mumbles something incoherent and shifts his position, but otherwise remains motionless.

I hurriedly put on running clothes in the dark and choke down some scrambled eggs with a glass of water. As nervous as I am, I may run the circuit twice.

The sun is just peeking over the horizon as I step outside. Everything is awash in brilliant pinks and subtle grays. It's going to be a gorgeous sunrise.

The cold air swirls around my exposed skin, causing me to shiver. I duck back inside to grab my light weight jacket, zipping it up in one fluid movement. I'm veritably bouncing with anxiety during my warm up walk, swinging my arms back and forth.

I don't know what to expect at this appointment. That's the scary part: the unknown. I picture Julie in my mind. If Ben is anything like her, then he'll probably put me at ease, too. Well, as much as possible.

No, he won't. It isn't possible.

I war with myself through the entire run and don't end up doing the circuit twice because the kids will be late for school if I do. I may run again after they leave.

I head upstairs to rouse Andrew first because he takes the longest. April and Sarah get up on their own. I poke my head in our bedroom; the sheets are pulled back and the bed is empty. The shower is running; Michael's up. I hope he slept well. He needs it. I also hope these long work days don't last.

Breakfast borders on chaotic. The kids all talk over each other. Andrew's very excited about his soccer game tonight. Sarah played soccer in grade school and is interested in hearing about it. April appears to be rambling on about her latest problems with some of the girls on the cheer squad to nobody in particular. From what I can decipher of her ramblings, it has to do with being on top of the pyramid versus something to do with the order of the cheers. She's actually talking to Mariah who's on the cell speaker phone next to her. Normally, I disapprove of cell phones at the dining table, but I am just too wound up to protest.

Michael gulps his breakfast, gets up from the table, and pours his coffee into a travel mug.

"You're not even going to have a cup of coffee with me?" I can't keep the disappointment out of my voice. This isn't how I wanted to start this day.

"I am hoping that if I get there earlier, I can get home earlier." He stirs cream and sugar into his coffee and screws the lid on.

"Oh. I hope so." I hug his waist and he gives me a quick peck on the lips.

"Good luck with your appointment today. Call me if you need to. I'll be thinking about you."

"Thanks."

Within a few minutes, the house is emptied in a whirlwind and I am alone.

I sigh and unload the dishwasher before putting the breakfast dishes in, wipe the counters and table. I glance at the clock and realize I have a few hours left before my appointment, so I finish running the circuit again. My body quivers and aches.

Even physically exhausted, the anxiety won't diminish. I glance at my cell and smile; April texted and let me know she arrived safely.

I climb the stairs slowly to shower and get dressed, groaning with each step.

What's proper attire for a counseling appointment? Should I dress up or dress down? I momentarily consider calling Brenda; she would probably know what's on trend for these types of appointments.

Is there an "on trend" for these types of appointments?

I don't know. But if I call Brenda, I'll have to actually tell her that I have this appointment and I have no intention of doing that. I'm on my own.

Dressing up would probably be over the top. It's not a date for crying out loud. I also don't want to show up in jeans and a T-shirt. That's too sloppy.

Just because I'm a mess inside doesn't mean I have to look like one on the outside.

Eventually, I choose casual slacks and a teal cashmere sweater. A silver rope necklace and small silver hoops finish the outfit. I comb my hair back into a low ponytail and give myself a once over in the mirror. Meeting my own gaze, I shrug.

"Just get it over with, Faith."

Time to go.

Whoa. It's time to go.

For counseling. Right now. To talk.

The familiar fear and anxiety rise up. I suck in a deep breath. I can't hyperventilate right now. I have to go.

I force myself downstairs, grab my purse and head into the garage. Sitting in the driver's seat, I rest my head on the steering wheel and take a few more deep breaths.

I hope I don't end up a crying mess. I almost lose my nerve and have my cell in my hand to call and cancel; I can tell that nice older secretary that I'm sick or I got stuck in traffic or something. I dial the first three digits when suddenly Julie's face comes to mind.

She was so confident that Ben would be able to help me.

I also think about Michael. I really, really don't want to have to tell him I chickened out at literally the last minute when he comes home tonight.

He was so happy when I made the appointment.

Groaning, I cancel the call I was about to make. With one last deep breath, I start the van and pull out of the garage. Gripping the steering wheel so hard my knuckles are white, I focus on breathing.

In. Out. In. Out.

Even doing the exact speed limit, my arrival is fast. I'm ten minutes early, so I take the extra minutes and sit with the engine off, trying to get a grip on my anxiety.

Finally, I can't put it off any longer.

Marching across the parking lot determinedly, I enter through the nearest double doors. There's a sign pointing to "Church Office" on the wall directly across from me with an arrow pointing to the left. I hope that's where I'm supposed to go.

Following the sign, I enter a small reception office. There's a plump, matronly older woman sporting a rather large bouffant sitting behind a modest oak desk. There are at least five pencils sticking out of her hair. She spots me and beams a smile.

"Well hello, hon. Can I hep you?" she drawls. This has to be the woman I spoke to. She even looks like I imagined. The brass name plate positioned on the front of her desk says "Mrs. Benson, Secretary."

"Uh. Yes. I'm…Faith Strauss. I have an appointment to see…Pastor Ben?"

She glances briefly at her desk calendar, and then returns her smile to me. "Yes, ma'am. Here you are! I'm Mrs. Benson. I spoke with you when you called last week. It's nice to meet you. Can I get you somethin' to drink, hon?"

My shoulders drop; I hadn't even realized they were so tight. The thought briefly crosses my mind to ask her for a glass of wine, but I doubt she'd oblige. Instead, I reply, "Yes, thank you. Some water would be lovely."

"Sure, hon. Just go ahead and have a seat. I'll fetch you some water and let Pastor Ben know yer here." She gestures to the love seat placed against the wall opposite her desk. As she waddles out from behind her desk, her pantyhose swishing as she walks, I allow my eyes to wander.

There is a narrow hallway to the right of the desk, some artwork on the walls that's of a Christian nature. They all have either pictures of Jesus with children or the glories of the heavens at sunset. Or is it sunrise? I don't know. There are also a variety of plants around and the soft sound of hymns being played overhead.

"Here you go, hon." Mrs. Benson, still smiling, hands me a plastic cup. "Pastor Ben will be with you in just a minute, sug."

"Thank you." I smile back at her, she nods and returns to her desk. I take a small sip of the water then reach over to place it on the table next to the love seat. The butterflies in my stomach are doing acrobatic maneuvers. It's all I can do to keep from jumping up and pacing the small space.

I concentrate on a small spot on the carpet about three feet in front of me and focus on slowly breathing in and out. I wonder if he'll have a leather couch or if he's upgraded to a modern, sleek version of a chaise lounge instead. I'm glad I wore pants. That could be even more awkward in a skirt.

Suddenly, a man emerges from the hallway and walks over toward me, his hand extended and a smile on his face. He's a little shorter than Michael with soft brown eyes and a kind demeanor. He doesn't appear threatening.

"Hi. I'm Pastor Ben. You must be Faith?"

I stand and grasp his proffered hand, which is warm. I wonder if he notices how clammy mine are. Probably. I groan inwardly.

"Yes. I'm Faith. Faith Strauss." Well, duh. I'm sure he knows my last name. Why did I say that? This isn't going well.

I'm so foolish. Can I go home now? Please?

"It's nice to meet you, Faith. Please, my office is this way." He releases my hand and indicates that I should follow him down the hallway. As he passes in front of me, I quickly wipe my hands up and down my pants willing them not to be clammy. We pass a closed door on the left and enter through the next door.

His office is well proportioned without being too spacious. He has a larger desk than Mrs. Benson, but it's obviously from the same manufacturer. The décor matches, as well. My eyes sweep the office briefly. I feel awkward.

Where's the couch? Isn't there supposed to be a couch?

As if on cue, Pastor Ben strides to a corner of his office where there are two leather chairs set up with a small table in between. The chairs are set slightly inclined toward each other in a conversational posture. He takes a seat in one and gestures for me to take the other.

"Should...should I close the door?" I ask nervously.

"No. When I meet with a person of the opposite sex, I always leave my door open. It doesn't allow for even a hint of impropriety. But don't worry, our conversation is still private."

I hesitate for a moment before taking my position in the second chair. It's surprisingly comfortable. My heart hammers in my chest and I gulp, nervously wiping my hands back and forth across my thighs.

I offer a tight lipped smile to Pastor Ben. Am I supposed to start talking or does he? I don't know what counseling etiquette dictates.

"Please don't be nervous, Faith. We're just going to say hi today and see how I can help you," he smiles gently. "I always like to open with a word of prayer, all right?"

I quickly nod.

Pastor Ben bows his head, closes his eyes and clasps his hands in front of him, elbows resting on his knees. I follow suit and bow my head with my eyes squeezed tightly shut, gripping my hands firmly in my lap.

His prayer is short and fervent. I haven't prayed with anybody in so long, it feels...odd, but comforting. When Pastor Ben says "amen" I open my eyes and take a deep breath.

"Can I get you some coffee or water? I may even have a Diet Coke, if you'd like." He swivels around to look into a dorm sized refrigerator that's half hidden behind his chair.

"Oh. Uh...just plain water would be fine. I left my cup out in the reception area. I can go get it." I start to get up, but he shakes his head, holds his hand up and reaches into the refrigerator to produce a bottle of water.

"Don't worry. Here's a fresh one for you." He smiles and hands the water to me.

"Thank you."

"You're welcome. Like I said, we're just going to say hi for the most part today, if that's all right with you." He opens a Diet Coke for himself and places two coasters on the table between us.

"Sure." I rub my hands back and forth on my thighs again and take a deep breath and let it out in a whoosh. "To be honest, I've never done this before. I don't know what to do."

He chuckles. "That's okay. Most of the folks that come see me say the same thing. I've actually been asked where my counseling couch is. I tell them that my couch is at home where it belongs."

I laugh nervously. I don't want to admit I wondered the same thing.

"So, Faith. Let me tell you a bit about me." He tells me about where he grew up, went to college, his wife, his relationship with God and how he came to be a pastor and counselor. It's interesting and I start to relax. He mentions that his wife has enjoyed our meetings and asks if I've enjoyed her treats. I enthusiastically tell him that I have, and so has my family.

When he's done, he lets me know in no uncertain way that what is said in the office, stays in the office.

"Thank you, Pastor Ben. I appreciate that," I say gratefully.

"I wanted to reassure you about that. In order for me to be of true and lasting help to you, I have to earn your trust and I want you to know that I take the confidentiality aspect very, very seriously."

I nod my head. "That's what Julie told me."

He smiles and asks, "So, Faith. Tell me about yourself. I already know you're married and have children. Would you like to tell me about them?"

The topic of my family always fills me with pride and is a very easy to talk about. I mention Michael and I have been

114

married for seventeen years and tell Pastor Ben where he works and what he does. I also launch into my Mom Speech about each of my children and how proud I am. I mention the challenges with April being an emotional teenager and how I appreciate that Michael and I are on the same page with parenting.

Pastor Ben lets me talk and talk, only interrupting briefly to ask clarifying questions or nod in understanding. I stop briefly to drink from the water bottle, relax into the chair and continue on.

When I've finished talking about the children and Michael, he suddenly asks me, "How was your own childhood?"

"Uh. It was…fine. Not perfect, by any means, but…fine."

"Oh. What made it just fine?"

I don't know what to say.

"Oh, uh, I don't know. It was…" I try to think of what word I can use that would be acceptable. "Not traditional. My mother raised me alone. My father left when I was really young."

"Oh. I'm sorry. Do you have any siblings?" he probes.

"Nope. It's just me."

"I see. How's your relationship with your mother?"

"I don't have one with her. I haven't spoken to her in…about twenty years. I don't even know where she lives."

Silence. Pastor Ben waits for me to continue, but I have nothing else to say.

"Why is that?"

"Well, we…just…drifted apart. She got into things that I didn't approve of, and…well, that's that." I shrug my shoulders and glance around the room distractedly.

Pastor Ben continues asking me questions about my family and upbringing, but I don't have much to say. It's not an easy task for either of us. I don't see the point. After a bit more time, he moves on.

"How about high school? Did you go to college after high school?"

"High school was fine. I did okay, played a few sports. The usual."

"What about college? Did you go after high school then?"

"Yes." Well, it wasn't right after high school…I gulp. My anxiety rises.

I wonder if Pastor Ben notices.

He pauses. "Tell me about that," he says quietly.

"Uh. I got a degree in computer science?" There's another pause.

Is it hot in here? I shift in my seat and take another drink of water.

He studies me for a moment. "Does talking about college make you nervous?" he asks.

I look down and think for a moment. "No. Not really. It just wasn't...that big of a deal."

His eyebrows rise. "Did you have friends? Get involved in clubs? Enjoy campus life? Do anything crazy in college?" he continues probing.

"No. I wasn't there for that. I was there to learn. End of story."

He doesn't seem satisfied and there's another long pause.

"Faith, I'll let you in on a little secret. When someone tells their counselor that it's the end of the story, it isn't." He smiles at me and glances at the wall. "You can tell me your story in your time, however, not mine. Our time is up for this week anyway. It has been a pleasure to talk with you today and get to know you. I would like to close in prayer, okay?"

"Sure. That would be nice."

After Pastor Ben prays, he looks up and says, "I would like you to come back at least weekly, if your schedule will allow. Will that work for you?"

"That's fine." I say, relaxing once again knowing I don't have to talk anymore. "Thank you. I'm sorry."

He blinks in surprise. "Sorry? Sorry for what?" he asks, genuinely surprised.

"This is going to be difficult for me," I say quietly.

"Faith, if it weren't difficult, you wouldn't be here. Please don't feel like you're odd or anything. You're not. You're normal. I suspect that life has just thrown some pretty tough curveballs your way. You'll get through it," he says reassuringly. "I'm here to help."

Quickly averting my eyes, I tear up and don't trust myself to speak. I just want to get out before my stupid chin starts its quivering thing. Instead, I clear my throat and nod quickly.

"Thank you," I say again quietly.

Pastor Ben stands up. "Would you like to meet each Wednesday at the same time? That way you have the same schedule each week."

"Yes, that will be fine."

"All right. I'll walk you out and let Mrs. Benson know that."

Mrs. Benson is clicking away on her computer, but stops and looks up when we emerge. She smiles warmly, looking expectantly at Pastor Ben.

"Mrs. Benson, please schedule Faith for the same time each Wednesday."

"Sure thing, Pastor Ben. I'd be happy to!" She addresses me and grins.

She scribbles the appointment on a calendar on her desk and then taps something into the computer.

"Do you need a reminder call, hon?" she asks me.

"No, thank you."

"All right, sug. We'll see you next week then. Have a good one now!"

Driving out of the parking lot, I exhale in relief. It wasn't that bad. Plus he wasn't old and didn't make me lie down on a couch.

Maybe I can do this. This session was easy, however. Just a getting-to-know-you appointment, like Pastor Ben said. Next week, we'll already know each other and have to move on.

The evening goes by in a blur of dinner and homework followed by Andrew's soccer game. April doesn't go. She has too much homework, but Sarah comes. Even though she's moved on to basketball, she still loves to watch soccer.

Sometimes I complain about being busy with my kids, but in truth they keep me sane.

Like when I want to keep my mind off things.

Sitting in my folding chair on the soccer field cheering Andrew on, I spot Brenda on the opposite side sitting next to and talking animatedly to a man I've never seen before. Their chairs are inclined toward each other and they're leaning in very close, talking.

Even on a soccer field, Brenda is dressed in the latest fashion. Squinting, I would swear even her folding chair looks like it's designer. Is there such a thing as a designer folding chair? Well, if there is, Brenda would have it.

I wave and try to get her attention, but she's engrossed in conversation with her companion and doesn't notice. I wonder if her nine-year-old daughter, Lisa, is in soccer now. That would be new; Lisa was involved in gymnastics the last I knew.

I pull out my cell and text her instead.

"I see you! Is Lisa in soccer?" I type and hit the send button.

I watch as Brenda pulls out her cell and glances at it. It looks like she cringed, but I must be mistaken. She's pretty far away. Her head whips around, eyes searching. I wave at her. She spots me and quickly returns my wave before her thumbs get busy on her phone.

My cell beeps with her response.

"No. I'm here watching a friend's niece play."

That's weird, I think, wondering who it could be.

"What friend? Anybody I know?" I reply.

As I glance up, she's moved her chair away from the man she was talking with.

"My friend Nate. He's sitting here with me. Wave hello!"

Nate? She's never mentioned a Nate before. I've certainly never heard of him. How does she know him?

I wave hello. They both return the wave, and I notice that he moved his chair away from her, too. Strange.

"Who's Nate?" I reply quickly.

"He's just a friend from work."

"Is Scott here, too?"

"No. He took the girls for pizza. I was bored, so came here."

That seems plausible, I guess. I'm sure she's just being nice. Maybe he and his family are new to the area and Brenda is just being nice.

"Okay. Want to sit over here with us?" I reply.

Her reply takes a few minutes; she's talking with Nate.

"Nate's kind of shy. I don't want to be rude."

What? Brenda's never been shy and she doesn't usually care if anyone else is, either.

"Okay. I'll see you Friday for lunch. Have fun!" I hit send and look over at the pair once again.

She and Nate have definitely moved their chairs apart.

I spend the rest of the game trying not to watch Brenda and Nate, but not being able to help myself. I don't want to think much about this or read into it. Brenda is one of my best friends and has been for a very long time.

There's nothing to watch. I force myself to focus on the game. Besides, I can talk to her on Friday.

Andrew's team wins the game two to one, so I take him and Sarah out for ice cream to celebrate. I get some ice cream for April, too. Otherwise she'd have a melt down over being left out.

It's seven-thirty when we get home. Disappointment stabs at me; Michael's car space in the garage is empty. So much for him getting home earlier today. I really hope these long shifts end soon. It's starting to feel like he's not here anymore.

I instruct Andrew to go take his bath and he heads upstairs, still excited from his soccer win and the ice cream. Poking my head around the corner into the living room, April is sitting on the sofa flipping through channels.

"Andrew won his soccer game, honey. So I took him out for ice cream. I brought you some. Do you want it now or later?"

She drops the remote on the couch, bounces out of her seat, and runs into the kitchen clapping. "Now! Where is it?" She looks around the kitchen eagerly and spots the bag on the counter. Before I can even follow her completely into the kitchen, she snatches the paper cup out of the bag and rips the clear plastic dome off to plunge the white plastic spoon into the ice cream.

"Uh, you're welcome, April." I shake my head.

"Oh! Sorry. Thank you," she mumbles, mouth full of ice cream.

"Did you get your homework done?"

She nods her head, eagerly scooping more ice cream.

I call Michael's office.

The phone rings three times before he answers.

"Michael Strauss. Can I help you?" he sighs into the phone. He sounds exhausted. He doesn't usually answer the phone so formally when I call.

"Hi, sweetie. It's me. Just wondering when you'll be home."

His voice softens. "Oh! Faith. I'm sorry – I didn't even look at the number, I just picked up. What time is it?"

"It's seven-forty-five. When are you coming home?"

"I'm sorry, honey. I didn't realize it was that late already. Let me wrap this up and I'll be home in about an hour."

"Okay. I'll see you when you get home. Drive carefully."

"I will. See you soon."

"Love you. Bye."

"Love you, too. Bye."

I hang up the phone with a deep sense of loneliness. Michael's working so much lately that he's only home to sleep and eat. I really wish I could talk to him. Sighing, I turn my attention to getting the kids ready for bed.

Waiting for Michael to get home, I grab a handful of M&Ms on my way into the living room to mindlessly flip through channels, not really seeing what's on. My mind is too wound up. April is still engrossed in her ice cream and has forgotten about whatever program she was watching.

Eventually, the garage door opens. I rise to meet him as he walks through the door.

His appearance startles me. He looks downright haggard. The circles under his eyes are a light purple and his eyes are red rimmed.

"Honey. Are…are you okay? You look awful."

"Well that's good. I would hate to feel this bad and not look the part." He attempts a smile, but it's only half hearted at best. He leans in to give me a kiss.

"Are you hungry? Let me heat up your dinner. Go sit down."

He rubs his face hard and plops into the dining room chair. "Famished." He runs his hands through his hair, leaving it sticking up in all directions. I can't help but smile. He looks like a much older Andrew with his hair like that.

I heat his dinner, pour him a tall glass of iced tea and hand both to him. He immediately stuffs large forkfuls into his mouth.

"Thank you, Faith. Sorry I am so late. I had hoped to get home sooner."

"It's okay."

"Did you eat lunch?"

He nods. "Yeah. We ordered Chinese. But that was around one. I haven't had anything since."

"How much longer is this going to go on? You can't keep this up, you know. It's not healthy for you."

Or us.

"I know, Faith. I know. It's not something I can help. I've got to do what I've got to do." He continues devouring his dinner.

"Are you going to be full? Do you want a sandwich or some fruit, too?" He's almost done with his dinner and doesn't look to be slowing down.

He nods. "Are there any more apples left? I love those Fujis."

"Sure." I rise to get the apple and wash it. I also refill his tea.

"Thanks, Faith. You're so good to me." He grins for real this time, but yawns right afterwards.

"You're going to bed early again, aren't you?"

"If you don't mind,"

I avoid his eyes. "Go to bed. You need your rest, Michael. You really do look beat."

"I am." Realization suddenly dawns on his face. "Oh! You had your counseling appointment today, didn't you? How did that go? I'm sorry, honey. I completely forgot while I was at work." He tries to stifle a yawn, but isn't successful.

People that try to stifle a yawn always end up having the strangest grimace on their faces. It reminds me of a gargoyle.

I desperately want to talk to him. How nice Pastor Ben was, how his secretary reminds me of my grandmother, and I want to share with him how anxious I am about next week. I also want to tell him about the strange incident with Brenda at soccer and that Andrew's team won. But he is utterly exhausted. He needs to rest.

It will have to wait. I can't dump this on him.

"It was fine. I have another appointment next week. Pastor Ben wants me to come weekly."

I'm so anxious about it, Michael. Pastor Ben was really nice and made me feel at ease today, but I'm really scared to do this. I wish I could tell you.

"Sounds good, honey. I'm glad it went well." He tries to stifle another yawn, but this one escapes full force. He pushes the plate away from him, leans back in his chair and munches his apple. "How did Andrew do at his soccer game tonight? It was tonight, right?"

"They won two to one. I took him out for ice cream afterwards. He was really excited."

"They won? That's great! I'm sure he did well as goalie."

I smile. "He did. He was all over that ball when it came near him. That boy isn't afraid to get hit." I shake my head remembering him diving for the ball. He took one in the face at one point and I cringed, but he grinned and jumped right up, ready for the next one.

Michael chuckles and puts his apple core on the plate with a sigh. "Thanks, honey. As usual, it was delicious. I'm going to go take a shower and go to bed, okay?"

"Sure. I'll be up in a minute."

I miss you.

He leans over and kisses me, picks up his plate and puts it in the sink to rinse and then slowly ascends the stairs.

I sit at the table for a moment, debating whether I should follow. Aside from loading the dishwasher, there's nothing else that needs to be done and if I go to bed, too, at least I'll be near him. Rising, I take care of the dishes and follow him upstairs.

After his shower, Michael falls into bed next to me with a groan and sighs deeply.

"You tired, too?" His speech slurs in exhaustion.

I glance at his form in the darkness, "Yeah. Even if you're just sleeping, I want to be with you."

His head turns toward me, but I can't make out his expression. "You okay, Faith?"

122

I miss you. I need you. I want to talk to you. "I'm fine."

Michael doesn't say anything further; he simply pulls me toward him with my back to him and wraps his arm around me. I feel his kiss on my neck. "Love you, Faith."

I snuggle into him. "I know. I love you, too."

It has to be enough. As much as I want to talk, now isn't the time. He couldn't stay awake if he had to.

Within seconds, his breathing evens out. He's asleep.

God, please let his long hours end soon. I need him. I'm sorry.

Chapter Thirteen

"What to wear, what to wear…." I mutter to myself, standing in my closet. I'm trying to decide what to wear for lunch with Brenda today. She's such a fussy fashionista and I know she'll give me the once over. For once, I'd like to impress her. Lunch yesterday with Lilly was easier – she doesn't care what I wear, as long as I come.

The bistro is casual, but in a trendy neighborhood. I finally settle on a dark charcoal skirt that flares slightly at the end so that it flips a little when I walk and pair it with a deep purple blouse that has an off center neckline. I keep the jewelry simple and go with gold this time rather than silver.

It's almost eleven-thirty, so I quickly touch up my make up and head out. I arrive with a few minutes to spare. Brenda is already there, which is unusual. She's sitting down at the bench in the lobby, waiting.

I see her before she sees me. Her thumbs are busily working on her cell phone. I walk over to her and when she notices me, she dumps her cell in her purse, grins and enthusiastically jumps up to squeeze me.

"Hi, Faith! How are you? It's so good to see you!" she squeals.

"I'm good. It's good to see you, too." I smile and squeeze her back.

She gives me the once over. "I really like that color on you. It sets off your eyes."

My eyebrows rise in shock. What? No helpful pointers? Wow. I did well.

"Thanks. As always, you look beautiful. You always do." It's true and she knows it.

After the hostess seats us and even through the placement of our orders, Brenda is her usual chatty self and talks about inconsequential subjects. She doesn't bring up the soccer game. I don't know if it's on purpose or not. It was only two days ago, after all.

Maybe it was nothing.

We receive our entrees and I can't stand it any longer. I have to clear this up, so I can let it go.

"Did you enjoy the soccer game the other day?" I ask casually.

Brenda drops the fork on her plate with a clank and gapes at me before quickly recovering her composure.

"Um...yes. It was fun! Andrew was a great goalie!" She says quickly and smiles, jabbing at her salad.

"So, how do you know that guy you were with? Nate, was his name?" I press her as I twirl my pasta.

"He's the new manager at the boutique, remember? I mentioned him when we were at your house. Why?" She stares at me innocently.

I shrug and continue to twirl my pasta. "Oh, that's right. I forgot. I was just curious." I keep twirling my pasta, even though it's more than securely wrapped around my fork. "Brenda, are you okay?"

She takes a sip of her tea. "Yes, I'm fine. Why wouldn't I be?"

"I don't know. I just want to be sure. It was...weird that you didn't come and sit with me. I felt like you were avoiding me or something."

She rolls her eyes. "No, no! It's just that Nate...is shy. And I didn't want to make him uncomfortable." She concentrates intently on her salad, carefully selecting which lettuce shards to spear.

"Oh." I'm not sure what else to say. She obviously doesn't want to talk about it. I'm probably making a big deal over nothing.

"He just started at the boutique and I am trying to make him feel welcome. His niece plays soccer and he asked if I would come and watch the game, so I did."

"Oh. That's...nice of you."

She flicks a brief glance at me before spearing a piece of chicken.

The silence that follows is awkward albeit brief before she changes the subject. The rest of our lunch conversation feels forced.

I mull it over on the way home. I don't know what's going on and asking her about it didn't clear anything up. She was definitely uncomfortable.

Could something be going on with this Nate guy? Surely not; she and Scott have always had a perfect marriage. Why would she act so strangely, both at the soccer game and at lunch?

I wish I could talk to Michael. He sees things differently than I do and could probably make some sense of it. A deep sense of loneliness washes over me. He's been working these crazy hours for the whole week. I hope he doesn't have to keep doing this much longer.

****

The long hours continue the following week. His weekends are even gone; if he's not at work then he's home sleeping. The kids whine, but they don't miss him as much as I do. I feel like a single parent. To compensate, I run more and longer.

It's not enough, but it's all I've got.

****

The second counseling session on Wednesday opens routinely; we sit in the same chairs as the previous week and start with prayer and some small talk. Just as I feared, Pastor Ben hasn't forgotten where we left off. I sort of foolishly hoped he would, but no such luck.

"Last week we were talking about your college years, Faith. You didn't have a whole lot to say about it." He smiles gently.

"Well, there really isn't much to say." I shrug. It's true.

"You told me you got a Computer Science degree. What year did you graduate from college?"

"Ninety-six."

His eyebrows lift and he thumbs through the pad of paper in front of him. "You graduated college in ninety-six?"

"Yes." What's this got to do with anything?

"But you graduated from high school in eighty-six? That's ten years, Faith," he says softly. "You told me you went to college right after high school."

Whoops.

"Well….I didn't say I went *right* after high school." I squirm in my chair.

"Well, perhaps not. But that was sort of implied. What did you do between the time you graduated high school and when you started college?"

I stiffen. My mouth goes dry and my mind blank. I stare at him. I can't move, not even to breathe.

Escape, escape, escape! *Run!!*

His eyes narrow as he studies me. "Faith, relax. I'm here to help you, but you need to tell me what to help you with. It's okay. Breathe, Faith. We're just talking."

I exhale sharply; I didn't realize I was holding my breath. My mind is frozen in terror. With panic rising, I start to hyperventilate.

"Faith, I need you to calm down. You're turning pale." He sits on the edge of his seat.

A hysterical giggle bursts out, and I clap my hands over my mouth to stop the action from morphing into hysterics. I close my eyes and try to calm down.

Pastor Ben is waiting for me to respond. I open my eyes, look at him, and shake my head.

"I'm okay. I'm…sorry," I reply hoarsely.

"I obviously hit a nerve. I believe perhaps this is the start of the discussion we need to have. Would you agree?"

I look at him incredulously, shake my head and then bob it up and down quickly. I can't speak.

He considers me for a moment. "Faith, I've touched something very deep. That's why you're here. You're not okay right now, but you will be." He pushes a box of tissue toward me. I reach out and shakily grab two. "Please share with me about that time in your life. I will help you through it. That's why we're both here."

I nod quickly again and focus on calming down enough to speak.

"I…I…" I stare at him helplessly. "I…don't know what to say." The words won't come.

They never have.

"Yes, you do." He smiles gently. "Just say what you know needs to be said and we'll go from there."

I nod, close my eyes, and breathe in deeply and exhale. My whole body is shaking. My heart slams against my ribs. Gripping the handles of the chair to keep from bolting out of the room, I realize I've got to do this.

I spit through my teeth, "I want to run out of here so bad right now."

He doesn't respond, instead he simply nods and waits.

With my teeth still clenched, I close my eyes. "I was…was…married!" I burst into tears and bury my face in a wad of tissues.

How humiliating. I should skip putting make up on when I come here.

He lets me cry for a few moments before responding. "That's a start, Faith. Now let's keep going. Tell me more. Why was that marriage so troubling to you?"

Where do I even start? Why am I here? Do I really want to get over this or not? Michael wants me to be here. I don't want to disappoint him.

But why am I here? Michael doesn't even know about my previous marriage. Is this a problem? Do I need to talk about it? Do I want to talk about it? Will it make any difference? Memories flash through my mind of all the effects this fear, this event, has had on my life. My anxiety with Michael's travel, my fear of losing him, my fear with April driving, and my fear of even thinking of Paul.

Fear, fear, fear. I'm so sick of being afraid.

Yes. YES! I want to get over this once and for all.

Pastor Ben is still waiting.

"You look like you're thinking hard about something," he prompts quietly.

128

I gulp and nod. "I am. I…want to do this. But it's really…hard. I mean really hard. I…I don't talk about…this. Ever." Hiccupping isn't making talking easy. I am panicky. I can only imagine what my face must look like. Looking down at my hands and fidgeting with the tissues, I whisper, "Michael doesn't know about this."

"You mean he doesn't know you're coming to counseling or…"

I shake my head. "No. He doesn't know I was…married before."

"Oh." His eyebrows rise, but there's not much else in the way of a reaction. "I see. Why haven't you told him?"

Looking down at my hands again, I shake my head, tears falling in earnest. "I…I just couldn't. It hurts too much."

"Tell me about that marriage, Faith. What happened that hurts so much?"

Shaking my head, I shred the soggy tissues in my trembling hands.

"That's why you're here. This is a safe place. I am going to help you. So, tell me about it. You can do this." He nods encouragingly, waiting patiently.

I square my shoulders, take a deep breath, and force myself to speak. I speak the words like I'm reciting lines for a movie, separating myself from them. "I got married at twenty. His name was…" Hiccup. Deep pain borders on agony. "Was…Paul." His name is nothing more than a whisper. A sob escapes.

There's nothing I can do to stem the flow of tears. The wad of tissues is now a tattered, soggy mess. I glance around for a trash can. He inches one toward me from under the table. I dump them in exchange for a fresh wad.

"We…we were…high school sweethearts and I…loved him…very much." I sob harder. So much for separation. Of course, my stupid chin quivers like jello.

"Keep going, Faith," he offers encouragingly.

I take a few deep, steadying breaths and fiddle with the tissues. "I…we…" My face crumples. I'm losing control. I collapse into my lap and sob so hard I'm sure Mrs. Benson will come running.

Surprisingly, she doesn't.

My determination wavers. Would having wisdom teeth pulled without anesthetic be easier? Maybe. My entire being disintegrates.

After a few endless moments, Pastor Ben asks, "Faith, tell me what you loved and enjoyed about Paul while you were married."

I hiccup loudly, pull myself up, and try to gain some semblance of control. I nod quickly. More tissues in the trash and another fresh replacement.

I try to tell him how kind, handsome and wonderful Paul was but can't continue. I can't share him. The memories are bottled away. It hurts too much.

"What happened to Paul? Where is he now?"

Wincing as though I've been struck, my mind recoils sharply.

No, no, no, no, no....

My wounded heart is cruelly twisted. I suck air in so quickly and so deeply that I clutch my chest and start coughing uncontrollably. It's only after a long moment that I realize the coughs are actually sobs and they're ripping from somewhere deep.

Control is gone; the grief has taken on a life of its own.

Pastor Ben places his hand on my arm and squeezes gently. "Faith, I see this is excruciating. Take a deep breath, calm down, and tell me what happened. You can say it and you will get through it."

It takes every ounce of strength I have to slow my breathing down and corral the sobs. It's physically painful.

"He....was....killed."

I can't go on. A dam bursts inside. I drown in its wake. The sobs overtake me. They'll never stop. I lose a sense of myself, of time, of where I am, everything.

I've gone hysterical.

Pastor Ben's warm hand on my arm is an anchor. "Okay. Okay. Faith, you took the first step. You've broken through your own barrier. You're going to recover."

Broken? Through?

I'm just broken.

Hysterical sobbing continues.

Pleading, I look at him through swollen eyes. "Please. I can't do anymore. I just can't...I can't..." I've had enough.

He looks at me gravely, squeezes my arm once more and releases it. "I understand. I believe you've walked through enough for today. You've made tremendous strides. This is the first time you've talked about this in a long time?"

"I...No." Hiccup. "It's...the first time I've talked...about it since...since..." Deep breath. "...it happened."

He backs up and his eyebrows rise. "Really? You've never talked about this before? To anyone? Not with your family? Nobody?"

"Nobody," I whisper, staring into my lap.

"Hmmm. That's why it hurts so much." He scribbles something on his notepad. "These sessions aren't going to be easy, but they are going to be good for you. Do you believe that?"

I don't know. This hurts far worse than I ever imagined. I nod reflexively as I reach for another wad of tissues. Surprisingly, the box isn't empty.

Suddenly, I stop nodding and start shaking my head, glaring at him.

"How can this possibly be good for me?! This hurts so much!" I spit through my teeth.

He sighs and a look of compassion covers his features. "Faith, you'll have to trust me. I do this for a living. The hurt won't ever go away if you don't let it out," he says gently.

"I don't know," my voice quivers.

My whole being quivers.

****

The drive home is a blur. Dumping my purse on the kitchen table, I crawl upstairs. I fall face down on the bed, curl up on my side, and sob myself to sleep. I am more exhausted than I've ever been.

Emotionally, physically, and mentally, I am spent...and lonely. I want Michael.

I wake with a start, feeling very disoriented. The sun is skewed at a weird angle. I squint and blink groggily. I try to remember what day it is and what's going on. There's a dull aching pain in my chest matched only by the throbbing of my head that jogs my foggy mind back to the present and reality. My body jerks reflexively as it all comes back with a jolt.

"Oh!"

The counseling session with Pastor Ben, the sobbing, crawling up to bed afterwards.

I jerk my head in the direction of the clock and sigh with relief. I still have an hour and a half before I have to pick up the kids. I roll onto my back stiffly. I hadn't moved from my curled up position. My joints pop and crack as I stretch. I am still fully clothed, shoes and all. I kick my shoes off and slowly roll to a sitting position. I place my head in my hands and sigh.

I might as well see how bad I look. I drag myself into the bathroom.

Groaning, I regard my reflection; it's much worse than I thought. My hair is matted to my head on one side and the top is sticking straight up. My make up is gone with the glaring exceptions of the smudge of lip color more off than on one side of my mouth and the remnants of mascara smeared under my eyes.

I'm hideous.

Turning my head this way and that, I give up. There's no salvaging anything. I head for the shower.

****

Dinner is subdued and simple. My body aches like I've got the flu. I am taken aback by how very much the session exhausted me. I would give my right arm to just crawl back into bed and call it a night, but Andrew has soccer practice and April can't take him because she has cheerleading.

I'm a zombie through the evening's activities, sitting as far away from other people as possible. It's all I can do to respond to questions when asked and not curl up on the grass like a toddler needing a nap.

"Mom? Can we talk later?" Sarah asks as I trudge into the house when we arrive home afterward.

"Honey, can it wait until tomorrow? I need to go to bed. I don't feel well. Would you mind making sure Andrew takes his bath and gets to bed?" I answer wearily.

"Sure. Are you sick?" she asks, entering behind Andrew.

I shrug. I would rather she think I'm getting sick than know the truth.

"What's wrong, Mom? You okay?" Andrew's concerned face turns up as he hugs me.

I smile wanly down at him and kiss the top of his head. "I'm okay, baby. I just don't feel good and need to go to bed. Will you be good for your sister, please?"

He nods his head quickly and squeezes me hard before releasing his grip. Suddenly his face crumples. "I wish Dad was home."

"I know, Andrew. I do, too." My already aching heart squeezes tight.

I turn back to Sarah. "Dinner's in the fridge. I'll see you in the morning. Love you." I give her a quick hug and kiss and slowly make my way upstairs.

I've had enough for the day.

****

A cool hand swipes across my forehead. "Faith? Are you all right?" Michael whispers.

I take a deep breath and turn toward his voice. I can just make out his shape sitting on the bed next to me as I force my eyes to open.

It's very dark out and everything is quiet.

"Hmm? Michael? What time is it?" My voice is thick with sleep, as is my mind. I rub my eyes. They are swollen and wet. Was I crying in my sleep? My heart throbs and aches in my chest in response.

"Almost ten-thirty," he murmurs. His hand brushes gently across my forehead again before resting on the side of the bed near my arm. He leans in and kisses me on the forehead. "You feel warm."

I clear my throat and stretch before answering. "I'm just warm because I've been in a warm bed."

"Sarah said you're sick and went to bed right after you got home from Andrew's soccer practice. What's wrong?"

I yawn and rub my eyes again. "It was just a…long day." I can't dump on him. I'm sure he's as exhausted as I am.

Acute loneliness washes over me. Fresh tears prick my eyes. I try to blink them away in the darkness before he can notice.

Michael is quiet for a moment. "Faith, what's wrong? How does a long day make you ill?"

There's a pause while I consider my words. I so desperately want to talk to him, need to talk to him, but he has enough going on.

I just can't. Now isn't the time.

I keep trying to blink the tears away as the waves of loneliness continue to lap over me, stinging my already raw nerves.

"Michael," I start, but my voice sounds wrong, too thick. I clear my throat and try again, working to make my tone light. "Please don't worry about me. I'm fine. I know you're exhausted. Come to bed. We'll talk…tomorrow."

I doubt that.

He doesn't answer me. Maybe changing the subject will distract him and give me a chance to compose myself.

"When did you get home? Did you already eat?"

I can tell from the angle of his head that he's staring at me, but hopefully he can't see my face anymore than I can see his. It looks like he's shaking his head from side to side. I can't be sure in the darkness. He remains silent for a long moment and then sighs heavily. He hangs his head.

"I got home about seven and ate then." His head lifts and turns in my direction. "I was hoping to spend some time with you because I've missed you."

My breath catches and another pang of loneliness rips through me. A sob builds in my throat, threatening to choke me. I clench my fists together to keep from losing control. The tears I unsuccessfully tried to quell dribble over into the hair at my temples. I am so thankful he can't see my face. My stupid chin is quivering. I bite down hard to steady it.

It takes a lot of work to steady my voice enough to answer him. "Me, too," I whisper.

Michael stares at me for a moment, and then suddenly leaps to his feet and flips the bathroom light on, his gaze on me. The light is nearest to my side of the bed. I'm suddenly illuminated in the yellow glow.

I turn my face into the pillow and cover my head with my hands, but I'm not fast enough.

He gasps. His hands gently try to move my hands away. I bury my face deeper into the pillow, trying to hide. He doesn't need anything else to worry about right now.

Least of all, me.

"Faith! Why are you crying? What's wrong? What happened?" he murmurs, desperate.

I shake my head, refusing to lift my face. The mattress gives as he lies down next to me and wraps his arm over me.

"Honey, please. What happened? Are you hurt?" His voice rises with anxiety.

"Nothing happened. I'm...okay," I mumble from the pillow.

"Okay? You're okay?! You've been crying, you hide your face from me, you won't talk to me, but you're okay?" He huffs and shakes me gently. "Faith, what the hell is going on?! Don't ignore me!"

A sob breaks from my throat and I slowly turn my face toward him. I can't meet his eyes. I don't want to dump everything on him, but I miss him so desperately. I bite down on my lip again.

He moves his face right in front of mine and forces my chin up to meet his gaze. He looks at me intently, searching my face. I return his gaze, but his face is in shadow whereas mine is not, so I'm not sure what his expression is. I hiccup and fight to keep from breaking down any further. I don't know how to answer.

"Faith, what's going on?!" he growls. Concern mingles with frustration in his voice.

Hiccupping again, my chin quivers uncontrollably. "I…I…I miss you, too." Another sob breaks through. "I…I had my counseling session today and…it was…hard." I give up talking. The tears flow as do the sobs and hiccups.

Michael holds me tightly.

"Faith. Oh, Faith. I'm so sorry. I wasn't here for you. I'm so sorry," he mumbles into my hair, continuing to hold and rock me gently.

I don't want him to be sorry. I just want him. Here. And he is here.

For now.

I wrap my arms around him, clinging tightly and squeezing tufts of his shirt in my hands like a child. Long moments pass and I'm even more exhausted. I also have a headache and my forehead is sore from crying. That hasn't happened since the days immediately after Paul died.

This thought puts me into a whole new round of crying that has Michael apologizing into my hair all over again. His apologies only intensify my guilt.

"It's not…your…fault," I manage to hiccup between sobs. "Please…stop apologizing."

He stops apologizing, but continues to kiss my hair and rock me back and forth. "I don't know what else to say, honey," he whispers.

There's nothing to be said. I just shake my head and continue crying into his chest. I don't know how much time passes. The crying eventually subsides into soft moans and occasional hiccups.

I am completely and utterly spent.

Michael pulls away from me warily, wipes the remaining tears from my face and kisses me softly. His face is illuminated better at this angle; he's not completely in shadow. His face is mere inches from mine. The fear and anxiety that are frighteningly apparent in his countenance stab me with guilt for breaking down like this in front of him. It's the last thing he needs. The purple shadows under his eyes are like bruises.

"I'm sorry, Michael. I didn't mean to do that. I'm sorry," I croak. My voice is rough and my nose is plugged. I must be a frightful sight; my face is so swollen I can barely open my eyes.

His face registers shock and he pulls back from me. "What? What do you have to be sorry for?"

"I shouldn't have broken down like that. You've had a long day. You don't need this, too. I'm sorry." My face crumples, but no more tears flow. There are none left. My head pounds. I push my fist up against my forehead.

He cradles my face in his hands. "Honey, you have nothing to be sorry for. But I do." His eyes search my face. "The session was really that bad, huh?"

I nod. "Yes, but…Pastor Ben said…it was good. So…" I shrug my shoulders.

"Are you sure you want to keep doing this? I've never seen you like this before. Ever. It scares me."

"Scares you? How do you think it felt to me?"

He looks at me with chagrin. "I can only imagine." He pulls back and props himself up on his elbow. "If you get to apologize, then so do I. Honey, I am so sorry that I wasn't here. That I haven't been here. I feel awful."

"Michael, it's not something you can help." I don't want him feeling guilty about this. It isn't right.

"Still. I would like you to forgive me."

"Okay." I squeeze my eyes shut, groan, and push my fist into my forehead again.

"What is it?" he asks gently.

"My head is pounding and my forehead really hurts," I moan.

"Oh! That's something I can fix. I'll be right back." He gets up carefully and disappears into the bathroom. He returns momentarily with two caplets and a glass of water. I take them gratefully.

"Tylenol?" I ask dismissively, swallowing them.

"No. I think you need something stronger. It's the pain pills from my knee surgery this past summer."

My eyes fly open and I stare incredulously at him. I rarely take anything stronger than Tylenol and even that on rare occasions. "What?!"

"Don't worry. They're not expired and are the right dosage." He reaches down and strokes my hair. "It will help you sleep. You could use a good night's rest, honey."

I sigh and shake my head. I've already swallowed the pills. Plus he's right, of course. I could use a good night's rest. "But my tolerance for that stuff is…"

"Low. I know, Faith. But you need this tonight." He gently strokes my hair for a moment longer. "I'm going to go get ready for bed and I'll be back."

"Okay."

Before Michael returns from the bathroom, I start to float on an imaginary sea, my eyelids and limbs turning to lead. The movement of the bed when Michael climbs in is just a gentle wave on the sea. He repositions me on my side. His body heat warms me.

Just before surrendering to the darkness, one thought escapes my muddled mind.

God. That hurt.

Chapter Fourteen

The sun streams in the window and I blink groggily, my tongue a fuzzy ball. My mind is saturated with molasses. It takes awhile to orient myself.

It's a school day, of that I'm sure. I reach behind me and feel the emptiness of the bed next to me and grimace. Michael is already gone, of course. I sigh and resign myself to another lonely day. I might as well get the kids up and moving for school.

I squint at the clock on the nightstand.

Eight-thirty!

I groan, rub my eyes and roll over. I sit up too quickly and the floor sways at a weird angle. I fall back onto the bed with a huff.

That's why I hate taking pills.

A few more minutes pass and I make another attempt at sitting up, slowly this time. I steady myself before standing up to go to the bathroom. They're already late for school, so what are a few more minutes?

My reflection in the mirror is an accurate portrayal of how I feel – horrible. My eyes are puffy and my face is swollen. I hope I don't have to go anywhere today. I can't remember and I don't care.

I cock my head to one side and am struck by the silence. I don't hear any voices or activity downstairs. The alarm didn't even go off. Where is everybody? Surely April and Sarah wouldn't leave Andrew to sleep in and miss school, would they? They must've thought I was sick and let me sleep, but Andrew, too?

I trudge downstairs and head into the kitchen to make coffee. There's a post it note on the front of the machine.

"Hi hon – Took the kids to school. Talk soon. Love, M"

"I wish we could talk, Michael," I mutter into the silence.

I close my eyes, press my fists against my forehead, and try to clear my mind. I really hate taking pills.

The morning is wasted. The fog in my mind doesn't clear until early afternoon, so I accomplish very little. I can't focus enough to get anything done. I don't have to spend any effort on keeping my mind away from the previous day's counseling session, however – my psyche cringes at even a whisper in that direction.

I have another appointment next week.

"Ugh!" I groan and shake my head, trying to dislodge the thought. "Yes, but I don't have to think about that today." Perfect. I've resorted to talking out loud to myself. That's about right.

Enough!

At one o'clock, I go for a run. That should get rid of the remnants of the fog. I quickly throw on my running clothes.

Heading down the driveway, I see Julie stooped in her front yard with her back to me, planting mums.

I hesitate for a moment, deciding whether I should call attention to myself or not.

Not now. If she's still outside when I get back, I'll say hello.

I turn on my heels and jog in the other direction. The run is slow, but feels good. I feel better even though I'm still mentally and physically exhausted.

When I return, Julie is still working in her garden and spots me. She smiles, rises, and walks toward me.

"Hi, Faith! Have a good run?" she asks cheerfully. Bits of dirt pepper the driveway as she claps her hands together in a vain attempt to clean them.

"Yeah, I'm just slow today."

"Oh? Are you feeling all right? You look…tired," she says carefully. I know she doesn't want to pry. Both she and Pastor Ben were emphatic that they don't talk about his clients and I believe them. I shake my head and snort a laugh. "Tired isn't the half of what I feel." I hang my head for a moment and decide to plunge ahead because I know Julie won't ask. "I had my counseling session with Pastor Ben yesterday and it was really tough."

Her expression is of genuine concern. She weighs her answer carefully. "Faith, you don't have to tell me about it. Honest. That's between you and Ben."

"I know, Julie. I know. But...I don't mind talking with you specifically because you won't ask." I smile.

She returns my smile. "I just don't want you to feel like you have to share anything with me, Faith. People go to counseling for a lot of reasons, one of which is confidentiality."

"True. But I believe I can trust you."

She reaches out and squeezes my arm. "Thank you. That's very kind."

"After I shower, do you want to come over for coffee? Decaf, of course."

She beams at me. "Sure! I'd love to. It'll give me a chance to get cleaned up, too. I'll come over in about forty-five minutes?"

"Sounds good. See you then." I turn toward my house, waving as I leave.

When Julie arrives as promised, we settle into the living room with mugs of steaming coffee. I don't want to talk about Paul with Julie. I know beyond a shadow of a doubt that I would break down again. She's my friend, not my counselor.

Julie is my friend. This woman whom I've only known for a short time is my friend. I feel a sense of deep kinship with her.

"Basically, yesterday I talked with Ben about something I've not talked about in...decades. It was emotionally and physically exhausting. More than I thought it would be. So, I'm still recovering."

Julie shifts in her seat, but remains silent. She eyes me over her mug as she sips.

"It sounds like it was especially painful," she says quietly. "I don't expect you to rehash it."

I smile gratefully. "Thanks. I don't want to. I think I'm just having a harder time because Michael is working so much lately. He's not here and I wish he was."

She nods in agreement. "That can be hard."

I sigh and swirl my mug, watching the coffee lap up the sides.

"Does your husband usually work long hours?" she asks.

"Just lately. There has been a shake up at work and he's had to fill in the gaps."

"So it will come to an end, eventually? The long hours, I mean."

"I keep hoping. It was only supposed to last a short while, but it seems to be dragging on." I set my coffee mug down on the table. "It's rotten timing because I just started counseling plus the kids have all their activities, too. I knew the counseling would be...difficult. But I didn't expect it to be this difficult. Actually, I don't know what I expected. I've never done this before."

"Faith, I know counseling is difficult, but I think perhaps it's more difficult to live with something that weighs you down, don't you?"

"I guess. I've decided that I am going to get through this process. I have to."

Julie smiles warmly at me. "That's the best you can do. It's the right thing."

Keeping true to her non-prying attitude, she deftly turns the conversation away from the counseling session and we spend the better part of an hour talking about gardening and baking, her two favorite pastimes. At the end of her visit, I'm refreshed and very much relieved.

******

Michael calls while I'm preparing dinner that evening. He tells me he'll be home early that night and hopes to be home early more often. I am cautiously thrilled. I can't get my hopes up; I can't take the disappointment. I'm barely holding it together between counseling sessions as it is, if the last two are any indication of how the rest will go. The sessions are short, but the recovery is brutal.

He keeps his word and arrives home at six o'clock that evening as we're finishing dinner. I leap up to meet him when I hear the garage door open. Andrew is close behind and quickly skirts around me to hug Michael fiercely around the waist before running back to his plate. Sarah and April shout their greetings.

Michael grins broadly and kisses me while engulfing me in a warm embrace. I sigh in contentment.

"How are you, sweetheart? Any better today?" he whispers in my ear.

I nod. "I'm better. Just sorry I missed you this morning."

"Me, too. But you needed your rest and those pills really knocked you out. You didn't even move when I got up or when I kissed you before I left," he murmurs.

I look at him, shocked. "I don't remember you kissing me."

"Like I said, you were out." He half smiles and glides over to sit at the table with a grunt. "Howdy, girls. Remember me?" he grins.

"It's about time you actually come home, Dad!" April replies teasingly. Sarah simply smiles.

He starts eating with gusto.

"Hungry as usual, I see. What did you have for lunch?" I ask.

He shrugs. "Sub sandwich. Nothing beats this, though."

"I'm glad you're home early."

"Well, if everything goes the way it's supposed to, this should be the new normal again."

A spark of hope glimmers in my chest before I squash it. Like I said, I can't take any disappointment right now. As evidence, my eyes prick with tears and I quickly drop my gaze before Michael can notice. I pick up my mostly empty plate and take it to the sink.

The kids, however, respond immediately and cheerfully.

His eyes are on me. "Did you hear me, Faith? I am hoping these long days will soon be a thing of the past."

"Yes, I heard you. That would be very nice," I try for enthusiasm.

I meet his studying gaze briefly, but then drop my eyes and return to the sink.

"So, kids. How was your day? I haven't been able to ask that question in quite awhile," Michael asks enthusiastically, turning his attention to the children.

****

When we climb into bed that night, Michael is unusually quiet. He is tense as I lie next to him.

"Are we okay?" he finally asks.

His question takes me by surprise. "What? What do you mean?"

"I don't know. Why aren't you happy that I will be home earlier? I thought that's what you wanted."

"Huh? What makes you think I'm not happy?"

"You weren't exactly…enthusiastic…when I mentioned I may be coming home earlier," he answers guardedly. "So again I ask, are you and I okay?"

I collect my thoughts. "We are fine, Michael. I would love it if you start coming home earlier. I just…don't want…to get my hopes up. You said you might be able to come home earlier. If you can't, I…I just don't want to get my hopes up, that's all."

"Is that what it is? You're afraid I wasn't telling the truth?"

"Michael, it's not that I didn't think you were being honest with me. I just…If you can't come home earlier, I don't think I can deal with the disappointment. I just can't take it right now." My voice and chin quiver. Tears prick my eyes. Again.

He wraps his arms around me. "Honey, I…," he pauses. "I am not trying to mislead you, honestly. These long hours will come to an end very soon. Do you believe me?"

"Yes, I believe that you believe it. I just don't want to hope for it and then…"

He holds me tightly and kisses me. He breaks away and breathes, "Faith, I…I have missed you more than you know. It tears me up to know that you're hurting so much and there's nothing I can do about it." His voice cracks. He turns his face into my neck and I feel his hot breath against my throat. He squeezes me so tight I can barely breathe.

144

My tears spill over and a sob escapes. My heart breaks for him.

He hurts for me.

I can't fathom why he should feel that way. I just want him to be all right; what shape I'm in doesn't matter.

"Faith," he groans. "Please don't cry anymore. I am so sorry."

The split of my heart widens as I realize that my crying hurts him. Another unwilling sob escapes me, and I tremble as I try to stem the tide of tears. I struggle to answer him. He groans again into my neck, never loosening his grip.

"Michael...please....don't."

He releases me and his face is in front of mine.

"What? You want me to leave?" His voice is quivering and strained. His breath is hot on my face.

I gasp, startled. "Leave me? You want to leave me?" I ask, bewildered and confused.

"You just told me don't. You don't want me to hold you?" he asks urgently, an edge to his voice.

I shake my head and close my eyes. My hands cling to him. "No, Michael. I don't want you to be upset about me. If you left me, I...I would die." I begin to sob. He envelopes me in his strong embrace, crushing my mouth with his. I barely have time to catch my breath. My chin quivers and I'm still sobbing. I wrap myself around him, clinging desperately to him.

"I'm not going anywhere. I promise," he murmurs against my ear.

"I...I need you...here. Michael," I manage to whisper. I bury my head against his neck. He pulls my mouth up to his and kisses me fervently.

My body responds and I squeeze him tightly. Suddenly, he's covering me and his mouth finds mine. I am aware of nothing but him.

His touch, his smell, his taste.

He saturates my whole being. There's no room for my fear, my pain. Not here. Not now. My raw, aching nerves are smoothed over with a soothing balm that flows from his touch.

I want more. I need more.

My heart is once again, for the moment, whole, complete, and utterly healed with Michael. I am always more and better with him than I am without him. I need him so much.

Perhaps too much.

A distant thought, a distant feeling pricks at the edge of my awareness.

I want too much. I can lose it all. God, please don't take it all away. Not again.

Chapter Fifteen

The shrill ring of the phone interrupts my musing over morning coffee the following week. Michael's work number blinks on the caller ID.

"Hello?" I breathe into the mouth piece.

"Hi, Faith. Good news – my hours are going back to normal. The team's hard work has paid off and the unfinished projects are back on track."

I offer up a silent prayer of thanks. "That's wonderful news, honey. When can you go back to normal?"

"Tonight. I'll be home by five-thirty."

He'll be home for dinner tonight; that's the first time in weeks. I'm stunned into silence.

"Hello? Faith, are you there?"

"Oh! Sorry, sweetie. I'm just shocked. And happy!" I blurt, gripping the phone.

"I thought that would make you happy. I'm relieved, too. These long hours have been really hard. For both of us."

"Yes. It has. I'm thankful they're finally over."

"Me, too. Look, I have to go. There's a final meeting about this right after lunch and I have a few things to wrap up before then, okay? Love you and I'll see you soon."

"Okay, honey! Love you, too. Bye."

Hanging up the phone, I sigh in relief that his long hours are finally ending. I won't have to be lonely anymore. This week's therapy session was as brutal as the last.

Pastor Ben continues to dig deeper and deeper. It's like going in for surgery each time. Anxiety builds in anticipation and I spend the following day or two in recovery. It consumes my life.

The good pastor assured me that it would get easier, but I have doubts. How can this possibly get any better? If anything, it's getting worse.

This week, he actually made me talk about how Paul died and the night I found out. I shudder to remember.

Hope sparks in me because Michael will be home earlier from now on. I am so relieved. It's been too long.

The other night made me realize that he misses me as much as I miss him. I hadn't considered that to really be a factor. I mean, of course he's been tired. But I didn't think he missed me. Not like I miss him.

My afternoon run is relaxed. I enjoy the crisp autumn air and the trees that are ablaze in color; they're bursting with crimson red, golden yellow, and burnt orange. The fallen leaves crunch under my feet.

For the first time in a very long time, I don't war with my thoughts. I simply enjoy the act of running and of just…being. It's foreign to me. I have the fleeting feeling that something is wrong. I'm sure it's just a residual after effect from the counseling sessions.

Walking up the driveway afterwards, Julie is stooped over in her yard, burying bulbs into freshly turned soil. I call out and wave hello to her, casually strolling over.

She straightens up, pressing the palms of her hands into her back as she arches upward. "Ugh! I've been bent over too long," she groans. "How's it going?"

"Pretty good. Michael is finally going back to normal work hours tonight."

"I'm so happy for you. I know it's been really hard with him working so much. I'm sure the kids are happy, too."

"They will be, but they don't know yet. He just called this morning to let me know and they're still in school. He said he'd be home by about five-thirty."

"Oh, sorry. We don't have kids so I forget about the school thing." Her expression clouds over for a split second.

"What are you planting?"

"Tulip bulbs. They don't last long, but they're so pretty when they poke through in the spring. Do you plant flowers?"

"Me? No. I can't grow anything green and gave up trying years ago. Never have been able to."

"Well, you can enjoy watching my flowers. I eat the calories in the kitchen and work them off in the garden."

"That's a balanced life," I joke. "Well, I'll let you get back to it. I need to go shower and get moving."

"Enjoy Michael!" She stoops over her flower bed again.

****

I text my friends that afternoon to let them know the good news. They know how difficult this has been. I get an immediate response from Brenda. I don't hear from Michelle. She's very busy and we hardly ever have the chance to talk. Her business consumes her time.

Lilly calls me back rather than texting.

"Hi, Faith. It's Lilly. I'm so glad Michael is going to be home earlier now. You need him there."

"Yes. It's been hard." I almost add that it's because of my therapy sessions, but stop short. I haven't shared that.

"I wanted to ask…is Sarah okay?" she asks hesitantly.

I blink in surprise.

Sarah? What's Sarah got to do with anything??

"Uh…yeah. As far as I know. Why?"

"Oh, I don't know. Shaun just mentioned that she's…having a hard time right now." Lilly's son is in the same school, but is one grade above Sarah.

"What? What does he mean 'having a hard time'? Like with her grades or something?"

"Faith, I really don't know. I just thought that's what you meant about it being hard without Michael around lately. I thought you were having to deal with Sarah."

My mouth pops open. I'm truly confused. The earlier feeling that something is wrong creeps over me, stronger.

"Lilly, what exactly has Shaun been saying?"

"Faith, I don't know anything. He doesn't say much. It's mostly hearsay."

My anger flashes. "Lilly, I don't care if it is hearsay; I want to hear about it because I don't have a clue what you're talking about. If it were Shaun or Shane, wouldn't you want to know?"

Lilly hesitates. "Yes, I suppose you're right." She takes a deep breath. "Shaun said that kids at school are…talking…about Sarah. He said she's hanging around with the wrong crowd and…may be getting involved with…things."

Ice crawls down my spine.

"What sort of things, Lilly?" I ask, working to keep my voice from becoming shrill.

She hesitates once again. "Shaun hasn't ever said specifically. I would assume it could be the…usual things that the wrong crowd gets into, Faith," she continues quietly. "Do you want me to ask Shaun to be more specific when he gets home?"

Now it's my turn to hesitate. I don't know what to do with this. Sarah? In with the wrong crowd? How could that be? This is Sarah, for crying out loud. My quiet, studious middle child. She's never given us, nor gotten into, any trouble. This has to be a mistake.

"Uh, yeah. No. I don't know, Lilly. Yes. Yes! Please do ask him to be more specific, if he can." I take a deep breath. "I'm just shocked. It's the first I've heard about anything."

"Faith, don't worry. It could just be much ado about nothing. Sarah's a good kid. Always has been. I'll call you and let you know what Shaun says."

Her tone is reassuring, but that nagging feeling in my heart won't go away. It's telling me that this most definitely is something to be concerned about.

"I'm also really sorry. I thought that's what you were dealing with. Is everything else okay?"

I don't want to share my therapy. Not after hearing this about Sarah. "Everything is fine, Lilly. I appreciate your concern."

After the conversation, I stand, staring at the table, unsure what to do.

I call Michael. His cell goes straight to voicemail, so I try his office number; same thing. I groan, remembering he had a meeting this afternoon.

Perfect.

Left to my own thoughts, my brain spins a web of potential problems. Could Sarah actually be involved in drugs? Sex? I dismiss that immediately. Certainly not that. She's only twelve and still a child.

What could it possibly be? I cringe, pondering the possibilities. Sarah's not terribly outgoing and has never been a popular girl, but she's always had friends. She's always willing to befriend those who others tend to shy away from. That's probably what Shaun has seen at school; Sarah just talking to the wrong crowd.

She can't be in it, of course. Certainly not in that way. Plus she's probably just missing Michael, too. His absence has caused stress on us all.

Yes, I'm sure that's it. It has to be. I can't imagine my Sarah getting involved in anything else.

The nagging feeling won't go away.

I clean furiously to get my mind off of it and throw myself into making an elaborate dinner, convincing myself that it's to celebrate Michael coming home. I plan to make a rib roast with garlic mashed potatoes, gravy, and oven roasted green beans.

There's plenty of time to figure out how to handle this before the kids get home. I don't want to confront Sarah; I don't even know what I could be dealing with. It could be nothing at all.

It has to be. This is Sarah.

It was just one small conversation with Lilly about some things that Shaun may have heard at school. Nothing concrete. It's really nothing at all.

Nothing except that nagging feeling in my heart.

When they tumble in the door, I plant a smile on my face and hide the worry that's eating at me.

"Hi guys! How was your day?"

Andrew drops his book bag on the bench and runs immediately for the basement door without answering me except a yelled "Hi, Mom!"

April can always be counted on to be the first to respond.

"It was an awesome day! An awesome week!"

She blathers on about her weekly activities and the latest social gossip. Superficially, of course. She never tells me details. I am her mother, after all. None of it captures my attention. I listen to bits and pieces of what she says all the while casting sideways glances at Sarah to see if anything looks amiss. She's her usual quiet self, her expression unreadable.

When April at last finishes her monologue, I turn to Sarah and ask, "Sarah? How about you?"

She regards me for a moment and answers flatly, "Fine, nothing to report."

She turns and bounds up the stairs two at a time. I simply watch her go, not knowing what else to do.

"She was pretty quiet on the way home, even for her," April murmurs.

"Do you know…if there's something wrong, April?" I ask her. Maybe Sarah has shared something with her.

She shrugs. "I don't know, but I doubt it. Nothing ever happens in middle school, Mom. Besides, it's Sarah. What could possibly be wrong?" She rolls her eyes and turns her attention to her cell phone, which has just beeped.

So much for that source of information. April's too wrapped up in her own life to notice anything. I hesitate for a moment, deciding whether to pursue Sarah or let her be. Maybe she'll share what's on her mind in her own time.

Walking slowly up the stairs, I gather my thoughts trying to come up with a game plan. I don't want to make accusations; what would I accuse her of? I don't know anything.

Hesitating at her door, my hand resting on the knob, I sigh and pull my hand away. Perhaps knocking would be better.

"Sarah?" I say gently, knocking lightly. "It's me. Can I come in?"

After a momentary hesitation, she responds. "Sure."

I enter slowly, peering around the door. "Are you okay?" I ask gently.

She is sitting cross legged on her bed with an open book in front of her and her cell phone resting next to it.

Her brow furrows for a moment before smoothing out. Her expression is undecipherable; she's always been so steady and unreadable. I have no idea what she's feeling or thinking.

152

"I'm fine. Why?" she asks.

My eyes search her face. "I don't know, honey. I just…I just want to know if there's anything bothering you. Is everything okay?"

She concentrates on something before answering. "Everything's fine." Her cell phone beeps. She glances at it, frowns, and then looks at me. "Really, I'm fine." Her tone is dismissive.

"Who's that?" I nod my head toward her cell.

She glances quickly at me. "It's just…Jennifer." Jennifer is Brenda's daughter and one of Sarah's best friends. She taps something quickly on the cell and holds it close to her.

"Oh?" I say expectantly. "How's she doing?"

"She's fine." Sarah looks at the book and then back at me, as though she's decided the conversation has ended. "Mom, I'm fine, really. Don't worry about me. Everything's good. I'm just…tired. It's Friday."

I don't buy it for one second but have nothing else to say.

"Sarah," I begin, still searching her face. "I just want you to know that you can talk with me about anything. I love you, okay?"

An emotion flickers briefly across her face, but is gone before I can place it. She hesitates. "I know, Mom. I love you, too. There's really nothing to worry about." She pauses. "What makes you think something is wrong?" There's a hint of suspicion in her voice.

I decide against telling her about my conversation with Lilly.

"Nothing really. You just seem more down than usual. More quiet. It's not like you. Is it because Dad hasn't been home much?"

"Yes," she answers quickly. A little too quickly. "I'm just missing Dad."

I'm not going to get anywhere. I'll have to wait to hear from Lilly and see if Shaun offered any further information.

"Well, you can feel better then. Dad called today to let me know that he's back on normal hours. He'll be home for dinner tonight. Want to come help me finish?"

"Not yet. I'll be down in a little bit. I want to finish more of this book first."

I push her hair away from her face. "Okay, honey. Come down soon, though." I kiss her forehead. "I love you."

She doesn't look up. "Love you, too, Mom." She's already engrossed in her book. I leave her to it and go downstairs.

The gnawing feeling in my heart doesn't go away. I hope Lilly calls soon. I'll be able to talk to Michael tonight, at least.

I busy myself finishing up dinner. Sarah joins me half an hour later. She's still wearing the long sleeved shirt she wore from school with the high neck line she's been favoring lately. Such an odd choice of clothing, especially since the weather isn't that cold yet. It's only early autumn.

A sinking feeling hits me. Oh God. I have heard of kids who cut themselves. That can't be it, can it?! Rather than demand to see her arms, I try a different tactic.

"Sarah, would you mind peeling the potatoes? I'm going to make garlic mashed potatoes with dinner."

"Sure."

"Don't you want to change into something more comfortable, honey? You've got to be hot in that shirt," I say casually.

"No. I'll just roll the sleeves up." She pushes them up over her elbows and washes her hands at the sink. The skin on her arms is smooth and healthy.

Of course she's not doing that. My imagination is working over time. This is Sarah; she wouldn't do that. She couldn't do that. I need to just stop worrying.

It's fine. Everything is fine.

Attempts at having a conversation with her result in clipped responses, at best and I give up. Sarah will talk when she's ready. She's just been stressed because Michael hasn't been home. Yes, that's it.

Michael arrives home for dinner ten minutes later than planned. My already anxious insides twist tighter while I wait. My nerves are forever raw. When he walks through the door, he is grinning from ear to ear and bears a bouquet of beautiful red and pink roses.

154

"Michael, they're beautiful!" I gasp as he presses the bouquet into my hand. The paper crinkles and I bury my face in the blossoms, deeply inhaling their heady perfume. I adore roses.

"Sorry I'm late, Faith. I wanted to get these for you. Hope you don't mind."

"Of course I don't mind! They're just so beautiful, Michael. Thank you." I smile and hug him. Andrew wriggles in between us to hug Michael's waist.

"Hi, Dad!" he blurts out. "I'm glad you'll be home for dinner now."

"Me too, buddy. I've missed you." Michael musses Andrew's hair and hugs him before turning his attention to Sarah.

"Hey, Sarah. How's my baby girl doing?" He hugs her and she folds herself in his arms.

"Good." Her response is muffled, her face buried in his shoulder. He kisses the top of her head and releases her.

He looks around. "Where's April?"

"She's upstairs in her room. Sarah, would you go get her and tell her Dad is home and dinner is ready, please?" Sarah nods and disappears.

I wait until I'm sure Sarah is out of ear shot, then whip my head around to Michael and say in a hushed tone, "Michael, we need to talk about Sarah after the kids go to bed, okay?"

Startled, he blinks in surprise and responds, "Okay."

Dinner goes very well – the conversation is lively and the kids want to fill Michael in on all he's missed since his long hours started. I try to listen intently for Sarah's contributions, but hers are rather typical – very short or not at all. She has always been content to let April and Andrew talk.

Now it bothers me.

Once dinner is done, the dishwasher loaded, and the kids are all upstairs, Michael approaches me in the kitchen.

"So, what's going on with Sarah?" he asks quietly.

My eyes dart toward the stairs and then back at Michael. I keep my voice low.

"Let's go upstairs and talk." He follows me upstairs. I pause and listen by each child's door. April's radio is playing softly in her room, Andrew is quiet and so is Sarah. I tiptoe across the hall into our bedroom and shut the door softly behind me.

"Honey, I'm not sure. But….there's something going on." In a hushed tone, I tell him about my conversation with Lilly, Sarah's unusual quietness lately, her sudden wardrobe change to long sleeved shirts, and what I think it all might mean.

When I'm done, he's quiet. He gets up from where he sat at the end of the bed and paces the room slowly. Suddenly, he turns to me, "Have you heard from Lilly yet?"

I shake my head. "No. She said she'd call me tonight and let me know. I don't know why she hasn't."

Michael glances at his watch. "It's already ten." He sighs in exasperation. "Maybe she forgot, or…maybe there was nothing to tell you. You can call her tomorrow. I'm sure it's nothing that can't wait until then."

My shoulders relax. I am making a mountain out of a mole hill.

"I'm sure you're right. I'll just call her tomorrow." I try to convince myself of this and ignore the increasing intensity of the nagging feeling in my heart.

I glance over at Michael and stop dead in my tracks.

Something about his expression is very wrong. I don't know why. He looks like he's thinking very hard about something. Not something good, I'm sure of it.

"What, Michael?"

He pauses for a long moment, his eyes searching my face with his arms crossed. Finally, he uncrosses his arms and moves toward me, placing his hands on my arms. "Faith, sit down for a minute. There's something I need to tell you," he says gently. I drop woodenly onto the bed, heart in my throat.

Oh, God.

My heart begins to pound. What could this possibly be?

"Honey, I…" he starts, but as he sees my face he stops, moves in front of me, and gets down on his knees and places his hands on my balled fists. He looks down at my hands, frowns, and smoothes them open before continuing. "Faith, breathe."

I release the air I hadn't realized I had been holding. "Michael," I blurt, "Just tell me whatever it is."

My hands begin to ball up again, but he holds them tighter, forcing them to remain open.

Michael studies me for a moment longer and then begins again, his voice low and gentle. "Faith, remember I told you I had a meeting this afternoon? About this whole mess and the long hours?"

I nod.

"Well, honey. That wasn't all it was about." At least he's not confessing an affair or something…I think. "The project is back on track now, but there are some complications."

He's not having an affair. This is a good thing.

"Michael, you had me scared for a minute!" His words sink in. Complications… "What sort of complications and what does that have to do with me? With us?" I ask, confused.

"Apparently, some very strict rules, laws actually, were…broken…by Gene before I ever came on board with the project. They are potentially criminal in nature and the authorities are investigating me and the rest of my team for any involvement."

"Huh? What? Investigating you? How? Why? You aren't a criminal. You just said it was before you ever came on board."

"I know, Faith. I know. But the investigation is widespread. Which means I'm on their radar."

"Why you? What does this mean?"

"Me, because I am the lead on this project. Or at least I am the lead now that Gene left. It means they are investigating all of our records with a fine toothed comb and interviewing us. It was sort of dropped in our lap this afternoon. We had no idea beforehand that it was even going on. Which, of course, makes sense, you know? If someone is doing something wrong, you don't tell them you're investigating. You just do it."

I shake my head. "What's going to happen?"

"Well, we weren't allowed to go back into the lab or our offices after we were informed of the ongoing investigation and we were assured that the company was being fully cooperative with the feds on this."

The feds? This sounds serious. "And?"

"And…we will just have to wait and see what unfolds. I wanted you to know about it and I don't know what the fall out is going to be. But believe me, there will be fall out. The company has been working on this for about nine years already, invested millions of dollars. If they find evidence of wrong doing, some will lose their jobs and others could be prosecuted."

"Prosecuted? You mean like go to jail? Did you do something wrong?" I ask quietly. I can't imagine he would.

His face registers hurt. "No! What…why would you think that?" He places his palm on his chest. "Why would you ask that?"

"No, honey. No. I don't think you would intentionally ever do something wrong, much less illegal. I'm simply asking. It was just a question."

He shakes his head. "Absolutely not, Faith. Intentional or not, I'm not sloppy about my work. I am diligent with the process and in my record keeping. I didn't get this far in my career by being sloppy," he responds defensively.

I have to diffuse this. "Michael, sweetie. I know. I don't know why I asked, really. Just forget it. I know that you'll be cleared in the end. What about everyone else?"

Again, he shakes his head. "Faith, everyone on the team is upstanding. But the feds don't launch an investigation without cause. I honestly don't have any idea. It's pretty scary, though." His eyes look off into the distance. A chill runs down my spine. "Very serious."

"Michael, what are you saying?"

"I'm saying that I bear responsibility for those under me. I don't know what's going to happen."

I gasp as shock and realization registers. "You mean…you could lose your job or…?"

"Let's not get ahead of this thing, Faith." He sighs. "I know that I haven't done anything wrong. It will be okay. I am, after all, innocent and I will fully cooperate with the investigation. I said as much this afternoon. If someone is doing something wrong, they will be held accountable."

I nod, speechless, trying to wrap my head around this. "But…if you are found responsible for something someone else did wrong, what does that mean?"

"Faith, don't worry about that. The fact is I am innocent. That will be shown to be true. In this country, we are still innocent until proven guilty. So we'll be all right."

"But what if, Michael? What if?!" I feel panicky.

Michael sighs, gets up, and moves toward the bathroom. "Faith, don't worry. It's going to be okay. I don't want to fight about this. Let's get ready for bed. I'm pretty beat and so are you. A good night's sleep will help us get some perspective."

Watching his retreating form, I stew in my emotions. I'm shocked, frightened, and just plain confused. How can this happen? He drops a bombshell like this on me and expects me to just roll over and go to sleep? Not likely. I jump up in a huff and tell him in a sharp tone that I'm going to check on the kids. His reply is muffled because he's brushing his teeth.

I open our bedroom door with more force than necessary and flounce down the hall. I check on Andrew first, who is fast asleep curled into a ball. April is also asleep, so I tiptoe in and cover her up; her covers are flung off the bed and she's sprawled out with her limbs in all four corners, mouth hanging open. I turn her radio and light off on my way out, quietly closing the door behind me.

Carefully opening Sarah's door, I glance over at her bed. She's covered from head to toe in her comforter. I smile and stride over to rub her back and uncover her face. As my fingers brush her back, it feels unusually cold and soft. I squeeze the lump and it's very soft. Too soft.

It's not her.

Frowning, I pull the comforter down a little and then whip it completely off the bed. Her pillows are lined up neatly. Her bed is empty. The gnawing feeling in my heart is razor sharp. Maybe she's in the bathroom. I dart into the Jack and Jill bathroom she shares with April.

Nothing.

I flip on her light and my eyes whip around the expanse of her room looking for evidence of her. My eyes stop at the window; it's been left cracked open about four inches, the curtains gently undulating in the chilly breeze.

She snuck out.

My heart sinks to the floor. I run into our room yelling, "Michael!"

My cry brings him darting out of the bathroom in his boxers, towel in hand. "What?! What's wrong?"

"It's Sarah. She's gone! Her window is open. She's gone, Michael!" I burst into tears.

He drops the towel, jogs past me and into Sarah's room. I follow closely on his heels. He immediately runs to the window and forces it wide open. Gripping the bottom of the window sill, he leans out and looks around. After a moment, he leans back in and turns to me. "I'm calling her cell." His voice is dark, his expression black.

"Oh, my God, Michael! Where do you think she is?! Why would she sneak out? Was she kidnapped? Did she run away?!" I cry hysterically.

"I don't know." He squeezes my arms briefly and then jogs back to our bedroom to retrieve the phone. I try to pull myself together and follow him. In the hall, I hear Sarah's cell phone bleating from her room.

She left her cell phone behind?

I turn around and race back into her room, Michael close on my heels this time; he must've heard it, too. As we enter her room, I notice her cell phone is lit up, vibrating, and sitting on the table next to her bed. It's plugged in, charging.

"Where is she, Michael?!" I yell. One hand goes to my stomach and the other to my heart. Both feel like they've been ripped apart.

Michael swears under his breath and rapidly pushes buttons on the phone in his hand. "I'm calling Lilly. Maybe Shaun knows where she went." As an afterthought, he points at her phone and gestures for me to get it. "Check her calls and texts. Maybe there's something on there." He glances at me and his expression softens. "Honey, don't worry. We will find her. I promise."

I nod numbly and grab her phone, ripping the charging cord out and flinging it away from me.

Please, God. Please, God, Please, God.

"Hello, Lilly? Hi, it's Michael. Sorry to call so late but we have a problem. Sarah is missing and we need to know if

Shaun told you anything. Any idea who she's with or where she may have gone?"

I can't hear Lilly's answer, so I turn my attention to Sarah's cell. Blinking and wiping my eyes to clear the tears out, I focus on the small screen.

I need to find Sarah.

It takes a moment to figure her phone out, but I finally navigate my way to her in box. As my hand scrolls through the texts, I notice there's several from a person named Matt that I don't recognize. I open the texts and as I read them, the air is sucked out of the room. I am horrified by what I've found.

I gasp and my hands shake.

"Michael…" I manage in a hoarse whisper. He is still talking to Lilly.

Suddenly, the cell is ripped from my hands and Michael is glaring at the black rectangle, his thumb scrolling up and down the screen. His expression goes from shock to comprehension and finally fury. I collapse onto Sarah's bed and hug her pillow tightly, burying my face in it. I inhale her scent and try to calm myself.

"Lilly, ask Shaun who Matt is," he speaks into the phone at his ear. His voice is calm, low and very deadly.

There's an eternal pause before Michael speaks again. "I don't have a last name. Does he know a…person…named Matt that Sarah knows or has been hanging around with?"

Another eternal pause.

"Very good. Does he know where this Matt lives?" Michael continues. He nods his head. "Thank you very much, Lilly." He's about to end the conversation when suddenly he says, "Sure. She's right here." He hands the phone to me.

I take it with a shaky hand and voice. "Hello?"

"Oh Faith! I'm so sorry! I was going to call you, but then we got busy with the game tonight and…oh, I'm so sorry! Please forgive me. If anything were to happen to Sarah…"

"I know, Lilly. Does Shaun know who Matt is?"

"He thinks he might. He told us what he knew. I hope it helps! Please let me know what else we can do. Tony wants to know if he should come over to help Michael."

"Hold on, let me ask." I cup my hand over the phone and ask Michael, "Do you want Tony to come over to help?"

He glances up at me, shakes his head, and returns his attention to Sarah's phone. He continues scrolling through the texts, black fury on his face.

"Michael says no." I answer. "I'm so scared, Lilly!" I choke out, crying. Lilly cries on the other end.

Suddenly, I hear Tony's voice on the line, "Faith, let me talk to Michael, please."

"Okay." I hand the phone to Michael. "Tony wants to…" Hiccup. "…talk to you."

Michael glares at the phone before taking it. "Yes, Tony?"

I can't make out the conversation and I'm becoming more and more hysterical as the text messages play over and over in my mind; so manipulating and vulgar in nature. There is very little innuendo there; it's blatantly sexual with a few "You know I love you" bits of garbage thrown in.

Sarah is only twelve-years-old! She's still a little girl! What kind of sick bastard is this Matt anyway to talk to a child like that?!

Finally, I am pulled from my own thoughts and pick up on Michael's conversation because he laughs. It's more of a chuckle, but I don't see anything that could be remotely funny.

"Yes, Tony. I guess it would be better to have you along." Michael's tone is a shade lighter.

I wonder what Tony could've said to Michael to change his mind and make him laugh. Michael ends the conversation and turns to me.

"Tony will be right over. He convinced me that I don't want to end up in jail for beating this kid to a pulp when I find him."

"Oh." Good point.

When Tony arrives, Michael is already dressed and waiting at the front door. Shaun and Lilly are with him. Lilly bursts in and grabs me in a tight embrace. Shaun lingers shyly in the background.

"I brought Shaun because he doesn't know the address, but has a pretty good idea of where this kid lives." Tony says, nodding toward Shaun.

"Yes, sir." Shaun's voice is quiet and uncertain.

"Is this Matt a friend of yours?" Michael asks, his voice snarling on the name.

"No, sir. He's a junior or senior in high school, I think."

I blanch and Michael's face pales. His lips become a thin line. That means this Matt is about seventeen-years-old; way too old to be interested in a twelve-year-old.

Lilly grips my waist, "They'll find her, Faith."

I place my hand over my mouth and close my eyes, nodding rapidly.

They have to find her. I hope they find her before…

I can't finish the thought. I don't want to.

Michael approaches me, grips my arms and kisses my forehead.

"Faith, I will find her. Don't worry. Lilly is going to stay here with you."

"Okay." I squeak and take a deep breath. "Hurry! I don't know how long she's been gone."

He nods, turning his attention to Tony. "Let's go," he growls.

"I'm driving, Michael," Tony replies. Michael merely nods and heads out into the night, followed by Tony and Shaun.

Once they're gone, I turn to Lilly. "Lilly, what's going on?!" I cry.

Lilly leads me into the living room and guides me onto the sofa, sitting down next to me. "Faith, I can't tell you how sorry I am. I didn't realize it was this serious. I really didn't. Shaun just told me little bits and I didn't think too much about it. Please forgive me!"

I shake my head. "Lilly, there's nothing to forgive. I'm just so worried about her! She's just a child! Who is this Matt anyway?!" His name is a curse word on my lips.

Lilly shakes her head. "Shaun didn't know much about him except that he's an older guy that hangs out with the other kids that Sarah's been hanging out with lately. He obviously goes to high school, but drives over to the middle school pretty much every day when school lets out."

My jaw drops. "He has his own car?!" I say incredulously. "That means he could've picked her up and then....and then... Omigod! Omigod!!" I approach hysteria again.

Dear God, where is she?! What's happening to her?!

Lilly is quick to respond. "I don't know, Faith. I don't know. It might just be his parent's car or something. We don't know. It's going to be okay." She rises. "I'm going to make some tea. I think we could both use it right now. I'll grab your chocolate," she adds as an afterthought and heads into the kitchen.

I sit on the sofa and bawl.

Lilly returns with the tea, places the bowl of M&Ms in front of me, and sits down. Grabbing a handful of M&Ms, I take the mug gratefully and sip the hot liquid, not knowing what else to do. All I can do is sit and wait for Michael to call.

And pray.

God, if you're there, hear me now! Please, please bring her home! I'm begging you, don't let him touch her! Don't do this! Please!!

Chapter Sixteen

Waiting is torture. Lilly's presence is helpful; she's comforting without being obtrusive. I want to call Michael a dozen times, but Lilly assures me he'll call when there's something to say. As a distraction, she puts in a movie. She asks for my input, but I really don't care. She chooses a comedy. Neither of us laughs. I'm not even sure what movie it is. All I see are colors and shapes moving across the screen.

This morning, I was entirely focused on recovering from this week's counseling session and elated that Michael's work hours were returning to normal. Now Michael is being investigated and Sarah is missing. My life has turned upside down.

Again. This can't be happening...

I have reached too far and too high. Everything really can be pulled right out from under me again. Just like last time...

Fear locks my heart in a vise grip. My mind recoils.

No, no, no, no, no...Don't do it again, God. Please! I'll do anything!

When the phone finally rings, we both jump. It's nearly midnight. The M&M bowl is empty. My mind spins out of control.

I lunge for the phone and answer it before the second ring.

"Hello! Michael?!" I yell into the phone.

"It's me, Faith. I have Sarah. She's okay. We're on our way home," he replies in a clipped, angry tone.

"What happened?!" I desperately try to pull any clues from his tone. "Where are you?"

"We're in the car and on our way home now. She's fine. We'll be home soon."

All I can tell is that he doesn't want to talk. At least I know Sarah is with Michael and she's safe. We end our conversation and I burst into tears again.

"Faith, is she okay?"

I nod and Lilly and I hold each other until I can speak. "Michael has her…," hiccup "…with him and he's…," hiccup "…on his way home."

"I'm so glad. I'm so glad," Lilly breathes in reply.

"Me, too." I try to catch my breath. "Sarah is on her way home." That's all that matters.

Lilly releases me and busies herself clearing the tea cups and the now empty M&M bowl, disappearing into the kitchen.

When Michael arrives, he walks through the door and throws me a warning glance that I don't fully understand. He's followed by Tony and Shaun. Finally, Sarah walks through the door. I practically knock her over as I grab her in a death grip of a hug, crying all over again.

"My baby! I'm so glad you're safe! Don't you ever do that to me again, do you hear me?! Never again!" I kiss her head and begin to kiss her cheeks when she scrunches up her face and pulls away.

"I know, Mom. I'm sorry! I didn't think…it was such a big deal," she replies, casting a sideways glance at her audience. It looks like her gaze rests specifically on Shaun, but I can't be sure. Right now, I don't care. My focus is entirely on her and that she's safe and sound at home.

"Not a big deal? Not a big deal?!" I huff. "Sarah, I…"

Michael cuts me short. "Faith, let her be. We'll talk about this tomorrow morning."

Bewildered, I look at her, but let it drop. Michael knows more of what happened than I do, and I trust his judgment.

Michael addresses Sarah. "Go upstairs and get to bed, Sarah. I may nail your window shut, by the way. So don't even think about it."

Her shoulders drop and her mouth becomes a thin line; she resembles Michael so clearly when she makes that face. "I'm not, Dad," she replies sullenly and disappears upstairs.

Michael turns to Tony and Lilly, his face and tone soften, and shakes Tony's hand. "Thanks for coming tonight, Tony. I appreciate your help. You too, Shaun. You're a fine young man." He nods toward the wary teenager lingering in the background.

"Yes, sir," Shaun smiles shyly at Michael.

I hug Lilly once more and thank her for her company before they depart. Michael locks the door behind them and deflates before my eyes. His expression is pure agony.

I inhale sharply and a new fear grips my heart. "Michael, what is it? What happened?" My hand creeps up to my throat. He takes a step toward me, shakes his head slightly, and folds me in his arms.

"I'm just glad she's home, that's all. Let's go upstairs to talk." He guides me up the stairs pausing briefly to listen at Sarah's door, sits me on the bed in our room where I remain stiff, and closes the door quietly behind him. He turns toward me, closes his eyes with his hands on his hips, takes a deep breath and lets it out. As he begins to tell me what happened, he paces the floor.

"Faith, she is okay. They didn't...I mean they weren't...you know. I was so worried about what...could have happened."

"Thank God." I exhale sharply and press my hands into the bed. "Then...what? You look as bad as I feel, but I don't actually know anything!"

"I know. Sorry," he replies, sitting on the bed next to me. "Well, we went to this kid's house and he wasn't there, but his parents were. They had no idea what was going on, only that he was out with friends tonight. We told them who we were and that we were looking for Sarah. I had her cell phone with me and showed them the text messages. They were as upset as we were." His expression darkens and he grinds his teeth. "They called his cell phone and found out where he was and that Sarah was indeed with him. They asked if I had tried to call Matt from Sarah's phone and I actually had. We tried that when Tony was driving over there, but he didn't answer.

"Matt told them he was on his way home and would bring Sarah. So we waited for them. I got to know his parents a bit, plus I learned more about this Matt kid. Apparently, he's been in trouble before and actually had a live in girlfriend last year. A live in girlfriend of all things, Faith! She got pregnant and miscarried. They eventually broke up. I don't know what kind of parents would let…"

He exhales sharply before continuing. "I already didn't like this kid and now I really don't like him. If Tony hadn't come, I don't know what I would've done when he walked through that door! Did you know he's almost eighteen-years-old? He swears he didn't realize Sarah is only twelve, but I think that's a load of bull. She's in middle school for crying out loud!" He's raising his voice the more he speaks.

"Michael, please keep your voice down," I caution him.

He takes another deep breath and gets up to pace the floor, continuing in a quieter tone. "So anyway, he walks in holding Sarah's hand and she's looking at me all scared; she knew she was in serious trouble. It was all I could do to keep from knocking his teeth in, even with his parents standing right there. That's where Tony came in handy. I'm so glad he convinced me to let him come."

I grimace thinking that I could've gotten a call from Michael in jail; him having been arrested for assaulting a minor. My mind whiplashes to the investigation. I blink and shake my head.

"Matt's parents, to their credit, jumped all over him as soon as he walked in. They started yelling at him that she was only twelve and what was he thinking. I almost didn't get a chance to say anything at all. He started yelling back that he didn't know she was only twelve." He stops pacing and faces me directly, "This is where it gets interesting. Then Sarah actually spoke up and told him that she thought he was fifteen! He had been lying to her the whole time, I'm guessing." He shakes his head. "I finally got a chance to get a word in and threatened him about coming near my daughter again. I demanded to know where he was and what they were doing. He said they had gone to a party, whatever that means. He said they weren't doing anything. His parents were very upset, and I am sure I left him in capable hands. From what they've told me, he's a handful. Then we came home."

"What could've happened? What if I didn't go check on her?! Where would she be and…what…would she be doing? Did you talk to her about the text messages we saw?" I cringe, remembering.

He shakes his head. "I didn't want to talk to her about it in front of Tony or Shaun. That's what we're going to have to discuss with her tomorrow. And I don't know that she's getting this back." He holds up her cell phone that had been in his breast pocket, then glances at his watch. "Well, today actually; it's already one. We need to get to bed."

"Yeah. This has turned into one hell of a day." I rub my face and yawn as waves of exhaustion roll over me.

Climbing into bed, I turn to Michael. "Michael, what are we going to do? What are we going to say?"

He shakes his head. "Faith, I really don't know. We will say whatever needs to be said. I can't believe this happened with Sarah. Of all our kids, I would've thought it would be April we'd have this discussion with. Never Sarah."

"I know. I'm shocked, too. Sarah's always been the one I worry the least about," I reply wearily and pause. "Maybe that's the problem. I never worried about her much and she just sort of slipped under the radar."

"Maybe. I don't know. I've never been a teenage girl." There's an edge of amusement in his voice.

"Maybe not, but you've been a teenage boy. How does that fit into the equation?" I retort.

He stiffens. "Not very well. I don't know what actually happened between them up to this point. We will have a long talk with her tomorrow."

"Yes. Michael, you don't think they…they…had sex, do you?"

"No! No," he answers quickly. "I can't wrap my head around that. She's just a child. Even though she did something very stupid doesn't mean she is stupid."

Shuddering to think of the alternative, I hope he's right. This is not happening. It can't be.

Michael is quiet for a long while. So long, in fact, that I think he's gone to sleep. Suddenly, he murmurs quietly, "Faith, I really don't want you to worry about the investigation."

It's my turn to stiffen. "Not possible and you know it."

He sighs and squeezes me against him, kissing the back of my neck. I close my eyes and try to relax. I don't want to face tomorrow.

God, I don't know how much more of this I can take. Please, please don't do this.

Chapter Seventeen

My dreaming subconscious tosses from scenario to scenario. In one, I am packing huge military style duffle bags only to find that I've packed nothing but Sarah's stuffed animals, but I can't find her. In another, I'm searching with increasing desperation through the empty rooms of my home looking for my family. Each room is wrapped in police tape. I end the search in our master bedroom where Paul's coffin is set up with flowers all around just like at his funeral.

I dread the day before my eyes even open on Saturday morning. When I wake up on this particular day, there is no disorientation as to the day of the week, the time, or what needs to be done; I'm acutely and painfully aware. I roll over and look at the clock.

Sighing heavily, I roll onto my back, placing my arm over my face. Michael stirs and presses close to me.

"Morning," he says thickly. "Sleep okay?"

"No."

He hugs my waist. "You were tossing and turning most of the night. Muttering, too, but I couldn't make out what you were saying."

"Bad dreams," I reply.

"I thought as much. Yesterday was a lot, wasn't it?"

"Mm hmm."

"Sorry," he murmurs. "What time is it?"

"Almost seven-thirty." I turn and look at him. "I don't want to do this day, Michael. I really don't."

He yawns before replying. "Me either, Faith. Do we have to do it so early?"

"No, but I can't sleep anymore. I would just end up dreaming again. Although if going back to sleep would make this day go away, I would."

He sighs and rubs his eyes. "I know, honey. I know. Are you going to try and get some more sleep? I'd like to. We went to bed so late."

"No, I'm going to make some coffee. You go ahead and sleep some more if you want." I kiss him quickly and roll out of bed.

He yawns again. "Okay. Get me up if you need me."

"Sure." I have no intention of waking him up. Everything that needs to happen today can wait until he's gotten enough sleep. As for me, well… I'll sleep when everything is as it should be.

I put on my robe and steal myself quietly from the room. Michael's already returned to a deep sleep, judging by the gentle snoring coming from the bed. I pad across the hall and check to see that Sarah is actually still there. She's curled into a ball on her bed and also gently snoring, just like her father. This time I see a foot and her hair, which is comforting. April and Andrew are sound asleep, as well.

Perhaps having the house quietly to myself for a little while will help me collect my thoughts and my strength.

As the coffee brews, I ponder recent developments and am overwhelmed. Tears spring into my eyes thinking about the investigation and Sarah's escapade. I can't believe it's real.

My world has gone crazy. Again. The thought makes me shiver.

There's absolutely nothing I can do about the investigation. I am powerless and it's frustrating. As for Sarah, that is so not happening. We are going to make sure Sarah doesn't see this Matt again, even if I have to ground her until she graduates from high school. Surely she realizes it was a mistake. I mean, whatever has been going on lately, I know that Sarah is still a good kid. She is level headed. Isn't she? This isn't normal for her.

The coffee maker sputters and wheezes to announce the completion of its task, interrupting my musing. I pour myself a cup and take it to the back porch.

The sun is rising just over the trees to the left of our property line. It's quite lovely on this crisp autumn morning. I've missed the actual sunrise, but the flaming orange in the sky reminds me that I haven't missed all of it. Leaving the French doors open, I settle into a padded wicker chair and clasp my hands around the steaming mug, inhaling deeply.

How I wish I could just exist in this moment without the nagging disquiet as a constant reminder of what lies ahead. I force myself to focus on the beauty of the sky, the crisp air surrounding me, and the cacophony of birds chattering away in the trees. Leaning my head wearily back into the chair, I turn my gaze heavenward.

God, work this out. Please work this out. Don't hurt me again.

Julie Jackson's smiling face floats into my head, startling me. Why would she come to mind? She's got nothing to do with any of this nonsense, but I smile thinking about her. She would probably make a good counselor just like her husband. Chuckling to myself, I take another sip of my coffee which has cooled considerably in the chilly autumn air. Maybe I'll call her later and talk about this. I'm sure she would have an interesting perspective.

For now I just want to enjoy my coffee and my back yard.

Lingering for another forty-five minutes and savoring one more cup of coffee, I do just that until I spy Andrew stumbling into the living room, yawning. He's probably hungry. Gathering myself and my now empty coffee cup, I sigh and reluctantly rise to meet the day.

Andrew collapses onto the sofa, rubbing his eyes with one hand while fingering the remnants of his baby blanket with the other. The blanket is nothing more than a stringy, significantly diminished swath of fabric, a mere shadow of its former self. Andrew has loved it nearly into extinction and refuses to give it up. Although I have noticed it's making less of an appearance in the past few months, he still drags it around on the weekends and it remains on his bed when not otherwise pressed into service.

"Hungry, bud?" I run my hand through his hair as I pass him on my way into the kitchen.

His mouth stretches into a large O as he nods.

"How about some French toast?"

"Uh huh," he answers sleepily.

I busy myself making French toast and bacon for breakfast. I turn the oven on warm to store breakfast for when the others wake up.

April is the next to make an appearance. Her hair is a wild, tangled mess and there are sleep wrinkles on the side of her face that make her look like she slept on a waffle iron. Not knowing what kind of mood she's in, I don't laugh out loud.

"Morning, April. Hungry?" I ask.

She simply nods and plops into a chair with her eyes more closed than open. "I smell bacon," she mumbles.

"Bacon and French toast, actually," I answer while plating her breakfast.

As she eats, she gradually perks up. Perhaps her mood is a good one today. That will be helpful.

"I'm going to meet with the cheer squad this morning. We're doing some new cheers and we need to practice extra for next week's game," she says around a mouthful of bacon and syrup.

"What time?" I ask.

"Nine-thirty." She jabs another forkful of French toast and shoves it into her mouth. "So I have to hurry."

"You've got plenty of time," I chide her. I keep my tone light with the next question. "April, do you know a guy named Matt at your school? He's a senior, I think."

She shrugs. "I know a couple of guys named Matt. Why?" she asks absentmindedly, smearing another forkful of French toast around the syrup on her plate.

"I'm just curious. Sarah has been hanging around with some…older kids and one high school guy named Matt. I wanted to know if you knew him. That's all." I avoid looking directly at her.

Her eyes bug out and she gulps her food. "It's not Matt Johannson is it?" She points her fork in the air.

I eye her warily, working to keep my face unreadable. "I don't know his last name, honey. Why? Who's Matt Johannson?"

174

Do I really want the answer?

"Only the biggest douche dog in school!" she replies. Seeing the expression on my face she quickly adds, "Sorry, Mom. It's just a term we use for guys like him."

"What does…that…mean, April?"

"It means he…" she stops herself short and quickly eyes Andrew, who is at the table, engrossed in his own breakfast. "He bags every girl he can get his hands on. So I hope it's not him."

A cold shiver runs down my spine.

Dear God.

"Me, either," I reply quietly, looking down at my now empty plate. I drag my fork through the remnants of syrup on my plate. I look up to see April staring at me, her eyebrows knitting together.

"Mom, what's going on?"

My eyes flutter to Andrew for a moment. "April, it's nothing. Don't worry about it."

"Uh huh," she replies unconvincingly. Shrugging, she finishes her breakfast with gusto, dropping the subject. She understands there are some things that don't need to be discussed in front of Andrew. From what she's mentioned of this Matt Johannson, I'm pretty sure she can assume this is one of those things. Once she finishes breakfast, she bounds up the stairs to change, returning rather quickly and sidles up to me at the kitchen sink. Andrew has disappeared to watch Saturday morning cartoons.

"Mom, is there something going on with Sarah?"

"I don't know, April. Dad and I are going to talk to her today." I turn toward her. "Do you know anything going on that we should be aware of?"

She shakes her head. "No. Sarah never gets in trouble. She's such a goody goody."

I scowl at her. "You say it like it's a bad thing."

She snickers and rolls her eyes. "No, Mom. It's a good thing!" She turns on her heel and is out the door. I yell my warning about texting me right before the door slams shut.

Once she's gone, I'm left to ponder whether the Matt from last night is this Matt Johannson. I hope it isn't, but I'm terribly afraid that it is. I hope we were able to nip this in the bud before…

I can't go there. Sarah is only twelve. I just bought her first bra a year ago. No. No. It can't be.

The shrill ring of the phone startles me.

"Hello?"

"Faith, it's just me," Lilly replies. "I wanted to know how you're doing this morning."

"I'm fine." I quickly peek around the corner, checking to make sure Andrew isn't within ear shot. "Michael and Sarah are still sleeping."

"Did you guys talk with Sarah last night?"

"No. Michael wanted to wait until this morning. We were all so keyed up last night. Thank you for coming over. Thank Tony and Shaun for me, too."

"I will. I am still so sorry! I feel absolutely horrible."

"Please don't. I am so thankful Shaun stepped up and we did find out before…well, you know."

"So nothing happened?"

I close my eyes and grip the phone tightly. "Actually, we don't know what happened. I am just praying *that* didn't happen. We haven't talked to her yet." I swallow loudly. "I just can't think that it did."

The phone is quiet for a moment before Lilly responds. "I know, Faith. I know. I don't have any daughters, but I think of all our kids as my own. I hope for the best, too." It goes without saying that she's referring to my, Brenda's, and Michelle's children. We have all watched them grow up and are like aunties to each other's children.

"I know, Lilly. I know. I'll keep you posted. Hey, would you mind if I send Andrew over to your house while we talk to Sarah? That would really help a lot. This isn't something we want to discuss in front of him."

"Not a problem. I want to help however I can. Send him over whenever you want. We will be home all day. It's going to be okay, Faith."

"Thanks. I'll send him over shortly."

After our conversation, my heart feels even heavier. How can this be okay? Even if we were able to stop Sarah before the

176

worst happened, it still got very close and who knows what else may happen.

Plus that stupid investigation…

When I inform Andrew that he'll be playing over at Lilly's house, he jumps up with a whoop and runs upstairs to change. I retrieve my cell phone from its charging base and head upstairs to change my clothes so I can drive him over.

I tiptoe into our room and close the door quietly behind me. When I turn around, Michael is staring at me from the bed.

"Sorry. I didn't mean to wake you," I whisper.

"S'okay. I woke up a little while ago." He yawns and rolls over to grimace at the clock. "Whoa. It's almost ten o'clock." He scratches at the scruffy growth on his chin and falls back onto the bed.

"I'm going to drive Andrew over to Lilly's house to play today and April is at cheer practice. I thought we should talk to Sarah alone."

"Yeah," he replies quietly. "Is she up yet?"

I shake my head. "No."

Michael stretches once more and then heads into the bathroom while I change. Andrew knocks excitedly on the bedroom door.

I open the door and he spills into the room. He looks around until he spies his father coming out of the bathroom tying his robe around his midsection.

"Dad! I'm gonna go play at Shane's house!" he reports excitedly.

"I heard, buddy! I'm sure you'll have a good time. Behave yourself, all right?"

"I will!" He hugs his father fiercely and then grabs my hand, pulling at me.

"Hang on, Andrew! I want to hug daddy, too," I laugh.

Andrew drops my hand, rolls his eyes, and sighs impatiently.

"Breakfast is warming in the oven and I'll be back in a little while. You'll need to make some fresh coffee." I turn my full attention to Andrew. "Get your shoes on and we'll go."

Andrew bounds down the stairs and I follow quickly on his heels.

When I return home, I walk into the kitchen and see Sarah sitting at the table mulling over, rather than eating, her breakfast. Michael is sitting at the table with her, coffee mug grasped firmly between both hands. Both are staring silently and grimly at the table. Michael's mouth is a thin line and Sarah looks utterly miserable.

"Morning, honey. Did you get enough sleep?" I ask Sarah, making an attempt at being cheerful.

She nods, but doesn't answer. Michael glances up at me, despair and frustration written on his face. I shrug my shoulders and shake my head. I don't know where to begin, either. I certainly don't think it should be before breakfast and coffee.

I clear my throat. "Michael, why don't you go sit outside with me? It's such a lovely morning. I'll grab a cup of coffee and meet you out there."

He raises his eyebrows in question, but I simply jerk my head toward the door, encouraging him to go. He sighs and frowns at Sarah for a moment before ducking outside.

I walk over to Sarah, wrap my arms around her shoulders and kiss the top of her head. "I love you, Sarah. I hope you know that," I say quietly into her hair. "Finish your breakfast. We'll talk later. Everything will be fine." My voice sounds much calmer than I feel.

"Love you, too, Mom," she replies just as quietly. I pat her shoulder once more then fill a coffee mug for myself and join Michael out on the patio, closing the French doors behind me.

"What are we supposed to do, Faith? What are we supposed to say?" Michael asks, his eyes darting around the yard. "I mean, I really never thought we'd have to do something like this with Sarah."

I shake my head and take his hand, which he grips tightly. "I don't know, Michael. I really don't know. I'm not ready for this, either. I guess we'll just have to wing it. I think it might be best to just let her talk first. Find out what's been going on. I know one thing; we need to let her know that we love her. Yes, we're angry, but I for one am just…confused. I don't know where this came from or why."

"I'm angry. I want to tear this Matt limb from limb. I blame him mostly. I also want to yell at Sarah for being stupid. She's not a stupid kid!"

"Well, you can't do that. He's not our problem and she's our daughter. You're angry because you love her, right?"

Michael nods.

"Are you angry at Sarah?"

His head whips toward me, his lips pressed in a thin line. "Yes. No. A little. I thought she'd know better than this. What was she thinking?!" His fist pounds the arm of the chair.

"Michael, that's what we need to find out. Being mad at her will just make her clam up. You know she's never been one to talk much anyway. Let's just give her a chance to explain herself. There's a reason she's done this and we won't find out if we yell at her."

There's a light rapping on the glass. Sarah is staring at us from behind the glass of the French doors. I motion for her to come outside. She opens the door and pokes her head outside.

"Mom, Miss Julie is at the front door for you."

"Oh! Okay. I'll be there in a second. Thanks, honey."

Sarah nods and steals a sideways glance at her father before disappearing inside. Michael's face is pained.

"I'll be right back." I say, bending over and kissing his head. He sighs and blows at the steam in his mug.

Julie is standing on the front porch, holding a small foil covered dish. The aroma of cinnamon wafts up to my nose.

"Hi, Julie. How are you this morning?" I ask, trying to keep my voice light.

"Good morning, Faith. I'm doing well, thanks. I just thought you might like some more coffee cake. I am working on a chocolate chip cranberry recipe and wanted you to try it." She offers the dish to me. As always, it's still warm.

"That's so thoughtful of you, Julie. Thank you."

She grins broadly. "It's nothing! I'm just glad I have someone to share my kitchen experiments with."

I consider her for a moment, deciding if I should share what's going on or not.

"Julie, I can't go into details right now, but can I ask you something?" I tear up and struggle to keep my emotions in check.

Her expression morphs into one of confusion and concern. "Sure. What's up?"

I shake my head and close my eyes, searching for the right words. "I…I would like you to pray for us, for our family. There are some serious things going on right now and we don't know what to do."

Julie places her hand on my arm and squeezes. "Of course I will, Faith. Can I pray with you right now?"

Startled, I blink a few times. "Uh…here? On the porch? Right now?"

She smiles gently. "Sure. Why not?"

"All right," I say quietly.

Julie closes her eyes and I follow suit. As she begins to pray, I feel the tenuous grasp on my emotions fall away. A sob breaks through and then another. Julie wraps her arms around me, the bulky foiled dish in between us. She continues to pray and I continue to sob.

Her words penetrate my heart in a way that I've not felt in a long time. Slowly, a deep sense of peace wraps around me like a warm blanket on a bitterly cold night. When she's done, I feel a sense of refreshment deep in my heart. It's the sort of relief one feels when plunging into cool water on a hot summer day.

I wipe the tears from my eyes and smile when we pull apart. She smiles warmly in return and chuckles.

"Amazing what God can do when you ask, isn't it?"

"Yes. Thank you so much, Julie. I'm sorry you only came over to give me some coffee cake and I end up dumping my problems on you."

She shakes her head. "It's no trouble. I'm blessed that I can help you when you need it. Did it help?"

I grin. "Yes. I feel better, actually. Is that weird?"

She laughs. "No, that's not weird. I believe God is letting you know that He is with you, right here, right now. He loves you."

I shake my head. "But your prayer was perfect. You don't even know what's going on."

She shrugs her shoulders. "I don't have to. God knows. He'll take care of it and show you what to do. Trust Him."

"I am trying." I balance the foil covered dish on my hip and squeeze Julie as hard as I can with my free arm. "Thank you, Julie. You really are a blessing."

"Any time." She smiles and disappears up the walkway without another word.

I go inside and close the door behind me, pondering what just happened. I want to cling to the peaceful feeling, afraid it will disappear with Julie.

I look around for Sarah. I can't find her on the main level, so I place the warm cake on the kitchen counter and head upstairs. Maybe she went to her room. I find her sitting on her floor reading a book.

"Sarah, honey. Are you okay?"

"Yeah. Are you and Dad ready to yell at me?" she asks sullenly.

"Honey, no. We're not going to yell at you. But we do have some talking to do. We want you to stay here in your room until we come get you."

"Okay. Can I have my phone back?"

I shake my head. "No. I'm afraid not."

She sighs and returns to her book. When I join Michael on the back porch, his head is resting on the back of the chair and his eyes are closed.

"Michael, you okay?" I ask quietly as I sit beside him.

He turns to me with a pained expression in his eyes. "No. Nothing is okay. I don't know what to do." He places his open hands on his lap with palms upward, signifying the emptiness there. My heart aches for him.

Mulling over how the prayer with Julie had just helped me, I wonder if it might help him, too. I'm not Julie and I can't pray like she does, but it may be worth a try.

"Honey, I just had a very nice conversation and prayer with Julie. She stopped by to bring some more coffee cake. I don't know why or really how, but I feel better now; more at peace. Do you want to pray together and see if it will help?"

Michael gapes at me with more than a little surprise on his face. "You just prayed with her on the front porch? Really? Did you tell her what's going on?"

"No, I didn't tell her. I just asked her to pray for us because we have a lot going on. Yes, we prayed right there on the front porch. It was amazing, Michael. I can't explain it except to say that I feel better. I think we should try it."

He seems to consider something, then finally shakes his head and throws his hands up. "Sure. Why not? Let's give it a go." He shifts his body to face me, looking awkward. "How do you want to do this? Should we kneel, hold hands, cross ourselves, what?"

"I guess it doesn't really matter. At my counseling sessions, Pastor Ben just sits in his chair, clasps his hands, and closes his eyes. Maybe we should hold hands?"

He smiles ruefully. "I guess. It just feels awkward."

"I know. But it can't hurt, right?"

Michael nods. We hold hands, bow our heads, and close our eyes. I wait for a few moments and….nothing. I glance up and see Michael staring at me, looking confused.

"Uh…did you want *me* to pray?" he asks sheepishly.

Oh.

"Only if you want to. Would you rather I prayed? I don't think it matters."

"I'd like you to pray. I'm out of practice."

We bow our heads and close our eyes once again. Feeling awkward, I plunge ahead using some of the same words that Julie used. My prayer is simpler than hers because I'm not as good.

I ask God to help us figure this out, give us the right words to say, and help us make the right decisions. When I say amen, I open my eyes and look at Michael. His eyes are slightly misty, which I ignore. He's not an outwardly emotional man.

"Do you feel any better?"

He blinks and looks at me. "Well, the earth didn't move." He shrugs. "Like you said, it can't hurt. Let's go talk to Sarah." He rises and reaches for my hand.

Here we go, God. Come with us, please.

Chapter Eighteen

Sarah looks up from her book when we enter her room. She carefully marks her place before setting the book on her night stand and facing us. She crosses her arms, waiting for us to speak.

"Sarah, let's go downstairs and talk," Michael says gently, reaching a hand toward her.

Sarah nods and walks past her father ignoring his hand, arms still crossed, and turns to go downstairs. Michael looks at me as if to say "here we go" and drops his hand. We follow her silently.

Michael and I sit together on the sofa. Sarah positions herself in the chair farthest away from us, keeping her arms crossed while her eyes bore holes in the floor.

Michael sighs. "Sarah, would you like to sit here so we can talk better?" He indicates the chair next to us. She quickly shakes her head. Michael glances over at me.

"Okay, Sarah. Sit where you feel the most comfortable," I say gently, nodding at Michael.

Michael shifts in his seat and clears his throat. "Sarah, we need to talk about last night, of course. But more importantly, we want to talk about what led up to last night. Your mother and I are very…confused. More than a little shocked, too. Only you can shed light on what's been going on that caused you to sneak out like that. That's so unlike you."

Silence.

"Sarah, this isn't a speech. This is a conversation. This means you have to talk, too," Michael continues softly.

"I don't know what to say," she replies, her voice barely audible. She uncrosses her arms and begins to pick nervously at her cuticles.

Perhaps asking questions will get her talking. "How did you meet this Matt guy?" I ask.

"At school."

"Sarah, he's in high school. How could you have met him at school?" Michael answers sharply. I shoot him a warning glance.

She rolls her eyes. "I know, dad! I met him at school after school."

"Sarah, please understand," I reply quickly, squeezing Michael's hand. "You're stressed about this and so are we. We're very concerned because we love you."

Sarah flashes a glance at me. There are tears pooling in her eyes.

"Oh, Sarah," I close my eyes and shake my head. When I open them, the tears are streaming down her cheeks. She's barely holding herself together. I've been there myself, so I recognize it.

Instinctively, I cross the room and wrap my arms around her. For a moment, she stiffens, but soon the sobs wrack through her body. Michael joins me and engulfs us both in his arms. We simply hold her until she cries herself out; nobody speaks for a long time.

Michael is the first to break the silence. "Well, aren't we all a mess." His attempt at a joke causes Sarah to snort as she rubs furiously at her eyes.

"Sarah, honey. Please understand that more than anything, we want to understand where this has come from and how you got involved. It doesn't make any sense," Michael offers.

Sarah nods and leans back. Michael and I sit across from her, closer this time. She hiccups occasionally.

After a few moments, Sarah haltingly begins to tell us her side of the story. She met Matt after school when she had begun hanging out with some of the more popular kids in her class. Sarah isn't clear how Matt knew these kids in the first place and it's not important. She tells how she thought it was cool that an older guy would find her interesting, as she put it. I notice

Michael's jaw working when she describes how Matt gradually expressed more of a physical interest in her. Sarah blushes profusely when she gets to that part and doesn't go into much detail. Normally, I would appreciate that, but in this case I need to know how far they went.

Once she finishes talking, I grip Michael's hand tightly as I carefully consider my words. "Sarah," I clear my throat. "Your father and I saw the text messages from him on your phone."

Her face goes from beet red to ghostly white when realization dawns on her; her eyes bore holes in the carpet again. She nods once.

I clear my throat again. "We, ah, are very concerned about what he said to you in those messages. Did you and Matt...kiss or...anything else?" I swallow hard. Michael tenses. Both of us hold our breath, waiting.

Sarah squirms. I remind myself to breathe.

"We...we just made out. That's all." She continues to avert her eyes and squirm.

"What does made out mean to you, Sarah?" Michael asks slowly.

She squirms even more. "We just...kissed and stuff."

I glance at Michael and his face is pinched. I try a different path.

"Sarah, we want to be sure we understand what you've gone through. At twelve-years-old, there are things that can be very overwhelming and confusing. Was the kissing like when we kiss you or was it...more than that? And what other stuff did you do?"

Sarah sighs and shifts in her chair. "Geez, mom! Do we have to talk about this? Really?" The tears pool in her eyes again.

"Yes, Sarah, we do."

She closes her eyes, leans forward and buries her face in her hands before she speaks. "We...we kissed with...tongue. He...felt under my...shirt sometimes, too." Though her words are muffled, each one individually and distinctly pierces my heart. Michael sucks his breath in sharply and I close my eyes, trying to control my reaction. I don't want her to clam up now.

Oh, dear God. Let that be all.

"I'm sorry to hear that, Sarah. He was wrong to do that," I say softly, working to keep my voice even. "Did you do anything else?" My mind unwillingly flashes to the content of the text messages and my heart hammers.

So help me God, I swear I'll send him to prison… Please say no. Please say no.

She squirms again, her face buried in her hands. Agonizingly, we wait. Finally, she pulls her hands away from her face and works her cuticles furiously.

"No. He…wanted to, but I was…scared," her voice trembles.

Simultaneously, Michael and I sigh in relief.

"That's a good kind of scared, Sarah. I'm glad you were afraid. You're very young and you don't need to be involved with boys right now, much less older ones," Michael replies, his voice strained. I can only imagine what he's thinking. I'm sure it involves some blood shed on that boy's part.

"I am so glad, Sarah! So glad." Placing my hand on my chest, I feel the pounding there. "What were you scared of?" Fear of whatever Matt wanted to do? Fear of us? What?

God, how I wish I had the power to read minds.

Her face is crimson. "I don't know. Just scared," she responds in an almost inaudible whisper. Her cuticles have commanded her attention once again.

"Are you scared of us?" I prompt her.

She shrugs. I glance at Michael and he shrugs, too. He has no idea, either.

"Sarah, remember. This is a conversation and we need to hear from you. I know this is embarrassing for you. It's embarrassing for us, too. We want this over with like you do, but we have to know. We love you and will always do what's best for you."

She nods briefly, once. I wait for her to speak. Michael squeezes my hand and waits silently, too. A long moment passes and I wonder if she is going to speak again. Finally, she does.

Sighing heavily, she says, "It..it was just nice to have someone pay attention to me for once! I'm always in the shadow of April or Andrew or my other friends. Nobody remembers me or even notices me! It's…frustrating." She rubs her face and falls back into the chair, glaring at the ceiling.

Relieved, I relax the tension in my shoulders. This is something we can fix.

"Do you feel like we ignore you? Is that why you liked Matt's attention so much?" Michael asks.

She nods.

"Honey, I'm so sorry about that. Your mother and I never intended to ignore you, ever. We didn't know that you felt that way. You've always been such a good kid. That's why this really shocked and scared us. It was just…so unlike you."

Her gaze whips to her father. "That's the problem. I've always been sooo good. Nobody ever pays attention to me! I feel like wall paper. Boring old wall paper. I'm tired of being so good all the time!" She pounds the cushion with her fist.

"Sarah, I understand how you would feel that way. I'm sorry we've made you feel like that. We certainly didn't mean to," I reply gently.

"I guess," she sighs. "Can I get my phone back now?"

I look at Michael and he flicks a glance at me. "Not right now. Your mother and I need to discuss it. One thing is for sure, you are never to have contact with Matt again, do you understand?" he replies sternly.

She nods. "Yeah. I mean, I don't think I want to anymore anyway. I didn't realize he was that old!"

"Sweetheart, didn't it occur to you that freshman in high school aren't old enough to drive?" I remind her.

She looks bewildered before her face crumples in comprehension. She buries her face in her hands. "Oh, wow. I am such an idiot!"

"No, you're not. He's the idiot and I want to…" Michael starts before catching himself. Instead, he presses his lips together. "Sarah, sneaking out last night was a really bad decision on your part and you have to be disciplined for that. You really scared us. Do you understand?"

"Yeah," comes her muffled reply.

"You are going to be grounded to this house for three weeks and you won't get your cell phone back for at least that long, or until your mother and I decide that you're going to be safe with it again. We are going to delete and block Matt's number, as well. Anybody else you want to confess right now that we should delete while we're at it? Because believe me, if anything even close to this happens again, you may never get your cell phone back or leave the house again. Plus I'll put bars on your bedroom window. So help me, God."

Her shoulders drop. "No, that's all."

Enough has been said about that, so I move on. "Sarah, what do you want to see changed to help you feel more noticed, at least by us?"

She sighs and meets our eyes. "I don't know. Dad, are you ever going to be home anymore??"

Glancing over at Michael, his expression is one of sadness and...guilt? My anxiety returns. I swallow hard, waiting for Michael's reply.

"Yes, I am going to be home more."

I glance at him. Will he?

"Is there anything I can do differently, Sarah? I want you to know how very much I love and appreciate you. It may not seem like it now, but being a good kid is a real blessing to us." I smile.

She snorts. "Yeah, whatever. I'm such a boring person. Look at April! She gets all kinds of attention and she's crazy!"

I can't help myself; I laugh out loud. Michael chuckles, too.

"Honey, she's not crazy. She's your sister and she's, well, just...boisterous. But that's her personality. You're steadier, and believe me, I appreciate that. I love all of your different personalities, but I couldn't take it if you were all the same," I reply.

Sarah shakes her head. "I guess. But it's still frustrating." She pounds the cushion with her balled fist.

"I know, Sarah. I know. You're a lot like I was at your age. I liked to read books and mostly kept to myself. There were times I felt ignored, too. But please know even if you don't have gobs of friends or get much attention sometimes, the friends that you do have are better and will last. Jennifer and Shaun have always been good friends to you, haven't they?" Jennifer is Brenda's daughter who is the same age as Sarah.

Sarah smiles wryly. "Yeah. I probably should talk to Jennifer, though, and apologize. I…I've ignored her a lot lately trying to fit in with the popular kids at school." Suddenly she blushes and her face becomes agitated. "Oh, no! Shaun was there last night. God, I'm so embarrassed. I can only imagine what he thinks of me."

"I'm sure he doesn't think badly of you, Sarah. He was very helpful. We were glad he knew where you were," Michael replies.

Sarah groans.

"Honey, the cell phone is off limits but you can go in the kitchen and call Jennifer if you'd like to. I think our discussion is done, unless you have something more you would like to say. You can call Shaun, too, if you'd like."

She shakes her head and rises. I intercept her, my eyes questioning with my arms outstretched. "Hug?" She ducks her chin and allows me a brief squeeze before disappearing into the kitchen.

Once she's left, I turn toward Michael and shake my head with my hands pressed to my temples before collapsing on the sofa. "I am glad that's over."

"No kidding. I don't want to do that again," he replies. "Thankfully it didn't go any farther than it did."

Suddenly, the weight of everything grows heavy on my shoulders. Counseling and my long buried grief, losing my grip on parenting, Michael's investigation at work…what next?

Enough already! I have been swallowed by my own hell once before, and I don't relish a repeat performance. Like a hand instinctively recoils from the heat of fire, my mind and heart recoil from the pain.

I have heard the phrase God will never give you more than you can handle. I think that's hogwash. Does He or doesn't He care? Forget the chicken and the egg question; that is the real question of life.

Michael interrupts my musings. "What are you thinking about?" He's poised at the kitchen door with his arms crossed, leaning against the wall.

His question startles me. "Huh?"

"I mean, I realize there's a lot going on, but you look like you're really concentrating on something. I'm just curious to know what."

I can't share it with him. Not right now. Deciding on a safe detour, I reply, "Let's go upstairs and talk for a second." Halfway up, I ask in a low voice, "What are we going to tell April and Andrew about this?"

"Oh. I don't think we need to tell them anything about it. It's none of their concern."

We enter our bedroom and I close the door behind us. "Yeah, I think you're right. But I'm pretty sure April already knows a little anyway. I had asked her this morning if she knew what was going on with Sarah and she seemed to know who this Matt kid was. Or at least someone like him. There's a Matt Johannson at her school that has a bad reputation. Sort of fits the profile of this kid."

Michael rubs his face. "Wow. Why didn't she tell us? I'll talk with her about that."

"I don't think so, honey. She didn't seem to know anything about what Sarah was up to. I mentioned the name Matt and that's the Matt she mentioned. Plus like you said, it's not their concern."

"Well, yeah. But April is her big sister. That does come with responsibility," he counters.

"Michael, I'm sure she didn't know. All she did was make the connection between the Matt I mentioned and this Johannson kid. That's all."

He nods in concession. "Okay. But I want to talk with her about it so she can keep her eyes peeled in the future."

"Let's keep in mind that Sarah doesn't want to feel ignored. Maybe we can start here? I think we should ask her if she'd like to share this with April first. Let her be in control of that part of it, at least. If she says no, then we don't share it with April."

"It's worth a try. Let's go ask." Michael opens the door.

Safe detour, indeed. I don't need to share where my thoughts have been going. I am relieved, but there's an unsettling increase in the distance between us.

I dismiss it and push it away. It's necessary for now. There's a lot going on and besides, we're fine.

Secrets have a nasty way of being discovered.

The wayward thought causes me to stumble before I catch myself on the stair railing. Michael instinctively reaches out to steady me. "You okay, honey?" he asks.

"Uh…yeah." I chuckle nervously. "I'm just klutzy, I guess."

As we enter the kitchen, Sarah is just placing the cordless phone on the cradle.

"How did it go? Did you call Shaun?" I ask.

She nods. "It went fine. I called Shaun and you're right. He was just as embarrassed as I was and he didn't really want to talk about it, either." She begins to walk past us out of the kitchen, but Michael puts his hand on her arm to stop her.

"Hang on, Sarah. We have a question for you."

She rolls her eyes. "What now?" Her tone isn't disrespectful, just weary.

He smiles encouragingly. "Well, we want you to feel that you are in more in control and not ignored, so we just wanted to ask what you'd like to do about April." He pauses for her reaction.

She looks confused. "Uh. What do you mean?"

"Well, your mother and I feel she should be…accountable to you as your big sister. She could've helped nip this in the bud if she'd been more aware of what was going on because…Matt goes to her school. We want to know if you'd like to share, ah, what happened with…him with your sister." Michael still has a hard time saying Matt's name without sneering. I can't blame him.

"Dad, I really don't want to talk about this anymore. I just want to forget it, and I really don't want to tell April!" she cries.

"Sarah, think about this. Are you sure? She does go to high school and…"

"Dad! I am serious, I don't want to talk about it anymore with anybody and especially not with April!" she fumes as she storms past us and stomps out of the kitchen.

We both look at each other. The look on Michael's face is so hilarious that I snort, trying in vain to quell the desire to burst out laughing. First, I chortle before bursting forth in raucous laughter. He looks like he just had a firecracker go off behind him; his mouth is a large O and his eyebrows have risen almost to his hair line. At seeing my reaction, his eyebrows reverse course and knit together.

"What's so funny, Faith?" he asks flatly.

I collect myself enough to respond. "Oh, sweetie! You should see your face! I'm sorry, but you just look…so…" I burst out laughing again.

Michael crosses his arms and waits for me to finish. "I'm glad you find me amusing. I still don't get the joke," he responds dryly.

After catching my breath, I find the words to apologize. He accepts the apology, albeit grudgingly. "I still don't know what was so funny," He mutters.

"It was just your expression, honey. Honestly. It was funny! I wasn't laughing at what Sarah did. It was just your face." The thought makes me laugh again, but I rein it in to more of a chuckle.

"Good, because I would swear that girl just morphed into April. She's never reacted that way before." He points his finger and full arm in the direction of Sarah's now departed back.

"I know. You're right. Well, she is twelve and maybe she's starting to get hormonal and moody. But it could also just be what she said; this is embarrassing for her and she's really tired of talking about it," I respond. "I think we should let her."

He sighs. "Yeah, I hope that's all it is. God, don't let her get like April!" He lifts his eyes heavenward, exasperated.

"I'll say amen to that," I murmur.

Did you hear that, God? Please. Don't do this.

Chapter Nineteen

Sundays are lazy and today is no different, except for the underlying tension that permeates the air. Sarah is silent and sulky, recovering from yesterday's embarrassing talk. We decided it would be best to let her go through the emotions of what she has done and work them out without further interference from us. We've said our peace and doled out the proper discipline. She has chosen to spend the day in her room, only coming downstairs when necessary.

Andrew remains blissfully oblivious to the underlying tension, and April is self absorbed, although she did ask about it at breakfast. The innocent inquiry sent Sarah into another minor fit, at the end of which she left the table without finishing her breakfast. She hasn't left her room since, but Michael checks on her periodically to be sure she's still there.

"Michael, I really don't think she's going to sneak out anymore. Let her be," I chide him as he descends the stairs for the third time.

"I can't help it, Faith. I didn't think she'd sneak out at all before, but she did," he counters.

"Sarah snuck out?!" April's head pops out from the kitchen. She looks shocked and amused.

Crap.

Michael rolls his eyes. "Yes, April. Sarah snuck out the other night. She's grounded. Enough said."

"Holy cow!" April crows. "I can't believe it. Little Miss Goody Two Shoes snuck out! Ha!"

"April! That's enough," Michaels snaps. "She may not have done that if you'd been keeping better tabs on what's been going on at school!"

I shoot him a warning glance, but he ignores me.

"What? What's this got to do with me?" she huffs angrily, folding her arms defensively across her chest.

Realizing the cat's out of the bag, I decide to see what further information I can get from her and quickly intervene. "April, do you remember that Matt Johannson you mentioned the other morning?"

"Yeah, so?" she asks. Suddenly, comprehension dawns on her face and her mouth drops open. "You mean she snuck out with him?!" Her nose wrinkles in disgust. "Oh, gross!"

"We think he's the one, but we don't know for sure. Regardless, nothing serious happened and Sarah is really embarrassed about the whole thing. She didn't want you to know." I shoot a glance at Michael and he ducks his head. "So please don't bring it up to her."

"Whatever," she chortles. "I just can't believe she did it, is all. Who would've thought?" She shakes her head and snickers.

"April," Michael growls. "This is not funny. Your sister is only twelve-years-old and I expect you to look out for her. Did you know anything about this?"

"God, Dad! No, I didn't know anything about this. Whatever this is," she responds sarcastically. "Besides, maybe you would've known about it yourself if you'd been home more."

Her target hits its mark and Michael sucks his breath in.

"Watch your tone, April," I scold her. "That's not fair. Your father isn't intentionally staying away. He has to work. You'd do well to remember that he's the one that puts a roof over your head and clothes on your back."

Michael shakes his head. Her comment has cut him deeply. "April, I am sorry I've not been home more. I want to be. That's why I need your help, especially with your sister. Mom and I can't do everything."

April's expression is defiant at first, but quickly turns remorseful. "Yeah, I guess. Sorry, Dad. That was a low blow. I just wish you were home more."

"Like I said, I'd like to be home more, April. For now, I should be. But I can't always control my schedule."

"I guess," She sulks. "But it still sucks."

Michael shoots her a warning glance. "April, you know we don't like that word."

She rolls her eyes. "Sorry," She mutters as she heads upstairs.

Feeling deflated, I plop into the nearest chair. "Michael, do you remember when they were small? Like just toddlers? I felt like I was going to pull my hair out. Nap times, sleepless nights, tantrums, potty training, always picking up messes. It never seemed to end. But I'm beginning to think that was the easiest time. Sure it was physically more demanding, but this, this is hard. At least with a toddler, they may sneak out of their crib, but they aren't sneaking out of the house!" I sigh and look at him. He's shaking his head, hands on his hips, looking as deflated as I feel.

"Yeah, I remember. You always looked so frazzled back then." He smiles affectionately. "They used to run around the house and you'd practically follow them with a Dirt Devil trying to vacuum wayward Cheerios." He chortles and rubs his face. "This is wearing me out. All of it."

"Me, too." The magnitude of everything overwhelms me. "Michael, are we going to be okay?" My voice comes out as a whisper.

He looks up, surprised. "We'll be fine. Everything will work out." He closes the distance between us and wraps his arms around me.

I hope so.

I plunge ahead with the first thought in my mind. "Michael," I begin carefully. "What happens next in this investigation?"

He stiffens and pulls away, holding my shoulders at arms length. His eyes meet mine. "Why do you bring that up now?"

A shiver of panic ripples down my spine. I don't want him to pull away.

"I…uh…isn't that sort of what we were talking about?" I ask, slightly confused.

He sighs. "No, not really. I was talking about what's been going on at home."

"Well, I'm concerned about everything, Michael. This investigation is a big part of that."

He drops his arms. "Faith, I told you not to worry about it. Don't you trust me?"

I jerk my head back sharply. "Trust you? Of course, I trust you. It's not about me trusting you. I simply want to know what's next. That's all."

He turns to walk away. "I already told you. I will be cleared in the end, so don't worry about it."

Anger unexpectedly swells up and my spine stiffens. "Michael Strauss, don't you walk away from me without answering my question!" My voice is louder and sharper than I intend, and he whips around to face me, his eyes wide in shock.

"Faith, you've never raised your voice to me before. Why are you acting like this?"

My mouth drops open in surprise. "What? Why am I acting like this? Are you serious?"

His brow furrows. "Faith, what's gotten into you? First Sarah, now you?"

That did it. "Michael, how dare you say that! I am dealing with more than you can possibly…" I begin, but pull myself up short. I close my eyes, take a deep breath and lower my voice, casting a furtive glance around for prying ears. Finding none, I continue. "I'm sorry I raised my voice, Michael. But all I asked is what happens next in this investigation. That's all. Instead of answering my question, I feel like you're…brushing me off, even attacking me."

He blinks in surprise. "I am not attacking you, Faith. I simply ask that you trust me about this. It's going to be fine."

Throwing my hands up, I groan in frustration. "Michael, I do trust you. This is not about trust, it's about information. Just answer me, please." I'm practically pleading with him.

He shakes his head, and then continues. "Fine. Basically, they're sifting through all of our paperwork with a fine toothed comb and are looking for any discrepancies they can find. They want to make sure that we have the proper permits, consents, and that all procedures and regulations are being and have been followed. What happens next is determined by what, if anything, they find." He looks at me with equal measures of frustration and expectancy. "Does that answer your question?"

"Yes, it does, Mr. Smarty Pants." As soon as the words are out of my mouth, I know they sound childish, but I can't help myself. "Was that so hard?"

The corner of his mouth twitches and he coughs out a laugh. "Mr. Smarty Pants, Faith? Really?"

"Well, it fit the situation!" I jerk my chin up. "Was that so hard? I don't want to fight with you, but you wouldn't answer me."

"All right. I'm sorry, honey. I just felt like you were questioning me, not the investigation."

I shake my head. "I wasn't. I just wanted to know what was next. That's all."

"Okay. I'm sorry, Faith. It's just a sensitive subject for me. My work is very important to me, and this investigation has all of us on edge."

"I'm sorry, too. I didn't mean to raise my voice." I smirk at him. "At least I didn't stomp my feet and storm upstairs."

He smiles and shakes his head. "Yeah, but I thought you were going to. After the last couple of days, I think just about anything outrageous is possible."

"I want to ask some more questions. I am not questioning you, Michael. I'm just curious."

Michael stiffens for the briefest of moments, but then relaxes, crosses to the sofa and pats the cushion next to him. "I doubt I'll have any more answers, but fire away." He gestures with a flourish of his arm.

I sit next to him and turn toward him, tucking my foot under myself. "What kind of discrepancies could they find?"

"Well, there are any number of things. Timing of the application to when the trial started, the procedures and if they've been adhered to, documentation of the volunteer responses to the drug and whether any of the expected benefits are realized or any side effects have manifested. That's a hard question to answer. Really, the investigation is going to consist mostly of them sifting through our documentation and interviewing us. Although the timing of Gene leaving the company and these problems are…suspicious, to say the least."

He stops and shakes his head. "Honestly, I'm baffled. I always thought Gene was meticulous, but I'm finding that perhaps he had some sloppy tendencies."

"Really? What kind of sloppy tendencies?"

He shakes his head and searches for the right words. "Well…there are some holes where there shouldn't be. I've been trying to put a puzzle together, but I don't have the complete picture to reference and the pieces are scattered. That's not…normal…for us as a company, or for me. I just don't know." His gaze becomes distant. "I…I'm afraid they are going to find something wrong, Faith." At my expression, he quickly continues. "Not with me, Faith. They're investigating everyone who has any fingerprints on this particular trial. I know I haven't done anything wrong, but I'm not so sure about Gene. That can very well trickle down and affect everything. Worst case scenario, the whole thing gets scrapped and we have to start from scratch. If that happens, it will cost the company a boat load of money."

I don't understand the nuts and bolts of what Michael does, but this doesn't sound good. "Michael, what I'm most worried about is how that's going to affect you, which affects us. I'm not concerned that you'll be prosecuted; how could you be? You've done nothing wrong. But if the company loses money, much less a lot of money, how is that going to affect us? Would you take a pay cut?"

He smiles and pats my leg. "Honey, like I said; don't worry. I didn't do anything wrong, so I'm not going to be penalized. My boss Frank doesn't seem worried about it, either. If they do find something wrong, I may very well be the one that helps them find it and I just want to make everything right. It is my job, after all. Let the chips fall where they may, I know I can sleep at night. So no, I'm not worried about my job or my pay."

His words are a balm to my nerves. I desperately want to believe him. "I'm so glad, Michael. I know you're a good man and I do trust you."

"That's all I ask, Faith. It's all I need."

****

198

"Mom, are you guys fighting?" Andrew asks quietly. His question startles me and I drop the bowl I was rinsing to place in the dishwasher into the sink.

I look over to see my youngest standing just to the side of the kitchen door, peering up at me, worry creasing his brow. "What, sweetie? No, we're not. We had a disagreement, but we're okay." I reach for the dish towel and dry my hands off, then bend down to meet his gaze. "Why do you ask?"

He looks down at his feet and shuffles back and forth. "Well, I heard you guys yelling earlier and Sarah isn't happy, either. S'not right."

"Sweetie, Sarah disobeyed us and is grounded, so she isn't going to be happy about that. Daddy and I had a discussion and yes, we raised our voices. That shouldn't have happened and we already told each other we were sorry. Everything is okay. I promise."

He raises his eyes. "Really?"

"Really. I love you, Andrew." I squeeze him fiercely and kiss his head, drinking in the sweet scent of my little boy. He squeezes me back, smiles and scampers off. His worries are so quickly and easily erased. I envy the sweet, precious, and innocent trust of children. If only life could stay that simple.

Life is never simple.

Chapter Twenty

The next two weeks go by in a tense blur. Breakfast, school, sports, dinner, rinse, repeat.

I cancel my Wednesday therapy sessions both weeks. I can't open the Paul drawer in my head. Not right now. I may actually lose my mind if one more thing happens. It's like creeping timidly along in life, peering around the corners of every minute of each day, afraid of what waits.

I don't have mental or physical strength to face anything. The M&M bowl empties frequently. I don't even go for my usual runs; I'm so exhausted, all I want to do is nap.

Sarah accepts her punishment in silence, going through the routine. April just looks smug, but doesn't say anything. I hope she's making amends with Sarah, but I don't ask.

Not right now.

Michael comes home from work each evening earlier as promised, but looks as exhausted as I feel. We both numbly go through the motions of life. I am afraid to ask about the investigation and he doesn't offer any information.

It's going to be all right. It has to be.

****

I curl up on the sofa for my now almost routine afternoon nap on Thursday. An annoying, repetitive sound penetrates my slumber.

Knock. Knock. Knock.

I roll over and try to push the annoyance out of my mind. I want to sleep a little more before I have to get dinner going and the kids come home.

Knock! Knock! Knock!

My brow furrows at the persistent, annoying sound and I flop onto my back and sigh.

KNOCK! KNOCK! KNOCK!

My eyes fly open. The door. Someone is knocking on the door. I rub my eyes and sit up.

KNOCK! KNOCK! KNOCK!

"Good grief. Don't knock the door down," I mutter as I push myself up and try to smooth my hair, wondering who it could be.

I approach the door and open it. There are a number people standing on my porch with black jackets and ball caps with the letters DEA emblazoned on the front. One gentleman steps to the front and thrusts what appears to be an opened wallet in one hand and a wad of papers in the other at me.

"Good afternoon, ma'am. I'm Special Agent James with the Drug Enforcement Agency. Are you Mrs. Strauss?"

I stare at him dumbly and nod. "Yes," I answer automatically. I'm fully awake. The opened wallet is his badge, but I'm not sure what the wad of papers in his other hand is all about.

"We're sorry to inconvenience you, but we have a warrant to search your home in relation to an ongoing investigation at SML Pharmaceuticals…." He keeps talking, but I don't hear what he's saying. While he talks, I have a surreal flashback to the moment I learned of Paul's death.

The similarities are too frightening. I grip the doorway to steady myself. My knees begin to buckle. I take an unsteady step back and suck in my breath as a wave of coldness washes over me like a bucket of ice water. I close my eyes. Suddenly, there are hands gripping my arms and leading me into the living room.

As I sit, or rather am seated, on my own sofa, the man that introduced himself as Special Agent James squats in front of me.

"Are you okay, ma'am?" he asks, his voice cold and professional.

More people are pouring into my home. I hear the clatter of metallic equipment mingled with the sound of footsteps.

I look at him and feel my heart hammering in my chest. "Uh…no, not really. I…uh…just woke up from a nap and now…you're here and…I, uh…" I don't know what to say.

The world, my world, is spinning.

"Ma'am, I'm Special Agent James with the DEA and we have a warrant to search your property." His tone is quiet, but cold. He places the wad of papers, which I now understand to be a search warrant, on my lap. I look down at the papers, not really seeing the words. Comprehension is sinking in.

I shake my head. "I don't understand. What's going on? What are you looking for?"

"Ma'am, your husband's company, SML Pharmaceuticals, is under investigation and we are looking for any evidence that may be useful in that investigation. We can't be more specific than that. I'm sorry." A glass of water is thrust into my hand and it startles me. I look toward the face that belongs to the hand that gave me the water. It's a woman. She smiles, but the smile doesn't reach her eyes.

"What am I supposed to do?" I breathe. It may sound stupid, but it's honest.

"There's nothing that you need to do right now, ma'am. Just let us do our job and we'll be out of here as quickly as possible. I suggest you stay here, perhaps lie down. How are you feeling?"

"Uh…I'm okay." I shake my head and rub my forehead. "Does my husband know you're here?"

"No, ma'am. But you're more than welcome to call him, if you'd like. We just ask that you allow us to do our jobs."

I nod numbly. Looking around for the first time, I realize there are a lot of people moving around my house; three immediately head into the home office and some are climbing the stairs. All of them are carrying boxes.

My head snaps up. "What are they doing going upstairs? There's nothing up there but our bedrooms and bathrooms!" I stand to protest. Special Agent James holds his hands up and stands in front of me.

"Ma'am, as I said, the warrant allows us to search your property. All of it. I promise that we aren't going to make a mess, but we have to be thorough. It's our job," he says in that same cold, business like tone. It's getting on my nerves.

"I think I'm going to call my husband now." I walk toward the kitchen to retrieve the phone.

"Yes, ma'am."

There are two people going through the drawers and cabinets in my kitchen, one is looking under the silverware tray in the drawer and sifting through the papers I keep there. There's nothing suspicious in that pile; I keep all of my kitchen appliance receipts and owner's manuals there. Although I understand why they're here, the action infuriates me.

I press my lips together to keep my silence, ripping the phone from the wall and punching in Michael's office number. Although they appear to be ignoring me, I turn my back on the people in my kitchen and face the wall, wrapping my free arm protectively around my body.

Michael answers on the third ring. "Hi, Faith. What's up?" he answers wearily.

"Michael, there are people here searching the house. They're from…" I whip my head around to read one of the hats. "…the DEA. They have a warrant!" Tears spring to my eyes. "What's going on, Michael?" I cry, voice shaking.

Silence meets me on the other end.

"Michael, are you there?" I ask in a quavering voice.

"Uh…yeah. I don't know, Faith. I honestly don't know. I have no idea what's going on. How many people and when did they get there?"

I take a deep breath and sigh, which actually turns into a hiccup. "Um…about fifteen minutes ago. I don't know how many (hiccup) people. They're everywhere, Michael! What am I supposed to do?! I don't understand what's going on!" I start sobbing and press my head against the wall.

"Honey, I'm coming home. I'll be there as soon as I can. Don't worry."

Hiccup. "Okay. Please hurry, Michael!"

"I will. Calm down, honey. I'm on my way." Click.

I place the phone back in its cradle and walk woodenly into the living room, practically falling into a corner chair. A hand on my arm makes me jump. It's the same woman who gave me the water.

"Ma'am, my name is Special Agent Riggle. I'm sorry we've upset you, but please understand we will be as efficient and quick as we possibly can. We are sorry for the disruption to you. Is there someone you'd like me to contact for you?"

I stare at her, confused. "Contact for me? For what?"

She smiles gently. "Just to come sit with you. A friend perhaps? You seem very upset."

I blink at her. "Of course, I'm upset! I was just lying down, minding my own business and you people come barging in and start rummaging all over my house. How can I not be upset? My house is going to be a mess! Plus I don't understand anything of what's going on."

Her eyes are sympathetic. "Yes, ma'am. I'm very sorry that we have to be here. We will be quick, I promise. We aren't going to leave your house a mess. Is there someone you'd like me to contact?"

I shake my head, grabbing a tissue from a box on the side table. "No. My husband is on his way home."

"Very well. Please don't worry. This will be done and over soon." She rises and places the same glass of water she gave me earlier on the table next to me, smiles, and walks away without another word.

I swear if one more person tells me not to worry, I'm going to…

"Faith? Are you here?" It's Julie.

Oh, Lord. How embarrassing.

"I'm in here, Julie!" I call from my corner chair. I don't think my legs will support me very well. I curl them under me.

Julie appears around the corner, her face one of fear and deep concern. When she spies me, she crosses the room quickly, bends down, and squeezes my shoulders.

"Oh, Faith! What's going on? I saw two white vans out front and people in black coming and going and thought you were being robbed! Then I saw the letters across their jackets and hats and just plain got confused. Are you all right?" She pulls a chair up next to mine and holds my hand in hers.

I shake my head, close my eyes, and let my head fall back against the chair. "I don't know, Julie. I simply don't know. They're with the DEA and have a warrant to search our house. I just called Michael and he's on his way home. I don't know anything else." The tears start to flow; I hear tissues being pulled from the box and gentle dabbing on my cheeks. I open my eyes.

Julie is wiping away my tears.

"I'm so sorry. This is just awful and so scary, I'm sure." She clucks her tongue and continues to dab my tears. I place my hand on hers to stop her.

"Julie, you don't have to do that. Really." I take the tissues from her and look at her for the first time. Her eyes are wide and her brow is creased with worry.

"Well, other than pray, that's all I can do." She smiles at me. "Do you need something to drink?" She makes as though she's about to rise, but I shake my head quickly and gesture to the glass of water at my side. "Oh, I didn't notice it there." Her eyes sweep the room. "Wow, Faith. What a party you have going on here, huh?"

I snort. "Yeah, it's a real chandelier swinger." I survey the room with her. "Julie, I really don't know what's going on. They just showed up awhile ago with a warrant and now they're everywhere."

"Oh."

As usual, Julie doesn't pry. And as usual, I want to tell her everything. I tell her what I know about the investigation at work and Michael's role in it. She nods occasionally. When I'm done, she is silent for a moment.

"Faith, I think your husband is right from what you've told me. I'm sure Michael is innocent. This is probably just a procedural thing. It's best to just let happen whatever is going to happen. Trust God, He'll get you through it." She pats my hand. "Do you want me to pray with you now?"

I throw my hands up in the air. "I don't care, Julie. Right now, I really just don't care. I can't take anymore." New sobs emerge and I reach for another handful of tissues.

"I know, Faith. I know. I am going to pray for you anyway." She begins to pray and I close my eyes and let her. I don't feel anything remarkable, but I like when she prays. It's soothing. When she says amen, I open my eyes and look around at the people still pawing quietly through every nook and cranny of my home.

The thought occurs to me that I honestly just don't care. I don't care if they rip up my carpet; I know that I know they aren't going to find anything wrong. I believe my husband when he told me he's innocent of whatever has gone wrong at that company. I know he is.

He has to be.

"Faith, do you want me to stay here with you until Michael gets home?" she asks quietly.

I smile at my friend. "Yes, please. This feels like such...an invasion."

She pats my hand and settles in her chair next to me. "Then that's what I'll do. We'll just sit and watch this unfold."

That's exactly what we do. We sit in companionable silence, only talking occasionally. When Michael walks in the door an hour later, I'm almost calm thanks to Julie.

He's angry and bewildered at the sheer number of people and the activity in the house. So far, the agents have apparently found nothing of consequence because boxes are being returned empty to the white vans parked out front. Their demeanor has relaxed, too, as they continue to find nothing.

Michael's eyes crisscross the room, landing on me in my corner chair. He quickly closes the distance between us and pulls me to my feet in a bear hug.

"Honey, I'm so sorry about this. Are you okay?" he murmurs into my hair.

I nod and wrap my arms around him. "I'm better than when I called you." I gesture toward Julie. "Julie has been kind enough to sit with me."

Julie smiles at Michael and offers a short wave in his direction. He smiles in return. "Oh! Julie. I didn't see you sitting there. Sorry."

"That's okay. You've got a lot on your mind at the moment." She rises. "I better get going now that you're home. Faith has had quite a fright with all this going on." She sweeps the room with her hand.

Michael grimaces and reaches his hand toward Julie. "Yeah, this is crazy. Thanks for being with her." Julie shakes his hand. "I'll see you out." He moves toward the front door, scowling at the DEA people he passes. Julie and I follow him.

"I'll continue to pray for you guys. Faith, let me know if there's anything else I can do. I'm just next door." She smiles, waves, and disappears down the walk.

I turn toward Michael. He laces his fingers in mine and leads me back into the house, through the living room and out onto the back patio, pulling the door closed behind him.

"Faith, I am sorry about this. I had no idea this was on the horizon. I spoke with the rest of my team and my boss; this is happening to all of us. The office is shut down today and tomorrow because we're all reeling from it." A dark cloud descends over his features. "They came and searched the office this morning and left with boxes and boxes of documents and other things. God, I hope they find whatever they're looking for soon, so things can get back to normal." He rubs his face wearily and paces the patio.

I drop into a chair. "Michael, I don't know what to say. This really shook me up. I mean, they're searching my home! What do they expect to find here anyway?" I look up pleadingly.

He squares his shoulders and plants himself directly in my line of sight. "They're hoping to find evidence of wrongdoing. But there's nothing here. Absolutely nothing. I don't bring anything out of the office, ever. So let them tear it up in there!" He jabs his hands angrily toward the house. "I need to go see who's in charge and find out how much longer they're going to be."

He yanks the door open and disappears into the house. A sound like a helicopter's blades whirring fills my ears. A traffic helicopter perhaps? I've never heard that here before…

I wearily dismiss it, lean back and close my eyes and let the afternoon sun warm my face despite the autumn chill. I can almost forget what's going on around me, but not quite. After a few minutes, Michael returns to the patio. I open my eyes and peer up at him.

"Honey, they're almost done, and as I said, they've found nothing." His voice is calmer and more than a bit triumphant. "Do you want to come back inside?"

I shrug my shoulders. I am slightly chilled. "I guess."

He offers his hand and pulls me up. We walk together into the house, and I survey the activity as it winds down. Special Agent James approaches me, apologetically smiling.

"Ma'am. Sir." He tips his head in both of our directions. "I apologize for any inconvenience this may have caused and especially for causing you distress, Mrs. Strauss. We had a job to do and appreciate your cooperation in it. We've completed our task and are just wrapping things up. Do you have any questions?"

"Did you find anything at all during your search, Agent James?" Michael asks quietly.

"No, sir. We did not." Special Agent James replies in the cold business tone I've come to know.

"I thought not," Michael says, unable to keep the smugness from his voice. "I would appreciate it if you and your team would leave as quickly as possible."

"That's our goal, sir." He tips his head at Michael and turns on his heel.

As the last of the DEA agents gather their equipment and head out the door, Michael closes the door quietly behind them and turns to me. "I don't ever, ever, want to go through something like this again."

"Me, either. I feel like everything is falling down around me and I'm drowning."

A pained expression crosses his face. "I'm sorry, Faith. I never meant to put you through this. Honestly, I had no idea they'd search our homes."

I shake my head. "I know. I'm just glad it's over and they found nothing. Maybe they'll leave you alone now."

"I hope so." He sighs and pulls the sleeve of his shirt up to glance at his watch. "It's almost time for Andrew to get out of school. I'll go pick him up." As an afterthought, he adds, "Do the girls have sports today?"

I nod and walk into the kitchen, when I suddenly realize that I didn't take anything out for dinner. With everything that happened this afternoon, I totally forgot about it.

"Craaaap!" I yell.

Michael pops into the kitchen. "What? What's wrong?" he asks, bewildered.

"I didn't take anything out for dinner!" I cry, tears welling in my eyes.

Why do I want to cry about this? It's so stupid.

Michael regards me for a moment and his eyebrows climb his forehead in surprise. "Faith, don't worry about it. It's just dinner. Want to order a pizza instead?"

"Whatever." I throw my hands up in the air. "God! When is life going to be normal again, Michael?! I can't even take care of my family!" I start to sob.

He wraps his arms around me. "Hey, hey. Faith, it's okay. You're still upset over this afternoon. It was frightening; that's understandable. It's okay, honey. Relax." He rubs my shoulders.

I pull away from him. "Michael, I feel like I'm losing my mind. What else is going to go wrong? I just don't want to do this anymore."

"Honey, there's nothing you have to do. You're going to be okay. Everything is okay. Take a deep breath. Listen, I'll pick up a pizza after I get Andrew. Maybe we'll watch a movie tonight or something? Get your mind off of everything?"

He just doesn't get it.

That's because he doesn't know.

I shake my head to dislodge the thought. Michael is still looking at me. I had better answer him and get a grip on myself. Forcing my expression to smooth out, I respond, "Yeah, maybe. That sounds good. Go get Andrew and I'll see you in a little while." Thinking quickly, I add, "I think I'm going to go change and go for a run. I haven't been in a couple weeks and I'm sure that will help."

He relaxes, smiles, and kisses me. "Sounds like a plan, honey. Be careful and I'll be home soon."

When Michael disappears through the garage, I grab a fistful of M&Ms and climb the stairs to change. Perhaps a run will do me some good. I've neglected that for too long; it's time to get back on track. Once outside, I walk out to the driveway and spy Julie elbow deep in one of her flower beds. I call out to her. She turns around and waves.

"How did everything go?" she yells from her dirt pile.

"Good. They didn't find anything, of course. What a time waster. I'm going out for a run!" I yell back.

She nods and turns her attention back to her flowers.

As I begin my run, I clear my mind. I imagine the stress as layers of grime on my body and let the wind and the pounding of my footfalls strip it away with every step.

Just when it starts to work, I feel winded more quickly than usual and my hips start to ache. I shrug it off; after all, I haven't run in nearly two weeks. I'm out of shape. That's got to be it. I hope it's not my age. The forties aren't that old, after all...

I press on, but it isn't long before I'm sucking wind and can't continue. I slow my running to a walk, gasping for air. I place my hands on top of my head and try to slow my breathing down, but it still takes longer than normal. It's a full five minutes before I can catch my breath. I forget running the full circuit and turn around to go home instead.

By the time I get to my house, I'm exhausted like I'd run a marathon. The garage door begins to chug open and I turn around to see Michael's car coming around the bend. I wave and wait for him to pull up.

He rolls his window down and asks, "Did the run make you feel better?"

"Hi, mom!" Andrew yells from the back seat.

"Hi, sweetie!" I greet Andrew first before addressing Michael. "Yeah, I'm just more tired than usual. I haven't run in almost two weeks. I guess I'm already out of shape."

He grins and winks. "You look good to me."

"Uh huh." I smile and wave him into the garage, following behind.

Andrew spills out of the car and runs around it toward me. "Hi, sweetie. How was your day?" I ask as he squeezes me.

"Good! I have no homework tonight and dad picked up pizza for dinner!"

Laughing, I reply, "I know, sweetie. Get your book bag and go wash your hands. I'm sure you want your pizza while it's still hot."

He bobs his head up and down and just as quickly whips around the car, grabs his bag, and bolts into the house before Michael has even exited the car.

"Did the run help?" he murmurs quietly, watching me.

I nod. "Yeah, but I really am tired. I only got about halfway through before I had to turn around." Sighing, I add, "I shouldn't have skipped the last two weeks. It really set me back."

"Don't sweat it, Faith. You'll get back to normal in no time." He kisses my cheek and holds my hand as we walk into the house.

"Listen, Michael. I'm sorry for my…break down earlier. I don't know where that came from."

Michael shrugs. "It was out of character for you, but this afternoon was quite the shocker." He sighs and shakes his head. "I never expected something like that."

"Me, either." I head to the cupboard and grab plates and glasses. "I'm afraid to ask what's next."

"After this, I honestly have no idea. Hopefully, this was the worst of it." He leans back and looks toward the hallway. "Let's talk about it later. I don't want to talk about it with the kids around."

"Agreed." I place the plates and glasses on the table and move the pizza boxes over to the table, too, portioning two slices on each plate. The pizzas are simple cheese: the kids' favorite.

Andrew's bounding footsteps on the stairs announce his arrival for dinner. Within seconds he bursts into the kitchen and heads directly for the table. Michael and I join him. While Michael and Andrew dig heartily into their pizza and Michael gets more slices, I barely manage to get through one slice of mine. It's just not appetizing. My nerves are raw.

Once dinner is complete, I load the few dishes there are into the dishwasher and cover the remaining pizza to save for April and Sarah.

"Honey, are you feeling okay?" Michaels asks.

"Huh? Yeah, I'm just not that hungry, I guess. Still stressed from today."

"Understandable." He kisses my neck and sends shivers down my spine. "I'm going to see if they left a mess in the office."

"Mm hm. I'm going to shower." I turn and offer a smile.

I absentmindedly grab a handful of M&Ms to munch on. Noting the time, I realize April and Sarah should be home in about forty minutes; Thursdays are gymnastics for April, and Sarah has basketball. I grab my cell from my purse and text April to ask if everything is okay. Within minutes, she texts back that everything is fine. Tucking the cell away in my purse, I climb the stairs to take my shower.

Afterwards, I return to the kitchen to grab some more M&Ms and come across a glass baking dish that belongs to Julie. It had been tucked back into a corner of the counter and had once contained one of her many baked goods offerings. Considering it, and Julie, for a moment, I am flooded with what a wonderful friend she's been to me. I decide to return the dish now and thank her not only for her continued kindness, but for her friendship. I realize guiltily that our relationship is one sided; she's always doing something for me but I haven't done anything for her.

I put on my shoes and gather up the dish. As I pass the home office, I peek in and tell Michael that I'll be back in a few minutes.

His head pops up from the file drawer and he glances in my direction while sifting through papers in his hand, "Where are you going?" he asks absently.

"Just next door. I have one of Julie's dishes to return."

"Okay. Have fun." His full attention returns to his task.

I walk up to Julie's door, admiring her skillful hand with flowers as I pass her latest colorful works of art. The beds are bursting with fresh, dark mulch and mums in every autumn color imaginable.

It takes a few minutes for her to answer once I've knocked and I can tell that her typically easy smile is a struggle. That in itself is unusual, but the fact that her eyes are red and swollen catches me off guard.

Julie has been crying.

My smile disappears. "Julie. Hi. What's wrong?" I immediately advance to her and put my free hand on her arm.

She shakes her head and tries again to smile, but her mouth only quivers. "I'm sorry, Faith. I'm just a bit of a mess right now." She chokes out a chuckle and claps her hand over her mouth.

I'm really worried. What could possibly cause her to be so upset? She's always so strong and cheerful. "Julie, what's wrong?"

She again tries to smile and gestures for me to come in. I've never been in her home before. Fresh guilt washes over me; she's always come to my door, but I've never come to hers. Her home is adorable and suits her personality perfectly; it's warm, welcoming, and very tidy.

I follow her to the sofa and sit opposite her as she collects herself. "Would you like something to drink?" she asks, shakily.

My mouth pops open in surprise. "Seriously, Julie? You're obviously upset and you're offering me something to drink?"

"Well, it's what I do," she shrugs.

"Julie, thank you but I don't need anything to drink. Can I ask what's got you so upset?" Only then do I realize that I'm still holding on to her baking dish. "Oh! I came over to return your dish. I'm sorry I didn't return it earlier." I offer it to her.

"That's okay. It's not a big deal." She smiles at me and takes the dish, placing it on the coffee table in front of her. "Uh...well," she starts, but doesn't finish.

I wait quietly for her to continue, simply placing my hand over hers and squeezing it gently.

She closes her eyes and takes a deep breath. "I...ah...took a pregnancy test today, and...it's....negative...again." Tears pool and spill over as a sob escapes before she places her hand over her mouth once more.

Oh, wow. I never even thought... God, I have been so selfish.

"Oh, Julie. I didn't know. I'm so sorry..." I don't know what to say.

Her smile peeks through the pain in her eyes. "It's okay. I haven't shared our...struggles...with you. You have so much going on already. I don't want to burden you."

Her words pierce me. How can I be so selfish to not notice my friend hurting? She's been so good to me and I haven't been anything to her. Tears burn my own eyes at the realization of the depth of my selfishness.

"Faith, don't cry! It's okay." She offers me a tissue.

I look down and see a new depth of meaning there beyond the simple offering of a tissue. Even suffering through her own pain, she continues to offer comfort to others. To me. Wow. I look at her and cry. Our eyes meet and lock. We clutch each other and cry for quite some time, one friend embracing another.

After seemingly endless moments we pull apart, both wiping fiercely at our eyes and chuckling. Her smile has returned with more strength than before and I find myself smiling, too.

"I'm sorry to make you cry again today, Faith. I'm sure you've had enough of that."

I shake my head fiercely. "No, Julie. You didn't make me cry. I made me cry. I can't believe how selfish I've been. Whenever you've come over it seems like I've always got something going wrong and you've been there. Praying with me and encouraging me. I haven't done anything for you. I'm such a terrible friend. Please forgive me." I drop my head and stare at my hands.

"Faith, no. You've been a good friend to me. I like having you guys as neighbors. Please don't feel bad about yourself."

"Julie, you are struggling with something that is…incredibly hard. I can't even imagine it, except that I know it's difficult. This isn't about me. What can I do for you?"

Julie continues to smile and starts to share the struggle she and Ben have had with infertility their entire marriage; ten long years. They've suffered through four miscarriages, none of which have gone past the first trimester. They so desperately want children, but haven't been successful. It's a deep source of pain for them both. Julie was late for her period by almost a week and was so sure that it was because she's pregnant. But the test turned up negative…twice. Her disappointment is palpable. Ben doesn't know about this particular setback yet.

"Oh, Julie. I'm so sorry. I had no idea. Are you going to tell Ben?"

She looks up, raw pain in her eyes. "No, I don't think I'll tell him this time. What would be the point? I just need to stop crying before he gets home."

"Have you guys tried infertility treatments? I'm sure they can do some amazing things…" I don't know what else to say that would be helpful.

She shakes her head. "We can't afford it. We did look into it a few years ago, but it's just so expensive."

"Do you…ah…do you know why you can't have children?" I ask carefully. Perhaps that's asking too much.

She doesn't even flinch. "Not really. We went through testing, of course, about a year or so after trying to get pregnant. We didn't get a definitive answer, really. Just that we…can't." She shrugs.

"Julie, I can't tell you how sorry I am." I squeeze her hand. There's nothing else to say that would be helpful. "Is there anything I can do for you?" I ask desperately. I wish I could ease her pain, but I am useless.

She smiles and squeezes my hand in return. "No, not really. We never imagined we would have to walk this journey, but I know God is still good and if He wants us to have children, we will." Her smile is difficult, but the radiance on her face is unmistakable.

I'm taken aback. Where does she get this from? If I were facing infertility, especially for ten years, I wouldn't be able to say something like that; much less say God is good. I have my doubts, based on my own experiences. What kind of God does this to a person like Julie? If anyone deserves to be a mother, it's her. A ripple of indignation undulates through me.

"How can you say that with what you're going through?" I blurt and immediately regret it. "I'm sorry. I shouldn't have said that."

Her expression puzzles me; she's not offended, which is what I expect. She doesn't even look surprised. "Faith, God is sovereign. Who am I to question His ways? Sure, I can ask Him anything I want to, but He doesn't have to answer me, at least not like I may want Him to. There is a purpose to this; there's a purpose to everything He does. Is this painful? Yes. Do I wish we didn't have to go through this? Yes. But just because I choose to follow Him doesn't mean that life is going to be easy or pain free. It simply means we never walk our journey alone. And our lives have real meaning beyond the every day. That is how I can say something like that." There's passion behind her words. She believes what she says with every fiber of her being.

I shake my head and marvel. "I don't know what to say. I know you believe it, but I am just not there yet. Granted, I haven't suffered with this, but I have suffered." I drop my eyes. "I just don't see how he can do some of the things he does."

"Faith, I don't have all the answers. But I trust the One that does. Like I said, I don't like this, but I know there's a purpose in it. I have faith in that and in God." She frowns for a moment. "This isn't the best example, but it's sort of like electricity, I guess. I don't understand why when I flip a switch on the wall a light turns on, but I trust that every time I flip that switch, the light will turn on. Understanding isn't necessary for it to work. It just works. That's how faith is. Just because you don't understand it doesn't mean it isn't true."

I consider her words and shake my head. "I guess. It's just hard for me to accept it."

She smiles. "You'll get there, Faith. Someday."

****

"I'm back, Michael!" I call out as I walk through the door. Silence greets me, so I pop my head into the home office. Michael has his back to me and he's leaning on the desk with his head down, like he's reading something.

"Honey, I'm home." I repeat.

Michael glances over his shoulder and slowly turns to face me. His expression stops me dead in my tracks and confuses me; he looks hurt, bewildered, confused, and furious all at the same time. His lips are pale white and he's glaring at me. He's never done that before.

A thick tension immediately chokes the air between us. My heart hammers in my chest and a lump builds in my throat. What could possibly make him look at me like that?

216

"What…" I begin, but choke on my own word. I try again. "Michael, what's wrong?" I squeak. "Why are you looking at me like that?"

He continues to silently glare at me for a moment longer before slowly holding up a sheet of paper, which is shaking. I note a flash of yellow with the white sheet of paper. An opened envelope? I vaguely remember seeing a yellow envelope awhile back….

"Who is Paul Peterson?" he asks quietly, the quiver in his voice matching that of his hand. "And for that matter who is Faith Peterson?"

For a brief moment, crystal clear comprehension clicks into place; the letter from the Colorado Department of Corrections. That letter arrived weeks ago and I never opened it.

How did he…? When…?

I see myself in my mind's eye; I had thrown it in the drawer and forgotten about it. He must've gone through the desk and found it.

And read it.

GOD, NOOOO!!!!!!

My mind snaps. I can't breathe. I suck in, but nothing reaches my lungs.

White dots dance in front of my eyes. I feel a nauseating sense of spinning. Not a slight kind of tipsy spin, but a the-floor-is-falling-out-beneath-me-while-the-house-collapses-on-me kind of spin.

There's a strange sound coming from somewhere. I can't identify the source.

Gravity doesn't exist. Suddenly, I'm weightless and being sucked into a tunnel. Deep blackness envelopes and consumes me.

Everything goes mercifully quiet and still.

I knew it. I'm going to lose everything.

Chapter Twenty One

Nothing. Nothing surrounds me. Nothing is a soft, comforting darkness. A warm blanket enveloping and penetrating my core. There's a peripheral irritation, a growing sense of disquiet somewhere in the distance.

That last sensation is bothersome; I like the soft darkness of Nothing better. I want to stay, but the disquiet continues to come closer, growing, chasing away the comfort of Nothing.

Even knowing it's futile, I try to cling to Nothing.

Garbled sounds coming through a tube; voices. Indecipherable words. My head turns from side to side. A moan escapes my throat.

What's going on?

The disquiet grows into an all too familiar fear and anxiety. The comforting blanket of Nothing is almost gone.

I'm so disappointed.

Where am I?

The voices are getting closer and more urgent. I can make out some words. Michael's voice coupled with an unfamiliar one.

"Should take her in….took a spill…is she going to be okay?...heart rate…normal sinus rhythm…all vitals look good…"

My eyes flutter open briefly, and I squint at the bright light in my face. I close my eyes and turn my head away. There's something soft, familiar there; the couch. I'm on the couch.

"Honey? Faith, can you hear me??" Michael's anxiety-laden voice in my ear. There's pressure on my hand; he squeezes it. There are other hands on me, too. Something very close rips sharply. Startled, I turn my head and squint at the activity before me, trying to make sense of what I see.

Michael's face is closest to mine. His expression is pained. He places a hand on my forehead. There's a young man kneeling next to me with another young man standing at my foot; the one at my side is curling up a blood pressure cuff to stuff it into a bag at his side. That must've been the ripping sound I heard a moment ago. They're both wearing uniforms of black pants with white shirts that have emblems emblazoned on the front.

As I unwillingly return to full consciousness, my mind is flooded with the realization that I must've passed out and Michael called for an ambulance.

The scene before me is eerily familiar. Not in a good way. That's twice today. I swallow hard, willing Nothing to return.

It doesn't.

Just for once, please give me what I want and let me go, I silently beg.

"Mrs. Strauss? Can you hear me?" asks the young man kneeling at my side as he makes eye contact with me.

"Yes," I croak. I clear my throat and try to sit up.

"Just lay down here for awhile, Mrs. Strauss." He places his hands on my bare shoulders. I realize I don't have a shirt on and there are wires jutting out in various places around my chest.

This just gets better and better. At least my bra is still on.

"You passed out and should just lie down for now. Can you tell me your first name and what day it is?"

I give him the information.

"Now, follow my finger with your eyes while keeping your head still," he continues. I nod as he moves his finger from side to side then up and down.

"Do you have any pain anywhere?"

I consider his question and flex my muscles. I shake my head.

"I feel fine. I'm just embarrassed." I manage a half smile.

He returns my smile. "There's no need for embarrassment, Mrs. Strauss. You didn't do anything to be embarrassed about. It appears you're just fine. We recommend you go in for observation because you passed out. But you don't have a significant health history, and all your vitals are normal as is your heart rhythm. Your husband witnessed the incident and says you didn't hit your head. So the choice to go to the hospital is yours."

I shake my head quickly. "I would rather not go to the hospital, thank you." I'm beginning to remember why I passed out. I gulp loudly. "Can I sit up now?"

"Yes, ma'am, but sit up slowly and remain seated for a few minutes. Let me know if you feel dizzy or anything, okay?" He offers me his hand and Michael places his arm under my shoulders to help me, too. I feel like an invalid.

A shirtless invalid.

Good grief.

I slowly sit up with the offered help and tell the young man that I feel fine. Well, I don't have any dizziness at least and I'm sure that's all he's interested in.

"Can I put my shirt back on, please?"

"Let me remove the electrodes first. Your rhythm is still normal, even with your change of position. Your heart is in really good shape, actually. Your husband says you run?" he inquires as he efficiently removes the stickers and wires. I appreciate his professional manner. Michael hands me my shirt and I quickly pull it over my head.

"Yes. Yes, I do run."

"Well, that's a good thing. I wish more people I saw were physically active." He smiles while packing up his equipment.

A nod is all I can manage.

"Are you sure you prefer not to go to the hospital with us?" he asks again.

"Yes, I'm quite sure," I respond.

He nods and turns his attention to Michael. "Mr. Strauss, would you please sign here." He indicates a point on a sheet of paper and hands him a pen.

Michael signs the paper and hands it back. The uniformed young man separates a pink sheet from the clipboard and hands it to Michael with a smile and a "You folks have a nice evening" before he and his partner head to the front door.

It's at this point I realize there are more people in the room. Julie hovers in the corner and Pastor Ben is standing beside her.

Perfect. Can it get any better? I can't possibly imagine how.

Michael follows the paramedics out and closes the front door softly behind them. I sit on the sofa with my head in my hands.

Dear God. What a day. Plus the local pastor saw me shirtless. Just perfect.

I'm exhausted and overwhelmed. The sofa sinks as Michael sits down next to me.

"Faith, how do you feel?" His voice is quiet but strained.

I look up to see Pastor Ben and Julie advancing to sit down, too. Their faces are mirror masks of concern.

"Foolish. What happened?" I ask him, dropping my hands into my lap.

"You scared the life out of me is what happened. You turned white, your eyes rolled back and you just dropped like you'd been shot. I almost caught you before you hit the floor, but I'm afraid you're going to be sore and bruised tomorrow. You hit the floor pretty hard. At least you didn't hit your head. You were out cold for about forty minutes. I thought you'd stopped breathing at first." He pauses to shudder. "As soon as I got to you I made sure you were breathing and then ran for the phone."

I close my eyes and moan. "Good grief..." My head suddenly snaps up, remembering who else was home at the time. "Andrew! Where's Andrew?" I whip my head around looking for him.

"He's in his room right now. He either heard you fall or heard me yell or both because he came running in. He was pretty scared, but he's quite a smart little guy." Michael shakes his head and smiles half heartedly in admiration. "He was calmer than I was at first. He held your head and was talking to you."

"Oh, Andrew." My eyes well with tears at the thought of what Andrew saw and what he may have thought about it. My poor little boy. I turn toward Michael. "Does he know I'm okay? Bring him here. I don't want him to be scared."

Michael nods and rises, heading to the stairs.

"Faith," Pastor Ben speaks up. "Andrew is a fine young man; very calm for his age. I talked with him, with Michael's permission, and he's okay. Really. I explained that you passed out, what that means, and that it's something that happens sometimes, but it isn't serious."

"Thank you, Pastor Ben. My God, I don't know what to think right now." I lean over and place my head back in my hands. After a few silent moments, I peer at Pastor Ben and Julie through my fingers. "I don't mean this to sound rude, but what are you guys doing here anyway?"

They look at each other for a moment before Pastor Ben nods at Julie. "I was out working on my flowers and saw the ambulance stop at your house, so I ran over to see what happened," says Julie. "Michael asked me to stay. He wanted Ben to come over and…ah…" She looks questioningly to her husband for support. Ben nods at her again and places his hand on her knee.

What's going on?

Suddenly, Andrew comes bounding down the stairs. The look on his face makes my heart ache; the worry creasing his brow is more than I can bear. I grin widely and hold my arms out to him, which he promptly enters, albeit carefully, and sits next to me.

"Mommy," he whines. "Are you okay?"

"Yes, sweetie. I'm fine. I'm sorry I scared you." I smooth his hair and kiss his forehead. "I just passed out and fell down. It's not a big deal. Daddy said you were a big help. Thank you. I'm so proud of you."

His little chest puffs up. "We took first aid at school and I held your head like they showed me. I didn't get scared," he says solemnly.

I hear the garage door open and look to Michael who rolls his eyes and sighs. "The girls are home," he says.

I've completely lost sense of time; I didn't realize how much had gone by. Of course, the girls should be home by now. What am I going to say to them? What am I going to say to any of them? I look desperately at Michael who avoids my gaze, his jaw working.

Heaviness descends on my heart.

Julie clears her throat. "Michael, may I take Andrew and the girls over to my house? I made some cherry chocolate cookies earlier today and there are too many for us to eat alone." Julie winks at Andrew. "They're really good."

Andrew perks up. "Oh! Dad, can we? Please?" Then he turns to me and the concern returns to his face. "Unless you want me to stay with you."

"I wouldn't want you to miss out on those, honey. I'll be fine. Cross my heart." I scrape my fingers across my chest. His face brightens.

April and Sarah walk into the living room, both with puzzled expressions on their faces at the scene before them. They look from me to Michael and then to our guests.

"Uh…hi. What's going on?" asks April. Sarah stands a few steps behind her sister.

"Your mom…wasn't feeling good today and passed out, so I called 911. Pastor Ben and Miss Julie are here," he gestures to the pair. "Because they saw the ambulance and wanted to know if they could help. That's very kind of them." He smiles a tight lipped smile at them. They both nod.

"Mom, are you okay?" asks Sarah, concern clouding her features.

I nod and force a smile. "I'm okay, girls. Really. It was just a fluke."

Julie quickly intervenes. She rises and approaches the girls. "It's nice to officially meet you two. Your mom has told me about what fine young ladies you are." She offers her brightest smile to them.

April's mouth pops opens and she exclaims, "Oh! You're the lady next door that bakes really good stuff! It's very nice to meet you, too!" She grins widely.

Julie laughs and Sarah relaxes, but remains silent. "Yes, that's me. I was just talking to your father; would you girls like to come over to my house with your brother for a visit? I made a batch of cherry chocolate cookies today that I'd love to share with you."

Both girls look expectantly toward Michael. He nods. "Sure. Go ahead. We ordered pizza for dinner, so take the box from the counter with you. Eat your dinner first." He points a finger at them. They both nod and head to the kitchen, but not before both turn their gaze on me, wordlessly asking a question. I shake my head and smile at them in what I hope is a convincing way.

Michael turns his gaze on Julie and his expression softens. "Thank you, Julie. That's very kind of you," he says quietly.

She shakes her head and waves him off.

"I already had pizza, so I can just eat cookies!" Andrew exclaims excitedly. He leaps up and scampers toward the door, grabbing Julie's hand and pulling her along. She laughs and shoots a glance back toward Pastor Ben before disappearing, who smiles and waves. Within seconds, all four have left the house and silence dominates like a physical presence.

Pastor Ben is the first to break it. "Michael, would you like to sit down? There are some things you two need to discuss."

My eyes widen as I watch Michael approach hesitantly. My heart hammers. I cringe into the sofa and glance from Michael to Pastor Ben and back to Michael.

Michael doesn't meet my gaze and sits on the other end of the sofa, away from me. I look at Pastor Ben, pleading with my eyes. I don't know what to do or say. I am trapped. Normally, I would run away.

In my current condition, I wouldn't make it to the end of the driveway.

Pastor Ben smiles encouragingly at me. "Faith, Michael knows about Paul." I suck in my breath and close my eyes, clutching my stomach with one hand and clapping the other hand over my mouth to keep from screaming. "He read the...ah...letter you received. Right, Michael?"

"Yes." Michael's voice is hoarse and thick.

When Michael says nothing more, Pastor Ben clears his throat and continues. I open my eyes narrowly and look at Pastor Ben.

"As you can imagine, Faith, Michael is...confused, and hurt. I...ah...spent just a few minutes talking with him when I came over." Pastor Ben nods at Michael who remains stiff at his end of the sofa. "He asked me to stay and talk with you two tonight. He allowed me to read the letter, as well. This is a lot to deal with. For both of you. Apparently, it was unopened when he found it, so I assume you've not read it?"

I shake my head.

"I see," Pastor Ben sighs. "So you don't know the contents of the letter. Faith, I shared some of what we've discussed in our counseling sessions with Michael simply based on the information in that letter. He knows that you were married before and that your first husband was killed by a drunk driver."

I start to sob. I'm going to lose it. Mentally, I curl into myself, balling my hands into fists, attempting to keep from becoming hysterical.

"Why didn't you read the letter, Faith? How long have you had it?" Pastor Ben asks.

I suck in my breath a few more times, trying to calm myself to no avail. I close my eyes. "I just couldn't. It came…weeks ago, I guess. I don't remember exactly." I steel a glance at Michael and he's rigid, glaring at the floor, his hands clasped firmly together. His jaw works furiously.

Pastor Ben continues. "Faith, I think it's important for you to read that letter. It was addressed to you and as I have told you in our sessions, you need to face these things in order to deal with them. That's how you're going to recover. Now I'm here tonight because I want to help the two of you deal with it together. Although Michael hasn't known about it, it has affected him, Faith. It's affected him because it's affected you."

Shocked, I stare at him. I thought that all along I was dealing with it. I started counseling and I've done everything I could to protect my family. It's blowing up in my face. As proof, Michael won't even look at me.

Pastor Ben addresses Michael. "Michael, would you like to go get the letter, please?"

Michael nods stiffly and disappears into the office, reappearing moments later with the letter in his hand. He hands it to Pastor Ben, who accepts it, smoothing it out. Pastor Ben looks at me and holds the letter out to me.

I cringe further into the sofa, clutching the cushions and stare at the letter as though it's a viper about to strike. Feeling panicky, I shake my head furiously and whisper, "No! I can't. Please don't make me do this!"

"Faith, I know how deeply you're hurting. But Michael doesn't. He loves you and wants to understand and help you, but you have to tell him. You can't keep this a secret anymore."

I look desperately at Pastor Ben, begging and shaking my head, the tears spilling over. "No."

Suddenly, Michael, who is still standing next to Ben, blurts out, "Faith, what the hell are you so afraid of? Why didn't you tell me about any of this? We've been married for seventeen years, for crying out loud! Why would you keep something like this from me?!" The anguish on his face is raw. "You really don't trust me, do you? You never did."

His words cut me. "Michael, no! I trust you. I do! Please don't think that. I couldn't tell you. I couldn't tell anybody! It was…it was…" I start to sob.

Pastor Ben intervenes. "Michael, I understand how you can interpret this as a lack of trust on her part. But I sincerely believe that's not the heart of the matter. Faith, take some deep breaths and tell your husband the truth. It's time. You need to let it out."

I look up at the ceiling and try to take deep breaths, mentally begging for help.

This hurts too much! God, don't do this to me! No, no, no, no, no…

Moments go by. I struggle to collect myself and my thoughts. Pastor Ben waits patiently. I turn my gaze on my husband. He's waiting in stony silence.

He still won't look at me. Anguish permeates his features.

With one final deep breath, I release what's inside. "I'm sorry, Michael. So very sorry. I never meant to hurt you. That was the whole point. I didn't want to hurt you or anybody else. When…when…Paul," I cringe. "…died, I…a part of me died, too. We were so young and…it wasn't supposed to happen like that! He was killed! Ripped from me!" I look pleadingly at my husband. "I buried part of me when I buried…him. I buried everything! I kept going each and every day, but I hurt so bad that I didn't think I would ever live, really live, ever again." I look at him, my chin quivering uncontrollably, tears pouring unchecked down my face. "Then I met you. I never thought I would love or be loved again. But then there was you. You made me feel like maybe there was hope. I am so broken and I never wanted to talk about it. The pain was so raw and so deep when we met. I couldn't bring it up then.

"If you saw how…damaged I was, I am, maybe you wouldn't want me. The pain is still raw and it's still deep. More and more time went by and I just thought I could ignore it and it would eventually go away. But, I'm just not…whole, Michael. I never will be and I know you deserve better than that. Better than me!

"You're a good husband and father. I know that if you ever found out," I drop my eyes and stare at my hands that are now calm, and my voice is inexplicably getting stronger. "If you really knew how broken I am, then…you wouldn't want me anymore. I just thought it would be best to never bring Paul up. He's been gone for a long time, and I…I can't risk losing you. I mean, you and the kids are my whole world. Don't you understand? I can't survive another loss like I did with Paul. I just can't. I won't! I thought you would never have to know. I love you. I loved him, too, but he was taken from me. I mean, why do we have to do this? Why do I have to risk this? I would do anything to keep what we have." I direct my question at Pastor Ben. "Why do I have to do this?"

Ben is smiling.

I want to slap him for it. "Why are you grinning at me? What's so funny about this?" I blurt.

"Faith, do you feel any different?" He turns to Michael. "Do you notice something here?"

I look over at Michael; he's staring at me and looks…bewildered. There's no other word for it. His gaze rests on me for a moment longer and then shifts to Pastor Ben. He clears his throat. "I…uh…I don't know what to say. I don't know what to make of any of it."

Pastor Ben leans his elbows on his knees and looks earnestly at me. "Faith, I have a few questions. Do you mind?"

I shrug my shoulders, confused, and warily wait for him to continue.

He regards me for a split second before asking his first question. "What did Paul go to college for?"

I wipe my eyes. "Oh. He was going to law school to be a lawyer, of course. Why?"

"What area of law did he want to practice?"

"He wanted to become a prosecutor. He always had a good heart and wanted to put bad guys away." I chuckle. "That sort of fit his nature. He was the kind of guy that if someone needed help, he wouldn't hesitate. He'd help in a heartbeat. A lot of people would look around to see if someone else is going to step up, but not Paul. He would run to help if he had to, ignoring everything else.

"This one time, we were walking down the street and we heard a woman cry for help. He immediately ran toward the scream. This lady was actually being mugged in broad daylight! A guy was pulling on her purse and she was hanging on for dear life. Paul jumped right into it and even chased the guy down, waiting for the police to arrive." I glance over at Michael. "You sort of remind me of him, you know. You've got the same good heart. It's one of the things I love about you." Michael's face relaxes a degree. He walks toward the sofa and sits down, still on the other end of the sofa.

Pastor Ben continues with his questioning. "What else did you love about Paul?"

I smile, remembering. The tears continue to flow. "He was hard working, spontaneous, and had a great sense of humor. He could make me laugh so hard I couldn't breathe. Oh, he could make the funniest faces! It's like his face was made out of rubber or something. Michael, he would've cracked you up." I chuckle. "This one time, he actually put his lower lip over his nose and made his eyebrows do a wave. It was the funniest thing I had ever seen!" I chortled. "Of course, we were in church when he made the face and I had to get up and leave the service because I couldn't stop laughing. Oh, was I mad at him for that." I continue to laugh for a minute. As my laughter dies down, I realize I had forgotten about Paul's funny faces. How could I have forgotten that?

"Faith?" Pastor Ben asks.

I raise my eyebrows at him in response.

"This is the first time you've talked, really talked, about Paul since he died?" he asks quietly.

I blink at him. I realize the pain is smaller, slightly more bearable.

I can think of Paul, and the deep, searing pain associated with him, with his memory, doesn't burn as deeply. I gasp.

"Oh, my God. You're right. What…what does this mean? Why? What happened?"

"I think this secret you've kept, the pain and the fear, is just like poison. You've kept it inside all these years, and now that you've let it out, it can't hurt you as much anymore. That's what you've needed to do all along. Get it out."

I look over at Michael. Pain still laces his features. "Michael, can you please forgive me? I am so sorry. I don't want to lose you."

"Faith," he starts, then clears his throat. "This is…a lot to take in. I find out today that my wife that I've known for years, have three children with, and have loved, was married before me. It's not that you were married that bothers me, but that you never told me about it." He shakes his head. "I…ah…really don't know what to do with this or how to process it. I feel like I don't know you like I thought I did." He looks at Pastor Ben and shrugs. "What am I supposed to do?"

Pastor Ben regards Michael for a moment before quietly answering. "What would you like to do?"

Michael stares at the floor. "I don't know. I just need some time to think." He rises and walks across the room, hands on his hips, facing away from us.

From me.

Ice flows through my veins. My throat closes.

I knew it. I'm going to lose it all again. I can't lose Michael. Please please please please…

"That's understandable, Michael. This is painful for both of you." Pastor Ben gestures toward me. I'm horror stricken. Is this the end of my marriage? I won't survive if that happens.

I won't want to.

Is God going to make me trade one pain for another?

Michael turns around and faces Pastor Ben. "I asked you over here because I was hoping you could tell me, tell us, what to do." He raises his hands helplessly and shakes his head. "I'm really at a loss."

Pastor Ben nods. "As I have always done with Faith in our sessions, I suggest that we have a prayer. All right?"

Michael rubs his face, plops into a chair on the other side of Pastor Ben and nods his head.

Pastor Ben prays briefly but sincerely. He asks for wisdom, guidance, healing and peace. He mentions both me and Michael and prays for each of us specifically. When he finishes, I open my eyes and look immediately to Michael who is still boring holes in the carpet.

Seeing that neither one of us is going to talk first, Pastor Ben starts the conversation. "Michael, why don't you tell Faith how you feel about this?"

Michael looks incredulously at Pastor Ben. "How I feel?" He turns his gaze to me.

Finally.

"I am…angry. That's what I feel. Anger. I can't believe that you didn't trust me. This isn't like keeping a small secret, as though it's an embarrassing moment you just want to forget, or an ex-boyfriend. No! This…you were married, Faith. Married. It obviously has affected you tremendously. It's affected us. All these years…" He closes his eyes and shakes his head. I lean myself toward him, wanting to close the distance between us. I'm afraid he would reject me if I came to him now.

"Your fear about me travelling, April driving, and your running…always the running," he continues. "Now I understand where it came from. I have wanted to help you. But you never let me know what was wrong, you never let me in. You'd just turn into a…block of ice and shut down or literally take off out the door. I'm your husband, Faith. I thought I knew you. Why didn't you ever tell me?"

I have to fix this!

"I thought…" I begin. "Michael, I…when you came along, you were perfect. You made me feel like maybe I could be okay. I thought that you would be able to help me just because you were there. I didn't tell you then because I figured if you realized what a mess I was, you'd leave. I mean, nobody wants a project. So I stuffed it away. I tried, have always tried, to keep myself together and not let you or the children know. What would've been the point?"

230

Michael's eyes flash. "The point is that I'm your husband, Faith. Marriage is about trust and trust deals with truth. You didn't trust me with this. How do you know I would've left you if you'd shared this with me?"

"Wouldn't you have?" I blurt out reflexively. "Will you?"

Michael shakes his head, his brows burrowing into his eyes. "Is that what you think of me?" He places his hand on his chest, fresh pain crossing his features.

"Oh, my God." I bury my face in my hands. I've just made it worse.

"Faith," Pastor Ben intervenes, "Michael feels very strongly that because you kept this from him it means you don't trust him. Is that true? Did you keep this to yourself because you don't trust Michael?"

I drop my hands and glare at Pastor Ben. "No! Absolutely not!" I turn my gaze on Michael. "This has never been about trust!"

"Hasn't it?!" Michael retorts. "How can it be about anything else?"

"Faith, Michael. Both of you need to take a breather." Pastor Ben addresses Michael. "You asked me here to help you. I'm going to. I don't have a bone in this dog fight, so I will give you my professional observation." He leans forward and rests his elbows on his knees. "First of all, we all hear the words that are spoken, but, and this is especially true when we're hurt, we don't typically listen to what's being said. We filter what's said through our own pain and interpret, or misinterpret, the message being conveyed." He pauses.

"You are both speaking from a place of hurt. Faith, you were hurt because of Paul's untimely death and the circumstances that surrounded it. Michael, you're hurt because you were never told that your wife was married or about her late husband. Am I correct?"

We nod in unison.

"Michael, what I'm hearing is that you're hurt because you believe that Faith didn't trust you enough to tell you about it." Michael bobs his head once. "But the truth is that for her, it had to do with her not believing that she is worthy of you and she told you a little while ago, but I don't think you heard her, that she didn't share her pain with anyone?" He turned his attention to me. "Isn't that right, Faith?"

"Yes."

"Not worthy of me? What do you mean you don't think you're worthy of me?" Michael says incredulously, staring at me. "What would make you feel like that? Did I make you feel like that?" he asks.

I stare at my hands, considering my words carefully. I don't want to make this worse.

"Michael, I have always known I'm...I'm just not good enough. I mean, Paul was a great guy and so are you. God took Paul away from me and, well...I'm still afraid he'll take you, too," I whisper. "Because I didn't deserve either one of you in the first place."

Michael's mouth is agape. "I don't understand how you can think that, Faith. Why?"

I look at him, desperation on my face and in my heart. "Michael, I came from nothing. My family isn't important much less intact. I am not gorgeous, successful, or have any major accomplishments in life. There's nothing great about me and...now you know what a huge mess I am. I kept my ugliness from you and now..." Fear strangles my heart. "I don't want to lose you because of it." Miserable tears pour down my cheeks.

Michael's expression softens. "Faith, do you really feel that way about yourself?"

"Yes." I drop my gaze into my lap, my hands balled so tightly my knuckles are white.

Michael sighs and rises from his chair, crosses the room and sits next to me. "Faith, have I ever made you feel this way?"

"No, Michael you didn't make me feel this way. This is just who I am!" I cry. "I know who and what I am and that I don't deserve you. But I can't lose you. I can't survive it. Not again."

Michael's warm hand covers mind. "Faith," he begins gently, his voice thick. "You're not going to lose me. Not over this. Not over anything. I love you."

I can't share that my fear is deeper than whether he'll leave me. I'm afraid he'll be taken. When I raise my gaze to meet his, there's such love and sincerity in his eyes. I can't help myself; I plunge into his arms and hold tightly to him. His arms wrap around me and hold me just as tightly, whispering words of love into my ear.

"Michael, please forgive me for not telling you about Paul. I'm so sorry," I mumble.

His hand smoothes my hair and he replies, "I forgive you, Faith."

"There's something else here that needs to be addressed," Pastor Ben interjects after a few moments.

Michael and I separate from each other, keeping our hands laced and look at him.

"What do you mean?" asks Michael.

Pastor Ben turns his gaze on me. "As I said earlier, we all hear, but don't necessarily listen to the message being conveyed. Faith, you said that God took Paul away from you. Is that what you really believe to be true?"

I nod. It's true. "God did take Paul away from me."

Pastor Ben reflects quietly for a moment. "And that you feel you don't deserve the husband you have or the one you had and that's why God took Paul. Correct?"

"Yes," I whisper.

"In our sessions together, you've shared quite a bit with me and I would like to put the pieces together to give you a clear picture of why you have this belief. May I?" he asks.

I blink a few times and glance over at Michael. He's waiting for me to respond. I nod.

"Faith, God is not vengeful toward you. He doesn't see you the way that you see yourself. You are precious to Him. He loves you more than you can ever possibly imagine. Think about your own children, how deep your love for them is. How, no matter what they do, you will never stop loving them or ever love them any less. Do you watch them to see when they mess up just so you can punish them? Or do you instead watch over them, hoping they make the right choices, and hurting for and with them when they make the wrong ones? You know they're not perfect and you have never expected them to be. You simply want the best for them in every way. Does that mean life will always be easy and without difficulties, hurts, and challenges?

No. That's just life. But you'll always be there for your children, right?"

"Yes."

"You shared with me that you never knew your father, correct? That he abandoned you and your family when you were a child?"

I nod.

"You also shared how difficult it was growing up with a single mom and the struggles you went through as a result. When you married Paul, you thought you had finally escaped the pain of your upbringing. That Paul was your savior?" he continued.

I nod again.

"But he died. It was a horrible, unexpected tragedy and that hurt you very deeply. You blamed God for that. You know that God is all powerful and He can do anything. So He should have stopped that, shouldn't He?"

"Yes!" I answer emphatically, anger rising in me. Pastor Ben is right; God should have stopped that from happening.

"I want to help you see how what has happened in your life has shaped how you view God, but that your view is not the true image of who He really is. You've transferred your feelings of abandonment from your earthly father, who was an imperfect human being that was prone to making mistakes, to your heavenly Father who is perfect and makes no mistakes. Your earthly father abandoned you, but your heavenly Father never will. He did allow the tragedy of Paul's death, but He didn't take Paul from you. The man that chose to drive drunk that night took him from you. Your heavenly Father was waiting to catch you in His arms when that happened. God loves you."

Hot tears cascade down my cheeks. My breath catches with each intake of air.

Pastor Ben continues. "God has never left you, Faith. Instead of running to God, you ran away from Him when Paul died. You were broken and He wanted to heal you, but you wouldn't let Him. You thought you'd been abandoned again. But you weren't. He has always been waiting for you to return to Him. He continues to orchestrate things in your life to tell you how much He loves you." He gestures at Michael. "Paul was taken from you, but Paul never was your true savior, Faith. You only have one Savior and His name is Jesus. You told me that you accepted Jesus into your heart when you were a child. He never left you, either. God gave you another wonderful husband that loves you and cares for you. He gave you three beautiful children to love and raise." He pauses to chuckle. "He even moved Julie and me next door to you because He knew what was coming and that you were just about at the end of your rope. He knew you would need us here. That you would need Him here."

Crying hysterically at this point, I see the picture Pastor Ben is painting of my life as one that I never saw before. God doesn't hate me or see me as worthless; He isn't mad at me and waiting to hurt me. He does love me.

I hear paper crinkling and look up through my tears. Pastor Ben is holding the infamous letter that started all of this, offering it to me. "Faith, you need to read this."

"I...I...I can't. I can't see it! I'm c-c-crying too....hard!" I blubber.

Michael rises and takes the letter from Pastor Ben. "Faith," his voice remains thick with emotion. "I'm going to read this to you. All you have to do is listen."

I can't respond. I'm blubbering too much. I try to compose myself, but the hiccupping is its own entity at this point. All I can do is focus on breathing and listen. And sob.

Michael sits down next to me, smoothes out the letter, and clears his throat before beginning.

"Dear Mrs. Peterson,

My name is Victor Fergus. I wanted to write you and tell you that I am truly sorry for what I did. I don't know if you'll get this letter or not. Heck, I don't even know if your last name is still Peterson, but I feel this is something I have to do. Confession being good for the soul and all that. So I'm going to write it anyway.

I admit that I killed your husband Paul. I made the stupid mistake of getting drunk and getting behind a wheel. I wish I could take it back and do things over again because I would do it differently. But I can't take it back. All I can do is ask you to forgive me. I don't deserve your forgiveness, but I'd like to ask all the same.

You see, I have found Jesus in this prison and he's forgiven me now. I want to forgive myself, but I want you to forgive me, too. I don't think I can feel completely right without at least asking you. It's a lot to ask, I know. Like I said, I don't really know if you'll ever get this letter or not, but I need to write it just the same. I am not going to make any excuses for my behavior. My whole life has been one excuse after another and I'm not doing it no more. I'm finally owning up to what I've done and I'm spending the rest of my life in prison for it. Well, I'd be in prison anyway, but I'm still owning up to it.

Anyway, thanks for your time and I do hope you can forgive me.

Sincerely, Victor Fergus"

Michael sets the letter down on the coffee table before us, and he and Pastor Ben wait for me to respond. My hysterics have died down enough for me to speak. The tears, however, continue to flow.

"I…uh…I'm shocked. Wow. That's not what I thought it would be," I start. "Actually, I don't know what I was expecting, but…not that."

"It's a good thing, don't you think?" asks Pastor Ben.

"I don't know about good. But it's not bad, I suppose."

Pastor Ben chuckles. "What I mean is that man is seeking your forgiveness, Faith. He's acknowledging that he did something very wrong and is doing what he can to make it, if not right, then at least better. How do you feel about that?"

I consider the question for a moment, especially in light of everything Pastor Ben has said. He certainly has altered what I thought God was like; he's brought my view of Him back to more of the image I had of God when I was a child, before life got in the way.

If God loves me like that, then everything else is truly okay. I'm still sorry for Paul's death and I wish it hadn't happened, but then I would never have known Michael.

Or April, or Sarah, or my sweet little Andrew. My heart squeezes thinking about my children.

Mulling this over, I glance over at Michael. He's such a handsome man. He's my husband, my partner. God did give him to me. He's been everything that Paul probably would've been to me.

Wow.

Forgiveness. What a concept. Should I forgive this Victor Fergus? Can I?

"I'm not sure how I feel about it. How am I supposed to feel about it?" I ask.

Pastor Ben settles back into the chair and crosses his legs. "Faith, I can't tell you how you're supposed to feel about anything. You just feel what you feel. The question really lies in the letter itself. This man, Victor, is seeking your forgiveness. Will you forgive him?"

"I don't know that I should. I mean, what he did was wrong. He killed a man. He killed my husband and has put me through hell all these years. Why should I forgive him?"

"Why indeed," Pastor Ben responds quietly. "So you think he doesn't deserve forgiveness?"

"No, he doesn't. He's evil and does evil things."

"Hmmm. What do you think God has to say about that?"

I shake my head. "I don't know. Maybe God can forgive him, but I don't think I can."

Pastor Ben nods his head and remains silent for a moment. "Faith, the Bible tells us in Matthew chapter six verses fourteen and fifteen that if we forgive people that wrong us then God will forgive us for our wrongs, which are our sins. But if we don't forgive others, then God can't forgive our wrongs or sins, either."

He looks at me and I feel heaviness in my heart, sort of an uncomfortable itching inside that makes me squirm.

"Does this in any way perhaps change how you regard his request for forgiveness?" he asks.

"So you're telling me I don't have a choice about it? But I'm not a bad person! I don't do really bad things like what he did!"

"Faith, sin is sin in God's eyes. There are no greater or lesser sins; they're all the same. Each and every one of us needs forgiveness. Romans three verse twenty three says that all have sinned. That means you, Michael, me, and Victor. All of us have sinned. All need God's forgiveness."

"But…how can I forgive him? That's like saying what he did doesn't matter. That Paul didn't matter. That what he did was okay."

Pastor Ben smiles and shakes his head. "No, Faith. That is not what forgiveness means at all. Most people think that by forgiving someone you're saying that what they did was okay and they're free to do it again. They're free to hurt you or to harm you or someone else.

"The real truth is that forgiveness isn't really about them at all. It's about you. It's about letting go of the anger, the resentment, the bitterness that the sin fosters in you and the destruction it will cause. You already know how that has worked in your life. I mentioned to you earlier, when you first started talking about Paul, how the pain you had was like a poison. Well, some of that pain was just a symptom of the underlying problem of unforgiveness. Basically, holding on to unforgiveness is like taking poison hoping that the one that you won't forgive will die from it. It doesn't work like that. Poison kills the one who ingests it. Unforgiveness is poison to your soul. Forgiveness releases that poison and gives it no more hold on you."

"So I have to forgive him?"

"Faith, what do you think?"

I sigh. "I have to forgive him. But it's hard! I'm still angry about it."

He chuckles again. "I never said it would be easy. It's also not about how you feel about doing it. Never make decisions based on how you feel; they'll always be wrong. Just remember that you were first forgiven of your sins by your heavenly Father. How can you not do the same for someone else?"

"This is some heavy stuff, Ben." Michael interjects. "I mean, these are things I've never considered before. Faith," he turns to me. "What Ben says is right. I just know it. I've never heard it put that way before, but it makes sense."

"Would you like to pray again, Faith? You can tell God anything you'd like to and He'll listen."

Flashes of my conversations with Julie bounce around in my head and how she's basically said the same thing to me many times. "Yeah, but can you start? I'm out of practice talking to Him and don't really know what to say."

"Sure. Prayer isn't about lofty language or following a formula. God is God to everyone and He speaks whatever language you do. Just think of prayer as a conversation with God because that's what it is."

"Ben," Michael interrupts. "I…ah…I feel like I need to know about this forgiveness you've talked about. I need to know God, too." His voice cracks.

Pastor Ben regards Michael. "Michael, have you ever asked Jesus to forgive your sins, cleanse you from the inside, and be your Savior before?"

"Ah…no. I don't believe I have."

Pastor Ben walks Michael through the plan of salvation, quoting from the Bible as he speaks. He talks about how we are all born into sin, that we can never work our way into heaven or earn God's forgiveness through doing or being good enough. He talks about how Jesus had to sacrifice Himself on the Cross in order to cover all our sins. Acceptance of Jesus as the Son of God and asking for His forgiveness is all we have to do. When he finishes, he asks Michael if he believes that Jesus is the only Son of God, and if he believes that Jesus died on the cross to forgive him of his sins, and to restore him to God and in relationship with God through Jesus.

"Yes, I do," Michael replies, his voice strong.

"Then repeat after me as we pray." Pastor Ben bows his head and leads Michael in prayer.

As the words flow from Pastor Ben's mouth and then are repeated out of the mouth of my husband, I feel like my heart is going to burst out of my chest. I am so full of love for my husband and for what's taking place that I almost can't stand it.

When their prayer is complete, I look over at my husband and see peace in his countenance; the kind that I have only seen in the faces of sleeping children.

It's amazing to behold.

"What's going on inside?" asks Pastor Ben, addressing Michael.

Michael shrugs and shakes his head. "Well, I just feel…right. Like I've done the right thing. Is that normal?"

Pastor Ben laughs. "Yes, that's normal. Everyone feels something a little different. Some get all giddy and jump up and down; others just feel a deep sense of peace."

"Yes! That's it. That's what I feel – peace." Michael grins at me. "Interesting. I guess I did it right."

Pastor Ben smiles and turns his attention to me. "Well, Faith. Let's move on to you and your forgiveness of Victor. Are you ready to do that?"

I marvel at my husband for a moment longer before responding, "Yes. I am. I'm still angry at him, but I'm trusting in what you said that it's the right thing to do regardless of how I feel about it. I really don't like the part you said about God not being able to forgive me if I don't forgive him, so…I want to do it."

We bow our heads, Michael and I holding hands, and Pastor Ben begins to pray. This time, I repeat after him at first. Midway through, Pastor Ben pauses. I wait a moment and look up. When I make eye contact with him, he simply nods at me as if to tell me to go ahead on my own.

"Oh! Uh…okay. God, I want to forgive Victor Fergus for…killing Paul. Help me to do that. I don't feel like I want to, but I know I need to. Just help me…and thanks. Amen." The uncomfortable itching I had felt in my chest disappears, startling me. "Pastor Ben?"

"Yes?"

"I…had a sort of, I don't know, weird bad feeling in my chest while we were talking about forgiving and stuff, and now it's gone. What was that and why did it just all of a sudden go away?"

"It very well could have been the Holy Spirit convicting you of your need to forgive."

"Oh." Duh; I should've figured that much out on my own, I suppose. "That makes sense."

This launches a whole new discussion about the Trinity, Michael being the chief asker of questions for Pastor Ben who patiently answers each of them. I am as intrigued by the questions and answers as Michael is.

He is very hungry to know more about God and the Bible and Pastor Ben happily feeds that hunger. I don't know how long we sit in conversation, but we are eventually interrupted by a light knock on the front door followed by a called out "Hello?"

It's Julie.

"In here!" Pastor Ben calls out.

Michael glances at his watch and exclaims, "Holy cow! It's almost nine o'clock!" He leaps to his feet. "Ben, I'm so sorry! I didn't realize how quickly time had passed."

Pastor Ben rises and stretches. "It's not a problem. I am just sorry that I've taken up your entire evening."

Michael approaches Pastor Ben to shake his hand as Julie's smiling face comes into view. "You didn't take up our evening, we took up yours." Michael turns toward Julie. "I'm sorry, Julie. We didn't mean to hold your husband hostage for so long."

Julie waves him off. "Nonsense. Ben always has time for those who need him." The adoration she has for her husband drips from her tongue. "Besides, I had a lovely time with your children. What a joy and a blessing they are! Such good manners."

I smile at my friend. Acting impulsively, I rise and cross the room to give her a hug. "Thank you, Julie. For everything."

"Oh! You're welcome, Faith. It's my pleasure," she responds with a laugh of surprise.

"Are the kids on their way home?" asks Michael.

Julie nods. "They were getting their shoes on, gathering their books and such. By the way, they did their homework, too. I thought I'd sneak over here to be sure it was an okay time for them to return."

"What you mean is were Michael and I in a heap of a mess over here or not, right?" I laugh. "And thanks so much for getting them to do their homework, too."

Julie's cheeks pink for just a moment. "No biggie. And I wouldn't put it like that. But, yes; I wanted to be sure it was okay for them to walk in on it."

"It's actually a perfect time. They need to get showered and get to bed. We could've gone on with our discussion all night if you hadn't come when you did. I have to tell you, your husband is one smart man, Julie." Michael turns to Pastor Ben with a smile. "Ben, thank you seems so inadequate for what you've done for me, for us, tonight. But thank you."

Pastor Ben shrugs. "You're welcome. I'm glad I could be of service."

Suddenly, all three kids burst into the room, talking animatedly. Even Sarah has something to say. April and Andrew still vie the hardest for attention through volume, however.

"Okay, okay! Calm down and talk one at a time," I laugh. There's a brief infinitesimal moment of silence before they all start talking again. Apparently, they've all got something to say and want to say it now.

Michael claps his hands together twice to get their attention. "All right, kids. We want to hear what you have to say, but we can't hear all of you at once." He points to Andrew. "You. Upstairs with me. Let's get your shower and you can tell me whatever it is you want to say."

Andrew slumps forward before throwing his head back, and trudges up the stairs. "Aaawww! How come I have to goooo?" Michael looks back, smiles and waves before disappearing up the stairs with Andrew.

Sarah is silent, but April sighs heavily and rolls her eyes. I turn my gaze to the pair. "Girls, please thank Miss Julie for having you over this evening."

"Thank you, Miss Julie." They say in unison.

"Your cookies were the bomb! My cheer squad will love them!" April blurts.

I look inquisitively at Julie.

"Oh. I promised to make them for her cheer squad next week. Is that okay?" she replies.

"Of course," I grin. "As long as it's no trouble for you, I know the girls will love it."

Her smile takes up even more real estate on her face. "I would love it and it's no trouble at all."

April squeals and claps her hands. "I have to go let them know!" She turns on her heel and disappears up the stairs.

So much for having something to say.

"Did you enjoy yourself, too?" I ask Sarah.

Pastor Ben interrupts me. "Faith, we really need to get going and let you guys do your thing. Thank you for opening up your home and your heart tonight. I know you and Michael are going to be just fine."

Suddenly, a thought dawns on me. "Oh, Pastor Ben! I'm so sorry. I just realized we kept you for hours here basically having a session." I grimace. "I'm so sorry. I'm sure that's the last thing you want to do at the end of your work day."

"That's all right. I haven't seen you at the office for a couple of weeks anyway, so I guess I owed you one. Well, have a good night!" He places his arm around Julie's waist and guides her out. She grins and waves as they disappear into the night.

I smile and turn to find Sarah studying me with a guarded expression. "Mom, what's that all about?"

Oh, no.

Suddenly, I'm bone weary. I rub my forehead and gather my thoughts before answering. "Sarah, it's been a very long day and I'm very tired. Your father and I had to work some things out. Everything is okay." I smile at her. "It's better than okay, actually."

Her expression remains unchanged. "Uh huh. You've missed some sessions with Pastor Ben? Whatever." She turns on her heel and walks upstairs without another word.

Well, God. I guess everything is not okay, is it?

Realizing that I'm actually praying, I continue.

Okay, God. Um…there are still messes in my life. I'm sure you've noticed. I screw things up a lot and I need your help. Please help me with Sarah. Help me to know what to say to her, and please let her hear what I'm really saying and not just the words, like Pastor Ben said. Also thanks for what you did tonight. That was awesome! Bless Pastor Ben and Julie. They've been so helpful to us. Amen.

Chapter Twenty Two

Friday dawns with a sense of peace. The bleating of the alarm clock announces it's time to face the day; breakfast needs to be made and the kids need to get to school. For the first time in an eternity, Fear isn't my constant companion. It's unsettling.

I think I can get used to it. I want to get used to it.

Rolling over, I clamp my hand on the alarm clock to shut it off, then stretch and yawn widely.

"Oh!" I exclaim, unable to help myself. The intensity of the soreness in my body takes my breath away. Every joint and muscle in my body screams in protest. Michael told me I'd probably be sore today following my fall.

I glance over at my husband and can't help but smile though every other movement makes me wince. He continues to softly snore. With his office closed today, he can sleep in. He's earned it.

I see him in a whole new light. He's my partner; he knows about me, and yet somehow still loves me.

Climbing out of bed is torture. Tying my robe as I pad slowly and painfully downstairs after waking the children, I continue to chew on yesterday's events. It doesn't seem real that only yesterday my world was turned upside down, and yet here I stand, feeling stronger than ever despite being sore. The DEA tore through my home and Michael found out about Paul.

What I had feared most and tried to bury, didn't end up burying me.

Oatmeal for breakfast is the quickest thing I can think of that will allow me to lie down as soon as possible, which I am desperate to do. I slowly stir the oats into the boiling water as

Andrew bursts into the kitchen, squeezing me around the waist before I can stop him.

I cry out. Andrew pulls back quickly.

"I'm sorry! Mommy, are you okay?" he asks, his forehead creasing.

I turn to smile, hoping to convince him as much as myself. "Yes, I'm just really sore from falling yesterday. It's sort of like when you get hit by the ball in soccer; I'll be fine in a few days." I kiss the top of his head.

His face brightens. "I'm glad. Sorry I hurt you." This time he hugs me very lightly and carefully before sitting down at the table, burying his face in the latest comic book.

Just as I place oatmeal in front of him with bowls of brown sugar, fresh berries, and nuts in the middle of the table for everyone to share, April and Sarah both enter, grab their bowls from the counter and sit down, as well.

"Good morning, girls. Did you sleep well?" I ask, groaning as I sit down to join them. Not being especially hungry, I just sip my coffee.

"Fine," Sarah mumbles. April nods and dumps spoons of brown sugar, nuts, and berries into her oatmeal before plowing in. Suddenly April spies my awkward movements.

"Mom, what's wrong? You're moving like an old person," she asks around the oatmeal in her mouth.

"April, please don't talk with food in your mouth," I reply wearily, deflecting her comment.

"Mommy fell down yesterday, so she's sore today. Sort of like when I get hit by soccer balls," Andrew blurts, also with a mouth full of oatmeal.

Sighing, I repeat, "Andrew and April; please don't talk with food in your mouths." I turn my attention to April. "Yes, I fell down when I passed out yesterday, so I'm pretty stiff and sore this morning. I'll be okay in a few days."

I want to talk to Sarah, but don't really know how to approach the subject. Michael and I didn't discuss what or how much we were going to share with the kids about what's happened. I know it's not good to keep secrets between us, but I really don't think the kids need to know.

They're just kids, after all. Even though she's eyeing me, Sarah isn't in the mood for talking. I'll discuss it with Michael before bringing it up.

Once the kids finish breakfast and are on their way to school, I survey the few dishes that need to be loaded and leave them for now. My body is screaming for respite. Limping into the living room, I lie down on the sofa with a sigh and close my eyes.

Why am I so sore? This is ridiculous. I just fell, for crying out loud. I feel as though I've been beaten.

Maybe I am getting old. I won't be able to run for at least a few days.

"Perfect!" I grumble aloud. "I may never get back in shape." I've been eating a lot of M&Ms lately and my clothes have been getting tighter.

Maybe I can walk instead for now…

Rolling onto my side causes me to gasp.

Okay, maybe not today. I settle deeper into the sofa cushions instead, trying not to move.

I must've fallen back asleep because, in what feels like seconds later, Michael's gentle shaking brings me into consciousness.

"Faith? Honey, wake up," he says quietly.

I can hear the phone ringing in the background, but it cuts off rather quickly. Perhaps it went to voicemail.

I slowly open my eyes. "Huh? What? What time is it?" I ask groggily, looking around me, my gaze finally resting on Michael.

His face looks pinched and his lips are a thin line. "It's about nine-thirty."

There are voices mumbling quietly in the background coming from the television.

Suddenly, the telephone rings again. Michaels purses his lips, sighs impatiently, rises and instead of answering the phone simply shuts off the ringer.

Puzzled, I try to sit up only to gasp in pain and fall back. He approaches me quickly, concern now mingling with anger on his face.

"Honey, are you okay?"

"Just sore, like you said I would be." Thoroughly confused, I ask, "Michael, what's wrong? Why didn't you answer the phone?"

"Because of this," he says, grabbing the remote and turning the volume up on the television.

I look briefly at the television and again try to sit up, this time with Michael's help. Once I'm in an upright position, I give the television my full attention. I see the logo for Michael's company captioned in the upper right corner and the stereotypical young blond anchorwoman is talking about the investigation into SML Pharmaceuticals.

"...the DEA, with full cooperation from SML Pharmaceuticals, raided not only the corporate offices of that company yesterday, but also the homes of its top executives. As you can see from this aerial footage of one of those executives' homes, whose name is Michael Strauss, they were pretty busy. They also raided the homes of..."

The anchorwoman's voice continues, but all I see is my home on the screen and my mouth falls open.

"Oh, my God, Michael! That's our house!" I yell, rising to my feet in spite of my body rallying in protest. "Oh, my God! I thought I heard a helicopter yesterday! I didn't think anything of it! Oh, my God!"

Michael gently pulls me down on the sofa. "Lovely, isn't it?" His voice seethes with anger. "This is just perfect, absolutely perfect. The phone has been ringing off the hook for thirty minutes. That's with an unlisted number, too. I got a call from my boss Frank about forty minutes ago, and he told me to turn on the news because he'd just been informed that it had made the news. That's when the phone started ringing. Every media leech under the sun is calling wanting a comment." He angrily rises to his feet and paces.

"I watched the story already on another channel, and they didn't even mention that they found nothing in our home." He scratches the scruff on his chin and takes a deep breath. "Nice objective coverage, isn't it?" he asks rhetorically, gesturing at the screen.

I stare blankly at the screen and watch the images revolve. Our house disappears from view and another one shows up; same scenario, different house. I wonder which house, and which family, is being exposed now.

The chirping of my cell phone breaks my trance and causes me to jerk painfully. Michael growls and disappears into the kitchen, returning with my cell.

"It's Michelle," he says, handing me the phone before grabbing the television remote to turn it off.

"Hello?" I ask, pressing the little rectangle to my ear.

"Faith? Faith, are you okay? I just saw the news and…I don't know what to say!"

I sigh. "Yeah, we're okay. We just turned on the news." I glance at Michael. "I don't know what to make of it. They came yesterday and made me feel like a drug lord or something. It was terrifying, but what they don't mention on the news is that they found nothing in our home. Nothing!"

"I'm sure they didn't, Faith. You guys are good people and I know this will work itself out. How are you holding up?"

"We're…" I search for the right word. "Stunned. I mean, Michael's company is under investigation, which means they're all under investigation. I just don't understand why this made the news, Michelle! My God, don't they care about the families?"

"No, they don't, Faith." Michelle's voice is laced with indignation. "They don't care anything about anyone! I'm so sorry about this. Please let me know if there's anything we can do. Richard and I are here for you."

Suddenly, my cell beeps with another call and I glance at the tiny screen. "Thanks, Michelle. Listen, Lilly's calling me now, too. I better answer it."

"No problem. Just keep me posted. Love you!"

"Love you, too." I end the call and answer Lilly. "Hi, Lilly."

"Faith! I just saw your house on the news. What's going on? Are you guys okay?"

I repeat almost the exact same conversation with Lilly that I did with Michelle. Just as I'm done, there's a knock on the front door which Michael disappears to answer. My cell phone beeps again. This time it's Brenda. I shake my head as I end my conversation with Lilly to answer this latest call and repeat the conversation once more.

As much as I appreciate my friends, I'm overwhelmed. As I am ending my conversation with Brenda, Michael walks around the corner with Julie trailing close behind.

Once I've completed the last call, I turn my attention to Julie.

She smiles ruefully. "Good morning, sunshine," she says. "Another day, another problem?"

I can't help but laugh. "You got that right. I wouldn't be me without a problem, right?" Sighing, I gesture for her to have a seat.

She shakes her head and offers her latest foil covered creation to me. "I'm not staying, just dropping off some cookies."

My mouth drops open, again. "Seriously? At nine o'clock in the morning? Julie, when could you have possibly made these? I mean, you left my house late last night and I assume you slept. Do you bake in your sleep or something?"

She laughs me off. "Maybe I do and maybe I don't. Don't worry about it. I tried a new recipe and hope you guys like it. They're salted peanut butter chocolate chip cookies." She smiles broadly. "And this nonsense going on with the news, don't worry about that. God knows and remember: He'll take care of you. He's not surprised by any of this." She looks from me to Michael, hands him the plate and then turns on her heels and leaves.

Michael and I look at each other blankly. He relaxes and shrugs, turning to take the plate to the kitchen. Almost as an afterthought, he turns back to me and asks, "Do you want a cookie?"

"Actually I don't, thank you. I think I'm gaining weight already because I'm not running. Plus it's not even lunchtime!" He disappears into the kitchen and my stomach growls in response. "I haven't eaten breakfast yet."

Groaning and grunting as I rise, I head for the kitchen where Michael has peeled the foil back and stuffed half of one cookie into his mouth.

I put my hands on my hips and glare.

"What?" he asks innocently, stuffing the other half of the cookie into his mouth while I watch. Once he swallows, he turns his attention to me, but I notice his hand reaching for another cookie.

"You're actually going to eat cookies right now?" I ask incredulously.

"Isn't that one of the privileges of being a grown up? I can eat cookies for breakfast if I want to," he states defiantly, stuffing half of yet another cookie in his mouth. "Besides, you seem to keep up with your M&M bowl, so don't judge me."

Before I can be insulted and fire off what I hope to be a well timed retort, I realize he's teasing me and settle for scowling instead. I turn my back and pull eggs out of the refrigerator. "They must be good."

I can smell the rich chocolate coupled with peanut butter and a hint of brown sugar, but the scent doesn't appeal to me. Not right now.

He nods vigorously, "Oh, yeah. I like the crunchy salt on top. It sounds weird, but it works. They're nice and gooey…" He sounds almost lustful, causing me to chuckle as I heat a pan.

"Michael, what are we going to do about this nonsense?" I ask moments later, slowly scraping the eggs around the pan.

He turns from draining the glass of milk he had poured for himself after having eaten four cookies and shrugs. "I like what Julie said. I also like everything Ben said last night. Just let God take care of it. I am innocent and I know it. I'm also sick of dealing with it. Enough already." He turns to me and grins. "Let's just let it be and enjoy my day off."

"But don't you want to call Frank or something? See what he says about it?"

"I already talked with Frank, and besides what would be the point? I've done nothing wrong. Period. Let the fools in the media do what they will; it won't affect the truth that I'm innocent and it won't affect my job. People's attention spans are short. They won't remember this story much less my name by next week. Besides, Frank is off for the day just like me. We'll decide what to do on Monday."

I'm flabbergasted. What a difference a day makes. "Are you serious? You really just don't care?"

250

"It's not that I don't care, but what can I do? I'm innocent, Faith. The DEA came and left empty handed. There's nothing for me to do."

I slide the eggs onto my plate and sit down, with another groan, at the table. Michael comes behind me and kisses my neck. I shiver in spite of myself. He chuckles and sits next to me, his hand on my leg.

"You know, there are wonderful ways to spend a day off without kids," he murmurs, kissing my neck again. Another shiver runs down my spine. "We won't even have to leave the house." His voice is hoarse. My heart quickens.

"Michael, you are so bad," I murmur in response, forgetting my eggs. "Maybe it's just the sugar talking. You're all hyped up on cookies and milk."

He coughs out a throaty laugh as his hand moves farther up my leg. "Does it matter?" His lips leave a trail of fire on my throat. He gently pulls the robe and strap of my nightgown off of my shoulder and kisses the skin there. He pulls the material farther down to reveal more of my flesh and suddenly he stops and gasps, pulling away. Startled, I look at him questioningly.

"Why did you stop?" I ask.

He looks shocked and horrified; he's staring at my chest. I follow his gaze and gasp, too. There's a nasty black and blue bruise blossoming out from under my right arm that edges unevenly up my chest wall and onto my arm and shoulder. I yank the material out of the way and pull my arm up. Michael sucks in his breath. The discoloration that travels down my rib cage darkens even more and disappears beneath the material.

"My God, Michael. What is this?" I ask in an incredulous whisper.

Michael clears his throat and gently pulls the material back up to its original position. "I think you really fell hard yesterday. Maybe we should take you to the hospital, Faith. You could have some broken ribs or something."

"Are you serious? I'm sore. But I'm not that sore."

His face is pained. "Honey, that looks awful. I mean, really awful. Have you looked at the rest of yourself?"

I shake my head mutely and pushing the eggs aside, start to get up. Michael quickly intervenes and handles me as though I'm a fragile piece of glass. Ever so carefully, he helps me up.

"Michael, I'm okay. I just walked in here on my own. I think I can manage." I smile, but he ignores me. He simply guides me out of the kitchen and up the stairs.

"Honey, I'll go into the bathroom and check myself out." I sway my hips from side to side suggestively. "Want to help?" I ask, winking at him.

My attempt at seduction falls flat. "Faith, please. You could be seriously injured."

Oh, well. It was worth a try.

I turn my back to him and go into the bathroom, closing the door behind me. I remove my robe and nightgown and stand in front of the full length mirror. It's difficult to keep my shock from becoming audible, so I clap my hand over my mouth instead.

I am covered from chest to knees in bruises, the bruise on my right shoulder not withstanding. I must have fallen on my right side because it bears the brunt of the ugly discolorations. Not only is the bruise on the right side of my chest especially nasty, but there's one just as ugly blossoming on my right hip that reaches down my leg like an arthritic hand print. I turn to view myself from the back and it isn't any better. The big bruises on my chest and hip wrap around to my spine.

Moving my limbs and torso gingerly, I take note of the pain that I feel assessing for any especially painful areas that relate to my bruising. I am very sore, to be sure, but there's nothing more that I can detect aside from that. I take a few deep breaths, focusing on whether the action causes any sharp pains in my ribs and happily note that it does not; so no broken ribs, just as I thought.

"Faith? Are you okay? How do you look?" Michael calls from the other side of the door, concern evident in his voice.

Regarding myself in the mirror, I'm unsure how to respond. Should I let him see this or not? I give myself a quick once over.

Definitely not.

"Uh, I'm okay. It's…uh…not as bad as it looks. Really." I reply, quickly trying to cover up with my robe, wincing at the pain the movement causes.

"Are you sure? What I saw looked really bad, Faith. Don't downplay this." Suddenly the door opens and Michael enters. I'm scrambling to tie my robe as he approaches me. He reaches for the tie of my robe and I take a step back.

"Michael, don't," I warn him, placing my hand over the tie. "Please."

Michael presses his lips together and his eyes cloud over briefly. He takes another step toward me. "Faith, no more secrets." He raises his eyebrows and removes my hand.

Reluctantly, I let him. He carefully unties my robe and unfolds the garment, pulling it away from me. He sucks in his breath and his mouth falls open as he surveys me.

His eyes rake slowly up and down the length of my body. He gently turns me to the side and follows the bruising around to the back. "Oh. My. God. Faith, we need to get you to a hospital now. This…you could have some serious damage. How bad do you hurt? Don't lie to me."

I look my husband in the eyes and hold his face in my hands. "Yes, I hurt. I'm very sore, but there's nothing damaged, Michael. I can move everything and there aren't any sharp pains anywhere, not even in my ribs. I just fell hard. That's what you said. I'll be fine. The bruising always looks worse the next day. It will get better. I don't want to go to the hospital."

"But, Faith honey," he says thickly, his eyes misty. "You look…awful. I'm really worried you may have injured something inside. I just want to make sure. Please?"

I sigh heavily and wrap the robe around me, cinching it, being careful not to wince. I have got to convince him not to make me go to the hospital; it would be such waste of time. Besides, hospitals always stink of antiseptic. Yuck.

"Michael, I know you're worried, but trust me. I am not downplaying this. I am very sore, that's true. But I moved around a lot this morning already and I honestly don't feel anything that might be out of sorts. The bruises are ugly, but they're just bruises."

"Faith…" he begins, but I cut him off.

"Michael, look. I promise that if I feel anything that's out of sorts or if anything changes for the worse, I will go to the hospital, okay?"

He studies me for a moment before pointing his finger at me and replying. "Faith, if anything changes, you will tell me or so help me, I will call for an ambulance. Understand?"

I scowl, but nod. At least he's not going to make me go to the hospital. He helps me into the bedroom and leads me to the bed.

"Michael, I would rather not lie down. I didn't even finish my eggs," I protest.

"Oh, sorry. Let's go downstairs and I'll make you some new eggs. They're probably cold anyway. You can rest on the couch."

"All right," I sigh and allow him to guide me down the stairs, taking them slowly. Once he has me settled on the sofa with fluffed pillows (not really necessary), he disappears into the kitchen.

I close my eyes. Within minutes, he appears with my breakfast on a tray, which I wave off as I slowly rise from the couch with a groan.

"Faith, don't get up. Just sit there and relax."

"Michael, I am not an invalid! I am sore, but I'm okay. I appreciate that you're concerned, but let me eat breakfast at the table," I snap irritably, and immediately regret it. "Honey, I'm sorry. I don't mean to snap at you. It's just that I...I don't know."

My emotions are out of sorts.

"It's okay. You're stressed and you're sore. I would like you to take it easy, but I guess eating breakfast at the table is easy enough." He follows me to the table and sets my breakfast in front of me as I gingerly sit down. "I made you fresh coffee, too. I think it's almost done."

He ducks into the kitchen and returns with two steaming mugs, one of which he places before me.

I take a bite of the eggs, and then another. They're fluffy and delicious. "Thanks, Michael. They're perfect." I spear another bite. The more I eat, the more my appetite picks up until before I know it, I'm scraping the last bits of yellow off my plate.

Michael sits, observing me.

"Want me to make you some more?" he asks, chin propped in his hand.

I shake my head, pushing the plate away. "No, I'm full. It was really good, though." I smile. "Thanks."

He smiles crookedly. "No problem." He rises and removes my empty plate, patting my arm very gently. "I'll load the dishwasher. You relax and put your feet up. Want me to help you onto the couch?"

I shrug him off. "No," I groan, rising, "I can make it." I slowly make my way into the living room and sink carefully onto the sofa.

Michael groans from the kitchen.

"What's wrong?"

His head pops around the corner, his expression dark. "There are thirty-two messages on the machine."

"What? From who?" I blurt, sitting upright, immediately regretting it as my body screams in protest. I sink back.

"Faith, just lie down and rest, will you? I don't know who they're all from. I scrolled through most of the numbers and don't recognize but a few of them. My guess is it's the media." He rubs his face. "I'll listen to some of the messages just to be sure, but if it is, I'm not returning any of the calls. They can talk through the PR person at work. I'm also going to leave the ringer off. Anyone that really needs to get hold of us knows our cell numbers."

"This is a nightmare. Why did they have to put our house on the news? I really, really have had enough."

Michael sighs and mutters, "Amen to that," before disappearing into the kitchen.

After a few minutes, he calls out, "Yep. It's the media all right!" I assume he's deleting messages because I hear an occasional "beep beep" as he punches buttons on the phone. Eventually that sound is replaced by the sound of dishes being rinsed and loaded. Once he's done, he sits on the sofa next to me with a sigh.

"Faith, we need to talk about some things."

I open my eyes and look at him inquisitively.

What now?

He relaxes back and crosses his legs, clearing his throat. "First of all, I want you to promise that you won't keep secrets from me anymore. I...that really bothered me, Faith. It hurt me, too. I tried so many times over the years to find out what was wrong and why you were so fearful, but you never even hinted at what was wrong. Can you understand how that hurt me?" He turns to me, his expression pained.

"Yes," I sigh. "I'm really sorry, Michael. I told you why last night, though. I just couldn't."

He nods and grabs my hand, rubbing it between his. "Yes, I know what you said. I still wish you had shared it with me a long time ago. I feel like you didn't trust me enough." He pauses, raising his hand to stop me as I begin to protest. "I also know what Ben said and I'll keep that in mind. The trust thing still lingers in my mind, though. I just need to hear you tell me that you won't ever do that again. I'm your husband and that should count for something."

"It does count, Michael. You are everything to me." I squeeze his hand. "I won't do that to you again. I am going to keep going to counseling with Pastor Ben and get this all worked out. I promise."

Michael smiles and strokes my cheek with his other hand. "I just needed to hear you say it. We both have things to work through, don't we?"

I smile ruefully at him.

"That brings me to my next thought. I think we should go to church this Sunday, as a family. I'd like to go to Ben and Julie's church," Michael continues.

"Oh." I blink in surprise. "I think that would be nice. I'd love to go to their church."

"One more thing." He rubs his hands together. "I think we should tell the kids about Paul." He eyes me carefully, weighing my reaction.

I'm taken aback. "Uh...why? Why do we have to tell them anything about it? I see no reason why we should have to do that, Michael."

"Faith, if there's anything that became crystal clear to me last night is that secrets, even old ones, are dangerous. This was a huge event in your life. I deserved to know about it, you didn't tell me and when I found out it, the way I found out…well, it hurt. Our children deserve to know the truth, too."

Wincing, I weigh my words carefully. "Michael, I told you I am sorry about that. I never meant to hurt you. But they're kids. They don't need to know about it. Besides, what exactly would you want me to tell them anyway?"

"I'm convinced we should tell them about this. They're not stupid; they are wondering what happened yesterday. I mean, you did pass out. That's not exactly a cough and a sneeze. We can stick to the facts about it and just tell them what happened with Paul's death. But I would be willing to bet they're going to have questions. You need to be ready to answer those questions. It's the right thing to do."

I can't give a coherent argument as to why not. The depth of fear and agony I had before is gone and I don't want it to return. Keeping it all inside for so long was poisonous.

God, what should I do?

There are times that I wish I would hear an audible voice from heaven telling me what to do. But no; I'm met with silence. I sigh and throw my hands up.

"Fine. I'll tell them tonight when they get home." My heart squeezes. "But, what exactly am I going to say, Michael? You know how hard that was for me last night."

He reaches over and squeezes my knee, very gently. "Honey, I think maybe we should pray and ask God to give us the right words."

I blink in surprise. "Pray? Really? You would do that?" I ask incredulously.

He shrugs and smiles. "Why not? It worked last night. No reason it shouldn't work again."

"Okay. Do you want to pray right now or do it later?"

"I don't think it matters. Let's go ahead and do it now." He holds his hands out to me and I place my hands in his. He scrunches his eyes shut and I close mine, as well.

He sighs before beginning. "Uh… Dear God, please help us to know what to say tonight to our children. This is hard for both of us and we…uh…really aren't sure what to say. So…thanks, and amen." I open my eyes and find my husband grimacing and looking questioningly at me. "How was that?"

I smile and lean over to kiss his cheek, ignoring the pain the movement fosters. "I think it was perfect."

Wasn't that perfect, God? Thanks for Michael.

Chapter Twenty Three

My stomach is in knots. Pressing my hand into my abdomen, I'm surprised I don't feel a physical lump there. It doesn't seem possible to feel this amount of anxiety and not have something to show for it.

Taking a deep breath, I sit up straighter in the chair and wince. I look around the kitchen table at the four most important people in my life, regarding each of them individually. We've just finished dinner and cleared the dishes.

Waiting until after dinner to discuss recent events was difficult. When the children came home from school, they had already heard about the news fiasco that descended upon our home and family. With technology that provides instantaneous information each and every second, it didn't take long for them to hear about it from their friends and even some teachers who, thankfully, were diplomatic.

I had wrongly assumed the children would have been shielded from it at least during school hours.

April and Sarah are anxious and fearful and blasted Michael with questions. Well, April blasted at a ratio of four to one over Sarah. To my surprise, Andrew thinks it's cool; sort of like Bonnie and Clyde. Michael tried to set him straight, but Andrew is convinced that we're going to be rich and famous simply because we are on TV. Nothing we say is going to reduce his euphoria over the whole business.

Michael is talking to the children, slowly introducing the subject of Paul. He looks calm, authoritative and completely in control.

I'm so jealous.

April is paying attention, but I wonder where her mind is. She's got a good head on her shoulders, most of the time. She's both bubbly and detached, a remarkable combination I hope and pray will serve her well in life.

When my gaze rests on Sarah, I can't help but feel a squeeze on my heart. I never thought sweet, smart, calm Sarah would ever have done what she did. But she's human and will make mistakes.

I pray she doesn't make too many and doesn't make any big ones.

I also hope everything else that is going on, including the bombshell I'm about to drop, doesn't send her off the deep end. Our relationship is fractured lately and I hate that.

Finally, my gaze rests on little Andrew. So young, so innocent, and so very sweet. I adore all of my children, but Andrew holds a special place in my heart. Perhaps because he's the youngest and, therefore, my very last baby. Maybe it's because he's my only son. I don't know.

I pray that as he grows he'll become a strong man of character like his father. It's hard for me to picture him as a man; no matter how old he gets, I still see My Baby.

With trepidation, I wonder what the effect of what I'm about to share will have on him and his view of me.

My heart lurches.

When my gaze returns to Michael, I tune in to what he's saying. He's still talking about the investigation.

"As I've said, the DEA did come here and search the home yesterday, but they found nothing. Not. One. Thing." He taps the table with his index finger emphasizing each word. "So the investigation will continue as far as the company is concerned, but I know that I'm innocent, and that's all that matters. In the end, everything as far as our family is concerned is going to be okay." He looks pointedly around the table at each child. "Got it?"

Sarah and Andrew nod their heads and April interjects, "But, dad, it's so embarrassing! I mean, all my friends are talking about it and saying stuff." She crosses her arms. "Do you have any idea what that's like?" She looks at her father, agony etched on her face.

Michael reaches across and squeezes her forearm. "I know this is hard, believe me. But it will all blow over soon. Trust me on this; by next week they will have forgotten about it."

"Not likely," April mutters.

"All my friends are talking about it, too! It's way cooler than the babies our teacher's hamster had," blurts Andrew, grinning broadly. His chest is puffed out in pride. "Dad's a star!"

Michael and I both chuckle.

"Not a star, Andrew. Just mentioned on the news," Michael reminds him.

Andrew bounces in his seat. "I know. That's awesome!"

"Sarah," I ask quietly. "How are you feeling about all of this?"

Sarah stares at the table for a moment before lifting her gaze. Her face is an unreadable mask. "I don't know. I don't like it." She glares at Andrew. "But there's nothing I can do about it. It is what it is. I just want it to go away. I don't like the looks and stares I got at school today."

"I'm sorry for that, Sarah. Truly, I am. I had no idea this was going to be in the news until it just showed up on the screen." Michael's jaw works. "I wanted to protect you guys from it and I couldn't. For that, I'm sorry."

Silence hangs in the air like ripe fruit. I decide to pluck it.

"Your father never meant for you guys to be affected by this. It's ridiculous. He's been working these long hours trying to fix whatever mess has been made by other people in the company. That's why he was gone for a few weeks and why he's not home a lot right now."

"Thanks, Dad," Sarah states quietly, followed by mumbled agreements from April and Andrew.

Michael nods and clears his throat. "There are some other things we need to discuss as a family, too." He ventures a glance at me. I blanch.

I don't want to do this. Please, please, please don't do this to me, God!

Michael reaches over and squeezes my hand. I grip tightly onto his.

He clears his throat again. "As you already know, your mother passed out yesterday. What you don't know is why."

I keep my gaze on the table; I can't look up. Will this damage them beyond repair? Will it damage my relationship with them beyond repair? I squeeze my eyes shut. This could be the culmination of all my fears coming true.

Michael plunges ahead. "Your mother received quite a shock yesterday. I…ah…found a letter in the desk that contained some information your mother hadn't shared with me before. It was a deeply personal and very painful bit of your mother's history that she didn't want to share." Michael gently tugs on my hand and I look up at him, eyes wide. "Do you want to tell them, sweetheart?"

I am too terrified to respond.

Before I can formulate a response, April blurts impatiently, "What?! Is mom a man or something?!"

That breaks the tension.

Michael starts to chuckle, followed by Sarah, and then me. The chuckling turns to laughter, and in spite of the pain it causes me, I can't help but join in, my free hand gripping my side as I intermittently gasp and laugh.

As the laughter subsides, Andrew chimes in, mouth agape, "Is that possible?" he asks breathlessly, eyes wide and eyebrows practically disappearing into his hairline.

That starts a whole new round of laughter that takes even longer to subside. When it does, I wipe the tears that have rolled down my face, tears of mirth as well as pain. Sarah and Michael are also wiping their eyes.

I turn to my youngest and shake my head, "No, honey. That is not possible. I am not a man." Michael chuckles again before bringing the conversation back to earth. "Faith, would you like to tell the kids or do you want me to tell them?"

I shake my head, blow out my breath, and respond, "I think I should tell them."

Lord, will you help me?

"Your father is right. It is something that I've kept a secret since before I met your father. It…I was very hurt by it and thought that if I kept it a secret, it would just go away." I look at Sarah; she's listening very intently. "But it didn't. Secrets are like that; ignoring them doesn't make them go away, it just gives them more power over you. It had a horrible grip on me since it happened and now…now it's time to tell you about…" I pause for a moment and look to Michael, who nods in encouragement. "…Paul."

I wipe my hands on my thighs and take a deep breath. "Paul was my first husband. We were only married a few years before he was…killed by a drunk driver. I was devastated by it. The letter your father found was from that drunk driver who killed him. That letter arrived weeks ago and I hadn't opened it. I was too frightened about what it might say. I don't know that I ever intended to read it. Then your father found it. He read it and was very shocked and hurt to find out that I had been married before and never told him." I squeeze Michael's hand. "He has forgiven me for hurting him like that and for keeping the secret from him."

I look at my children; Andrew looks puzzled, Sarah is tight lipped, and April's mouth has fallen open. "I am also sorry that I kept it from you guys. I thought keeping it from you would protect you, but I was wrong. There's nothing about keeping a secret that protects you. Please forgive me."

"That's it? That's the big secret?! That's not a big deal, Mom, really. When you look at everything else…" April waves her hands around. "That is so not a big deal. I mean, I'm sorry it happened to you and to…Paul, but why would you keep it a secret in the first place?"

Her response shocks me into silence momentarily. "Well, April, Paul's death was a big deal to me. It…I was in love with him and we were so young when he was killed. I felt…destroyed by it. I felt like, well, that I was such a mess afterwards that I didn't really think I could ever be okay again." My gaze once again turns to Sarah. "Sarah, that is why I have been going to counseling with Pastor Ben. I know that you were wondering about that last night. It caught me off guard when you asked. I didn't know what to say."

"You could've just said the truth, Mom," Sarah responds bluntly.

It stings.

"Sarah, that's what your mother is doing now. Give her some credit, okay? This is something she's dealt with, alone, for a very long time," Michael interjects. "I don't think we can understand the level of pain your mother has suffered for so long. This isn't easy for her."

"Sorry, Mom," Sarah says quietly. "But I just don't see why you kept it a secret in the first place. I'm with April. What's the big deal?"

I chuckle darkly. "Experiencing a loss like that, it…changed me. It shattered me and made me fearful that I could lose someone else that I love, too. I was scared when I met and fell in love with your father. I tried not to." I smile at Michael. "But I ended up loving him anyway. That love made me scared. Then as each of you made your appearance, I was even more scared that I would lose you, too."

April twitches in her seat. "That's why you're so psycho with the calls and stuff, isn't it?" She points a finger at me.

Michael groans, "April, do not call your mother psycho, please."

April grimaces and her voice softens. "Sorry, Mom. You know what I mean though, right?"

I nod. "Yes, I know what you mean and yes, that's why I've been…particular…about hearing from you when you're driving around. That's something I'm going to work on. I am choosing not to live my life based in fear anymore."

Saying the words out loud settles it in my mind. That's exactly what I want.

I feel a small hand on mine and turn to see Andrew looking earnestly at me. "Mommy, do you feel better now?"

My heart melts at his simple words and my eyes mist. "Yes, honey. I feel much better now." I lean over and kiss his forehead. He pats my hand.

"Gosh, I'm so glad you're not a man!" he blurts.

Smiling at Andrew, Michael asks, "Do you guys have any more questions about any of this?"

The children look around at each other and us and slowly shake their heads. "Are you sure? We are making this a new Strauss family rule: no more secrets. So ask away."

A few moments of silence linger before Sarah speaks up, "Mom, is that all you are seeing Pastor Ben for? What happened last night that you needed him here? I mean, are you guys having trouble?" Her voice quavers.

"No, honey. We are fine. I was the one in counseling, but only because of my...problem. They came over initially because they saw the ambulance and stayed because we needed them to help us sort through dad finding out about Paul. It was a shock for him and he didn't understand why I kept the secret. He was very hurt and I didn't know what to do to make it right. We are now sorted out and we're okay."

Sarah looks from Michael to me and back to Michael. "Dad? Is that the truth?" she asks.

"Yes, Sarah, it is," he tells her gently. "Don't worry. Everything, and I do mean everything is going to be just fine. As a matter of fact," he turns to me and smiles, "we have made a decision, too. We are going to start going to Pastor Ben's church this Sunday as a family."

"Are we going to have to go, like, every Sunday?" April groans.

"Well, I believe so. Yes, we are," Michael says firmly.

April rolls her eyes. "But I only get to sleep in on the weekends! That's so unfair!"

"Good grief, April. It's not like we have to be there at the crack of dawn. Church starts at eleven o'clock," I sigh, exasperated.

She sighs in return. "Fine. Whatever." Her mood reverts to sullen.

That went over like a lead balloon.

"I think you'll survive, April." Michael admonishes her. "Besides, I believe God has helped us get through all of this and He's going to continue to get us through everything. It's only right that we give Him an hour or so once a week. It's the least we can do."

The children look shocked to hear Michael talk like this. He's never really brought God into the picture before. A wash of shame comes over me, realizing my part in this; I turned my back on God and never introduced my children to Him.

Oh, God. Please forgive me.

The children say nothing more and we get up from the table, going our separate ways in the house. The girls go upstairs and Andrew heads into the basement, I assume to work out one of his various battle scenes. Passing through the kitchen, I grab a handful of M&Ms.

"That went better than I expected, for the most part," I express to Michael who nods in agreement. "I'm surprised at their reaction about Paul."

"I'm not surprised. Kids always have an interesting perspective on things. They don't fully appreciate what a painful experience you had because they haven't experienced life much. So for them, it wasn't a big deal," Michael muses.

"Well, I hope they never do have to experience that level of pain," I respond quietly.

"Nobody should, Faith. Especially not you." He kisses the tip of my nose and ever so carefully wraps his arms around me.

I smile and wrap my arms tightly around him, but only for a moment as such strain causes me to wince. Michael releases his light hold on me and steps back.

"Faith, do you want to take a warm bath or just lie down? I'm sure you're tired."

My shoulders slump. "I think I'd just like to go to bed. I'm beat."

Michael escorts me up the stairs and into the bedroom. He starts to follow me into the bathroom, but I protest. "I can get myself ready for bed, Michael. I'm just going to wash my face and brush my teeth. I don't need help with that."

He sighs and places his hands on his hips. "Well, I'll just wait until you're in bed before I go downstairs to wrap things up. I'm pretty tired myself and I'll join you shortly." He regards me. "You looked so awful this morning, Faith. I just…I just don't want to leave you for a moment yet. I still think you should go to the doctor."

I look at his reflection in the mirror as I rub cleanser onto my wet face. "I already told you, I'm very sore but I'm okay. If I notice something different or worse, I won't hesitate to go. Right now, I just need to rest."

Once I settle myself under the sheets with a few groans, Michael kisses me and murmurs, "I won't be long." He rises and clicks the light off as he disappears into the hallway, closing the door behind him.

Rolling carefully onto my side, I sigh and close my eyes. For the first time in a long time, I'm too tired to mull over anything. I am utterly exhausted. In what feels like mere seconds later, the bed gives way under Michael's weight as he slides in carefully beside me, wrapping his arm very gently around me.

"Hi, shweetie." My words are slurred.

He chuckles and kisses my neck lightly.

"Just sleep, Faith," He whispers into my ear.

I promptly comply, slipping quickly back into unconsciousness with one final thought.

Thank you, God. I'm grateful.

Chapter Twenty Four

"Let's all rise for the benediction." Pastor Ben's voice carries across the sanctuary at the conclusion of his Sunday morning sermon. Michael cups my elbow and helps me to a standing position, for which I am grateful. The soreness is still very much present, much to my dismay, and his.

Try as I might to mask my pain, Michael remains very concerned. We bow our heads and close our eyes as Pastor Ben prays.

Once the prayer concludes, Pastor Ben beams from the pulpit, "Now let's turn around, shake a hand and share a moment of fellowship one with another!"

Michael and I turn around and are immediately met with eager handshakes and smiles from those around us. Once we've greeted and been greeted, our family heads toward the main entrance and the receiving line with Pastor Ben and my dear friend Julie at the helm.

They both spy us at the same time and their grins widen. Pastor Ben pumps Michael's arm. "I am so glad to see you and your lovely family in the audience today!"

"Well, I said we'd be here, and here we are!" Michael responds enthusiastically. "It was a wonderful sermon, Pastor Ben, very timely." He glances around at our family. His sermon focused on forgiveness and the healing it provides.

"It certainly was," I remark, nodding. I turn my smile to Julie and, before I can stop her, she reaches in and squeezes me in a hug.

Not being able to help myself, I wince and yelp, causing her to pull back quickly, concern washing over her features.

"Faith, are you okay?" she asks, placing a hand gently on my arm.

I am quick to smile at her in reassurance. "Yes, I'm fine. I'm just really, really sore from falling the other night. It's nothing. Really."

Michael sighs loudly next to me and places his hand protectively around my back, resting on my hip. "She says she's okay, but I want her to go to the doctor. Perhaps you can talk her into it, Julie. She won't listen to me." He gives me a stern look.

Julie nods. "I think you should listen to him, Faith. I wouldn't think you should be that sore. Perhaps it's better to be safe than sorry."

"I will if I have to, but I still think it'll go away on its own."

"Don't mess around, Faith. I may not bring you anymore baked goodies!" She wags her finger at me and I grin as Michael moves us along; we're holding up the receiving line.

As we make our way to the car, Michael murmurs in my ear. "Told you so. You should listen to her and let me take you to the doctor."

I turn toward him to glare. "I promised you I would go if it got any worse. It's not getting any worse." I don't mention it isn't getting any better. Perhaps I am getting older (eek!) and it just takes longer to heal.

Another thought occurs to me; perhaps it's like any other sore muscle; I need to work it out to get rid of it. I've rested too much. That must be it. Michael barely let me walk to and from the bathroom yesterday.

Pulling out of the parking lot, I share my thoughts with him. "I think I'll try to go for a run this afternoon."

Michael physically jerks in his seat.

"Are you crazy?" he asks incredulously, his mouth wide open. "Honey, you need to rest, not run!"

"Seriously, think about it. Maybe I've been resting too much. Whenever I have a sore muscle, it needs to be rested a little bit, certainly. But the soreness goes away more quickly if I work it out. I have been so lax lately about running. I'm out of shape."

He doesn't respond immediately. He simply shakes his head and grips the steering wheel harder. His jaw is working, but I know better than to interrupt him. I change the subject and address the kids instead.

"So, what did you guys think about church?" I look through my mirror to see their faces; twisting around is too painful and I don't want to give Michael any more ammunition against me.

Andrew is the first to respond. "It was okay. Can I bring something to do next week, though? It was kinda boring."

At least he's honest.

"What sort of thing do you want to bring?" I ask him.

"I don't know. My action figures, maybe."

"I don't think that would be a good idea, Andrew. You should be quiet while Pastor Ben is talking. You can bring a book if you'd like."

That satisfies him; he nods.

"Girls? What did you think?" I ask.

April is the first to respond, naturally. "It was okay, I guess. Pastor Ben is funny."

"Yeah, he told some great stories," I reply.

"I liked it," Sarah says quietly.

My eyebrows twitch up at her response. "I'm glad, honey. Did you guys see all the kids there? There was a good mix of ages, from what I noticed."

They all nod. "Did you guys see any friends from school?" I ask.

Again, they all nod.

That's encouraging. I look over at Michael who has remained silent.

"That's good, don't you think, Michael?" I ask him.

He nods briefly and replies, "Yes."

Michael is not in the mood to talk. The rest of the ride home is quiet between us. Any chatter occurs in the back.

Once home, I move as quickly as I can toward the stairs, planning to change clothes for my run before Michael can mount another protest. As I pull on my shirt, he bursts into the bedroom.

"Are you seriously going to go for a run, Faith?!" His voice is rather loud and I tell him so.

"Of course I'm being loud, Faith! I really don't think you should be doing this!" He plants his hands firmly on his hips.

I finish smoothing my shirt over my hips and approach Michael, wrapping my hands around his waist. His hands remain firmly, stubbornly, planted on his hips. "Honey, I'm fine. Why won't you believe me? Do you really think I would hurt myself? I promise to take it easy and go slow, okay?" I grip his chin and force him to look me in the eye. "Okay?" I ask again.

He glares at me for a moment and rolls his eyes, shaking his head. "Faith, I am not comfortable with you going for a run, but I can't stop you, either. Just go on the short circuit, all right? I want you to take your cell phone, too." He places his hands on either side of my face. "If you have any and I do mean any pain, you call me and I'll come get you. Understand?"

I nod, grin and kiss him lightly on the lips. "I promise. And I'll be just fine, you'll see."

I actually feel better just anticipating the run. I've really missed it - the feel of the pavement under my feet and the wind in my face. The air is crisp and it should be very refreshing indeed.

He releases me and follows me out of our bedroom and down the stairs. I work hard to keep from grimacing when I take the steps.

Maybe this isn't such a good idea.

I quickly dismiss the thought as nonsense. I won't push too hard, but I really want to go.

"Do you want to at least eat lunch first?" Michael asks, worry written all over his face. I look over his shoulder and see the activity in the kitchen; the kids are assembling sandwiches and doling out potato chips onto plates as they talk over each other.

Strangely, the food isn't appealing.

I shake my head. "I'm not hungry right now. I'll eat something when I get back." In an effort to erase the worry from his expression, I add, "I need to work up an appetite first."

Noting the failure of my effort, I avert my gaze, grab my cell and quickly tie on my shoes as I head out the door. No sense in beating my head against a wall. He'll just have to deal with it until I get home.

My usual warm up consists of a rapid walk past a few houses followed by running at a good clip. I'm only able to walk at what would be considered a quasi-leisurely pace, which annoys me tremendously.

When I try to pick up the pace, the aches in my body work ferociously against me, transforming me from feeling annoyed into full blown anger.

My body is betraying me!

Through gritted teeth, I grumble, "I'll teach you who's boss, body!" as I start to jog.

The ripples of pain that course through my body almost force me to stop.

Almost.

I will work through this if it kills me.

My determination rapidly dissipates. The level of pain that assaults me can't be denied or ignored. There isn't an exact spot on my body I can point to that hurts. It's an all over body pain that takes my breath away the more I run.

I finally slow to a stop and grimace.

"Maybe this…wasn't such…a good idea." I speak to nobody in particular, as there is nobody around.

I catch my breath, dismayed at the fact that I have to actually catch my breath. I didn't even go very far! I look over my shoulder and realize I've gone less than half a mile. How can I possibly be out of breath?!

I pull out my cell to call Michael, but stop. If I call him and he comes to pick me up, then he'll just be more worried. I can't do that to him. I haven't injured myself. I've just over estimated what I can do. It has only been a few days since I fell and a few weeks since I ran.

I can make it.

I turn around and walk home, slowing my breath as I go. The pain recedes to severe achiness and I work at trying not to walk like a ninety-year-old that forgot her cane.

When I finally reach the door, I slowly turn the knob, open the door, and walk quietly inside glancing around to see if anyone's close by. Spying nobody, I creep inside and close the door as noiselessly as I can.

I lean my forehead against the closed door as a moan escapes my lips, wrapping one arm around my midsection gingerly. I turn around and jerk back against the door reflexively, gasping; Michael is standing right behind me. He must've snuck up.

The pain engendered by smacking against the door causes my eyes to prick with tears. I try to blink them back, unsuccessfully. It really hurt.

Anxiety covers Michael's face. "Honey, I was about to come looking for you. Do you feel any better?"

I cover my mouth with my hand, but it's doesn't matter. Unable to help myself, tears fall down my cheeks and a sob escapes. I shake my head.

Michael gently forces my face up and softly wipes the tears from my cheeks. "Why didn't you call me?" he asks thickly. "Are you hurting more?" His voice is strained.

"I'm sorry," I hiccup. I hate that. "I didn't want to worry you."

"Faith," he growls and mutters something about wanting me to trust him. "When are you going to learn that by not telling me, you do worry me?" He sighs and pulls me over to the sofa and sits me down, me grimacing the whole time. "Can we go to the hospital now?"

I sigh. "Michael, I will make an appointment tomorrow morning to see the doctor. I really don't feel like spending the night in the emergency room only to hear them tell me that I'm getting old and will take longer to heal. Just give me some Tylenol for now."

He stares at me incredulously. "No, Faith. We are going to the hospital right now. I let you talk me into not taking you the other day and I let you talk me into the run. I am done. You could have serious internal injuries. I'm getting my keys and I'll have April keep on eye on things. We are going."

"Michael, I…" I start, but he interrupts.

"Enough, Faith. I am taking you. End of discussion." His tone is one of unwavering authority. I no longer have a choice. I sigh and close my eyes, lying carefully back on the sofa cushions.

"OK, Michael. Can I have some Tylenol first, please?"

His face softens. "Of course. All I want is for you not to hurt." He disappears and returns quickly with the tablets and a glass of water.

The children take their father's side about my going to the hospital; I feel betrayed by that, but realize they're just as worried about me as Michael is. If I allow myself to be honest, I am more concerned now, too.

After arriving at the hospital, I'm surprised to be led into an exam room rather quickly. "Slow day today, I guess?" I quip to the young nurse escorting me into a room.

She smiles and cheerily replies, "Yeah, sort of!"

She gestures toward the backless gown neatly folded on the gurney. "Go ahead and put this on. You can leave your underclothes on. I'll be back soon to finish getting you set up. The doctor will be with you shortly." She disappears after closing the curtain behind her.

I sigh and turn toward Michael. "Well, it's come to this. I have to put the lovely backless gown on and be prodded by strangers. I hope you're happy. God help me."

He chuckles and pulls the gown up from its folded position, hanging it limply in the air toward me. "Faith, you know why you're here. Let's be sure that you're okay. So, put this on. I want to watch." He grins mischievously.

I snatch the gown from him and throw it back on the gurney as I begin to remove my clothing, grimacing at some of the movements. As I pull my shirt over my head, Michael gasps.

Once my face is clear of my shirt, I look over at him questioningly. His face is turned away. I look down and realize why he reacted that way.

The bruising is still horrific.

Great.

"Michael…" I start, not sure what to say. "I'm going to be okay." To ease his discomfort, I quickly put the gown on, struggling with the snaps and where they are supposed to go in relation to my arms. For the life of me, I will never understand why they make hospital gowns the way they do. I'm sure they have a purpose; it's to frustrate the heck out of people like me.

"Okay, I'm covered. You can look at me now," I retort sarcastically.

He turns to face me. His expression makes my heart ache; his eyes are glistening. He actually looks afraid. "Oh, sweetie! I'm really going to be okay." I reach for him and he closes the distance between us, but only holds my hand. He pulls the wheeled stool over and sits down next to me, leaning his forehead onto my forearm. I comb his hair with my fingers. "Please don't worry, Michael. Please."

He takes a moment to lift his head. When he does, the tears have spilled over. The pain in my heart is worse than the pain in my body. Just then, there's a gentle knock on the door and a male voice, "Hello? Mrs. Strauss?"

Michael quickly wipes his face as the curtain is pulled back and a young man in his thirties walks in wearing green scrubs and carrying a clipboard. He walks up to me and offers his hand. "Hello. I'm Dr. Rider, one of the senior residents here in the emergency department." I shake his hand and he offers his hand to Michael, as well. "Are you Mr. Strauss?"

Michael clears his throat before responding. "Yes."

Dr. Rider smiles and addresses me once again. "So, I see that you passed out and fell a few days ago and now you feel worse? Is that right?"

I nod.

He lifts a sheet on the clipboard and peruses it. "I also see that your husband called 911 when it happened and you were examined. That's good." He lifts his head and addresses me directly again. "Can you tell me how exactly you're feeling worse this afternoon? What made you decide to come to the emergency department today?"

"I'm just really...sore. I can't explain it specifically. There isn't one spot that hurts more. I just sort of hurt all over. It's a...deep ache."

"Actually," Michael interjects. Dr. Rider turns toward him, eyebrows raised. "Dr. Rider, you need to look at Faith's body. She's horribly bruised all over, especially on her right side, and she..." he looks pointedly at me. "...decided it was a good idea to go for a run today, even though I told her she shouldn't. So I made her come in today. She didn't want to."

Dr. Rider scribbles something on his clipboard and then addresses both of us. "Mrs. Strauss, do you normally like to run?"

I nod emphatically. "Yes, very much. I have run for years and love it."

"Were you able to run as you normally do today?"

I glare at Michael and then look at my lap. "No. I could barely break into a jog." My cheeks burn. "It hurt too much. I ended up just limping home instead." I snort a laugh, trying to lighten the mood.

It doesn't work.

"What kind of pain are you having? You mentioned aching and it being all over, but is there anything in particular you could say about it?"

I shake my head. "Not really. I just…hurt." I shrug my shoulders.

"Have you had any bleeding not related to your monthly cycle? Have you experienced any nausea, vomiting, or unusual urine or stools, in terms of frequency, color or anything?"

I think for a moment. "No."

"Okay, Mrs. Strauss. Would you mind lying on your back, please? I'm going to examine you." He gets up, closes the curtain, walks over to the sink and washes his hands. I look over at Michael and he helps me to a lying position, covering me with the sheet up to my waist. He looks into my eyes, his expression pained and fearful.

I cup his face and silently convey reassurance to him.

Dr. Rider turns toward me with a smile. "I'm just going to feel your stomach for now, okay? You let me know if anything I do hurts." He pulls the sheet down and lifts the gown. His eyes bug briefly before he quickly smoothes his expression. "Oh. I see what you mean, Mr. Strauss." His eyebrows crease. "Mrs. Strauss, I need to see where the bruising goes, okay?"

I nod mutely, glancing at Michael, who turns his head away.

Dr. Rider pulls the sheet down farther, following the lines of the bruising along its path. "Does it go around your body over here, as well?" He indicates my right hip and leg.

I nod.

276

"Can you turn on your side a little, please?" I comply, wincing all the while. Dr. Rider's hand gingerly feels along the edges of the bruise to my spine. "Does this hurt when I press here? How about here?" He presses in a few places along my hip and spine, but the pressure doesn't increase my pain, so I shake my head each time.

"It doesn't hurt any more than usual when you press," I tell the doctor.

Once he's done examining my leg and hip, he pulls the sheet up to cover my lower half and lifts my gown, looking behind him to be sure the curtain is indeed closed, which I appreciate.

Once again, I see the doctor's eyes bug out briefly before his professional mask returns.

Michael's gaze remains averted.

"Same drill, Mrs. Strauss. Let me know if it hurts more when I push, okay?" I nod and he begins to feel my body, pressing here and there. He spends extra time along my chest and rib cage encouraging me to let him know if it feels at all worse when he presses. I nod to the direction, but shake my head to his prodding. Nothing makes the pain any worse, thankfully.

"Okay, Mrs. Strauss. Go ahead and lie on your back and I'm going to examine your belly." I comply, wincing as I make myself comfortable. I glance over at Michael and he's staring at my face, worrying all the while from the look on his.

Dr. Rider begins to press and roll his hands on my stomach, which makes me wince occasionally. He notices.

"Mrs. Strauss, does it hurt when I do this?" He presses on my abdomen and I wince, nodding my head.

"What kind of hurt is it? Is it sharp, dull, radiating?"

I consider the options and concentrate on what it feels like. "It just feels like…pressing on a bruise. It isn't sharp or anything. It's just really sore."

Dr. Rider removes his hands and pulls my gown down over my body once again. "Okay. I am going to order a CT scan. It will give us more evidence of anything that may be going on." His eyes scan my arms. "Has the nurse started an IV on you yet?"

Michael's head snaps up. "Do you think there's something wrong? How hurt is she?" His voice is strained.

Dr. Rider smiles at Michael. "Mr. Strauss, it's just a precaution. You brought her here to be sure she's okay and that's what I'm going to do. Did the nurse come in yet?"

I shake my head. "No."

The doctor chuckles. "Looks like I jumped the gun. I'll send her in so we can get things moving along. I'll have the nurse draw some blood for tests and you'll need an IV before you can get the CT scan." He looks at Michael. "Please don't worry, Mr. Strauss. We're going to check her out completely and be sure everything is all right." With that, he disappears behind the curtain and I hear the door latch closed.

Within minutes, the nurse that escorted me into the room reappears with a large plastic tote clutched in her hand. There are all sorts of individually wrapped pieces in it.

She smiles broadly. "Sorry. Dr. Rider tends to get ahead of himself. He forgets to let us do our job before he does his." She washes her hands as she explains, "I need to get an IV in your arm and draw some blood before we do anything else."

She quickly dries her hands and pulls two purple gloves from a cardboard dispenser on the wall. She plucks supplies out of the tote and efficiently places them on the small rolling metal table she's pulled up next to herself.

I'm fascinated watching as she quickly puts an IV in my left wrist and deftly draws thick burgundy blood from the IV into an endless supply of skinny glass tubes with different colored stoppers before hooking the IV up to a large bag that drips slowly into my veins. The label on the bag says "Sodium Chloride 0.9%" on it.

The nurse notices me reading the label. "It's just a saline solution. There's no medication in it. We just do that whenever we have someone going for a CT scan." She smiles. "Do you have any questions?"

We shake our heads.

"Either I or Dr. Rider will be back soon. We don't know how long it will take to get you to CT, but hopefully not long. It's a Sunday and we're slow, so it shouldn't take long." With that, she disappears behind the curtain and the door latches in her wake.

After a few moments, I break the silence. "Well, at least things seem to be moving along. It's taking a lot less time than I thought it would."

Michael stares at me for a long moment before responding. "Faith, I would never make it without you." His voice is thick.

I turn toward him, shocked by his statement. "Michael, what are you talking about?"

His eyes mist over. "I mean, if anything ever happened to you…."

"Honey, nothing is going to happen to me. I am fine. Please don't worry." I place my hand on his cheek, rubbing his cheekbone with my thumb. "I'm sorry you're so worried."

Michael closes his eyes. "I have a better understanding of what you went through…with Paul."

I absorb this for a moment. "Yeah. But don't go there. Please don't go there over…this."

He shakes his head and closes his eyes. The moments pass in silence, Michael intermittently kissing my hand, my face. I, in turn, kiss his hand and run my hands through his hair. Eventually, there is a knock on the door and the voice of the nurse interrupts.

"Mrs. Strauss, they're ready for you in CT. Mr. Strauss, you're welcome to accompany your wife, if you'd like," she says cheerfully as she readies me for the journey.

The CT scan is boring and intermittently loud. Fortunately, I am not claustrophobic or there would've been problems. It feels like a lit up coffin, so I simply close my eyes and imagine myself elsewhere. Once back in the exam room, I try to talk with Michael, but he isn't much for conversation.

When I can take it no longer, I ask, "Michael, would you like to pray?"

He looks at me, a whole host of emotions dancing across his face; flashes so brief I can't identify one before another takes its place.

"I have been, Faith," he says flatly.

I blink. "Oh."

The silence continues.

When Dr. Rider finally makes his appearance forty-five minutes later, both of us jump when he knocks.

"Hello again, Mr. and Mrs. Strauss," he nods at Michael before addressing me. "The results of the CT scan are good. There are no internal injuries or broken bones. You do have a lot of soft tissue injury but it's nothing that requires intervention."

Michael lets his breath out in a whoosh.

Dr. Rider places his hand on my arm. "I can only imagine how sore you are, Mrs. Strauss. But that should gradually get better. You just need time to heal." He wags his finger at me. "No more running for at least two weeks. Give your body time to heal. I prescribe rest. I will also prescribe a good muscle relaxer and narcotic pain reliever for you, too. If I were in your shoes, I would certainly need it."

I vigorously shake my head. "I would prefer not to take those, if you don't mind. I don't react well to them."

Dr. Rider furrows his eyebrows. "I didn't see any allergies in your chart..." He flips through pages on his clipboard.

"No, I don't have any allergies. I just don't like them. They make me loopy."

"She won't take them," Michael warns. "Trust me."

Dr. Rider purses his lips. "All right. If you don't want them, I won't prescribe them. I just think your recovery would be much more comfortable if you did." He shakes his head and scribbles some more notes in his chart. "Do you want anything for pain?"

I shake my head. "No, I'll just take Tylenol."

He continues to shake his head. "All right. That's your call. I also want you to follow up with your family doctor in two weeks. You should be completely better by then. If for any reason you aren't feeling better in about four days, however, I want you to come back." He gives me a stern look.

I nod. "Okay, Dr. Rider. I will. Thank you so much." I start to rise, but he stops me.

"Hang on there. The nurse needs to come in and remove your IV plus give you discharge instructions. You'll be out of here soon enough. You take care, all right?" He smiles and Michael rises to shake his hand.

"Thanks, doctor. I appreciate everything you've done," Michael says, pumping the doctor's arm.

"Not a problem. Good call on making her come in. She's a tough lady, to be sure." He grins at me before ducking out.

After what seems like a longer time than I would've expected to simply disconnect and discharge me, I finally hear the door unlatch and the curtain is pulled back. Instead of the expected nurse, Dr. Rider stands before me looking...off somehow. He has what I assume is my chart in his hand and his gaze seems to study us both as he pulls the chair up to sit down.

Puzzled, I turn carefully and painfully onto my back. "Dr. Rider, I didn't expect to see you again so soon."

He shakes his head and takes a deep breath before answering. "Well, I didn't expect to need to see you again so soon."

Michael stiffens beside me.

My mouth suddenly goes dry.

"Doc, what's wrong?" Michael asks, his voice very low.

"Well," he starts. "There's nothing wrong, per se. It all depends on how you look at it." He regards us both again, a lopsided half smile on his face. His expression only deepens my confusion; if something is seriously wrong, why would he grin about it?

I reach for Michael's hand and he immediately grasps mine tightly.

"What I told you before about your CT is true; you have no internal injuries or anything, but what I failed to do was to look at your blood tests beyond just checking for some particular results that might mean you have internal tissue damage that would require further interventions, which you don't have and don't need. For any woman from about the age of fourteen through to their fifties, there are standard blood tests that we draw, most of which come back negative."

Lord, let him get to the point before I explode!

"One very important test came back positive." He looks from Michael to me. "Mr. Strauss, Mrs. Strauss, you are pregnant."

What are you doing, God?!

Chapter Twenty Five

Silence. Dead silence. After a bombshell like that is dropped, shouldn't there be shrapnel or some loud *Bang!* or something?! I mean, really? Is that too much to ask?!

"Uh…" my voice shakes.

"Excuse me?" Michael asks incredulously. "Did you say Faith is pregnant? Are you sure?"

Dr. Rider smiles, nods, and turns the chart around to face Michael, pointing to a specific point on the paper. "Yes, sir. It says so right here. You two are expecting." He turns the chart back around and flips through the sheets. "From your last stated menstrual cycle, you are in your first trimester, of course."

"Uh…" I say again.

Michael's mouth is open. He looks as shocked as I feel. My hand slowly creeps to my abdomen as the doctor's words begin to sink in.

I'm pregnant. Pregnant. With child. Pregnant.

My mind reels, flipping through recent memories, clues that would point to something so obvious. My erratic period that I attributed to early onset menopause, my lack of appetite, wanting to sleep a lot, my tightening clothes…

HOLY CRAP!! I'M PREGNANT!!

Michael and Dr. Rider both jerk. I clap my hand over my mouth; I just yelled out loud. Grimacing, I mumble, "Sorry," through my hand.

Dr. Rider looks warily at us. "Well, this has obviously come as a shock to you both." He looks directly at me. "Mrs. Strauss, I'm afraid I'll need to do a pelvic exam as well as an ultrasound to see if the baby is okay. All right?"

I nod mutely.

"You mean something could be wrong with the baby?" Michael asks.

Dr. Rider turns his attention to him, his tone reassuring. "This is simply a precaution, just like the CT scan. She is complaining of a lot of deep soreness, but she hasn't had any bleeding." He looks to me for confirmation and I nod. "The only way to be sure is by pelvic exam and ultrasound."

Michael slowly nods. "Yes. Okay. Let's get this done." He turns to me. "I just want to make sure she, that they, are okay."

I'm a "they" now. Wow.

My hand returns to my stomach, pressing slightly. Of course, I know I can't feel anything, but still...

Dr. Rider said something to me, but I wasn't paying attention. "Hm? Sorry, what?"

Dr. Rider chuckles. "I was just letting you know that I need you to remove your underclothes, please. I will be back in about ten minutes. Do you have any other questions?"

My eyebrows rise. "Of you? No. Of God, yes."

Dr. Rider blinks, smiles, and rises to leave. He sticks his hand out to Michael. "Congratulations, Mr. Strauss."

Michael looks startled, taking Dr. Rider's hand robotically. "Thank you." His mouth twitches.

Dr. Rider pumps his hand once before disappearing. I close my eyes, resting my head on the gurney.

After a few silent moments, Michael clears his throat. "Ah...Faith? You need to get ready for the exam."

"Oh! Yes, of course." I quickly accomplish the task. Well, quickly for me at the moment; I'm still very sore and that soreness is excruciatingly poignant. I hope I...we...are okay. Suddenly remembering my stupid attempt at running this afternoon, my eyes prick with tears.

Michael squeezes my hand. "What are you thinking?"

"How incredibly stupid I am." My stupid chin starts its predictable quivering and tears escape, landing in a soft *plop, plop, plop* on the hospital gown.

Michael's head jerks back. "What? What do you mean how stupid you are?"

I gulp air, determined not to start bawling. "I tried to make myself run today, Michael! I could've done some...some serious...damage to...our...our baby! Omigod!" Here come the hiccups... "Michael, we have a baby!"

...And here comes the bawling...

Michael sighs, gets up, and gingerly wraps his arms around me. "Yes, Faith. We are going to have another baby." Then he does something totally unexpected.

He starts laughing.

It begins as a soft chuckle, morphs into a chortle, followed by a full on belly laugh. I stare at him like he's lost his mind; he looks like he's heard the best joke of his life. I can't for the life of me understand what is funny about this.

"Michael..," hiccup, "what on earth is so funny?!"

He takes a moment to collect himself. "Faith, it's not funny. It's wonderful! I was terrified the doctor had missed something really bad and he was trying to let us down carefully. But, now...We are going to have another baby!"

"Yes, but what if something has gone wrong because of me?" My eyes fill again.

Still smiling, he looks at me tenderly. "Faith, let's just get through the exam. We will deal with whatever happens. Maybe nothing is wrong at all. Whatever happens, nothing is your fault. You didn't know, honey. We didn't know." He kisses me lightly on the lips as the door unlatches. Michael repositions himself to sit in the chair next to me again.

Dr. Rider peers around the corner followed by the nurse, carrying a different tote this time and pulling in a piece of equipment I recognize as an ultrasound machine. My hiccups haven't subsided, and I'm sure I look a mess.

Dr. Rider's face takes on a grim expression. "I know this has come as a shock to you both. This is obviously an unplanned event in your lives. We do have counselors on staff should you need any advice about your options..."

Michael immediately holds his hands up in the air. "Dr. Rider, let me stop you right there. We know what our *options* are." Michael curls his fingers in a quotation gesture as he says the word options, "and the only real option for us is to have a baby."

Dr. Rider doesn't lose his grim expression, but rather turns his attention to me. "Mrs. Strauss, you are obviously upset. How do you feel about this? Would you like to know what options are available to you?"

I blink in surprise before comprehension dawns on me, what he means by options.

"Oh! No, you don't understand. I'm upset because I'm afraid I may have harmed our baby by my…" Enter chin quiver, stage left. "…stupidity at trying to run today. That's all."

Dr. Rider continues to regard me. "Are you sure, Mrs. Strauss?"

Michael stiffens at my side, but remains silent.

Peace settles over me. Everything is going to be fine. I don't know what fine means, but I do know that it means this new little person is meant to be.

I take a deep breath. "Dr. Rider, I appreciate that you're just trying to do your job. But let me be clear: I am surprised and even shocked about this, especially at my age. I am not, however, unclear about the fact that I am going to have another child. Nothing is going to change that." I squeeze Michael's hand and he holds mine firmly.

Dr. Rider finally turns his gaze on Michael and his stance relaxes. "I'm sorry, Mr. Strauss. I hope you know that I see a lot of situations in my position here that are less than optimum, and I have to be sure that I look out for my patients and not always take things at face value."

Michael nods tersely at him. "I understand, but I don't have to like it. I hope you understand *that*."

"Yes, I do," Dr. Rider responds. "Let's move forward with the exam and see how baby is doing, shall we?"

As they busy themselves making preparations for the exam, I lose myself in thought about what this all means. I'm in my forties, for crying out loud. I thought we were done. There's also a lot of risk for women my age. I'm scared. Peace washes over me again. I don't fight it. What would we do if something happened? I don't know. There's also risk involved with me personally. I didn't have any problems with my other pregnancies, but that was a long time ago. I'm older now. I've had hip pain for quite a few weeks already, even before the fall. I wonder how that will be as I get bigger. Will I get stretch marks worse now because I'm older, too? Good grief.

My mind bounces from thought to thought, concern to concern, scenario to scenario.

Dr. Rider interrupts my musings. "Mrs. Strauss, are you ready to begin?"

"Yes." I scoot into position as the nurse begins to hand the doctor instruments.

Once the exam is over, Dr. Rider moves on to the ultrasound, squirting warm goo onto my stomach. The nurse repositions the machine so that we're able to see the screen. We both glue our gaze to the fuzz that fills the screen. Michael leans over me to get a better view. As Dr. Rider moves the wand into proper position, forms and shapes emerge and recede.

Suddenly, what looks like a dark kidney bean shape fills the screen surrounded by a thick lighter colored layer of the same shape.

"That's the womb..." Dr. Rider moves the wand. Within the dark shape a much smaller shape appears that wiggles and bounces around. "And there's your baby."

I gasp. Michael chuckles. "It looks like a Mexican jumping bean," he muses.

The nurse giggles and Dr. Rider chuckles. "Well, I've never heard it put quite that way before, but I suppose it does."

"Is the baby okay, Dr. Rider?" I ask anxiously.

"Well, so far so good. He or she is very active and that's always a positive sign. Let me look around a bit more." He continues to click on the machine and move the wand around.

After several, very long moments he sighs and replaces the wand on its perch on the machine and wipes my stomach with a towel. "You both can relax. Everything looks perfectly fine and very much intact. There's no damage that I can see from either the exam or the ultrasound."

Much to my dismay, I burst into tears as Michael stands to shake the doctor's hand. "Thank you so much." He pumps the doctor's hand vigorously. "But, why is Faith so banged up and sore? I mean, she's a very healthy woman and everything. Are you sure there's nothing wrong? You saw the bruising."

Dr. Rider shakes his head. "Well, from my experience, not being an OB/GYN, pregnancy does some crazy things to women's bodies."

The nurse snorts, "Ain't that the truth!" and winks at me as she busies herself cleaning the table and assorted machinery.

"It could simply be that she's really sore from the fall because she's early in her pregnancy, nothing more, and nothing less," Dr. Rider continues. "We've done the CT and I've examined her. I find nothing to be wrong other than she's sore and bruised."

"I'm just so glad that I didn't hurt him." My voice quivers more than I'd like. At least the hiccups have ceased.

"No, you didn't." Dr. Rider smiles at me. "Kelly will go ahead and take out your IV like I originally promised and I'll write your discharge orders. Of course, they're different this time. You need to make an appointment to see an OB/GYN as soon as possible to start your prenatal care. How many children do you have?"

"Three," I respond.

"So you know the drill then, right?"

I nod. "I'm a little rusty, but I think I remember."

"How old is your youngest?"

"Nine," Michael answers.

"Oh, that's not so bad. I'm sure it'll come right back to you!" He pats my shoulder and shakes Michael's hand again. "Congratulations to both of you. I wish you the best." He nods at the nurse and disappears.

The nurse efficiently removes all traces of my time in the hospital from my body and goes over the discharge instructions with an emphasis on rest and making my first prenatal appointment.

On the way home, Michael is lost in thought.

"So, what do you think?" I ask.

He smiles briefly, squeezing my hand. "What do I think? I think it's…incredible. Unexpected, but still pretty incredible. I can say with certainty I didn't see that one coming. How about you?"

Drawing a deep breath, I blow air out forcefully. "I don't really know what to think. This is crazy, Michael. I mean, I'm pregnant. I'm forty-three years old! I'm too old to be pregnant. How did this happen?" I blush as I realize what I've just said. "Never mind. You know what I mean."

Michael sighs. "Yes, I know what you mean, honey. But you are not too old to be pregnant, obviously. There are a lot of women who have babies at your age."

"Yeah, but I never wanted to be one of those women. I never pictured myself being in my sixties at my child's high school graduation. Gad, that's ridiculous! I may be in a walker."

Michael laughs out loud. "You? In a walker at sixty? I highly doubt that, Faith. You probably won't even be using a walker in your eighties."

"Hmph." I cross my arms and stare out the window.

"Faith, let's get back to the point. How do you feel about this other than your age?"

I consider his question. "I'm scared. But I also have peace about it. This little boy or girl is meant to be here and meant to be with us. I'm so thankful I didn't hurt him. I am concerned about…birth defects and stuff. That's another reason I didn't want to be in my forties having children."

"I know, Faith. I know. I thought about that, too, but didn't want to bring it up if you didn't. You have enough on your mind."

"So you're concerned about that, too?" I ask quietly.

Michael takes a moment to answer. "Yes."

"What'll we do, if that happens?"

He shrugs his shoulders. "Deal with it. It's still our child, right?"

"Yes."

Silence fills the gap for another few moments before Michael breaks it. "How do you want to tell the kids?"

I bury my hands in my face. "Lord. I hadn't even gotten that far yet. Can we wait for awhile? Please? I think we've had enough heavy discussions lately."

"Yeah. You need to rest when we get home."

I look out the window for the remaining ride home, each of us left to our own thoughts. My mind flips back and forth from one thought to another like an endless run on sentence.

I am actually pregnant. I…we…are going to have another child.

Lord, if it's not too much to ask please, please make this child healthy! Please.

This is followed by a twinge of guilt. Should I even ask for that? I don't know, but it's what I want. Just a healthy child. Oh! I almost forgot…

Sorry, God. Thanks for letting me and the baby be okay. Amen.

As we pull into the driveway, Michael turns to me. "Wait for me to come around and help you out." I don't have time to formulate a protest before he exits and scurries around the van.

After helping me into the house, he asks, "Where do you want to lie down? Upstairs or on the sofa?"

"I'd like to lie on the sofa. It's too early to go to bed, Michael."

He guides me gently to the sofa, fluffing pillows before allowing me to sit, and then lie down. "Do you want a blanket, too?" he asks.

I shake my head and sigh. "No. Stop fretting, Michael." I give him a stern look. "The doctor said I'm fine. I just have to let my body heal." The house is unusually silent. "Where are the kids?"

His brows furrow and he cocks his head to one side. "I don't know." He bends over and kisses me on the forehead before ducking into the kitchen. "There's a note here. They went over to Julie's house. I'll go get them and be right back."

I nod and let my head fall back on the sofa, closing my eyes.

Michael's soft footfalls diminish as he heads toward the front door followed by a soft "click" as the door latches behind him. My hands immediately move toward my abdomen and the little life growing there.

"Wow." I open my eyes and look toward the ceiling, "Okay, God. I don't know what you're doing here, but please stop with the surprises. I'd rather just have a surprise bouquet of flowers and some M&Ms instead. I think this is the topper. I can't stand anymore. You hear me?"

Silence. I close my eyes and try to tame my thoughts.

Some time later, the sound of the door bursting open startles me, followed by a gaggle of voices; the kids are all talking over one another. I don't even try to decipher what they're talking about.

"Shhhhhh!! I told you guys your mother needs rest," Michael warns them sternly, casting a glance in my direction.

I shake my head and sit up, grimacing with the movement. "It's okay. Did you guys have fun at Julie's house?"

They all start talking at once again. Michael rolls his eyes, cups his hands around his mouth and yells, "One! At! A! *Time!*"

They pause briefly and Andrew speaks up first, leaving April with her mouth agape. April wanted to be first, naturally. She snaps her mouth closed and glares at him before plopping herself into a chair with a "Hmph!"

Sarah follows behind and sits down across from her sister.

"It was great! She made us those salty chocolate chip cookies again and I ate four!" Andrew reports proudly, holding up four fingers.

My eyebrows rise. "Four, Andrew? Are you going to be hungry for dinner?"

He bobs his head up and down rapidly and turns to his father, "Can I go play downstairs?" I guess his report is finished; cookies are all that matter. Suddenly his face crumples, and he comes to sit gingerly next to me. "Mommy, are you okay now? Did the doctor make you all better?"

My heart squeezes. I smile and pull him in close. "Thank you for asking, sweetie. I'm just fine." I look at Michael meaningfully. "Everything is just fine. The doctor just told me to rest and the soreness will go away on its own." I kiss the top of his head.

"I'm so glad." He reaches in to hug me very gently before bouncing off the sofa and scrambling for the basement. Maybe Andrew will get a brother this time around. That would be nice.

"I only ate three cookies," April whines, obviously upset at being thwarted in her attempt to take her self-appointed rightful place as The First to Speak. "But I did get to help her make them."

"Well, that's good, honey. Are they easy to make?" I ask.

She nods, her mood improving now that she's being allowed to speak. "Yes. I think I'll make them for my friends next time! Plus I got to lick the spoon, too. She let Andrew and Sarah split the bowl." She jerks her head toward her sister. "Mom, how come they don't have any kids? I think they'd make great parents."

I cringe internally, trying to freeze my face into a mask. I hadn't thought about this; how am I going to tell Julie I'm pregnant? They've been trying for so long...

"Uh...they've been trying, honey. They really do want kids, but it just hasn't happened yet."

April turns white and her eyebrows shoot up, eyes wide.

"I told you, April," Sarah says smugly.

I dart a glance at Sarah as Michael comes to sit beside me. "What do you mean, Sarah?"

Sarah looks at us both, her arms crossed. "April asked Miss Julie why they don't have any kids. I thought Julie looked really uncomfortable. She changed the subject without really giving an answer. Then she excused herself and was gone for awhile after that. A whole batch of cookies baked before she came back and she seemed fine, I guess. But I told April there was probably something wrong about why they don't have kids. She didn't believe me." She turns her glare on April. "Dummy," she mutters under her breath.

"Sarah!" Michael barks. "Apologize to your sister."

"Sorry April," Sarah mutters.

"Mom! Dad! I swear I didn't know," April retorts. "I was just curious. How could I have known?!"

"It's okay, April. It's just a sensitive subject. Did you apologize to Miss Julie?" Michael asks.

She grimaces and shakes her head.

"We didn't bring it up again," Sarah interjects on her sister's behalf.

Michael and I look at each other for a moment. "That's probably wise. Just let it go this time." He turns his attention to April. "But think before you speak next time, April."

"Geez, I'm sorry!" April huffs, pounding the chair with her fist. "I didn't know!"

I try a different tactic. "April," I start calmly. "I know you didn't do it intentionally. It was an innocent question, and I'm sure Julie knows that."

April's face softens and she nods. "I really didn't mean to hurt her, Mom. She's so nice."

"I know, sweetie." I change the subject. This is just something else I have to tuck away in my brain to chew on later; how to tell Julie I'm pregnant. "What are we going to do for dinner?"

Not being particularly hungry, I determine to eat anyway. I have to.

Michael shrugs his shoulders. "I think soup and sandwiches will be fine. You didn't take anything out this morning, did you?"

I shake my head. I hadn't given it any thought, actually.

Michael claps his hands on his thighs as he rises. "All right then. Soup and sandwiches it is! Are you guys hungry or did the cookies fill you up?"

They both acknowledge they're hungry for dinner.

"Why don't you girls come help me and let your mother rest? Faith, you're going to eat, right?" he asks. Translation: You're going to eat for the baby, right?

I smile wryly at him and nod. "Yes, Michael. I'm hungry." Translation: Yes, I'm going to eat for the baby. Grateful for the respite and knowing that my rest now has a higher purpose, I return to a lying position and close my eyes.

OK, God. I got nothing. You've rendered me speechless.

Chapter Twenty Six

The last month has flown by. The bruises eventually went from nasty black and blue to a putrid green, then yellow, and finally faded completely. I am very grateful for that; Michael can stand to look at me now without a pained expression. He still treats me with kid gloves, however. It's annoying at times, helpful at others. It all depends on the day and my corresponding mood.

The soreness doesn't so much disappear as shifts. My pelvis and hips continue to ache constantly, except when I'm still. It takes a conscious effort not to grunt every time I rise from a sitting position. My clothes are getting even tighter and I am noticeably more tired. I'm not sure if the tight clothes are from the growing baby or because I've had to stop running or both. Starting about a week ago when the bruising was finally gone, I tried to run. But I couldn't stand the bouncing action; it hurt too much. I tried power walking, but the aching in my hips made that uncomfortable, as well.

On this frosty morning, I'm simply strolling through the neighborhood. Any faster and my hips scream in protest. I try to look like I have a purpose to this exercise by pumping my gloved hands back and forth with determination. It's wise to take it easy; my first OB appointment isn't until later this week. Even though my initial exam was good, I don't want to have, or cause, any problems.

"God, please don't make my pregnancy any harder than this." I mutter as I come around the corner to my own street.

Julie is raking up what smattering of leaves their tiny tree has managed to shed. Cringing internally, I realize there's no way to avoid her seeing me before I can get to my front door. I feel bad about that.

I haven't totally avoided Julie since getting the news of my pregnancy, but I haven't exactly gone out of my way to seek her out, either. I see her every week in church, of course. Michael is more determined than ever to make this a regular Strauss family activity, and I agree. We still haven't told the kids about the pregnancy, and I come up blank every time I try to think of how to break the news to Julie. When we tell the kids, we'll have to tell Ben and Julie; the kids won't be able to keep that a secret and I don't want her finding out through them.

God, this is going to break her heart. I don't want to do that!

Maybe God will make Julie pregnant, too. Wouldn't that be wonderful? We could share the joy together rather than having to hurt over it. We could compare notes on appointments and how we feel, maybe even host each other's baby showers… As I mull this over, Julie interrupts me.

"Howdy, stranger!" she calls out enthusiastically. "I haven't seen you much except in church. How are you?" She drops the rake and walks toward me, smiling.

I plant a smile on my face and try very hard to make it look genuine. She is a great friend and I love her, after all. She hugs me gently before pulling back. Her brow furrows.

"Faith, are you feeling completely better now? You look…off. You okay? I'm surprised you're not running."

Oh, Lord. Give me the words.

I shrug it off. "Yeah, I'm okay. The bruising is finally gone. I'm just tired, I guess. I haven't exercised in so long that it's going to take time to get back in shape."

I can't tell if she's convinced or not, but she moves on. "How are you guys holding up?"

The investigation into Michael's company hasn't come to a conclusion and we are still on edge. Fortunately, Michael's prediction about the public's short attention span has panned out. Andrew clings to his belief that we are famous and tries to play it up as much as possible. He even tried to sell his autograph at recess for a quarter, but there were no takers. He was very disappointed.

"We're doing okay. It's stressful, of course. My sessions with Ben are really helpful. He's helping me work through everything, including this investigation. Michael is doing what he can, and the investigation has shifted away from him and most of the top management, but it's far from over." I sigh. "I really hope it's at least done by Christmas. I really don't want to carry this over to next year."

Especially considering what, or who, else is coming next year...

"I can understand that. You've had quite the year already. You deserve a break."

I snort before I can stop myself.

You have no idea, Julie.

"I would agree with that. A break would be nice. How are you guys doing?"

Julie shrugs. "We're fine. Just gearing up for the Fall Festival at church and the upcoming Thanksgiving and Christmas seasons. There are always lots of activities and such going on." She snaps her fingers. "That reminds me! I'm not sure if you might want to do something to get your mind off everything else, but we are always looking for women to serve on various committees. We have the hospitality committee; that runs year round." She starts ticking them off on her fingers. "There's the Thanksgiving basket committee, the Christmas decoration committee..."

"Julie," I interrupt her. "Uh...I appreciate that you've thought of me and I normally would love to do something like that, but I don't think I should take anything else on right now." I'll be busy enough with a new baby in a few months. "I...I just don't think I would be able to focus on it properly."

"Are you sure, Faith? I know you would be such an asset to the ladies and the church as a whole..." she continues.

I shake my head. "No, really I shouldn't. There's enough going on right now to keep my head spinning. Besides, until the investigation is resolved, we really don't know what's in Michael's future."

"Okay. But some of the committees are short term..." she tries again.

I remain firm, knowing Julie doesn't know the real reason I can't. Unfortunately, she will soon enough. "I'm really sorry, Julie. I just can't."

Her face flashes disappointment briefly. "I understand. But if you change your mind, let me know. Your help will never come too late." She shivers. "Gosh, it's cold out here! I better go finish raking. You go inside and warm up."

We exchange hugs and part ways. Latching the door closed behind me, I look up.

"Hey, God. It's me. Would you please make Julie pregnant? Please? I mean, they really want a baby and she's such a sweet person and if anybody deserves to be a mom, it's her. Pretty please? Amen."

I wander into the kitchen scooping a handful of M&Ms as I pass through, shoving half of them in my mouth immediately. I had planned to go upstairs and change, but halfway up a horrible wave of nausea hits. I clap my free hand over my mouth. In a flash, I determine the downstairs bathroom is closest.

Bolting down the stairs, I barely make it to the toilet in time to drop on my knees and wretch loudly into the waiting pool of water.

Oh, no! Not the chocolate!

Yes, that's my first thought. Don't judge me.

Wretching noisily into the toilet, I drop the remaining M&Ms all over the floor. They make a *clickety clack* sound as they scatter. Heaving one last time, a few M&Ms crunch under my knees.

Struggling to catch my breath, I fall back onto my bottom and pull my knees up to my chest shakily. I had forgotten how bad morning sickness can be. Waiting a few moments longer to be sure the nausea has completely passed; I drag myself to a standing position at the sink. I'm pale and covered in a sheen of sweat. Splashing cold water on my face, I rinse my mouth out, squeeze my eyes shut and flush the toilet without looking. I don't want to risk a whole new round of heaving.

I take the stairs much more slowly this time, hoping to avoid more nausea.

The next wave of nausea doesn't hit until after my shower. Perhaps bending down to dry my legs or turning around to hang the towel up caused it. However it hit, it hit just as fast and hard.

Lunging for the toilet, I drop to my knees again and wretch…and wretch…and wretch. Dry heaving is the absolute worst. Is there anything more humiliating than dry heaving into your toilet while naked?

Once the nausea subsides, I opt for underclothes and my robe. I'm worn out and it's only lunchtime.

Lunch time. Food. Ick!

"No food. Bleh." I shudder and crawl into bed instead. Hoping to take a quick nap, I close my eyes and curl onto my side. Sighing, I instantly drift into unconsciousness.

****

A warm hand on my forehead followed by soft stroking on my head rouses me. "Faith? Honey? You okay?"

I struggle to open my eyes. "Hm? Michael?" I yawn and roll over, blinking. "What time is it?" I slowly push up on my elbows, becoming more awake and aware. Michael shouldn't be home yet. I glance over at the clock and my eyes bug. It's almost three o'clock.

"Gah!" I sit up quickly and instantly regret it. The strong wave of nausea that's becoming irritatingly familiar rolls over me again. I push Michael out of the way in my desperation to get to the bathroom.

"Faith?" Michael asks, following closely on my heels. "What's wrong?"

Unable to answer him, I dive onto my knees in front of the toilet and wretch once again.

"Oh." The faucet turns on briefly and suddenly a cool cloth is on my forehead. "Sorry, honey."

Still unable to answer, I barely catch my breath before another wretch undulates up from my toenails. The toilet, a willing receptacle if ever there was one, remains maddeningly empty. I've got nothing to show for my effort.

That's disappointing. There should be at least one toenail, for crying out loud.

Once the desire to heave mercifully dissipates, I fall back on my bottom and lean against the wall to catch my breath, clutching the cloth to my face with shaky hands. Michael rubs my arm.

"I'm so sorry, Faith," he says. He sits down next to me and puts his arm around me, pulling me over to place my head on his shoulder. "How long has this been going on?"

I shake my head and take a few more deep breaths before pulling the cloth away to answer him. "Since this morning. I went for a very slow walk because apparently that's all I'm capable of anymore. I came in to take a shower, but had to throw everything up first. Then I threw up after my shower, took a nap, and just threw up again." I smile wryly. "Lovely, isn't it? How was your day? And why are you home so early?"

He kisses my forehead. "You feel clammy. You haven't eaten or drank anything all day?"

"I did eat and drink, but none of it stayed down."

"Hmmm," Michael regards me. "I'll go get some water and you can at least sip it. Do you feel like eating some crackers or something?" He remembers the drill from my other pregnancies. Only with Sarah did I not get very sick. This one, however, may take the cake.

Cake. Oh, no…

I lunge for the toilet and dry heave all over again.

"Oh, Faith. God, I'm so sorry," he says remorsefully.

I can't even reassure him. I'm too busy trying to breathe between wretches.

"Mom? Dad?" April's voice is distant, but approaching rapidly.

Michael grumbles under his breath before answering her. I can't speak. "April! We're up here!" He kisses the top of my heaving head. "I'll be right back." He departs quickly, closing our bedroom door on his way out. I continue to gag into the still ridiculously empty toilet.

Once this particular episode is complete, I lie on the floor and curl up on my side, closing my eyes.

I hear footfalls and assume, correctly, that it's Michael. "Faith?" His voice is high pitched. "Honey, are you awake?" He drops down beside me, hand on my head again.

"I'm fine," I murmur. "I just don't want to move. I don't want to throw up."

"Let's sit you up slowly then. I can't leave you on the bathroom floor." He slides his arm under my neck and slowly pulls me to a sitting position. Thankfully, no nausea accompanies the movement. "Here." I open my eyes and he places a glass to my lips. I curl my shaky hands around it and sip slowly. I am parched and really want to rinse my mouth out; bile is nasty. I take another small mouthful. Still no nausea. Maybe, just maybe it has stopped for now.

Michael rises to rinse the washcloth, replacing it on my head. "I'm sorry, Faith. Truly I am."

I smile weakly. "It's okay. This too shall pass, right?"

He sighs heavily. "I hope it does and soon."

"What did you tell April? Are Sarah and Andrew home, too?"

He nods. "Yeah, they're all home. I told April you weren't feeling well. All three kids are really worried about you. Faith, we need to tell them what's going on. They need to know. We can't keep it from them, especially with you throwing up like this." His eyes dart around my face. "I don't mean this in a bad way, but you look awful. When they see you they're going to get scared and imagine the worst unless we tell them why."

I chuckle. "Well, at least I look as bad as I feel. I've got nothing else to show for it." I gesture toward the empty toilet.

Michael shakes his head and smiles. "That's one way to look at it."

"You never answered my question, Michael. Why are you home so early?"

"Oh! Well, Julie called me. Apparently, she came and knocked on the door, and when you didn't answer, she got worried. She practically banged on it because she knew you were home. She said you didn't look well when she talked to you this morning and was really worried about you, so she called me at work. Since I know you're pregnant, I was worried something had happened. I raced home to find you asleep in bed, looking very pale, I might add." His brows furrow. "Is this the first day you've thrown up?"

I nod and stand slowly. Michael is quick to offer his help, which I don't decline. I feel weak. Michael places the glass of water on the counter before helping me into the bedroom.

"Do you want to lie down again?" he asks.

"I'll sit in the chair for now."

"Are you sure?"

I nod. After settling me into the soft cushions of the corner chair, he retrieves the glass of water and presses it into my hand. "Better?"

"Yes." I take a deep breath and another sip of water. "I think you're right. We need to tell the kids. I don't want them to worry." A quiet knock on the door interrupts me.

Michael and I look at each other meaningfully.

"Yes?" Michael asks loudly.

"Uh…we're all wondering. What's for dinner?" asks Sarah from the other side of the door. "And why are there M&Ms scattered all over the bathroom floor downstairs?"

Michael looks at me, his eyebrows rising. "M&Ms?" he mouths silently.

Dinner…food.

I clamp my hand over my mouth and shake my head, expecting another wave of nausea to overtake me. Thank God, all I feel is a slight twinge in my stomach, nothing more.

"Hang on, Sarah. Go downstairs and I'll be down in a few." Michael stares at me, his eyebrows raised in a wordless question.

"Okay," Sarah answers. Soon, I hear her footfalls on the stairs.

I look at him and shake my head, dropping my hand to my stomach. "I'm okay. I was eating some M&Ms when the first wave of nausea hit me. I dropped them on the floor when I started throwing up. Sorry. Did you tell Julie I'm all right?"

"Yes. I called her when I went downstairs earlier."

I grip the arm rest and lean forward. "You didn't tell her I was pregnant, did you?"

"No. She is really worried about you, though. I can't imagine what she's thinking."

"I know. I have no idea how to tell her and Ben about this. It'll break their hearts." I place my hand over my chest.

"When we tell the kids, we have to be sure they understand they can't tell them yet. I want to be the one to tell Julie, Michael."

I'm going to need your help, God.

"You'll figure it out, Faith." He grimaces, reaching into his pants pocket. "I almost forgot. I brought these for you. I thought you'd probably not want anything else at the moment." He offers me a lunch baggie of soda crackers.

Chuckling, I take the baggie from him and open it, pulling out a cracker. "That's very thoughtful. Thank you. What are you going to feed the kids? I took hamburger out to thaw this morning." The thought makes me queasy and I swallow hard, closing my eyes.

"Faith…" Michael starts.

I hold up one hand to stop him, trying hard to settle my stomach before I continue. Once the feeling passes, I look up. "Just go make something for the kids. I'll come down when I feel better. These crackers will help." I nibble one corner to prove my point. "Maybe I'm more nauseated because my stomach is so empty."

"Okay. I hope the smell doesn't make it worse, though. We should talk to the kids after dinner."

I nod and nibble another bite. "Yeah, I guess you're right."

He kisses me and quietly slips out. I sink back into the chair and continue nibbling slowly. The queasiness is at bay for the moment. That really came on strong; it's never happened like that before. But then again, all of my pregnancies have been different, why shouldn't this one make its own mark?

Even though it's been a month since we found out, I am still in awe. It doesn't seem real, although puking is certainly making it real enough.

I eat one more cracker before I make a careful attempt at getting up to refill my glass of water in the bathroom. I'm so thirsty, but force myself to sip rather than gulp. I will do anything I can to avoid being brought to my knees again.

Satisfied with my attempts, I get dressed just as slowly and go downstairs. Simple yoga pants (hooray for stretchy waistbands…) and a T shirt are the easiest clothing to manage

302

without requiring too much movement. I hope the smell isn't too pungent, whatever Michael decided to make.

I grip my baggie of soda crackers and open the bedroom door. Moving to the top of the steps, I take a deep breath and identify the smells associated with spaghetti. It doesn't disagree with my stomach, so I slowly descend the stairs.

Michael is plating pasta and meat sauce when I enter the kitchen. He spies me and puts the plate down, quickly coming to my side.

He rubs my arms and kisses my forehead. "How're you doing?"

I shrug. "Not puking for the moment."

My attempt at humor falls flat. "You can go lie down on the sofa. I was just about to call the kids for dinner."

I look around. It's eerily silent. "Where are they?"

"Andrew's in the basement and the girls are in their rooms doing homework. Is the smell too strong?"

I shake my head, moving toward the living room and the sofa. "No, but it doesn't really smell good, either."

He follows me. "Is there anything else you want me to make for you? Something simple and bland?"

I shake my head vigorously. "No! Please, nothing except my crackers right now." I shake my baggie at him, settling down onto the sofa with a grunt.

"Let me know if you change your mind." He moves toward the stairs and calls up to the girls before calling Andrew up from the basement, then disappears into the kitchen to finish plating. Within minutes, they're all making their appearances. April is the first to spy me on the sofa, quickly followed by Sarah and Andrew.

"Gosh, Mom. You look like death warmed over!" April exclaims. "What's wrong with you?"

"I feel like death warmed over, honey. Don't worry, I'll be okay. It'll pass. You guys go eat dinner. I'm not very hungry." I wave them off.

Andrew looks worried and sits down next to me. "Mommy, I thought the doctor made you better."

Sarah lingers in the doorway.

I smooth his hair. "I'm okay, Andrew. Honestly. Remember when you got that tummy ache and threw up?" He nods. "That's sort of what I feel like right now. It will go away. Now go eat." I pat his back and he gets up, heading slowly for the kitchen.

Sarah has already disappeared. My heart reaches out to them.

Don't worry, kids. You'll know soon enough.

I hope they'll be good with it. I have no idea what their reactions are going to be. As has been the case so many times over the years, I'd be willing to bet they'll surprise me.

****

Dinner's almost done; I can hear the scraping of the chairs as they start to rise from the table.

"Kids, your mom and I want to talk to you guys in the living room once the table is cleared and the dishes are loaded," Michael calls to the kids as he appears from the kitchen and walks toward me.

He nods and asks quietly, "You ready, honey?" He sits down next to me and places his hand on my knee, giving it a gentle squeeze.

"As ready as I'll ever be," I shrug.

"Any more nausea?"

"Thankfully, no. The crackers helped." I gesture to the empty baggie on the coffee table.

"Do you want to eat anything else? Does anything sound good?"

I grimace. "No. I'm still not hungry."

He nods once and looks up. "Here they come," he murmurs quietly. The kids file in, wordlessly finding a seat. Sarah is the farthest away and I find that troubling. She's been distant since her incident and I don't know how to fix it. I don't know if this will bring her closer or push her farther away.

"Okay, parental units. Let's get this show on the road!" April proclaims. "What's wrong with you that requires a family meeting?" Her light-hearted words don't match her eyes; she looks scared.

304

I don't want to drag this out. I look over at Michael and he returns my gaze. "Do you want to start, Faith?" he asks quietly.

Taking a deep breath, I nod tersely and straighten my back. "Kids, we have some big news for you. It's good news." I look pointedly at April first, then Sarah, and finally rest my gaze on Andrew.

I might as well throw it right out there.

I squeeze my eyes shut for a brief second and proclaim, "I'm pregnant."

OK, God, there it is. What are you going to do with it?

Chapter Twenty Seven

Silence. We engender that reaction a lot. I wonder if it's genetic… Much to my surprise, Sarah is the first to break it.

"You're what?!" she yells, gripping the arm rests of her chair.

"I'm pregnant, Sarah. I'm going to have a baby," I reply quietly. "You guys are going to have another little brother or sister."

"Ew! That is so gross!!" chirps April.

"Cool!" is Andrew's reaction. I imagine now that he's both famous and cool, he won't know what to do with himself.

Michael shakes his head. "Listen, kids. We wanted to let you know because, well, you need to know. Your mother is due in about six months. Her first appointment is this week and we should get a more accurate due date then. That's why she's feeling sick. It's morning sickness."

"But it's not morning," Andrew blurts, looking confused.

I laugh. "Honey, it's called morning sickness because it usually happens in the morning. But it doesn't have to be in the morning."

"Oh." His face remains clouded over. "Then why don't they just call it any time sickness?"

"I don't know, sweetie."

Sarah sighs loudly. "Because any time sickness sounds dumb, Andrew!"

"Sarah, it doesn't sound dumb," Michael sighs wearily. "Be nice to your brother, please."

Andrew sticks his tongue out and we ignore it. There are bigger fish to fry at the moment.

"What do you think, Sarah?" I ask her.

She regards me, apparently thinking very hard about what to say. I tense up and squeeze Michael's hand. I'm surprised by her answer.

She shrugs. "I don't know. It's okay, I guess." She looks from me to Michael and back to me. This is the sort of answer I would expect from the old Sarah; very pragmatic. "Did you guys want more kids or something?"

"Uh, no, Sarah. We hadn't planned on having more children. But," Michael looks at me, "God apparently has other plans. Part of that plan includes one more child." He smiles at me and then turns his smile on Sarah. "So, we're going to have one more child in this family."

"Oh! Oh! I hope I get a brother!" squeals Andrew, bouncing in his seat. "Mom, can you ask God to give me a brother? That would be awesome!"

We both laugh at this most simple of requests. "It doesn't work quite like that, Andrew. But you can certainly pray and ask God anything you want. Just remember, He doesn't always have to give us what we want."

Andrew's enthusiasm won't be quenched. "I'm sure I'll get a brother. I think God knows how cool that would be! Woo hoo!" He jumps up and down.

We turn our attention to April and brace ourselves for the worst. "April, what are your thoughts?" She has the most disgusted look on her face; her nose is wrinkled and her mouth is open.

"It's just gross! I mean, you're old. How can you guys have more kids? This is so embarrassing." She buries her face in her hands.

"April, we are not old. There are a lot of couples out there our age that have toddlers and babies right now. Their first babies, I might add," Michael replies.

"Other than the fact that we're old, how do you feel about this?" I ask.

April throws her hands up. "Does it matter at this point? What's done is done." She sighs heavily and throws herself back in the chair.

"It matters to us. Everyone here," I look at each of them, "matters to us."

April looks at me. "I guess I'm okay with it, too. I mean, I thought maybe you had some horrible disease or something. So having another brother or sister isn't so bad, considering that. But I still think it's sort of gross for my parents to be pregnant when I'm in high school." She grimaces and shudders. Michael sighs.

Well, that's a better reaction than I could've anticipated.

"All right." Let's move on. "I really need you guys to keep this to yourselves for the time being. That means you can't tell your friends or anyone at all, but especially not Miss Julie. I want to tell her myself that I'm pregnant. Remember her reaction when you asked her about kids, April?" April squirms. "Well, I want to be sure to be the one to tell her when I'm ready. I don't want to upset her."

They all nod in agreement. Looking directly at Andrew, I say, "You, too, Andrew. You can't tell anybody."

He looks crestfallen. "Not even my friends at school?" he whines.

"Not even your friends at school. I'm sorry, but you have to wait a little while longer." I smooth his hair.

He throws himself back onto the sofa with a groan. "But, how long do I have to wait?"

Sighing, I look over at Michael. He shrugs. "It's your call, Faith."

Turning my attention back to Andrew I reply, "I'll let you know, Andrew. I will try to do that very soon."

"Gosh Andrew, if April can keep it a secret, then you can, too!" Sarah huffs and rolls her eyes. April glares at her.

What has gotten into Sarah lately?!

I squeeze my eyes shut. "Sarah, please."

"Do you guys have any questions?" Michael interjects.

"How long is the…sickness going to last, Mom?" Andrew asks.

My shoulders relax; this is easy to answer. "I don't know, sweetie. I hope it doesn't last too long. I don't like it any more than you do. It just depends. Sometimes it lasts for a few weeks or it can last a few months." I shrug. "It's hard to tell."

His eyes widen. "That long? That's awful!" His brow furrows. "I don't like that my baby brother makes you sick."

I squeeze his shoulders. "Oh, honey. The baby isn't making me sick. It is just part of being pregnant."

He looks mournfully at me. "Did I make you sick when I was in your tummy?"

Deciding on the easier course, I lie. "No, you didn't make me sick."

His face relaxes. "Good." He smiles, satisfied.

"Do you girls have any questions?" I ask. Sarah is deep in thought; oh for mind reading equipment not to be science fiction! April still looks mildly disgusted. A few moments of silence ensue.

Finally, Sarah simply sucks her lips in and shakes her head slowly before saying, "Nope."

I really wish she'd open up.

Rather than asking a question, April replies, "I have no idea how I'm going to tell my friends about this!" Her eyes dart between Michael and me before she modifies her statement. "I mean, when I actually can tell them about this, of course."

Michael claps his hands on his thighs. "Okay. If you guys don't have anymore questions, I think we're done. You can get your homework done if you have any or go take showers or whatever."

They slowly file out of the living room in pursuit of their own interests. Michael sighs, laces his fingers behind his head and sinks back on the sofa letting his breath out in a noisy puff. "Well, that wasn't so bad."

"Yeah." My thoughts are already elsewhere. "It went over pretty well. I'm more concerned with how to tell Julie."

"That's a tough call. There's not really going to be any easy way to break this news."

"Now that we've told the kids, I really do need to tell Julie soon, don't I?"

He nods sympathetically. "I think so."

"You know what's ironic about this? If this situation involved anyone else but Julie, I would be asking Julie or Pastor Ben for advice on how to break the news." I rub my face, suddenly tired even though I've slept most of the day. "I think I'll just go to bed and think about this tomorrow." Yawning to punctuate my point, I grunt as I rise from the sofa.

Michael looks at me incredulously. "Are you really still tired?"

"Weird, I know, but I just can't keep my eyes open. This pregnancy is kicking my butt. Maybe I am too old for this…"

Michael chuckles and rises to accompany me. "You mean maybe we're too old for this."

"We shall see!" I smile valiantly at him as I take the stairs slowly, Michael beside me. "You don't have to escort me to bed."

He shrugs and continues to follow closely behind me. "I don't have to, but I will."

"Fine," I mutter.

Once I'm settled in with no further nausea, I gratefully accept a goodnight kiss from Michael and barely register his leaving the room before I fall into unconsciousness with one final thought.

Prepare the way, Lord. Prepare the way. Please.

Chapter Twenty Eight

Peering at the wall calendar hanging above the house phone, I groan at how quickly time is flying. Halloween is creeping up and the holidays will be here before I know it. I haven't given any of it much thought. I'm trying to decide when to have Michelle, Lilly, and Brenda over to break the big news. I want to plan it no more than two weeks away. That gives me a deadline to tell Julie; I have to tell her first because I want to invite her over to meet my friends. For her to find out for the first time in front of everybody would be cruel.

My first OB appointment went well; everything is progressing normally. I'm due in early spring and about to enter my second trimester. I don't know which thought is more dumbfounding to me; the fact that it didn't occur to me I might be pregnant or that I actually am pregnant. Both ideas are ludicrous although they're my reality.

My obstetrician is a younger female doctor that took over the practice from the OB I had used for my three older children. Her bedside manner is very good, and Michael and I agree we're comfortable with her. Plus, she has two children of her own. Of course, we were counseled on the need to have genetic testing because of my age. She recommended waiting until my second trimester to lower the possibility of a false positive test. The possibilities fester in the recesses of my mind while we wait.

Skimming my finger over the neat row of days, it lands on the little square for next Friday; it's empty. I tap it twice then grab my cell. Taking a deep breath, I send a group text to everyone except Julie. I want to call her personally. I squeeze my eyes shut and hit send.

"There, it's done," I mutter, snatching a pen from the cup we keep full of pens and pencils, plus an odd nail file and paper clip, and scribble it on the calendar. My palms sweat as I contemplate dialing Julie's number. I have to tell her today or tomorrow so she can take some time to decide if she wants to meet my friends next week.

Pausing briefly to say a quick prayer, I dial. I press the phone to my ear and wait for her to answer. Her cheerful voice answers on the third ring.

"Good morning, Faith! How are you today?" she bubbles.

"Hi, Julie! I'm fine, just fine." I pace the kitchen.

I might as well get this over with.

Sighing, I continue, "I just wanted to call and see if you'd like to come over tomorrow morning for some coffee. I would love to talk to you about something."

"Oh! I would love to! Would you like me to come this afternoon instead? I don't have anything going on."

Afternoons aren't good; my morning sickness has been at its worst in the afternoon. "No! Uh, sorry. I...can't this afternoon. Are you available tomorrow morning?"

"Oh. Sure, no problem! What time is good for you? Would you like me to make some coffee cake, too?"

I bite my lip before answering; coffee cake doesn't sound good, nor does most food. My stomach roils in response. "Oh, gosh. Julie, please don't go to any trouble. I...I haven't been feeling too well lately and I'm afraid my stomach is...still sore." That sounds lame, even to me.

"Still? You're still not feeling well, Faith? Bless your heart. What can I do?"

I keep my voice even. "Nothing. Just your company will do. I'm okay, really. It's just...going to take awhile to get over this."

Julie doesn't sound convinced, but she doesn't pry. She agrees to come tomorrow morning at nine thirty. That will give me almost a full day to prepare what I'm going to say.

My cell beeps throughout the day with responses first from Brenda, who's always enthusiastic about everything, then from Lilly, and finally from Michelle. All three are available.

I spend most mornings lying down and most afternoons making my daily offering to the toilet bowl, sipping water or hot tea in between. Running is completely out; although the bruising is gone, the soreness remains. My doctor said it's normal for "older women like myself" to experience more physical discomfort with pregnancy. Naturally, I'm thrilled (not!). But this is my life right now.

Dinners around the Strauss house are composed of take out, delivery, or sandwiches. I can't stomach cooking, much less eating. The smells from the cartons and boxes are enough to send me out of the room. The kids are sympathetic, as is Michael. There's nothing they can do; I simply have to get through it.

Which I will….I hope.

****

Wiping my mouth as I rise from kneeling in front of the toilet for the third time this afternoon, I'm interrupted by Michael's entry into the bathroom. His sudden appearance makes me jerk.

"Sorry, honey. I didn't mean to scare you." He approaches me cautiously and kisses my cheek. "It's still no better, huh?"

I shake my head and grimace. "I at least kept my eggs down from breakfast this morning. It always hits in the afternoon." I splash water on my face and pat it dry. "I really hope it stops soon. It was never this bad with the others."

"Yeah, I remember." He follows me into the living room where I plop down on the sofa with a grunt; it's my bed away from bed. "Where are the kids?"

I rest my head back and gaze up at him. There aren't any sports practices today; it's Friday. "They're all downstairs. Michael, I really stink at being a mother right now. I mean, I can't cook, I can't keep my eyes open, and they're all avoiding me like the plague. What's going on?" My eyes well with tears.

He sits down next to me. "What do you mean they're avoiding you like the plague?"

"They're always upstairs in their rooms or downstairs in the basement. I don't tell them to do that. Why are they doing that?"

"Maybe they're trying to help you feel better." He looks sheepishly at me. "I sort of told them to leave you alone because of how you feel."

I groan. "Michael, I don't want them to avoid me. I'm not…I'm just pregnant. They…" I clap my hand over my mouth as a strong wave of nausea hits me. Leaping up, I run for the bathroom to resume my previous posture at the toilet. Michael follows and crouches beside me, rubbing my back as I heave.

Once the nausea passes, I clean myself up (again) and return to the sofa. This time I lie down and close my eyes. I hear the fabric of Michael's pants rustle as he silently sits in the chair next to the sofa.

"Michael," I say softly, turning my head to look at him. "I really don't like this. Tell the kids not to avoid me anymore, okay?"

He sighs. "I will. I'm sorry about this, too. I don't like seeing you suffer. I think it worries them."

"Yeah, I hope it doesn't last long." Although I hate to think of it, my mind turns to dinner. I don't want to eat, but my family needs to. "What are you going to do for dinner?"

He shrugs. "I think we'll just get pizza again."

A stab of guilt hits me. "That's twice this week, Michael. Isn't there anything else?"

He smiles crookedly. "It's quick and easy, Faith. It's not going to kill any of us to eat like this for a little while." He rises and bends over to kiss my forehead. "Besides, you'll be back on your feet in no time and making good food again. The kids will appreciate it more when you do." He grins, crosses the room and disappears into the kitchen to call for the pizza.

God, please make this go away soon. I really need to get back to taking care of my family.

"Oh!" I prop myself up on my elbows. "Michael!"

His head pops around the corner. "Yeah?"

"I am going to tell Julie tomorrow morning. Any ideas how I should break it to her?"

He looks surprised. "Oh! Uh…I don't know. Just break it to her gently. You've always been good with words. I'm sure you'll think of something." His head disappears back in the kitchen.

I fall back on the sofa, grumbling. "Thanks for the help," I mutter under my breath. Placing my forearm over my eyes, I mull over how to tell Julie in a way that won't hurt. Michael and I already have three children and this fourth one is a complete surprise. Julie and Ben have been struggling for so long trying to have just one child. I can't see how to make this easy.

The doorbell interrupts my musings; the pizza delivery has arrived. I hear multiple footfalls on the basement stairs as the kids burst into the room at the sound. Michael reaches the door quickly and retrieves the boxes. I steal myself for the onslaught of smells. Surprisingly, it doesn't bring another round of nausea. My spirits buoyed, I rise (grunting, always grunting…) slowly and join my family in the kitchen.

Andrew sidles up to me and hugs me gently around the waist. "Are you feeling any better?" he asks. His brow furrows suddenly as he steps back and rubs my lower belly slowly. "Mom, is that lump the baby?"

My hand immediately retraces the path his hand took. Activity suddenly stops in the kitchen and all eyes are on me. There is a definite pooch to my lower belly I hadn't noticed.

Wow. This is happening fast.

I smile down at Andrew and squeeze him hard against me, taking in his little boy scent. "Yes, I am, and yes, it is the baby."

"Cool! But it's so small. Aren't babies supposed to be bigger than that?"

"Yes, but it takes months and months before they're big enough to be born."

"Okay." He pats my stomach and then releases me, intent on grabbing the first slice of cheese pizza. It amazes me how he can so quickly go from one thing to the next.

"Mom?" April asks. "Can I feel?" I look at her and she has her nose wrinkled with her hands extended, palms up.

315

"Sure," I shrug and hold my hands away from my body. She approaches and places her hand on my belly. She presses gently a few times, a look of concentration on her face.

"It's so hard!" she says. "Is that what it's supposed to feel like?"

Sarah approaches cautiously and places her hand on my belly, too, right next to April.

"Yes," I laugh, glancing over at Michael. He's leaning against the counter with his arms crossed, taking the whole scene in with a look of amused gratification.

"Wow," Sarah says very softly. "There really is a baby on the way, isn't there?" She lifts her gaze to me and her eyes are glistening. Mine glisten in response. A mother's heart will always be threaded to the heart of her children.

I cup her face and rub her cheek with my thumb for just a moment; she still has slight baby roundness to her features I know will disappear all too soon. "Yes, there is," I whisper.

Sarah drops her gaze again. "Do you hope it's another boy or girl?"

"I hope it's a girl!" April chirps, dropping her hand from my belly. "Think about it, Sarah. We can dress her up like a doll and stuff! Wouldn't that be so much fun?!" She grins at her sister.

Sarah huffs a laugh. "Yeah, I suppose."

Andrew groans from the table, where he's already devoured one pizza slice and is working hard on his second. "I want a brother. There are enough sisters in this house." He looks pointedly at me. "Mom, tell them I get a brother this time!"

Michael chuckles and shakes his head. "Andrew, we don't get to choose if it's a boy or a girl."

"I know you want a brother, Andrew. Just remember that regardless of whether it's a boy or a girl, you're still going to be a big brother." I smile.

He considers this for a moment, chewing thoughtfully. "Yeah, but I still want a baby brother."

"You never said what you want, Mom." Sarah reminds me, dropping her hand. "Plus the pizza is getting cold." She turns toward the boxes and helps herself.

"Let's go ahead and eat and we can talk about it." Grabbing a plate, I pull a slice of cheese pizza out of the box. Michael looks questioningly at me.

"Honey, you okay to eat?" he asks.

"Why not?" I shrug. "I'm hungry and the smell didn't make me leave the room this time. So we'll see." Sitting down, I take a very small nibble and chew cautiously.

"To answer your question, Sarah, I really don't mind having another girl or boy. I have both and love it. Dad and I are just praying the baby is healthy and well."

"I still want a brother," mutters Andrew, glaring at his sisters as if to challenge them. April sticks her tongue out at him and he does the same.

"Okay, you two. That's enough or you don't get any more pizza." Michael's threat is toothless; he's grinning.

"I guess I don't care either way. It would be fun to dress up a little sister but I like little brothers, too," Sarah says, smiling wryly at Andrew.

"That's very sweet, Sarah." I reach over to squeeze her hand and to my delight, she squeezes back. The exchange settles something in me; she's going to be all right. I smile at Michael who is still grinning. It's another moment in my life I wish I could freeze.

We finish our dinner and conversation happily. The pizza stays down. What a relief. Perhaps things are looking up after all.

I am so grateful, God.

Chapter Twenty Nine

I glance at the clock for the twentieth time this morning. It's nine-fifteen. Julie will be here soon. My stomach is churning from nerves this time rather than nausea. I haven't decided what to say and don't know how I'll be able to get any words out anyway.

I measure out small scoops of ground coffee, decaffeinated now because I am pregnant, into the paper liner of the coffee maker. After pouring water into the machine, I hit the button to begin brewing. Instead of sitting down, I pace back and forth.

"Okay, God," I pray out loud. "She's coming over. I need you to be here and to protect her heart, please. Don't hurt her!" I whine at the ceiling.

The chiming of the doorbell makes me jump. With one final pleading glance at the ceiling, I walk toward the door rubbing my hands together. Taking a deep breath, I grasp the doorknob, plant a smile on my face, and open the door.

Julie's beaming face greets me as she wraps me in an enthusiastic hug.

"Good morning, Faith! How are you feeling?" she asks as I usher her through the kitchen and into the dining room to take a seat at the table.

"I'm feeling pretty good right now. The coffee is just about done, so I'll go grab our mugs." I smile.

"You're still not up for any coffee cake, though? I did bake some this morning just in case, but left it at home," she calls after me as I disappear into the kitchen.

"No, I'm sorry. You shouldn't have gone to the trouble," I chide her, returning with two steaming mugs to place on the table before retrieving the sugar and cream from the kitchen. She accepts her mug gratefully. "I hope it will get better soon." My stomach knots up anticipating what I have to do, so I simply swirl the cream and sugar in my mug, but don't sip any of it. Wanting to buy some time to gather my nerve, I start the conversation elsewhere.

"How are you doing, Julie? I'm sorry I haven't seen much of you lately."

She sips pleasurably from her mug. "Oh, we're fine. Nothing terribly exciting going on at the Jackson household. I'm more concerned with how you're doing."

I can't do this yet.

"I'm…going to be okay. Listen, I am having my girlfriends over for a party next Friday evening, and would love for you to come. It's Lilly, Michelle, and Brenda. I'm sure I've mentioned them to you before. Anyway, we get together for a girl's night every so often and I want to introduce you. This is the perfect opportunity to meet them."

My heart sinks into the floor; this will be so painful for her. It's probably stupid of me to invite her to this party, because that's where I'm going to announce my pregnancy, but I have to buy time.

"Oh, that would be lovely! I have to check my calendar, though. There's a ministry at the church that happens on Friday evenings and I can't remember if it's going to be that Friday or not. I'm part of the crew that volunteers to help with childcare. Can I let you know?" she asks, taking another sip from her mug.

I nod quickly, trying to maintain a smile.

Julie's face flashes confusion for a brief moment. "Faith, what's wrong? You're just not yourself."

Silence hangs in the air while I drop my gaze and stir my still full mug. The only sound is the *clink clink* as the spoon makes contact with my mug.

God, help me please! Help *her*.

I sigh and meet Julie's gaze, her face awash in patient concern.

Oh, that expression is going to change. I hate that I'm the one who's going to do it.

I grip my mug firmly with both hands and look at my friend. "Julie, I don't know how to tell you, so I just have to tell you. I have to say that I have really prayed about this, and I don't know why God is doing what He's doing. Please know that! You are such a strong woman of faith, and I have grown to care deeply for you. You're always doing such wonderful things, and you and Pastor Ben have both been so gracious and helpful. You've done so much for us and I don't know why this is happening..." I take a breath as my eyes fill with tears.

Julie looks even more confused. "Faith, honey, whatever it is just say it! You're not making any sense, and I don't have a clue what you're talking about." She laughs.

A tear falls down my cheek and I reach for her hand and grasp it tightly. "Julie, I'm sorry, but I've been sick lately because I'm...pregnant."

There. I said it.

My eyes scour her face trying to read her reaction. She freezes. A range of emotions flit across her face so fast that I can't decipher them. I can only imagine what they must be.

"Julie, I'm so sorry. Really I am! I don't understand this." More tears fall.

Julie's lips slowly begin to part in what looks like an attempt at a smile, but it looks more like the painful grimace of a person that's just been shot.

"I'm happy for you," She squeaks before clapping her hand over her mouth as she begins to sob, which, of course, makes me sob. I get up and make my way around the table, wrapping my arms around her shoulders, muttering over and over how very sorry I am. She shakes her head, buries her face in her hands and continues to sob.

Eventually, I lead her into the living room and we sit together on the sofa, both crying. She for the pain of her infertility and me for the pain my fertility causes her.

It's not fair.

I grab a fistful of tissues from the box on the side table and hand half to her. She blows her nose noisily and I do the same.

"Julie," I begin in a shaky voice. "Please know that I am so sorry about this. I really am. We weren't..." I stop myself just in time because saying that we weren't trying is not going to be helpful here. "I'm just so sorry."

Julie looks down at her hands for a few moments where she's nervously twirling the tissues into a wad. "Faith, I know. You haven't done anything to me. Don't misunderstand why I'm crying." She looks at me pleadingly. "I really am happy for you. I just…" She shakes her head and opens the wad to blow her nose once more. "I just don't understand. I know that I am not always supposed to understand, but there are times that I wish I did."

I don't know what to say, so I pat her knee and wipe my eyes. "I wish I could understand, too. You are such a doll and…I want everything for you that you want."

She genuinely smiles at me this time, although there's still a shadow of the painful grimace lingering. "Thanks." She takes deep breaths. "I am happy for you, Faith. How far along are you?"

I study her for a moment. "Almost four months."

Her eyebrows shoot up as she glances briefly down at my belly. "That far? Wow. I've never made it past three." Her gaze turns wistful and her eyes fill with fresh tears, as do mine.

"I'm sorry."

"Faith, it's okay." She shrugs, tears gently cascading down her cheeks. "God hasn't forgotten me. He has a plan." Suddenly her back straightens and her eyes harden. "He does." She swipes at the tears on her cheeks and her countenance brightens. Her beaming smile returns.

Unbelievable.

"I'm sure He does." I don't know what else to say.

Does your plan include children for my friend, God?

Defiant and a bit angry, I hope I haven't crossed a line with Him. I feel so fiercely that Julie deserves to be a mom.

How can He not make this happen? Let her hurt like this?

She nods vigorously. "Yes. Now," she rises and turns to me. "Let's go finish our coffee and throw this mess away!" She gestures to the wad of used tissues.

I follow her into the kitchen to throw our tissues away and then back to the dining room. I take a sip of my coffee and immediately spit it back out. "Yuck. Mine's cold. Do you need a fresh cup?"

Julie wrinkles her nose after sipping hers and nods, so we head into the kitchen to dump our mugs and refill them with fresh hot coffee from the carafe.

Expecting Julie to change the subject, she surprises me instead by asking how I'm feeling, what makes me sick, when, how often, and what makes it better. Then she asks about my OB appointment and wants to know every detail about it. I begin to realize that she's trying to feel what it's like to be pregnant through my experience. She doesn't want me to spare her any of the gory details with my puking and even asks if the nausea is the same as the flu. Our conversation goes on for over an hour. Finally, I have to stem the tide of questions because I am exhausted.

"Julie, I'm sorry to break this up, but I'm really getting tired. It's another part of pregnancy, at least for me," I tell her wearily.

She looks mortified. "Oh, Faith! I'm sorry. I should've thought about that. You do look tired." Her eyes roam my face. "Silly me. I'll just get out of your hair." She rises and takes her mug to the kitchen.

I follow her. "Julie, you know that party I'm having next Friday? Well, I am going to tell my friends at that party that I'm pregnant. They don't know yet and I wanted to tell you first. If you don't want to go, I'll understand. I didn't want you to be blind sided."

She places her mug on the counter and turns to me. "It's okay. I hope I can make it. It sounds like fun. I will check my calendar. Thank you for being so considerate, Faith. That means a lot." She gives me a quick hug and pulls away, a strange look on her face. "Can I ask you a question?"

I nod, not sure what could be left to ask.

"Can you feel the baby move yet?"

I shake my head. "No, not yet. But I do have the baby bump. As a matter of fact, the kids noticed it last night." I rub my hand over my lower belly, still shocked that it's extended.

She reaches her hands out, palms up. "May I?" she asks cautiously.

"Go for it!" I quip, thrusting my midsection out.

She slowly places her hands on my belly and closes her eyes, smiling. "Oh. I can feel a hard little bump there!"

I chuckle. "Weird, isn't it?"

She opens her eyes and beams at me. "No. It's wonderful!" She removes her hands and clasps them in front of her. "Thank you, Faith."

Once she's left, I pause for a moment after closing the door. I wonder if Julie is putting on a front, and is going home right now to cry her eyes out again. That's what I would do. She didn't seem to be faking it. I just hope she is as okay as she says she is, even though I don't see how that's possible. She's taught me a lot about faith and hope, but I don't think I could take it as far as she has with something like this. That's too much to ask.

My shoulders slump as I shuffle into the kitchen to turn the coffee pot off before plopping down on the sofa for a nap. Closing my eyes, I have one final thought before slumber wraps me in its warm embrace.

Give them a baby, God. Please. I know you're a big God and can do this. Please.

Chapter Thirty

"Mom. Mom! *Mom!*" April's voice interrupts my slumber. I reluctantly roll over and open my eyes. She's standing over me with her hands on her hips.

"What, April? What time is it?" I mumble, my voice thick with sleep.

She sighs dramatically and glares at me. "It's almost four o'clock, mom. How long have you been asleep? You look terrible."

"Lord," I rub my face, grunt to sit up and yawn loudly. "Most of the day, unfortunately. Sorry."

"What's for dinner?" she asks sarcastically.

I glare. "I don't know," I bark, grunting as I rise from the sofa. "You know, April, you're old enough to fix something to eat. I could use your help. I'm not enjoying this, either."

She pauses. To my shock she utters something unexpected. "Yeah, I guess so. Sorry. How are you feeling?"

I'm dumbstruck, even to the point that my mouth falls open. "Uh. Well, still tired of course and I have a full bladder and dry mouth, but otherwise I'm okay. Where are Sarah and Andrew?" I ask, shuffling toward the bathroom to take care of that most immediate need first.

"They're in the basement, I think," she yells through the closed bathroom door.

After completing my task in the bathroom and drinking an entire glass of water, I turn to April. "April, I'm sorry I snapped at you."

She shrugs. "I had it coming, I suppose. So, what should I whip up for dinner? Sandwiches? Soups? Lobster bisque?" She grins and I laugh.

"I think the lobster bisque would be lovely," I respond.

"Peanut butter and jelly sandwiches it is!" she replies, gathering the supplies.

I shake my head; I can't allow her to feed that to the family for dinner. "No, April. There's lunchmeat and cheese in there and we can at least make grilled cheese, so it's a hot dinner."

She returns the jelly to the refrigerator and rummages around in the pantry. "How about some cream of potato soup, too?" She pulls out a number of cans of soup and looks at me. I nod my approval.

"I will get better eventually, and this will only be a sad memory." I hand her a saucepan to heat the soup and look apologetically at her.

"I know. I just hope it's soon. I may never have kids if this is what it's going to be like," she muses, slathering butter on a slice of bread.

"April, it's only for a short period of time and look at what you get in return!" I gesture grandly to her, smiling.

"Ha! I wouldn't want to raise me!" she jokes.

The easy banter continues. I enjoy it so much I don't notice the absence of nausea. We've all just sat down at the table to eat when Michael walks in and surveys the sight before him, his gaze landing on me.

"Well, it's good to see you at the table with food in front of you, Faith. Is that a good sign?" he asks, joining us.

Can I get a hallelujah?

I smile and lean over to give him a kiss. "I hope so."

"Me too, Mom. I don't like seeing you sick," Andrew pipes in, his face in a frown. "I'll have to talk to my brother about that when he gets here."

"Here, here!" Michael adds. He looks down at his plate. "Well, at least it's hot."

"I made dinner, Dad!" April replies proudly, stuffing a large bite of grilled cheese in her mouth.

Sarah, Andrew, and Michael freeze and look at her in shock. She looks around proudly at each of them once, her expression slowly darkening to a glare for each one the second time around. "What? What's so shocking about that?" she challenges.

"You made dinner?" Sarah asks, bewildered, her spoon suspended in mid air. "I didn't know you could even turn the stove on."

April scowls at her sister, plops her sandwich back on her plate and crosses her arms. "Whatever, Sarah. What do you know about cooking anyway?" She reaches across the table and snatches her sister's plate and bowl out from under her. "Maybe you should go cook something for yourself!"

"Hey! Give that back!" Sarah huffs indignantly, dropping her spoon onto the table to retrieve the stolen dishes. The dropped spoon splatters onto Andrew's plate, causing him to rise in protest.

"Girls! *Girls!*" Michael yells. "That's enough! Sit back down in your chairs."

Sighing, I grab a napkin from the holder and hand it to Sarah. "Sarah, clean up your mess." She snatches it from me. "April, give your sister back her dinner." She does so reluctantly.

"What about mine?" Andrew whines. "She got soup on my sandwich!"

"Andrew, it's okay. Here," I swap his sandwich with mine. "you can have mine."

The solution satisfies him, but April and Sarah continue to glare at each other.

Michael orders the girls to apologize to each other and thanks April for helping out, complimenting her on the dinner. She's mollified for the moment, but both girls remain glum through the remainder of the meal. Fortunately for me, I'm able to keep down a whole sandwich and a bowl of soup.

Afterwards, Sarah clears the table and cleans up the kitchen while Andrew and April finish homework. Michael and I sit on the sofa to relax.

"How was your day?" Michael crosses his legs and leans back to rest his head on the sofa.

"It was good. I slept through the whole afternoon, but Julie came over this morning and I told her about my pregnancy."

His head snaps up. "Oh. How did she take it?"

326

"We both cried." I turn to face him. "Michael, I just can't imagine how she deals with this."

"So she was mad?"

"Mad?" I ask, shocked. "Not at all. Just really disappointed, but she didn't get mad."

"That sounds like her," he replies quietly. "I wonder how Ben will take the news."

"I don't have a clue. How would you take news like this?"

"I don't know. I can't go there, you know? We have three, correction four, kids now so…I don't know. I'd be upset, I guess. It's a real shame they don't have any children."

"Yeah, it was really sweet that she asked me lots of questions about my pregnancy. That was after we got done crying, of course. It was sort of like she was trying to know what it's like to be pregnant."

Michael is quietly thoughtful for a moment. "Why don't you ask if she'd like to come to the next OB appointment?"

"Huh? Why? Do you think she'd want to come?"

"I don't know, maybe. It sounds like she wants to be a part of this, and why not? Maybe it'll be good for her."

"Okay. I'll ask her tomorrow. She can say no if it's not something she wants to do."

"Mom!" April runs down the stairs, tumbling into the living room. "Mom! I need to go shopping, like, now!"

Michael and I both jump. "What are you talking about, April?" I ask, feeling slightly exasperated.

"Mariah already has her dress!" she cries, as if that one sentence will explain everything to her clueless audience.

Michael and I look at each other, befuddled. "Uh, April. What are you talking about? What dress?" I ask.

She slumps forward and then throws her head back in frustration. "The winter dance, Mom. It's coming up in a few weeks!"

Gasping, I clamp my hands on my cheeks. "Oh, April! I completely forgot about that! Sweetie, I'm so sorry."

"Okay, but I still need to get a dress. We need to go shopping!" Her voice takes on a whiny edge.

"Yes, April. We'll go shopping soon, I promise. Probably this weekend, okay?"

"We have to shop before all the good dresses are gone!" she continues to whine.

I sigh and rub my face. "April, the good dresses won't be all gone. I promise. We'll go this weekend. Besides, I need to get costumes for Halloween, too."

"Ugh!" she sighs. "Okay, but we better go this weekend or I don't know what I'll do!"

A thought pops into my head. "April!" I yell as she's about to disappear around the corner. She turns to look inquisitively at me.

"How would you like it if Miss Julie took you shopping this weekend? Then I'll take Sarah and Andrew to get their costumes." April gave up dressing up for Halloween years ago.

Her face lights up. "Oh, that would be so cool! I like Miss Julie!"

"Good. I'll talk to her and see if she's available."

"Yay! Did you tell her you're pregnant yet? I don't want it to slip out or anything," she asks.

How thoughtful.

I smile and nod. "Yes, I told her this morning."

"How did she take it?" her nose wrinkles and her shoulders tense.

"Well, she was upset at first, but she is okay now. She's a tough lady."

Her shoulders relax, and she smiles and disappears just as quickly as she appeared.

"Good grief, it's like a whirlwind with her," Michael mutters in amazement then leans in close to me. "Do you think we're going to have another one like that?" he asks quietly.

I have to laugh. "I don't know, but I hope not. One April is more than enough."

****

"Are you sure?" I ask Julie incredulously. She's just agreed to go to my next OB appointment. Her reaction took me by surprise; she actually jumped up and down and clapped her

328

hands. It's the sort of reaction I'd expect of someone who was just informed they'd won the lottery, not been invited to a friend's medical appointment.

"Yes, yes, yes!" she squeals. "I'm so excited, Faith! Will I get to hear the heartbeat and everything?"

I nod. "They do that at every appointment."

Her eyes open wide. "Oh! What does it sound like?"

"Uh, I don't really know how to explain it. It's sort of like a whispered *wow, wow, wow* sound." I had never really given it much thought.

Julie continues to ask me questions about the appointment, and I answer them as best I can. She also asks about my nausea, which has fortunately shown signs of diminishing the last few days. I still experience occasional waves, but the desire to puke is almost gone. I'm really tired of gazing into the porcelain bowl.

"I'm so thankful that you're allowing me to be a part of this, Faith!" She smiles.

"It's my pleasure. It's so fun to see your reactions. You're helping me to get more excited about it, too. This was such a shock for us." My cheeks burn at the insensitivity of my comment. "Oh, sorry. I didn't mean it that way."

She waves me off. "I know what you mean, and don't worry about it. Like I said, I believe God has a plan for me, too."

"Hey, listen. I have a favor to ask. I know it's super short notice, but are you available Saturday?"

She nods.

"Well, you know Halloween is coming up, and I still need to get costumes for Sarah and Andrew. April has a winter dance coming up, which I completely forgot about because of everything else that's happened." I roll my eyes. "I'd really appreciate it if you could maybe take April dress shopping Saturday? I know it's a lot to ask and…"

"Yes! I'd love to!" she interjects.

I blink, surprised. "Are you sure? April is a handful."

"Oh, she's fine. She's a nice young lady. She's just very expressive, and I don't mind. Do you think she's going to mind going with me?"

"Are you kidding? She adores you, Julie. I asked her about it already and she was really excited. I know she'll be over the moon that you said yes."

Her eyes shine and she drops her gaze. "You really do have wonderful children, Faith. I hope you know that," she replies quietly.

"Yes, I do."

"Thanks for letting me be a part of your life."

I don't know how to respond, so I change the subject.

"Did you get a chance to check your calendar for my coming out party?"

"Oh! Yes, I can make it. Is there anything you want me to bring, and what time is it?"

We discuss the details of the party, and I tell her a little about my friends. Everyone's coming. The menu is decided, and I tell Julie to add whatever she thinks would be best. She is eager to meet them. I think she'll be a good addition to our little group; how could anyone not like Julie?

Once she leaves, I catch up on the housework. As I begin cleaning, I'm shocked at how much I've let things slide. Cobwebs and dust abound where I never tolerated them before. My energy doesn't come close to my desire to clean. I only complete one bathroom and the living room before my eyelids begin to droop and a yawn escapes. Plus my back aches.

Nap time calls my name and I reluctantly heed the call. Instead of snuggling up on the couch, I rebel against the pregnancy and sleep in the guest room on the main floor, being sure to set the alarm clock so I don't sleep the rest of the day away. I won't let this pregnancy keep me down! I'll allow myself one hour….okay, maybe one and a half hours.

Turning away from the clock, I pull the covers over my shoulders, heave a sigh and close my eyes. Almost immediately, the alarm sounds and I roll over, annoyed. I'm sure I set the alarm correctly; it shouldn't go off just a few minutes later.

I gape at the clock as I realize it didn't go off a few minutes later. An hour and a half has gone by. My right hip is numb, testifying to the fact that I never moved from my original position.

Maybe this pregnancy is going to keep me down.

"No. Not going to happen," I mutter to no one in particular, rubbing my eyes with one hand and my right hip with the other, which throbs as the blood flow slowly creeps back. "I can do this."

Grunting as I heave myself to a sitting, then standing position I stretch my arms high over my head before catching a sideways glimpse of myself in the full length mirror in the corner of the room across from the bed. The image makes me frown; not only is my belly bulging but my backside seems to be growing in direct proportion to it. This is a high price to pay, indeed.

"My butt's getting bigger, too?!" I demand of the reflection. The image simply places its hands on its hips and twists to the side, frowning back at me.

"Aaaagh!" I yell, turning angrily from the mocking image to take my frustrations out on the bedding and pillows. I forcefully smooth them out and put them back into place. Intentionally ignoring the offensive mirror, I head for the kitchen because, blossoming backside or not, I'm hungry.

I keep it simple by just making a cheese sandwich and eating a banana to see if it will stay put. The puking has subsided, but not disappeared. A twinge of nausea rears its ugly head, but no lunging for the bathroom follows.

Yay, me!

Encouraged by this development, I push the envelope and make dinner for the family for the first time in a long while. I make the works: baked chicken, mashed potatoes, and green beans. The chicken isn't appealing; it's slimy and spongy in my hands, but I press on, only gagging twice.

With a deep sense of satisfaction, I spy each member of the family inhaling deeply and smiling as they walk in the door.

Michael, most of all.

"Honey! You cooked!" he declares exuberantly. "How are you feeling? You look tired, but better."

I hug him. "I am better. Still a little nauseated, but no puking."

He squeezes me quickly, but he's more anxious to examine what I've cooked. He lifts the lids on the pots and inhales deeply of the aromas.

"Oh…that smells good. Is it ready?" He's like a child on Christmas morning.

Andrew comes over and squeezes me carefully, always carefully now. "Mom, are you better?"

I ruffle his hair. "Much better, Andrew. Are you hungry?"

His head bobs up and down.

"Okay, let's eat!" Michael announces.

A chorus of voices and the clink of dishes fill the air as everyone but me loads up plates and fills glasses before heading to the dining room. I place a few spoonfuls of food on my plate, but skip the chicken. Even cooked, it still looks slimy.

As we all sit down and say grace, Michael notices the sparseness of my plate. "Is that all you're going to eat?"

I shake my head, taking a small forkful of potatoes. "I just want to be sure it's going to stay down first." I wrinkle my nose. "Plus the chicken is just…gross."

"I should probably eat less right now, too. I just know I'm going to have to get a bigger dress for the dance! Tom Parker probably already thinks I'm fat," April cries, negating her own words by ripping a large chunk of chicken off the bone with her teeth.

"Please, April. You're just fine the way you are," Michael replies than shovels a huge forkful of food into his mouth, moaning. Once he swallows, he adds, "I've really missed your cooking, Faith."

"Me, too," April and Andrew chime.

"I know. I'm sorry, guys. I should hopefully be better now." I take another tentative bite of food.

"Didja ask Miss Juwie about dwess shopping, Mom?" April mouths around her food causing her speech to garble. I am so tired of reminding her to not talk with food in her mouth that I remain silent. Won't she look classy at the dance in her nice dress, sauce dripping from her elbows to stain it as she spits food at her date?

"Yes, I did and she's happy to take you dress shopping on Saturday."

"Yes!" She fist pumps twice, spitting potatoes onto the table.

"Ew! Don't spit your food on me!" Andrew yells; he is sitting next to her. He pulls his plate further away from his sister and wraps his arm protectively around it, glaring at her.

April rolls her eyes and Michael growls a warning to April.

A wave of nausea rolls over me at the scene, and I close my eyes and take deep breaths, willing it away.

"Honey, you okay?" Michael asks.

I open my eyes, and they're all staring at me, although April and Andrew continue to eat.

I shrug it off and shake my head. "I'm fine. Just a little nausea."

"Way to make her sick, April," Sarah mutters.

April glares at her sister; Sarah glares back…. It's a familiar picture.

My dinner doesn't make a reappearance, thankfully. With the exception of the potato spitting incident, the evening goes well, and I crawl into bed that night satisfied that I can maybe function normally again.

Bigger backside notwithstanding…

Great, a bigger butt is what I've always wanted. On top of everything else, thanks so much for THAT. Sorry. Thank you, Lord, for this baby. I'm overwhelmed.

Chapter Thirty One

I'm trying very hard to be patient, but I'm weary to my core and just want Andrew to pick a costume already. He has spent the last three hours plucking through countless piles of super heroes, swamp creatures, and iconic cartoon figures to last a lifetime, but can't seem to settle on just one character to be for Halloween.

Sarah chose to be the Grim Reaper. It's odd, but I'll choose my battles wisely. I nostalgically remember when she wanted to be any and every Disney princess. Those days are long gone…or maybe not. Maybe we're having another girl. The thought brightens my mood briefly, until I gaze once again on Andrew; he wants a brother.

I just want him to pick a costume.

Working to keep my tone even while stifling a yawn (remember, Nap Time is calling my name), "Andrew, what about this one? You love this, right?" I ask and hold up a Jedi Knight costume with "Real Simulated Light Saber Included!" for his examination. He glances briefly at it before shaking his head.

"I did that a couple years ago." He continues to pluck and pull various costumes out.

I look over at Sarah, and she looks sympathetically at me. "Mom, why don't you go sit down and we'll come get you when he decides. I'll help him." She gestures to a bench just outside the mall store door.

I smile gratefully. "Thanks, Sarah. Try to get him to pick something soon. I really need to lie down." Walking toward the bench, I sit down on one end with a grunt and lift my legs, rotating my ankles. I sit back and people watch, keeping an eye on my children; I can just see Sarah's head over the racks.

There are so many different people walking around. Large and small, big and tall, young and old and everything in between. I allow my mind to wander and wonder where they've all come from, and where they're going. My eyes skim over each person that walks by. I devise stories about them before they disappear from view.

This one is a focused career woman, sure footed and powerfully dressed with eyes that say "get out of my way." That one is a cocky young man in baggy clothes with swagger, but no direction. He probably flips burgers for a living. I wonder what his future holds.

My gaze lengthens and lands on a couple walking parallel to me in the distance across the walkway. They are walking very close together as most couples do; she's closer to me, her face turned toward her companion. He's smiling at something she may have said. She bumps him with her hip, and he laughs, placing his hand on the small of her back in a gesture of intimacy. There's something familiar about the woman, but I can't place it. Suddenly her face turns in my direction, and I gasp in surprise.

It's Brenda!

That is most certainly not her husband, Scott. My mind boomerangs to the soccer game where I saw her sitting so close to a man, and then how she reacted at lunch when I asked her about it.

What was her co-workers' name again? Matt? Ned? Nate? Yes, that's it. Nate. Is that him?

I waffle between calling out her name and hoping against hope she doesn't see me. They look like a couple, not just a couple of friends. Choosing the second course of action, I get up quickly and duck into the store. I can't process this right now. Surely Brenda wouldn't...

"Sarah? Did he figure out what costume he wants yet?" I ask quickly.

"He's narrowed it down. You okay, Mom? Feeling sick?" she replies.

"Yes. I mean, no. I'm just tired. We need to get going. Get this one, Andrew." I tap one of the costumes he's holding in his hand without even looking at it, and pull the other one he was considering out of his other hand, throwing it back onto the pile.

"Hey! I'm not sure if that's what I want!" he protests.

Lord, not now.

"Andrew Jonathon, I said it's time to go. Now." I pull him toward the cash register and Sarah follows quietly behind. I never use their middle names unless I mean business, and right now, I mean business. I don't want to see Brenda. I wouldn't know what to say.

I quickly pay for the costume, snatching the bag from the cashier as soon as the transaction is complete, and leave the store, casting a nervous glance around the crowd before deciding which direction to go. The coast appears clear; there's no sign of Brenda or her companion.

Once we're in the van, I take a moment to draw a deep breath before turning to my children.

"Andrew, I'm sorry. I just really need to get home now. If you truly don't like your costume, we'll exchange it before Halloween."

"Okay," he sulks, fingering the package.

The ride home is sullen, and my mind is far away. I turn the event with Brenda over and over in my head, searching for possible clues she may have said to me or I may have seen between her and Scott that would reveal potential problems in their marriage. Granted, I don't spend much time with them together; we usually meet as girlfriends, not as couples. I haven't seen much of her in awhile. I've had so much going on in my own life. If she's wandered from him, having an affair… They have three kids! They'd be devastated.

"That would be awful," I mutter.

"What?" Sarah asks.

Grimacing, I realize I uttered my thoughts out loud. "Nothing. Sorry, I was just thinking out loud."

"But what would be awful?" she presses.

Gripping the steering wheel, I speak quietly hoping Andrew is otherwise engaged. "Sarah, it's nothing. Honest. Please just drop it."

She exhales an exasperated sigh and turns to gaze out of her window.

I really want our relationship to be repaired, but sharing this with her isn't an option, and I don't have a good cover story to tell. Sometimes, there's just nothing to be said.

When I pull into the garage, Sarah opens her door and jumps out of the van almost before it comes to a complete stop, and disappears quickly into the house, not even bothering to collect her costume bag. I don't try to stop her.

Andrew and I follow on her heels after gathering my purse and the bags. Realizing that I never did look at what costume I forced Andrew to get, I peer into his bag to see what it is.

Whoops.

It's a bumble bee.

He's going to hate that. Naturally, I think he'd look adorable, but somehow I don't think adorable is what he's going for.

I'm right.

Sarah is nowhere to be found and the house is silent. I drop my purse and the bags on the bench in the mudroom, cross through the dining room and enter the living room. Andrew follows me and falls face down, prostrate on the sofa, hands balled into fists. I shake my head and sit down beside him. When I place my hand on his back, he grunts for me to go away.

"Andrew, I'm sorry. Please forgive me. Look, we'll take it back. Maybe Dad can take you later today." I rub his back.

He turns his head to face me; his face scrunched into a scowl. "It's not that. I just want you to be *you* again. I don't want my baby brother anymore."

I'm taken aback. "What do you mean?"

He looks at me. "I mean you're always sick or tired and you get grouchy, too. I don't like it," he laments. "I want my old Mom back."

Heart aching, I try to answer carefully. "Andrew, I'm really sorry. This isn't going to last much longer. It's just part of being pregnant. The grouchy thing is my own fault, though. I'll try not to be like that. You don't mean you don't want a baby brother anymore."

Andrew remains sullen and unconvinced.

"Would you like to try on the costume? I think you'll make a...handsome bumble bee." I almost said adorable.

He continues to scowl, but his expression softens. He stares at the floor then at me. "Maybe."

"It's on the bench in the mudroom. Want me to help?"

He rolls his eyes. "No! I can do it myself." He sits up, slides off the sofa and sulks into the dining room. He reappears with the bag in hand and gives me a sideways glance before disappearing into the bathroom around the corner.

Realizing the house is still quiet, I get up and peer into the office, looking for Michael. I call upstairs for him with no answer. I don't recall that he told me he had anywhere to go this afternoon. I call his cell phone and he picks up after the second ring.

"Michael, where are you?" I ask.

"Hi, Faith! I'm over at Pastor Ben's house visiting. We were both out raking leaves and got to chatting. Are you home?"

"Yes. We got home a few minutes ago."

"How did it go? Did the kids get their costumes?"

"Yes, but it wasn't a complete success. Andrew may not like his costume."

I regale Michael with the details of the costume purchase. He sympathizes with Andrew, naturally.

"Honey, you shouldn't have rushed him. You know he's always slow to make a decision."

"Yes, but I'm so tired, Michael! Plus..." I need to talk to Michael about Brenda later, privately. "Well, there's something else. But I can't talk about it right now."

"Is everything okay?" he presses.

"Yes, everything is fine. I...I saw something at the mall I need to talk to you about, but later." I partially cover my mouth and speak in a low tone, just in case there are listening ears close by.

He pauses for a moment. "Okay. I'll be home in a little while." There are muffled sounds in the background. "Okay, okay, I will. Faith, Julie and Ben want to know if we'd like to come over for dinner tonight."

"Are Julie and April back from dress shopping already? They do realize that there are five of us to feed, right?"

"Yeah, they got back from shopping about twenty minutes ago." Michael asks if they'd like all of us to come and eat, and he's answered by more muffled background sounds. "Julie says the whole family is welcome for dinner, of course. She's making a big pot of chili with cornbread." More muffled sounds. "That is, if it sounds good to you. Hang on, let me give the phone to Julie!" he laughs.

Suddenly, Julie's voice fills my ear. "Hi, Faith! Does chili and cornbread sound okay to you? Or is your stomach still a little on the queasy side?"

"Oh, it's still a little queasy, but chili doesn't sound half bad. I haven't thrown up in a few days. What time do you want us to come over?"

We finish going over the details and I thank her; it's such a relief to not have to make dinner tonight. Plus I still need my nap. I hang up the phone just in time to see Andrew coming out of the bathroom. The corners of his mouth are turned down and his eyebrows are raised in a silent question.

"Well?" he asks, holding his arms out to the side. His skinny legs are jutting out of a yellow and black striped, lumpy, egg shaped fuzzy ball. He's also wearing a head band with bobbling black antennae.

He looks so adorable!

I restrain myself from saying so while pinching his cheek like a crazed aunt.

"I think you look like a bumble bee, although your legs will probably be cold. Maybe we can get some black sweat pants to wear underneath? What do you think?" Tights would look even more adorable, but again, I leave that be. Michael wouldn't approve of his boy wearing tights, no matter the reason.

Andrew looks down at his body, rubbing the fabric of the lumpy ball he's encased in. He shrugs his shoulders. "I don't know. Is it too baby-ish? I mean, I am nine and all." He grins impishly at me. "I like that it's so soft!" He continues to rub his torso.

I smile back at him. "Well, I think you look great. You're the most…handsome bumble bee of any I've seen!"

Don't say adorable, don't say adorable.

"Ha! Don't you look adorable!?" Sarah yells.

I whip around; she's halfway down the stair case descending slowly, smiling from ear to ear. I frown at her and turn my attention back to Andrew. He's squinting fiercely at his sister.

"I do not look adorable, Sarah. I look like a bumble bee," he corrects her.

"Well, yeah. You look like an adorable bumble bee!" she teases him.

"Mo-ooom! Tell her not to say that!" he whines.

I sigh and rub my eyes. "Sarah, please don't say that. Don't you think he looks handsome?" I turn my face away from Andrew, and try to signal her silently to agree with me. I know she knows what I mean and pray she goes along.

"Yeah, Andrew. You look *debonair* as a bumble bee," she answers flatly.

"What does that mean?" he asks, perplexed, not sure if he should take offense or not.

I'm quick to jump in. "It's an old fashioned word for handsome, Andrew."

He searches my face, trying to decide if I'm telling the truth or not. Finally, he reaches a decision. "OK. As long as I don't look adorable."

Time to change the subject.

"Listen, kids. Pastor Ben and Miss Julie have invited us over to their house for dinner tonight." Andrew responds with a *whoop*. "Miss Julie is making chili and cornbread. So go ahead and change back into your clothes, Andrew. I need to take a nap. Sorry, buddy." I look directly at Andrew. "But it won't be a long one. Then we'll go over to their house around five o'clock."

"Why can't we go over there now?" Sarah asks, her mood brightening. "Did she say what she's making for dessert?"

"I don't know if she's making dessert. We don't need to invade their home, Sarah. It's nice of them to invite us over for dinner, and that's good enough."

Suddenly, the front door opens and April spills into the foyer with a large garment bag in tow and Michael tagging along behind.

"Mom! I got the most amazing dress! You gotta come see it..." April the Tornado takes over. She whirls the garment bag in front of her dramatically and unzips it, still talking like an auctioneer. A beautiful dress emerges from the opaque plastic. It's a deep sapphire blue with just the right amount of sequins to sparkle without being gaudy, the hemline drops to about knee length (from what I can tell), and the neckline is rounded with straps wide enough not to be considered spaghetti.

"Oh! And Miss Julie thought this would look pretty with it." She pulls a beautiful white short sleeved shrug to wear over it. It's made from a shimmery material that accents the dress perfectly.

"It's beautiful, April!" I breathe, fingering the fabric of the dress. It really is stunning. "Job well done, I'd say. Did you thank Miss Julie?"

She bobs her head. "I still need to get shoes and probably some jewelry to go with it. I can't just let my neck be naked after all! Do you think I should get dangly earrings or just some diamond studs that match the sequins? Oh, and I better let Tom Parker know what color my dress is, so he can get the right kind of corsage. I don't want it to clash, after all…" She always refers to her date by his full name.

My eyes glaze over and I look to Michael for some relief. Andrew has already disappeared into the bathroom to change, apparently having no interest in this whole dress/dance business.

"April," he interrupts. "It's all very exciting, but don't you think you should put the dress away so that it doesn't get stained or anything? You mentioned you needed to make a phone call, too."

She pauses in mid-sentence, snaps her fingers, and begins to stuff the dress back into the garment bag. "Yes! I also need to call Mariah, too. I wonder what color she's wearing. Gosh, if she got the same color…" She zips the bag, pushes past Sarah, and takes the stairs two at a time, still talking to herself.

I hold my hands up and shake my head at Michael. "Wow."

"Mom?" Sarah asks.

"Hmm?"

"Can I at least call Miss Julie and see if I can come over by myself? I won't bother them."

I look to Michael. "What do you think? She could at least call and ask."

He shrugs. "Sure. I don't think it's a problem. She's just busy in the kitchen. I'm sure she'd love the help." He smiles at Sarah.

For the first time in awhile, Sarah's face actually looks animated. Rather than feeling envy the animation isn't for me, I am grateful that Julie is here for her. I just want what's best for my daughter.

"So, I can call her?" she asks, smiling and gripping her hands in front of her.

"Sure," I nod. "Go ahead."

She claps once, and disappears into the kitchen to retrieve the phone. Michael and I don't even have time to leave the foyer of the house before she returns.

"She said it was fine! See you later!" she calls out as she disappears through the front door and closes it with a slam.

Andrew emerges from the bathroom just as Sarah leaves. "Where's she going?" he asks.

"She's going to help Miss Julie cook dinner," Michael answers.

He throws his head back and drops his costume on the floor. "Aw! How come I can't go help, too?" he whines.

"Because I need your help," Michael replies. "I seem to recall you mentioning a battle that's going on in the basement. Wasn't Spiderman going to fight Poison?"

Andrew giggles. "Dad, it's *Venom*."

Michael winks at me. "Oh, that's right. I forgot." He knows very well what the names are. He's the one that introduced Andrew to superheroes and comic books in the first place. As they disappear into the basement, I drag my weary body up the stairs and rap lightly on April's door before opening it to poke my head in. She's rattling away on her cell phone.

She spies me and interrupts her chatter. "What's up?" she asks.

"I'm going to lie down and take a nap. Dad's in the basement with Andrew, okay?"

"Sure! Anyway, like I said..." she continues her conversation. I chuckle and close her door.

I set the alarm for an hour this time and burrow deep into the blankets of my bed. I really hope I get my energy back soon. I'm tired of feeling like a cranky toddler always in need of a nap.

****

The chili and cornbread are divine and I manage to eat two bowlfuls without difficulty. Julie is beaming and rightfully so.

"I'm afraid you won't have any leftovers," I muse apologetically.

She laughs it off. "That's okay. I'm just glad you all are enjoying it so much."

Michael and Pastor Ben are sitting on the sofa in their tidy living room joking and eating chili in bowls on their laps. Julie, the kids, and I have claimed territory at the dining room table. The living and dining room are one large room, so we can all talk together. The conversation threads flow easily around each other and there's plenty of laughter. Fortunately, April has modified her usual lack of table manners and avoids spitting food on anyone.

Andrew chose not to sit next to her, just in case.

"Guess what we made for dessert?" Sarah smiles conspiratorially at Julie.

"I hope it's those salty chocolate chip cookies!" April says excitedly.

"Nope. We made s'mores bars," she replies, lifting her chin in pride. "They are to die for!"

"S'mores bars?" I ask, curious.

Julie nods and explains. "Yes, they're a twist on traditional s'mores, which I love, but they aren't always practical to make. They have all the flavors of a s'more, but they're in a bar cookie form. I hope you'll like them. Is everyone ready for dessert?"

There's a round of enthusiastic "yes!" responses, mostly from the kids.

"Can I get them?" Sarah asks.

"Of course!" Julie responds, laughing. Sarah disappears into the kitchen, reappearing moments later carrying a large platter mounded full of little brown squares with toasted marshmallows on top.

"Wow, Julie. You made enough to feed the neighborhood," I joke.

"Maybe, but let's save the verdict for when the damage has been done."

The bars are really, really good. They're gooey and rich without being over the top sweet. My M&M addiction has taken a back seat because of my nausea. These taste so wonderful that I actually moan out loud on my first bite. I've really missed chocolate.

"Julie, these are amazing." I lick my fingers to be sure no morsel goes to waste. The kids are stone silent simply enjoying them and nod in unison at my comment.

"My wife is pretty talented." Pastor Ben grins, grabbing two more before kissing his wife on the head. "There's nothing she puts her hand to that isn't blessed."

In her usual self-deprecating way, she waves off the compliment. "I just like to bake."

"And garden," I add.

"And dress shop," April joins in.

"And talk," Sarah adds quietly.

Hmmm, I wonder what she talked to Julie about.

Julie looks overwhelmed and embarrassed at the same time. Clearing her throat, she rises and begins to stack the empty chili bowls. "You're all so sweet. Thank you."

I rise with a grunt and help her clear the dishes.

"Faith, please just relax. You don't have to help," she protests.

"Nonsense! You went to a lot of trouble, and the least I can do is help clean up."

"Actually, I think we'll do clean up while you ladies relax," Pastor Ben interjects. He and Michael rise and take over, ushering us out of the kitchen and into the living room. The kids are building a massive house of cards on the now cleared dining table. It looks to be rather impressive, if it doesn't collapse.

Once I settle down on the sofa, I yawn widely in spite of my efforts to restrain it. Julie notices.

"Still really tired, Faith?" she asks sympathetically.

I nod and let my head fall back onto the large cushions that encase her sofa. Her home is so warm and inviting; it's impossible not to relax.

"All she wants to do is sleep anymore," Andrew informs Julie from the table.

My heart squeezes.

"Well," Julie replies, eyeing me before directing her answer to him. "That's a normal thing with pregnancies, I think. Your mom needs extra rest right now to grow a new person."

"He's right," I sigh. "I do want to sleep all the time. It's annoying."

A shadow crosses Julie's features, making me regret my words.

"I'm sorry, Julie." I really need to be careful what I say.

She shakes her head and smiles. "It's okay. I know what you mean. I'd probably be annoyed if I couldn't keep my eyes open every day, too."

"Still..."

She waves me off with a flick of her wrist.

We say our goodbyes once the men are done cleaning up. The kids fuss about having to leave, but I'm sure Pastor Ben and Julie are ready to have their home back. I'm anxious to get home because I still want to talk to Michael about Brenda, and of course, I'm tired. I just hope I can keep my eyes open long enough to have a conversation with him.

After the kids have gone to bed, I choose to sit in the recliner rather than the sofa because I'd end up going to sleep.

"Michael, I want to talk to you about something. I need your opinion about what I saw and what I should do about it, if anything."

He sits on the sofa across from me and crosses his legs. "Shoot."

I tell him about what I saw at the mall with Brenda and the man she was with, whom I assume is Nate. I also remind him about the soccer game, and then tell him about her reaction at lunch when I brought it up. He listens quietly until I'm done. Once I've emptied my head of all of it, I wait for his response.

He takes a minute to consider what I've told him. Finally, he replies, "Wow. That's a lot, Faith. Are you sure about what you saw?"

"Really, Michael? I wouldn't make this up. I know what I saw. What should I do about it? She's coming over this Friday, you know. They're all coming over this Friday," I remind him.

He shakes his head and crosses his arms. "I don't know, Faith. This is shaky ground."

"But, Michael, I'm telling you there's something going on there. I don't know how far she's taken it, but it isn't right. She's my friend." I lower my voice. "Their kids are really close to ours, too. I mean, Mariah is April's best friend."

"I don't like getting involved in other people's marriages. I think you should let it be."

I shake my head. "I don't think I can. How would you feel if something like that happened to us? Would you want our friends to be quiet and ignore it?"

His eyes flash. "I don't even want to think about that. But no, I suppose you're right."

"You'd want someone to confront us about it?"

"Us? I don't think so. I'd want a friend to confront whichever of us was suspected of it first. It could be nothing, and I hope it is. If it really is nothing, telling them both would be an absolute disaster." He shakes his head. "Scott's a good guy."

"They're both good people, and I didn't mean I'd confront them both. I just want to ask Brenda privately about it, but I don't know what to say or how to say it. Maybe I'll ask Brenda to stay after the party."

"That sounds like a good idea."

"What am I supposed to say?"

"Just tell her what you saw, and ask her to explain it."

I shake my head. "I think that's too direct."

"Well, infidelity isn't something to beat around the bush about," he counters.

"Maybe it's not what it looks like." I'm rapidly losing hope for the situation. The more I think about it and turn the events over in my mind, the surer I am that whatever it is, it's wrong.

346

We continue to lob the idea of Brenda's potential unfaithfulness and how to confront it back and forth like a tennis match until finally, we agree that I do need to talk to Brenda, but that it needs to be done privately and not in connection with the party on Friday.

Satisfied that I at least have a plan, I tell Michael I need to get to bed. Sitting in the recliner was a wise choice because otherwise I would've been out quite awhile ago.

He smiles and rises, offering me his hand. "I thought so. I'm surprised you lasted this long."

Too beat to argue, I take his hand and head upstairs. Besides, what's to argue about? He's right. I'm exhausted.

God, I really hope Brenda isn't doing something she shouldn't be doing and please help me get this right. If I'm wrong, she'll never forgive me for accusing her and if I'm right...her family could be destroyed. Neither option is good.

Chapter Thirty Two

I spent time in church on Sunday praying about how to deal with Brenda. Not receiving any definite answer (e.g., a burning bush that talks or perhaps a mini parachute dropped from heaven with the answer neatly scrolled on parchment paper), I determine to call her. I can't keep mulling this over; it needs to be taken care of. Let the chips fall where they may.

Monday morning, I finally pick up the phone and call her.

"Hi, Brenda! It's Faith." I nervously pace the kitchen floor as soon as she picks up.

"Oh hi, Faith! How are you? Looking forward to Friday night? I know I am!" she bubbles.

"Yes, I am. Listen, I wanted to know if maybe we could meet for lunch, just the two of us."

"Oh, sure! I'm open all this week…"

Doing some quick thinking, I decide it would be best to meet after the party on Friday. She may not be speaking to me afterward.

"Actually, could we meet next week instead? My week's pretty full." I grimace at the lie.

"Sure! What day and where do you want to go?"

"How about…" I pause to look at my calendar. "Monday after the party? I don't care where we go, you can pick the place."

"Sounds good. What are you in the mood for?"

Pressing my hand into my bulging stomach, I had better play it safe. "How about something simple? Just a good soup and sandwich place. Any ideas?"

She chatters off a few different places and we decide to try The Bread Basket; Brenda's been there a few times and raves about their turkey club sandwich. We'll meet at eleven-thirty. I mark the information on the calendar and we say our goodbyes before hanging up.

Raising my face to the ceiling, I pray out loud (something I'm doing a lot lately). "God, help me here. I want to be wrong, and I don't want to accuse her falsely. Help! Amen."

My stomach rolls. I'm taken aback because this roll feels different. There's no nausea that would send me to the bathroom. Gasping, I realize the baby just moved. I press both hands to my stomach this time. My left palm is met immediately with a faint bump.

"Oh!" I had forgotten what the sensation felt like. It has been nine years, after all, since my last baby. Marveling in the moment, I close my eyes and start cooing to my belly.

Michael should know about this, so I pick up the phone and dial his office number.

"Hi, Faith. How's it going?" He sounds slightly distracted. I can hear papers shuffling in the background.

"Hi, Michael! I just felt the baby move!"

"Oh! Wow. Uh…that's amazing. Already? Isn't it a little early for that? Are you sure it was the baby?"

Snorting a laugh, I respond, "Yes, I'm sure. I felt something at first and then I put my hands on my belly and felt a bump."

"That's awesome. How are you feeling otherwise?"

"I'm good. I called Brenda, and we're going to lunch on Monday after the party. I was pretty nervous, so maybe that's what got the baby jumping around."

"Probably."

He still sounds distracted. "Michael, are you okay? Did I call you at a bad time?"

He sighs before answering. "Well, sort of. But it's okay."

"What's going on?"

"Just the investigation stuff." He sighs. "Personally, I'm okay. But I am helping put things together for my bosses and the authorities. It's not looking good for some others in the company. Which means it's not looking good for the company itself."

With everything else that's going on in our lives, I haven't asked about the investigation since the horrific invasion of our home by the DEA and the aftermath. I didn't want to know anything else about it. Is that selfish? Maybe, but it is what it is. "I'm sorry. What does this mean for you? As someone who works for the company, that is."

"I don't know. We'll just have to wait and see. This is a strong company, Faith. A good company. It'll survive, but I don't know what's going to happen."

He can't relay any further information over the phone, so we finish our conversation and hang up. Almost immediately, I dial Julie's number; I'm sure she'll be just as thrilled as I am about the baby moving.

She is. She actually squeals like, well, April.

As a matter of fact, she asks to come over and feel the baby move. When I agree, she hangs up before I can say goodbye. Within seconds, there's an impatient knock on the door.

When I open the door, her eyes are shining and her normally radiant smile is magnified to the tenth power.

"Can I feel?!" she asks excitedly, waiting a fraction of a second before placing her hands on my belly, her hands moving every few seconds in search of the elusive movement. She frowns. "What's it supposed to feel like?"

"Come on in, Julie. We don't have to stand in the doorway." I smile, ushering her into the living room.

She grimaces and follows me. "Oh, sorry. I'm just so excited!"

I laugh as we settle onto the sofa. "I am, too. But it's a fleeting thing, really. I was just standing in the kitchen and I felt sort of a roll in my stomach. But I didn't feel nauseous or anything else. Then it hit me what it probably was, so I put my hands on my stomach and felt a small bump against my hand."

Her eyes widen in wonder. "Wow," she whispers. "That's got to feel amazing, knowing that you're growing another human being inside you." Her gaze drops to my stomach.

My heart twists. "Yes, it is." I reach out and place my hand on hers and squeeze. "Julie, you're going to be a mom. I just have to believe that."

Her eyes glisten. "Me, too." Her radiant smile returns. "So, anything right now?" She gestures to my stomach.

I pause, concentrating. "Not at the moment. But remember, this is only the first time and it's early. Trust me, he or she will be doing somersaults before it's over."

Her shoulders slump slightly. "I'm so sorry I missed it!"

"Would you like some coffee? Maybe a little jolt of caffeine will get the ball, er, baby, rolling," I laugh. As if I need to ask; Julie never turns down coffee.

She nods and then frowns. "Is it okay for you to drink coffee?"

"Sure. I don't load up, and I'll make it half decaf. It's still early in the day."

Once the coffee is brewed, we fill our mugs and settle ourselves back into the living room. Fortunately, about fifteen minutes after I finish my second cup, the roll in my stomach returns.

"Julie! I just felt it again." I stand up quickly, and allow her to place her hands on my stomach, being sure to position her hands where I had felt the movement just a moment ago.

Suddenly she gasps and her jaw drops, her face one of utter shock and awe. She stares at her hands for a moment, her eyes shining.

"I'm guessing you felt it?" I ask when she doesn't say anything.

Her mouth remains wide open as she reluctantly pulls her gaze up to my face. She nods once and then returns her gaze to her hands, which are still on my stomach. She gasps again as another bump presses against her hand and a tear falls from her eye.

"I…I…amazing," she stutters.

"Yeah, I think this baby may be a pretty active one," I chuckle.

Julie remains silent, staring at her hands.

Am I doing the right thing? Is this hurting her too much?

I don't know what to say, so I just stand still and allow her the experience. Julie remains deep in thought, her expression still one of awe. Slowly, she closes her eyes and her lips begin to move in silence. She's praying.

Finally she opens her eyes, removes her hands, and smiles.

"Are you okay?" I ask, concerned.

"Yes, I'm more than okay. I'm at peace."

Searching her face, I see no trace of pain, anguish, or any sense that she's putting on a strong front. She looks like she says: at peace.

"What do you mean?" I inquire.

"Well, I am just leaving this in God's hands. He knows I want to be a mother in the worst way. For whatever reason, I'm not. At least not right now. If I don't become one, then I don't become one. I'm giving it to Him wholeheartedly." She raises her hands and shrugs her shoulders. "I give up!"

I bite my lip. "Julie, don't give up. You can't do that. You have to keep hoping!"

"Faith, I'm not giving up hope. I'm just giving my dream to God. That's all."

"Okay," I say, still confused.

She laughs and pats my hand. "Faith, don't worry. You'll understand eventually." She rises and takes her now empty mug to the sink. "I better get going. I left some brownie batter half mixed on my counter when you called. Would you like me to bring some over when they're done? They're raspberry truffle brownie bars, and they're going to be really good."

"Of course! What kind of neighbor would I be if I turned down anything you made? Besides, if my kids found out they'd never speak to me again," I laugh.

Once she leaves, I continue to ponder what she said. Call me crazy, but I can't imagine anyone going through something this painful and being okay with it. It just doesn't make sense.

You don't know what you don't know.

That still, quiet voice in my head again. Hmmm…wonder what that means. Swirling the water in my mug around before dumping it in the sink, I shake my head to clear it.

"Just give her a baby, God. Please," I say aloud. "She deserves one more than anyone else."

Silence.

****

My afternoon is devoid of anything but Nap Time. I have made it a routine to set the alarm so I have time to make dinner. Regardless of how I feel, sleeping the day away is not an option; I have my family to care for.

Unfortunately, when I wake up this time, rolling over causes me to bolt for the bathroom and lunge for the toilet, heaving until my body shakes.

There goes lunch.

Just as I'm about to rise, another wave hits and I drop back onto my knees, heaving again until I struggle to catch my breath. This time, nothing is extracted except my dignity.

Once I'm sure the episode has passed, I wash my face.

"Rats. I thought this was done," I mutter to myself, glancing at the clock. The kids will start getting home in about an hour. April has cheerleading practice today, so she'll be home later. I had planned to make a meatloaf, but the thought of rubbing raw hamburger in my hands makes me press my hand to my lips and squeeze my eyes shut. I opt for spaghetti and meat sauce instead. No meat touching required.

Only having to dry heave once while making dinner, I have a sense of accomplishment to have the meal complete and ready by the time everyone comes home.

When Michael walks through the door, his eyes sweep over the breakfast bar where Andrew and Sarah are engrossed in homework, then he takes one look at me and his eyebrows rise in question. "You feeling okay?" he asks, setting his briefcase down.

I look sheepishly at him. "Not so good today. I threw up a few times."

"Oh. Sorry, I thought that had passed." He envelopes me in a hug and kisses my forehead.

"I guess not." I rest my head on his shoulder.

"It looks like you made dinner anyway. Well done," he says, eyeing the pots on the stovetop. He lifts a lid and peers inside. "Spaghetti?"

I nod and turn my face away, a wave of nausea lapping at me. The noodles look like worms.

"Still queasy?" he asks, quickly replacing the lid.

I nod, keeping my eyes closed and concentrate on not throwing up.

"Go lie down if you want and I'll dish up dinner." He pulls dishes out to start plating food.

"Thanks," I reply and head into the living room, taking a glass of water with me to sip. "There's garlic bread in the oven," I call over my shoulder.

He grunts a response; I hear the oven open and the scraping sound of metal on metal as he pulls the cookie sheet out of the oven. I sit down on the sofa and close my eyes, taking a sip of water. The wave of nausea is dissipating.

Absentmindedly, I place my free hand on my belly bump. The motion is answered with a slight nudge. Smiling, I pat my stomach.

"It's okay. I know you can't help it," I say quietly.

This will all be worth it. I just know it.

My gaze wanders in the direction of the noise I hear in the dining room. The sounds of dinner intermingle with hushed conversation. They're probably talking about how their days went. I don't want to miss this.

Rising with the ever present grunt, I enter the dining room with my glass of water in hand and sit down at the table.

"You sure you want to be around food, mom?" Sarah asks.

I smile. "Yes, I'm sure. I don't want to eat, but I don't want to miss dinner, either."

"Good," Andrew chimes in as he stuffs a forkful of worms, I mean noodles, into his mouth.

I swallow hard and concentrate on his hair, which is sticking up in all directions as usual. He seems to have given up on the gel; too much work at the age of nine.

"So, how was your day?" I ask Sarah.

She's not tremendously talkative, but the conversation does flow eventually and I enjoy it as much as I can, forcing my thoughts to remain on the words rather than the food. Sarah seems more at ease than she has in awhile and I am grateful. I make it through the entire meal without having to leave the table. Andrew has plenty to say, especially since April isn't here. As he animatedly relays some point about his day, I find myself hoping that we do have a boy this time; Andrew could really use a brother. Being the baby, it's hard for me to picture him in the big brother role, but that will come in time.

The plates are empty, but the air is still filled with conversation when April bursts into the room. She obviously worked hard at practice; her hair is disheveled in its pony tail and her face is flushed. She dumps her bag on the floor next to the bench and immediately opens the cupboard to grab a plate.

"Hey, hold up there. Wash your hands first," Michael reprimands before she can touch anything else.

"Dad! I'm starving!" she protests, her hand suspended in mid air toward the stack of plates on the shelf.

"One minute won't cause you to die, April," he continues.

"Ugh!" she cries, slamming the cupboard shut. Once her hands are washed, she fills her plate, plops down at the table and begins to shovel food into her mouth.

The sight causes me to close my eyes and take deep breaths, trying to find my happy place.

"April, please slow down and chew your food," Michael says. "And close your mouth. Mom's feeling queasy."

The wet, slopping noises from where she sits cease. I open my eyes and cast a wary glance at her, afraid of what I might see. Aside from a smear of sauce on the corner of her mouth, the scene she portrays is safe enough for my gaze to remain.

"Sorry, mom," she says, appearing to be truly contrite. She deliberately slows her motions down and keeps her mouth closed when she chews.

"Thanks, April. How was cheer practice?" I ask.

She nods once, holding her finger up while she continues to chew and then swallow before answering. She glances at her father, and he smiles his approval. He hands her a napkin which she is quick to swipe across her mouth before dropping it on the table next to her plate.

"It went good. We were learning this new pyramid when Casey fell off the top. But she totally somersaulted when she landed, so she didn't get hurt. It was awesome! We were thinking about adding it to the routine, but coach said no."

Through the rest of her meal, she makes an effort not to talk with food in her mouth and even slows down enough to enjoy it. Sarah excuses herself halfway through April's monologue to finish her homework.

"Hold on, Sarah," I interrupt her departure, holding onto her arm. "I wanted to let you guys know I felt the baby move today."

There's a quiet chorus of excitement followed by the hands of my children being placed on my stomach and questions regarding how it felt. Michael lingers behind them.

"It felt like a little bump from inside," I inform them. "No, he or she isn't moving right now. Not that I can tell anyway."

Andrew grumbles his disappointment.

"Don't worry, there's going to be plenty of bumps to be felt in the next several months, Andrew. You'll get your chance."

"Is that why you felt sick again today, maybe?" Sarah asks.

I shake my head. "I don't think it works like that. It just comes and goes."

Slowly the hands drop from my stomach until only Michael stands before me, the excitement of the moment replaced by other pursuits; Sarah and Andrew to their homework and April to her plate.

Michael places his hands carefully on my stomach, the warmth penetrating me. "I can't wait to feel it," he says quietly. "I remember each time with each child."

I smile. "I know." I pull his face down and kiss him, which brings a groan from the table.

"All right parental units. That's enough of that. It's what got you in this situation in the first place." April snorts, looks down at her almost empty plate and pushes it away. "Now I'm not hungry anymore."

Michael and I pull apart, laughing.

I love my family, God. Thank you!

Chapter Thirty Three

It's Friday. I'll make my big announcement tonight, and I can't stay upright long enough to get anything accomplished. I'm either gulping deep breaths in an attempt to stay out of the bathroom or lunging for it to empty myself once again.

Why now? Why today of all days?

Heaving for what I hope is the last time (today, at least), I splash water on my face and regard my reflection. A sheen of sweat covers my hairline, and I look pale even to myself.

It's already one o'clock, and I've only been able to dust and run the vacuum once around the living room. Nothing has been finished; the dishes and silverware aren't even laid out. The party is supposed to start at six.

Of everything on the menu I planned, washing vegetables is the safest choice. The celery and carrots have been washed, but not cut or peeled and the broccoli remains piled in a colander in the sink. I can't even allow my thoughts to wander toward making meatballs, much less any of the other finger foods I planned. I am starting to believe I've been overly ambitious about the menu.

"This isn't going to work. I need help." Reaching for the phone, I quickly dial Julie's number and hope she's home. Fortunately, she answers on the third ring.

"Hello?" She sounds out of breath.

"Thank God you're home, Julie! I need your help."

"Faith? Are you all right? What's wrong? Is something wrong with the baby?"

"No! No, the baby is fine. It's me that has the problem. The party is tonight and I can't seem to stay out of the bathroom long enough to get anything done. Could you possibly come over and help me cook?"

"Oh, uh…sure. I can help. Give me about an hour, okay? I just need to…uh... finish up first."

It dawns on me that she could actually have something more important to do than be at my beck and call, and I grimace. "Julie, if you're busy, please say so. It's okay, really."

"No, it's fine. I'm just finishing up over here. I'll be there as soon as I can."

Hanging up, I feel a sense of guilt. I really shouldn't rely so much on her. She does have a life, after all. Looking around at my kitchen, however, I realize there's no way I can get anything done without some help.

When she arrives about forty minutes later, she looks flushed and her hair is damp.

She just got out of the shower? This late in the day? Maybe she was gardening…

"Hi, Faith! You do look sick," she says, her forehead creasing.

I wave off the comment and usher her into the kitchen. "As you can see, I've got almost nothing done. It's pathetic."

She shrugs her shoulders and places her hands on her hips. "So, what needs doing and where do I start?"

Struggling to hold back a heave, I hold my finger up and run past her heading for the bathroom. Naturally, I only dry heave. When I return, Julie is busy at the sink.

"Sorry," I say, pressing the back of my hand to my forehead to wipe away the moisture that has gathered. Why do I sweat when I puke? It's so unnecessary.

"Please, there's nothing to be sorry for. I feel sorry for you. I thought that was getting better." She moves on to peeling and chopping the vegetables.

"Yeah, I thought so, too. Listen, Julie. I think I caught you in the middle of something at home. If this isn't a good time, we can always order take out. Maybe I can send Michael to pick up some trays at the grocery store?"

To my surprise, she blushes and keeps on chopping. "No, it's okay."

Confused, I press on. "Really, Julie, if you need to go, I understand."

A giggle bubbles out of her and she blushes crimson.

"Sorry, I think I missed something." I sidle up to her and grab a carrot to peel.

She stops, sucks her lips in, and shakes her head. She remains silent for a moment before turning to face me. Her eyes don't quite meet mine.

This is getting stranger by the second.

"Faith," she begins, her cheeks burning. "Ben and I...ah...well, we're trying the rhythm method."

"The rhythm method for wha....?"

Oh. The *rhythm* method.

It's my turn to blush. "Oh, you mean...oh! So, you were...." I miss my mark with the peeler and drop my carrot in the trash can.

She nods and returns to her chopping.

"So, you and Ben were just..."

"Yes," she answers quickly.

I gasp. "Were you able to? I mean, did I...you know...interrupt..."

"No. We...ah...finished," she stammers. Her cheeks are the deepest crimson I've ever seen. Mine may be just as red. "He's on his way back to work now."

Enough said.

"Sorry, Julie. I shouldn't have pried. But, I will pray that you're successful in your endeavors." I grimace behind her back; perhaps that's the wrong choice of words.

She turns to face me. "Me, too." She smiles before turning back to her task.

We move through the menu in near silence, only speaking to share necessary information. We're both embarrassed. Unfortunately, I am completely unable to help with anything beyond the vegetables and some of the easier ingredients like cutting up bread for sandwiches. Everything else drives me from the room.

"Faith, why don't you do other stuff like finish cleaning? Being in the kitchen isn't good for you," Julie suggests. "I don't want you to throw up anymore."

I snort a laugh. "I'd like to not throw up anymore, either! You're right. I'll get the dishes set up and finish the living room." A wicked streak comes over me. "Maybe you'll be throwing up soon, too," I joke and grin mischievously at her.

Her cheeks flush crimson once again. "I hope so."

With the gracious help Julie provides all afternoon, everything is ready in plenty of time. The nausea dissipates so that by four o'clock, I'm confident enough to apply make up that will stay on.

Shooing Julie out the door to make her own preparations for the party after many hugs and thanks (and no further mention of the rhythm method from either of us), I survey all that we were able to accomplish.

"Wow." Julie has the food prepped, plated, and wrapped beautifully. All the trays of food look like works of art. She even arranged the vegetables in a swirl pattern using the different colors of the vegetables to achieve the effect. Upon closer inspection, she used hollowed out bell peppers as containers for the dip. She really has a knack for this.

****

Everyone arrives within minutes of each other and the house bustles with activity. My children are anxious to head over to Michelle's house with the others; April drives them over and is delighted at my new relaxed attitude when it comes to her driving. As a nod to me, April tells me she'll text me when she arrives anyway, which she does. How thoughtful.

Michael offers to stay behind and help me, but I decline. I nudge him to spend time with the guys; he needs his guy time as much as I need my girl time. The stress of the investigation at work and everything else in life is showing on his face lately, and I don't like it.

"Go on, Michael. Go enjoy yourself!" I give him a playful shove toward the door.

As he pulls on his coat, he turns to me. "Okay. Ben said he would drive, so I'll head over there. I'll be home in time to help clean up."

"Don't worry about it. You know my friends. They always help clean up."

Appeased, he turns and begins to disappear into the night on his own adventure. Well, "adventure" is a pretty loose interpretation for what he's going to do. If I'm not mistaken, they're just going bowling. As he's about to depart, he almost bowls Ben over on the front porch.

"Oh! Sorry, Ben. I was about to come and get you," Michael laughs as they steady themselves.

Seeing Ben, I blush remembering the afternoon of "rhythm method". I'm thankful the sun is already over the horizon; even though my blush is felt by me, it is seen by none.

"Hi, Ben! Have a great time!" I manage to blurt, surprised at the evenness of my voice.

He doesn't notice. He simply turns toward me and waves, disappearing into the night with Michael. I close the door and shake my head free of the thought.

There are many *oohs* and *ahs* over the buffet. I direct credit to Julie, who blushes with each bit of praise.

Julie is radiant in a turquoise cashmere sweater, the neckline of which is an interwoven satin sash tied with a small off center bow. Brenda eyes her entire ensemble with her usual critical eye, nodding her approval. Brenda is, of course, dressed in what I assume are matching designer pieces. She would show up in nothing less.

Seeing Brenda causes a knot to build in my stomach, so I force my mind elsewhere. I've had enough stomach issues lately; I don't want another reason for me to head for the bathroom. Not tonight.

Miraculously (how does she do it?), Julie arrives with a beautifully decorated chocolate cake topped with glistening whole strawberries along the edges and a burst of chocolate curlicues in the center.

Once everyone has made their acquaintance with Julie, we all fill our plates. I keep my plate sparse. Everyone settles into a comfortable spot in the living room, balancing the plates in their hands.

"So, Julie, what do you do for a living?" Michelle inquires.

Julie places her fork on her plate before answering. "Well, my husband is a minister, and I keep myself busy helping the church family and volunteering."

"Do you have children?" Brenda asks, smiling.

The knot in my stomach twists and I discreetly spit the bite of celery I had been chewing into my napkin, wadding it in my hand. What little appetite I had is gone. I want to glare at Brenda, but she wouldn't notice or understand it if she did. Instead, I look mournfully in Julie's direction.

She doesn't look bothered in the least. She clears her throat and responds very sweetly, "No. We've been trying for years, but it hasn't happened yet." Then her radiant smile appears.

My shoulders relax. Of course Julie would know what to say; I'm sure she's been asked this hundreds of times before.

Brenda's face pales for a moment. "Oh. I'm...I'm sorry. I shouldn't have..." she looks around for support.

Julie is quick to respond. She reaches across and pats Brenda's knee. "It's fine. It's not an unusual question, and you couldn't have known. Please don't worry about it. Do you have children?"

Brenda blinks. "Uh, yes. I have...three," she stammers.

"Boys or girls or both?" Julie continues.

"Girls. All girls," Brenda replies, still uncomfortable.

"Oh, that's nice." Julie smiles. "I'll bet they're as lovely as their mother."

Brenda blinks again and smiles shyly. "Well, I think they're beautiful. But I'm their mother, so of course I would say that."

"Oh, you know you have beautiful girls, Brenda," Lilly chimes in. "Shaun and Shane have been in love with them for years."

Michelle raises her glass into the air, grinning. "Here, here! All the girls in this group are gorgeous, moms...and future moms...included!" She points her glass toward Julie, who raises her glass, as well.

We all raise our glasses and clink them together. Since my usual glass of wine has been replaced by iced tea, I hope no one will notice, at least for a little while longer.

No such luck.

"Are you driving home later, Faith?" Michelle asks jokingly. Lilly and Brenda chuckle.

Trying to buy some more time, I reply innocently, "Excuse me?"

"Aren't you going to try some of the delicious Pinot Noir that Lilly brought? It's yummy." She swirls the wine in her glass.

I look to Julie and she gives me an encouraging nod. My hesitation and expression must've given something away, because Brenda chimes in almost immediately.

"What? What's going on, Faith?" she asks.

Taking a deep breath, I place my plate down on the coffee table and stand up. Turning to the side, I cup my bulging belly with both hands. "Ladies, I'm pregnant."

There's a long moment of stony silence before pandemonium erupts as everyone, with the exception of Julie, leaps up and there's a high pitched chorus of "Whoa!" "What?" "That's wonderful news!" "How far along are you?" "When are you due?" "Do you know if it's a boy or a girl?"

Hugs and hands on my belly ensue, and I'm unable to answer any questions with coherence for awhile. Once the initial reaction subsides and everyone takes their seats again, all eyes are on me.

"So," Michelle begins. "When are you due?"

"Late March."

"How are you feeling? I noticed you didn't eat much," Lilly responds, always observant.

"Oh, it's been awful; lots of throwing up and food aversions. But I'm getting through it. As a matter of fact," I gesture toward Julie. "Julie has been very helpful to me, especially today. She's the one who did everything. I couldn't have managed otherwise."

Appreciative glances are followed by an uncomfortable tension. Julie is the one to break it.

"Ladies, please don't be uncomfortable about this. I'm so happy for Faith. I really am. This is wonderful news for her and her family!"

"She really means it. Trust me; she's almost more excited about this than I am," I add my support to her statement.

"Were…were you guys trying to have another baby?" Brenda asks, casting a furtive glance toward Julie.

I shake my head. "Absolutely not. This came as a total shock."

"Are you concerned about the risks at your age?" Michelle asks.

"Yes, of course. But," I glance at Julie. "we're leaving it in God's hands. He let this happen, so He knows what's going to happen."

Julie smiles.

"Yeah, but," Brenda interjects. "aren't you worried about that?" She wrinkles her nose.

I consider her question before shaking my head. "No. I'm not. We will deal with whatever comes our way." I leave unsaid the fact that I've had so much worse in terms of worry over the years. This is nothing in comparison. "Of course, Andrew is sure he's going to have a little brother." I smile and pat my stomach.

The ladies shift in their seat. Brenda sips her wine.

"I think it would be wonderful to have two boys and two girls. Andrew is such a sweet boy; he deserves to be a big brother," Michelle replies. "Any more wine or iced tea, ladies?"

"I'll have some more wine, please." Lilly leans forward and hands her glass to Michelle. "I thought you looked a little sickly tonight, Faith. I didn't want to say anything. I know you've had a lot on your mind lately. Now to find out that you're pregnant, I'm just relieved!"

I don't mind sharing the struggle we had with Sarah and "that boy". They're all appalled and shocked by it, but relieved that it worked out. I am quick to point out the help that Lilly provided, which she is just as quick to dismiss.

The primary conversation continues to swirl around the baby, my pregnancy experience so far, and how we're coping. Julie involves herself in the conversation, and my friends start to relax around her; she has that way about her of putting people at ease.

After much discussion, I can't help myself; a yawn escapes. As if on cue, Julie rises and begins to retrieve empty plates. "I think you're worn out, Faith. I'll get the dishes done, so you can rest."

The rest of my friends take the hint and happily join in. They begin to efficiently and quickly clear and clean, insisting that I rest. Lilly even brings me a glass of water and asks if there's anything else I need.

Smiling, I respond, "No. This is wonderful! You guys are the best."

She smiles, squeezes my arm and joins me on the sofa. Laughter and conversation continues in the kitchen. I can pick out Julie's voice and laughter and am gratified that she fits in so nicely.

I never doubted she would.

"Faith, how are you feeling, really?" she asks, her tone serious.

"Honestly, we were shocked at first, but we're okay with it."

"Really? I think I'd lose my mind if I came up pregnant at my age and with my kids being the ages they are. I don't mean to put a negative vibe on you, but I just want to be sure that you really are fine."

I smile and squeeze her hand. "Lilly, you know me. I'm good with this. It's been a very...healing thing for me."

She looks at me, puzzled. "Healing?"

Preferring not to go into details, I simply respond. "I've had some...struggles lately. Sometime I'll tell you about it over a long lunch. This whole experience is helping me to come to terms with some things. Considering the alternative, this isn't so bad. It's another beautiful baby, not a chronic illness." I rub my stomach.

"I'm never one to intrude, Faith. You know that. But I hope you know you can talk to me any time."

"I know, Lilly. You're a doll and I appreciate it."

She doesn't pry any further, but instead rises and retreats to the kitchen.

Midway through the cleaning process, Michael comes through the front door and calls out, "Hello!"

"I'm in here, honey!" I yell. He comes around the corner, unbuttoning his coat.

"Hey. How'd it go?" he asks, leaning over to kiss me.

"It went well…" Before I can continue, Brenda, Lilly, and Michelle spill out of the kitchen congratulating and teasing him all at the same time. He accepts it all with grace.

Julie joins the group, wiping her hands on a dish towel. "Did you return my husband in one piece?" she quips, laughing.

Michael smiles. "Yes, I delivered him safely to his home and he's pretty tired. He kicked all our butts at the bowling alley, by the way. His swing is killer! I think he bowled more strikes than anything."

She nods enthusiastically. "Did he tell you he was the Holy Bowler champion three years in a row?"

Michael's mouth drops open before he laughs. "Seriously? That would explain a lot."

"Yeah, he doesn't boast much," She laughs before turning to me. "Well, everything's pretty much cleaned up. I think I'd better get home."

I rise with my typical grunt, and give her a big hug. "Thank you, Julie. Thank you so much."

She squeezes me and pulls away, her eyes glistening. "I had a wonderful time. It was so nice to meet you, ladies." She turns to each lady in turn and says her goodbyes with hugs, which are enthusiastically returned. She's going to fit in beautifully.

In the midst of the ladies getting their coats on to leave, my children return home. All of the activity is overwhelming, and I'm grateful when everyone goes home and I can finally catch my breath. I never did get my Nap Time today.

Once everyone is in bed, I crawl into bed myself, only stopping to brush my teeth and wash my face halfheartedly.

"You look so tired, Faith. More than usual," Michael mentions as I yawn so wide I know he can see straight down my throat.

I can only mumble in agreement. Michael turns the lights out and slips in next to me, drawing me to him. I feel him kiss my neck and whisper, "Sleep well, my love."

Yes…I am grateful for his love and for Yours, too. Thank you, Lord.

I slip into unconsciousness, grateful and content.

Chapter Thirty Four

I wonder if Brenda's already here.

Walking into The Bread Basket, I approach the host station manned by a beautiful red head with a warm smile.

"Hello! Welcome to the Bread Basket. How many in your party?" she asks, eyeing the seating chart in front of her.

"I'm actually here to meet a friend."

"Oh. We have two guests here already that are waiting for the remaining members of their party. Shall I show you around and see if either one is your friend?" she asks cheerily.

I nod and follow her into the dining room. Brenda spots me and waves enthusiastically from her booth. The knot twists in my stomach.

"That must be her," the hostess replies and ushers me to the table where a menu is already waiting for me. "Enjoy your meal, ladies." The hostess retreats.

Lord, help me.

"Hi, Faith! It's so good to see you again!" Brenda bubbles and reaches across the table to squeeze both of my hands in hers. "How was your weekend? Did you have any more morning sickness? You look better today, actually. But you do look thinner." Her eyes flick around my face, but don't appear to scrutinize my choice in clothing. That's a first.

I didn't spend much time concerning myself with what to wear. My mind is too full of other more pressing issues. Every article of clothing in my closet is getting tighter, and naturally, I have no maternity clothes. I'll have to shop very soon. I opted for comfortable jeans (the top button remains open) and a loose fitting maroon peasant blouse.

Brenda is, of course, dressed to the nines from her diamond drop earrings to her Louis Vuitton clutch. Today her colors are black and white with the exception of a crimson scarf draped artfully around her shoulders. Her freshly colored blonde hair has some darker tones to it this time; it's much more flattering to her face than the near white blond she usually sports.

"Well, I don't know about 'thinner'. Most of my clothes are already getting too tight. I'm feeling good today. Breakfast stayed down, but it was only a piece of toast. I spent most of the weekend resting. Michael took Andrew to his soccer game Saturday so I could sleep in. Were you there?" I ask innocently. This may be a good segue into the conversation I need to have with her.

She sips her tea and shakes her head. "No, Scott took Lisa this time. I had some things to do at the store." Lisa is her nine year old daughter that plays in the same league as Andrew.

The waitress arrives to take our orders, even though I hadn't been able to peruse the menu. Honestly, nothing sounds particularly good anyway. Brenda insists I at least try the chicken salad sandwich, so I opt for a salad and half sandwich with iced tea.

Once the waitress leaves, I continue. "How's everything going at home for you?" It's a broad enough question, maybe she'll open up.

"Oh, fine. Fine. How're things going for you? Your life is turned upside down right now, huh?" she laughs.

Rats.

"We're doing well. We're all getting used to the idea. But I'm not really looking forward to the diapers and sleepless nights again. It's been awhile." The waitress arrives with my tea and I eagerly sip some to buy some time.

Brenda laughs and agrees with me. "I'm sure you'll be fine. Maybe this baby will be the easiest one of all!"

Perhaps a different approach will work. "You said you had to do some things at the store on Saturday. You've worked there so long; I thought you had Saturdays off. What did you have to do?"

There's an almost imperceptible twitch to her mouth as she casts her gaze down for the briefest of moments.

"Oh, you know. Just inventory," she replies a little too casually just as our meals arrive. The waitress busies herself with placing our food down, and Brenda takes the time to collect herself. I study her the entire time while I decide if I should just come out with it and ask, or if I should take a gentler approach.

Something tells me that she won't ever come out with it if I'm not direct.

Taking one last sip of my iced tea, I dive right in.

"How's Nate doing?" I ask, reaching for my salad fork.

Brenda coughs and sputters. She had just begun to chew a bite of her sandwich. She hastily reaches for her napkin with one hand and her tea with the other.

Bingo.

"Are you all right?"

She looks at me wide eyed as she continues her recovery.

"Brenda, what's going on?" I ask quietly, placing my fork back onto the plate.

Placing her hand over her chest and taking a deep breath, she replies, "What do you mean? There's nothing going on." Her voice is a little too high pitched.

Closing my eyes for the briefest of moments for the briefest of prayers, I press on. "Brenda, I'm worried about you."

"Me? Why?" Her lunch remains untouched in front of her as does mine.

"Well, there are some…things I've noticed lately that have me concerned."

She blinks hard for a moment. "What are you talking about?"

My gut tells me I already know the answer to the question I don't want to ask.

The waitress bustles in and interrupts. "Is everything all right here, ladies? Can I refill your drinks?"

Brenda doesn't even look at her, so I reply hastily, "We're fine, thank you. We're just talking."

The waitress nods and moves on to her next group of guests.

"Brenda, I remember seeing you at the soccer game with Nate that one time. You guys sat awfully close to each other until I texted you. Then you moved your chairs apart and I would swear you looked…guilty or something. When you and I had lunch a few weeks ago and I mentioned Nate, you reacted sort of like you did now. I was out at the mall last week and saw you with another man. You guys looked rather…close. I saw him touch you." I look her in the eye. "Brenda, are you having an affair?"

Brenda visibly pales. She looks trapped. I can see the truth in her face and I gasp.

"You *are*," I whisper. My hands fly to my mouth.

She shakes her head slowly as her eyes fill with tears, lunch forgotten. "I don't know how this happened," she whispers, her voice shaky.

"Oh, Brenda." I reach across to take her hand, but she snatches it away and fumbles around with her napkin, blotting at her eyes so as not to ruin her make up. She's trembling. "I'm sorry." I don't know what else to say.

She waves me off as she continues blotting. I wait for her to speak first.

Eventually she looks mournfully at me. "I guess the cat's out of the bag, huh?" She tries to smile, but it looks more like a guilty, painful grimace.

"Brenda, what *happened*?" I ask. "I thought you and Scott were perfectly happy together."

She takes a sip of her iced tea. "I can only imagine what you must think of me."

"I don't think anything bad of you, Brenda. You're my friend. I just don't understand."

"Well, that's two of us." She tries to joke again, but it falls flat. "I mean, I've never done anything like this before and…it just sort of happened."

"So that was Nate I saw you with at the mall?"

The waitress interrupts again and places two fresh iced teas in front of us, along with our checks. "Ladies, are your lunches not to your liking?"

How does she sneak up like that?

Brenda rolls her eyes.

"The food is fine. We're just talking. I'm sorry," I smile at her. She is appeased for the moment and quietly walks away.

"Maybe we should try some of this chicken salad that you recommended." I pick up my half sandwich and take a bite.

Brenda picks at her bread. "I'm not hungry." She doesn't even look up.

I place my sandwich back on the plate and reach for her hand. This time she doesn't pull away. "Brenda, what happened?"

She chews on her lower lip. "I'm just so…lonely, Faith." When she looks at me, her vulnerability is so raw and intense that my heart aches for her. "Scott works such long hours, and he's not home even when he's home. We don't talk anymore, and he doesn't even do that much with the kids. It's been so long since we've had sex, and the last time we did I didn't even really need to be there. It's like I don't exist to him anymore!" Her eyes well with tears. "Oh, sure. He'll do *anything* for his clients, but his family? No, we get shoved off to the side like we're garbage." Her tone is angry.

"Does Scott know how you feel?" I ask quietly.

She replies with a snort of derision. "As if! We don't talk anymore, Faith. He doesn't *hear* me. We've gone our separate ways while still living in the same house."

"How did this thing with Nate start?"

"I hate to say it because it sounds so cliché, but Nate was just there for me when I needed someone to be there for me. He *listens* to me, Faith. I was working late one evening with him doing inventory, and I just started talking to him. I had a very frustrating day, and I needed to open up to someone. He didn't just nod and give grunts every now and then, pretending to listen. He asked me questions and even offered some advice." She falls back in the booth and closes her eyes.

"But how did it develop into more than that?"

She shakes her head and her eyes wander around the restaurant. "I…I don't know, really. He started out to just be a really good friend. You know I work a lot at the boutique, and he was usually working when I was. One day, he offered to buy me coffee, and I accepted. I didn't plan on doing anything like this, Faith. Please believe me. It was just coffee and talking. That's all."

I nod.

"Then we started meeting for lunch on a regular basis." She looks down at her hands and twirls her wedding ring around and around on her finger. Her cheeks begin to pink. "I don't remember the last time Scott and I sat down and ate together at home, much less anywhere else. Then one day, Nate mentioned that his apartment was just around the corner and perhaps we could continue our conversation there. So, I accepted." She presses her lips together.

My throat closes and I place my fork back on the plate.

"When we got to his apartment," her voice drops to a whisper. "We just kept talking. He told me about where he grew up and his dreams in life. I told him about the dreams I had for opening my own boutique some day…" Her voice is wistful as she looks into the distance. "Then, he…he held my hand and…one thing led to another…"

"Brenda, you don't have to…" I start, but she waves me off.

"Faith, I never, ever wanted to do something like this. But you have no idea how *good* it felt to have someone make me the center of their attention, and make me feel…beautiful." A tear cascades down her cheek unchecked as she bites her lip, her make up forgotten. "I felt like an absolute wretch afterwards."

"But you…you're still…?" I ask.

She nods, and covers her face with her hands.

"*Why*, Brenda?"

Her hands drop from her face and she stares defiantly at me. "Because don't I *deserve* to be loved, Faith?! Doesn't everyone deserve to be loved? And happy?"

"Well, yes. But…does Nate know that you're married?"

Another tear drops onto her lap. "Yes, he knows. That's what I complained about the most to him: my problems with Scott."

"Oh, Brenda. I don't know what to say. You know this is wrong. Have you and Scott ever considered counseling?"

She snorts. "Yeah, right. Scott doesn't think we have any problems." She crosses her arms over her chest. "That *is* our problem."

"Oh, boy," I sigh and place my napkin across my half eaten food. Brenda's remains untouched. "I'm so sorry, Brenda. This is awful."

"What are you going to do?" he asks anxiously. "Now that you know about me and Nate."

"What do you want me to do?"

She grips the table and leans forward. "Please don't tell Scott."

"Brenda, that's not my place. But you can't keep this up." My mind flashes to my own bout with secrecy and what it did to me. "You can't keep a secret like this. It won't work. You're going to throw away your marriage and your family. What about Mariah, Jennifer, and Lisa?"

Pain flashes across her features. "Trust me; I have thought about that a lot. I think about them every day, as a matter of fact." She begins to twirl her hair and the distance returns to her gaze. She muses silently for a moment before addressing me again. "Faith, I just don't know what to do. I don't see how Scott and I can make this marriage work. It seems like he checked out a long time before I...before I met Nate."

"Brenda, don't give up on your marriage," I plead. "You just need to break it off with Nate first, and try to talk to Scott again."

She looks incredibly sad. "Faith, I am tired of trying. I don't know how anymore."

"Listen, why don't you talk to Pastor Ben? He's Julie's husband, and he does counseling at the church we've started going to. I think he's a really good listener. Maybe he can help."

She shakes her head. "I don't know, Faith. I don't see how anyone can help at this point. It's such a mess. Besides, we don't even go to church much less that church."

"Brenda, there are no messes too big to be helped." I should know. "Pastor Ben doesn't just see people that go to church, either. He'll see anyone that needs to be seen."

She agrees to consider it and we notice the waitress eyeing us anxiously; we've basically camped out at her table for almost an hour and a half.

"Brenda, we should get going. Do you want to come back to my house and keep talking?"

She shakes her head. "No, there's nothing else to talk about." She grabs her purse and scoots out of the booth.

I quickly throw some cash on the table to cover the bill and follow her into the lobby of the restaurant. She's already on her way out the door before I grab her arm to stop her.

"Brenda, please wait. I don't want to end our...lunch like this." I almost said friendship. "Won't you come back to my house? I'll drive you and then bring you back, okay? Please?"

She sighs. "Faith, we're fine. All right? You and I are good. I hope." She looks down at her shoes.

"Brenda, I don't think anything bad about you, really. I'm sorry this has happened. It's just not like you. You're better than this," I plead with her.

"Apparently I'm not better than this, Faith. I've done it. I've really done it." Her voice quivers, and suddenly she starts bawling. I guide her over to a stone bench that's surrounded by bushes and slightly secluded.

It takes her a few minutes to calm down and rummage through her purse for some tissue.

"God, what have I done? I'm so stupid, Faith." She cries into her fistful of tissues.

"You're not stupid, Brenda. You made a mistake. Everyone makes mistakes." I try to soothe her by rubbing her back as she hunches over, sobbing.

"Yeah, like forgetting to pay the phone bill, or showing up late to work." She straightens up and turns toward me. Her face is red, swollen, and almost make up free. "I *slept* with another *man*, Faith! That's not the kind of mistake everyone makes!" She wails.

I have no idea what to say, so I let her cry and keep rubbing her back. After she's cried out, she sits up.

"Faith, I'm sorry about this. Sorry about all of this."

"You don't owe me an apology, Brenda. It's not me that you've hurt." She's messier than I've ever seen her. But then again, I've never seen her messy.

Glancing at her watch, she jumps up. "I have to go. I need to fix myself up before the kids get home from school." She hurriedly stuffs her used tissues in her purse and turns to leave, but hesitates before turning around.

"Faith, I don't want to tell Scott. But I will end it with Nate." Her vulnerability is achingly raw. "I will. I promise."

I hate to, but I have to tell her the truth no matter how much it hurts her. "Brenda, you can't keep this from Scott. You have to tell him. I promise you'll regret it if you don't." My secret about Paul almost ruined me.

Panic flashes across her face before she collects herself. A stone wall descends on her features. It's very unsettling. "That's not for you to decide, Faith." Her eyes narrow into slits. "I hope you're not threatening to tell him yourself."

It takes me a split second to realize she's misconstrued my words. "No, Brenda. Absolutely not! I just meant that secrets of this magnitude won't just go away if you ignore them. You have to tell Scott yourself."

Her eyes search mine before she responds. "I'll think about it, Faith." Her eyes flash toward her watch again. "I really have to go. We'll talk soon, okay?" She turns on her heel and walks quickly away from me toward her vehicle. I see her swipe at her cheek.

All I can do is watch her go, an unsettled feeling twisting in my chest.

"That did not go well," I murmur to myself before heading to my own vehicle and going home.

Okay, God. She admitted that she's having an affair. Now what? I don't know how to help her, and I really don't want her marriage destroyed. What do I do?

No answer, of course. But I've learned God works in His own way and in His own time. Ben and Julie have told me that many times, and I've seen it in my own life.

I just wish He would hurry up. I don't want to see a marriage and family destroyed...

Chapter Thirty Five

Brenda doesn't call me that day, or the next, or even the next. In fact, Friday rolls around and I'm deeply concerned. Worrying isn't helping my appetite. The nausea levels off, but doesn't disappear. If I'm not nauseated and not eating, then I'm anxious about Brenda and not eating. Michael doesn't try to hide his concern.

"Faith, you have to eat something. You can't just keep going like this. It's not good for you or the baby." He's eyeing me as I regard, rather than eat, my oatmeal at breakfast. The kids have left for school and I'm still sitting there with a full bowl in front of me. "You're shaking."

I notice the tremor in my hand as my spoon is suspended over the bowl. Sighing, I dig the spoon deep into the oatmeal and let it go, folding my arms in front of me. "Michael, I know. But I'm just not sure how to handle this." I had filled him in about Brenda.

He sighs. "Faith, there's nothing for you to handle. This isn't your problem. It's Brenda's and Scott's problem. Let it go. We are praying for them and that's all we can do. Please eat your oatmeal." He reaches over, picks up a spoonful of oatmeal and holds it in front of my face. The childishness of his action makes me giggle.

"Really, Michael? You're going to spoon feed me?"

His face remains serious, but I see the twinkle in his eyes. "If that's what it takes." He pushes the spoon toward me and I reactively push it away causing the oatmeal to fall off the spoon and plop onto the table with a wet *thud*. We both chuckle.

I wipe the mess up with a napkin and take a bite from the bowl, which I promptly spit out.

"It's cold," I lament.

Michael clucks his tongue and grabs my bowl along with his empty plate and disappears into the kitchen. He returns momentarily with a bowl of cold cereal and places it before me.

"There, now it's supposed to be cold." A twitch of a smile curls the corners of his mouth.

"Thanks," I reply wryly. I eat a small spoonful. I like corn flakes. So far, so good. I'm able to eat the entire bowl. I tilt the empty bowl in his direction and grin. "See? Done."

"That's a start anyway. Do you want any eggs? I don't have to be at work until nine."

I shake my head. "No, I better just let this settle. It's best to stop while I'm ahead." I rise with the ever present grunt, place my cereal bowl in the sink, and fill a mug with steaming fresh coffee, stirring in cream and sugar. At least my taste for coffee hasn't diminished.

"April's pretty stoked about tonight," Michael muses as he hugs me from behind, cradling my belly bulge before kissing my neck.

"You think so? I hadn't noticed." I chuckle. To be honest, stoked is an exceptionally mild description of how April feels about the dance tonight. She was practically on the verge of a stroke with excitement during breakfast, and I tell Michael so.

"That's about right." He laughs. "I hope she can make it through the day at school."

"Well, she'll have to. If I have to pick her up from school today, she won't go to the dance."

Once Michael leaves for work, I load the breakfast dishes into the dishwasher and head upstairs to shower. Pausing at April's door, I see her beautiful dress hanging from a hook on her closet door. It really is gorgeous. Stepping into her room, I finger the fabric of the dress and imagine how she's going to look. She'll be so beautiful.

My first child is going to a formal dance. She's growing up so fast. They all are. My hand is drawn to the bulge on my belly, and I think about this new child that's coming into our lives. What he or she will look like, whether it is a he or a she, what they'll be like, and how we'll be as new parents again.

My eyes gaze around the walls of her room. There are still traces of the little girl that she was intermingled with teenage paraphernalia. There are goofy candid pictures of her with her friends taped to her mirror and walls. Books that contain her sticker collection she started at the age of four are stacked haphazardly on a corner of her messy dresser. Make up is strewn over the rest of it. One drawer is open halfway and there's a neon yellow sock hanging out.

A fluffy piece of white furry fabric catches my wandering eye; it's sticking out between her pillow and mattress. My curiosity is piqued. Surely it's not prying to just see what that could be. It's not like I'm reading a diary or rifling through drawers.

Plucking the piece out from its hiding place, I find it's attached to a much loved and much used little teddy bear with one eye missing.

"Beary White!" I gasp aloud. I can't believe it. I thought that little bear was long gone. I received it as a baby shower gift when I was pregnant with April. It was the only stuffed animal in her crib and she latched on to it rather quickly. It went with her everywhere when she was little. It carried her through her first hair cut, her first dental visit, and her first day at preschool. She even kept him in her backpack in elementary school; just having him near was enough. I thought for sure she had outgrown him; he disappeared from our lives years ago. Or so I had thought. Yet here he is.

I stroke his soft furry belly and cradle his one-eyed little head as I realize that she still sleeps with him.

Hugging Beary White to my chest, peace washes over me. My little girl may be growing up, but she's still my little girl.

They're *all* growing up fast, but they'll always be my babies.

Carefully, reverently, I tuck Beary White back into the space between April's pillow and mattress and leave her room otherwise undisturbed.

"Thank you for that gift, God," I murmur as I head for my own room to shower.

****

That evening April descends the stairs slowly, smiling from ear to ear. Her hair is in a beautiful up do; I made an appointment for her at an upscale salon downtown to have her hair and make up done professionally.

April's dark hair is swept off her face into a loose knot on the crown of her head, her face is framed in soft curls and there are large, loose curls cascading down her back. Her blue eyes sparkle and shine like the diamonds that dangle from her ears and hang around her neck. Her make up is flawless and accentuate her natural beauty perfectly without making her look painted.

Lilly, Julie and I gasp.

"Oh, April! Baby girl, you look so beautiful!" I clap my hands together and try not to tear up, unsuccessfully.

Lilly insisted on coming over to see April's finished look; she recommended the salon. Her recommendation is well deserved.

"You are absolutely stunning, April!" Lilly chimes as April completes her descent and is immediately enveloped in a hug from her father.

"Dad, don't mess up my hair!" she protests while accepting the hug.

"You're going to be the most beautiful girl at that dance, April," Julie bubbles. "I knew that dress was the right choice. It's the perfect color for you. It really brings out your eyes!"

"Shaun! Shane! Come see how beautiful April looks in her dress," Lilly calls out to her sons who are playing in the basement.

Shane appears rather quickly and looks at April. "Cool." Lilly clears her throat and looks pointedly at him, gesturing toward April. Shane rolls his eyes before modifying his answer. "You look good, April."

April rolls her eyes in return. "Thank you, Shane," she replies woodenly, but winks at him. He grins and runs back into the basement to continue his games with Andrew.

"Where is Shaun?" Lilly asks. "Shaun! Come here, please!" she calls out again.

Shaun appears with Sarah in tow from the basement. They both have their hands clasped in front of them. For some reason, they look…different standing there so close together. I narrow my eyes at Sarah; she diverts her gaze. Her cheeks turn pink.

Lord. Here we go again.

I make a mental note to discuss this with Lilly later. Compliments are obligingly passed between the kids before Shaun and Sarah disappear into the basement once again.

The doorbell ringing causes April to shriek, which causes all of us to jump.

"April, calm down, please!" I hiss at her.

Michael simply chuckles and answers the door. A young man I reasonably assume is the famous Tom Parker stands stiffly in our doorway, wearing a tuxedo with a tie that matches April's dress perfectly. He's holding a clear plastic box with a corsage in his left hand and holding out his right hand to Michael.

"Hello, Mr. Strauss. I'm Tom Parker and I'm pleased to meet you. I'm here to escort April to the dance."

Michael smiles and shakes the boy's hand. "Why thank you, Tom. It's nice to meet you, too. Please come in. April's waiting." He ushers Tom inside. As soon as Tom sees April, his mouth falls open and his eyes bug out before he collects himself.

April walks eagerly up to Tom and grins, lifting her chin up to him. "Hi, Tom! You look so handsome!"

Tom blushes and drops his gaze, suddenly remembering the plastic container in his hand. "Oh! I…uh…got you a corsage." His eyes sweep the foyer for the first time and he notices the large audience standing before him. He blushes and takes a step back, bumping right into the wall.

Oblivious to his discomfort, April accepts the container from Tom and gushes over the beautiful corsage. Bouncing on the balls of her feet, she cries, "Oh! It's perfect!" She thrusts the corsage toward him. "Will you put it on me?"

"Oh, uh…sure," he stammers, retrieving the corsage with shaky hands. He fumbles around with the strap and it drops onto the floor. His face turns crimson.

Michael suppresses a laugh and retrieves the fallen corsage. It's still intact. "It's okay, Tom. Any man surrounded by so many beautiful women," he sweeps the room with his free hand. "would be nervous, too. Let me help you."

"Thank you, sir," Tom squeaks and clears his throat.

As Michael places the corsage on April's wrist, I try to make Tom more comfortable.

I approach him smiling, and extend my hand to shake his. "Hi, Tom. I'm sorry. We didn't mean to make you uncomfortable. I'm Faith, April's mother."

Tom shakes my hand and I can't help but notice his palms are sweaty and cold.

Poor kid. He's so nervous.

"It's a pleasure to meet you, ma'am," he clears his throat again.

I continue introducing Tom to Lilly and Julie, who are just as warm and receptive.

"Tom, would you mind spending a few minutes chatting with me? I think there are still a few things the ladies want to help April with before she's ready to go." Michael looks pointedly at me. "Would you like something to drink? A Coke, maybe?" He places his hand on Tom's back, and guides him into the kitchen.

Michael told me he wanted to have a talk with Tom before the dance. He wants the young man to know what sort of behavior is expected of him towards April and how she is to be respected. April deemed the whole thing embarrassing, but didn't demand that her father not do it. She knows her dad is here to protect her. Michael assured her he wouldn't embarrass her, but made it clear if she didn't allow him to have a discussion with Tom, then she wouldn't be allowed to attend the dance.

April grudgingly relented.

While Michael chats with Tom in the kitchen, the ladies and I gather around April and take pictures of her. She hams it up, of course. She loves being the center of attention.

Once Tom returns a few minutes later, we pose the two together for more pictures. I notice Tom flickers a glance at Michael before placing his hand around April's waist at an appropriate height. Michael nods almost imperceptibly.

Once they're on their way with a warning about the curfew (to which Tom said a firm "Yes, sir!"), the ladies and I chatter on about what a handsome couple they made and reminisce about our own high school dances. Michael looks amused.

Julie excuses herself and retreats to her own home. Lilly is about to gather her children and do the same when I pull her aside.

"Lilly, do you have a minute?" I ask.

"Sure," she replies, placing her purse back down on the bench. "What's up?"

We make ourselves comfortable on the living room sofa before I bring up the subject. "Listen, Lilly. Do you know if there's anything going on with Sarah and Shaun? It just looked to me like they were a little...cozy together."

Lilly looks at me sideways. "Well, since you mentioned it, I think Shaun does have a crush on her."

My eyebrows rise. "Really? How long has this been going on?"

She shrugs. "I don't know. I think it's been a month or two. He gets a little tongue tied around her. You know, tripping over his words and such. I think it's cute. He was insistent that he be allowed to come over tonight."

I try to keep a straight face. "Madam, what are your son's intentions toward my daughter?"

She giggles. "I don't think any thirteen-year-old can even define intentions, much less have any." We both laugh.

"Seriously, though. Especially after the incident we had over that....boy, I am really concerned about her. She's still not completely herself, and I wonder what's going on inside her head. You know she's never been one to share a lot, but now..." I sigh. "I just don't know."

"Faith, please don't worry about her or Shaun. I know my boy, and you know me."

I nod vigorously. "Yes, I'm thankful it's your son and not some stranger."

"Between us, we can keep an eye on them both. I better get going, though. I'm sure April is going to have a wonderful time." She leans in conspiratorially. "Did Michael read the boy the riot act in the kitchen or what?"

I chuckle. "Sort of. He just wanted to be sure that Tom knows our standards and anything less won't be tolerated."

Her eyebrows rise in surprise. "Oh. Well, that's very chivalrous of him, especially in this day and age. It's actually quite refreshing. I should bring that up to Tony…" she murmurs as she rises.

She calls down to the basement for her boys and sure enough Sarah is close on the heels of Shaun. I try not to stare, but I'm definitely observing their body language. I believe the feeling is mutual.

Standing at the door, they are almost toe to toe, breathily saying "Bye" to each other before waving shyly as each watches the other until they're both out of sight.

****

I fall asleep on the couch waiting for April's return, even though Michael insisted that I go to bed while he waited up alone.

The door opening rouses me from my slumber. Slowly I make my way to the foyer, trying to smooth my hair on the way.

"Hi, Dad! It was incredible!" April chirps from the doorway. Tom follows close on her heels.

How sweet that he escorted her to the door. Just as he should.

"Well done, Tom. You're fifteen minutes early," Michael says, shaking the boy's hand and clapping him on the back.

Tom's chest puffs out and he beams. "Yes, sir. I promised I would have her home on time."

"He was a perfect gentleman, Dad." April rolls her eyes.

Michael continues smiling at Tom. "I never doubted he would be."

Tom and April are allowed to say their goodbyes with a quick hug before Tom disappears into the night.

April is hyped up; she dances around the foyer with a phantom partner, humming to herself.

"I'm guessing you had a great time?" I ask as she floats into the living room.

She stops dancing long enough to bounce in front of me. "Oh! It was divine! We danced, we ate, we talked, we laughed…" She resumes her dancing.

"Tom treated you properly then?" Michael inquires.

She stops dancing and drops her shoulders. "*Yes*, Dad! He didn't even hold me very close as we danced like everyone else was doing. I think you really scared him! Thanks a *lot.*" She scowls at her father for a fleeting moment before the huge sappy grin returns.

Michael nods decisively. "That's a good boy."

I chuckle and shake my head. "April, it's almost eleven. We need to get to bed." Yawning, I head for the stairs.

"Oh, if only this night would never end…" She dances her way slowly up the stairs.

Laughing, I savor watching the absolute joy emanating from her very core as she reaches the landing, floats down the hall turning slowly in circles before floating into her bedroom and closing the door softly behind her. I bet she snuggles with Beary White tonight, maybe even rubs his ear like she used to.

April may be over the top emotional, but I have no doubt that she's going to live life to its fullest and enjoy every single moment. There are so many people in this world that live life dull. April is a vibrant color in a sea of gray.

What a wonderful creation she is, God. Thanks for letting me see that. And please protect her; I don't want her vibrancy to fade with time or because of life.

Chapter Thirty Six

"Faith? Are you awake?" Michael's voice is close to my ear.

"Hmph? What?" I say thickly, blinking at the sunlight peaking through the windows. By the softness and slant to the light, it's still early and it's Saturday. "What time izh it?" I slur.

"A little after seven."

Stretching and yawning, I roll onto my back. Michael hoists himself up on an elbow and looks at me, his forehead creased in worry. That catches my attention.

"What's wrong?" I'm fully awake.

His eyes wander over my face for a moment. "I…There was a meeting at work yesterday morning."

"And?" I hold my breath. This could be bad.

"Well, it looks like Gene is criminally liable for his actions. I can't be specific, but it looks really bad for him. He'll probably do prison time. There are a number of others that are culpable, as well."

"Okay. So what does that mean for us?"

"This is really going to hurt the company's reputation, first of all. It's going to take an incredible financial hit. So, there's talk that there will be across the board pay cuts for everyone in a managerial or executive position. That includes me."

"How much of a pay cut?" My mind flicks through our finances and fortunately, we live within our means and are savers, but still…there are limits.

"As little as five percent or as much as twenty percent. They're not sure yet."

My mouth falls open. "*Twenty* percent?! How...we couldn't do that, Michael."

"I know. That's what worries me," he replies quietly. "especially with a new baby on the way." His hand lands gently on my stomach.

"When will we know?"

He sighs and rolls onto his back, staring at the ceiling. "We should know by Christmas. I hope."

"But...that's a big gap, Michael. If your pay is cut by twenty percent, we...we may have to sell the house." The magnitude of the possibility is frightening.

He rests his forearm over his eyes. "I know. Trust me, I know."

"Is there anything you can do? Maybe get a job somewhere else?"

He drops his arm and frowns. "Faith, I've worked at this company for fifteen years. I've worked my way up and invested a lot of my talent there. I helped build the division I work in. I couldn't just leave. I love my job."

"But, if we can't pay our bills...."

He groans and closes his eyes. "I know, I know. We'll figure something out."

"We can always pray about it." I find his free hand and lace my fingers through his, squeezing.

He chuckles. "Yeah, we can." He turns to me. "Would you like to do the honors?"

I smile and say a very short, straightforward prayer. It's all I know how to do.

After saying amen, I promptly get up and dry heave into the toilet. Michael follows behind me, watching with concern.

"Faith, I know you're showing and everything, but you look like you've lost weight. I'm worried about you."

Wretching once again into the toilet, I can't respond. Once I catch my breath, I respond sarcastically, "Have you seen my rear end lately? I think it's taking on a life of its own. The bigger my stomach gets, the bigger it gets, too."

Tilting his head, he looks at my backside for a moment. "I love it. It's just right."

386

I give him a withering look and pull out the bathroom scale, turning it away from Michael. No respectable woman lets a man see her weight.

I'm twelve pounds lighter than I was two months ago. "Well, I have lost weight."

"How much?"

"Twelve pounds."

"Twelve *pounds*?" he asks incredulously. "Faith, that can't be good."

"What do you want me to do? I try to eat, but nothing stays down."

He shakes his head. "I don't know. But you need to do something. This can't go on. You don't look well. Maybe you're worrying too much about everything." Sighing, his head drops. "And I just gave you something else to worry about."

I wrap my arms around his waist and pull him close. "I'll be fine, and so will the baby. Let's go get some breakfast and see if I can't put a cork in it to keep it down."

He bends down to kiss the tip of my nose. "Is that all that's going on?"

"What do you mean?" I ask, puzzled.

His eyes search my face momentarily before he answers. "Well, I just…want to make sure you're not still keeping things from me." He frowns. "Is there anything else on your mind?"

We've still got some work to do, apparently.

"Micheal," I sigh. "I am not going to keep any secrets from you. I promised you that. Please believe me."

He presses his lips together before sighing. "Okay. Let's go get some breakfast."

We pad quietly down the hall; the kids are still asleep. Michael offers to make an omelet, but the thought of all those ingredients being mixed in eggs turns my stomach.

"Oatmeal?" he asks, rummaging in the pantry. "Could I put some raisins or nuts in it for you?"

"Just plain oatmeal, thank you." I busy myself making coffee as Michael prepares oatmeal. Once they're both done, I collect my bowl and head toward the dining room with Michael in tow. Passing my bowl of M&Ms, I pause. They would be really good in this oatmeal, I think…

I grab a small handful and plop them into my oatmeal. Michael gasps.

"Really, Faith? Oatmeal with M&Ms?"

I glance back at him over my shoulder, continuing my journey into the dining room. "It sounds good."

As I sit the bowl down in front of me, I stir the M&Ms around and around. The various colors bleed into the beige lumps of the oatmeal before the chocolate is finally released. My mouth begins to water.

Michael looks at me like I've lost my mind.

I take one bite and close my eyes, the corners of my mouth curling into a satisfied smile. "Mmmmm. This is really good! Do you want to try it?" I offer him a spoonful which he is quick to refuse.

"Fine, more for me." I stuff another spoonful into my mouth. Before I know it, the bowl is empty and I'm scraping my spoon around the interior so as not to miss a single chocolaty bite.

Michael also finishes his oatmeal, but the incredulous look hasn't disappeared. "You actually liked that?"

I nod. "Is there any oatmeal left?" My appetite has woken up.

Michael blinks in surprise. "Sure. I'll go make some more. You want a full bowl?"

"You don't need to make any more. Just whatever's left is okay."

He chuckles and rises quickly, reaching for my bowl. "Hey, if you'll eat it then I'll make it." He disappears into the kitchen and returns in record time with not just my bowl filled with oatmeal but my bowl of M&Ms, too. He places both before me, causing me to laugh.

"What's so funny?" Sarah stumbles around the corner, yawning and scratching her head.

"Your mother is mixing M&Ms in her oatmeal," Michael replies, smirking at me.

Sarah's head jerks up. "Huh? What? Why?"

Michael puts his hands in front of him, palms up and shrugs his shoulders. "I don't know and I don't care. Your mother is *eating*. That's all that matters."

I grab a larger handful of M&Ms and plop them in my oatmeal again, stirring to melt them, being careful not to spill any of the chocolaty oatmeal goodness over the sides of the bowl. This second batch tastes as good as the first. I take a second, larger mouthful.

"Thank God for chocolate," I mouth around my food, ignoring my own rule.

"Amen," Michael murmurs as he refills his coffee mug before joining me once again at the table.

"Mom, that's so gross," Sarah says, plopping down on a chair and resting her chin on her hands.

"Do you want some oatmeal, Sarah?" Michael asks.

"Nah," she says. "I think mom's ruined oatmeal for me." She rises and stumbles around the table, heading for the living room. "I'll just watch cartoons."

Once the second bowl is empty, I push it away with a satisfied smile. "I feel like a Thanksgiving turkey: stuffed!"

"Any nausea?" Michael asks.

I shake my head. "No. I feel fine."

"If you want to eat oatmeal with M&Ms for the next several months, that's okay by me. Just so long as you *eat*." He raises his mug in toast, and I do the same, taking a sip.

"Want to go sit on the back patio?" he asks. "It's nice this morning. You'll just need a lap blanket."

"Sure," I shrug. "Let me just refill my coffee, and I'll meet you out there."

We spend several quiet moments in the coolness, the blanket tucked snugly around my hips as we rock back and forth on the love seat-sized swing. Michael's arm is draped around my shoulders, and we are content to sip our coffees and listen to the birds.

The click of the French door that leads to the patio from the living room interrupts our reverie. Michael twists around. It's Sarah.

"Mom? Dad? Can I go to the movies this afternoon with Shaun?"

Michael is puzzled. "With Shaun? Lilly's boy? Why?"

"Sarah, who else is going?" I ask.

"His mom is taking us, of course. I think she's going to stay for the movie, so Shane is coming, too."

"Would you mind if Andrew comes? He doesn't have any soccer games today."

She grunts her dissatisfaction. "Why does Andrew have to come?"

"I'm sure Shane would like to have him come along. They're good friends, Sarah."

Michael looks at me, still puzzled. "What am I missing?" he asks quietly.

I shake my head and whisper, "I'll tell you in a minute." I address Sarah again. "So Andrew can come with, right?"

She rolls her eyes and her tone is flat. "Sure." She retreats into the house, closing the door.

"What gives?" Michael asks.

"I think Sarah and Shaun have a crush on each other."

Michael's eyes bug out. "What? When did this happen?" His head falls back on the swing. "We just got done with that other...boy. Now this."

"I first noticed it last night. At least we know Shaun and he's basically her age, too. This has nothing to do with that other incident, Michael. She is growing up, you know."

He sighs and looks at me. "Yeah, I guess. Still...she's awfully young."

Sipping my coffee, I shrug. "We can't stop it, but we can guide her. Shaun's a good kid, and I know Tony and Lilly are good parents."

He mutters his agreement, but his mood is sullen.

The door bursts open and Andrew spills onto the patio. "Mom! I'm going to the movies today with Shane!" He's wearing his teddy bear pajamas and his hair is disheveled. There's a drop of milk on his chin; he must've gotten a bowl of cereal.

"I know, sweetie. Do you know what movie it's going to be?" I ask, trying to match his enthusiasm.

"I don't know. I don't care. I get to go to the *movies*! Woo hoo!" he cries, and then disappears into the house, leaving the door wide open.

Michael rises to close it.

"I think I'm ready to go inside," I say.

He turns and offers his hand. I take his hand and grunt to a stand, following him inside. The television is on, but Sarah and Andrew are both at the table eating cereal.

Michael reaches for the remote and clicks the television off. Andrew immediately protests. "Dad! I was *listening* to that!"

"Sorry, buddy. We don't need to waste electricity."

"Aaawww!" Andrew replies. "It's not a waste if I'm listening to it, is it?!"

He has a point. Michael shakes his head. "Sorry, Andrew. When you're done eating, you can turn it back on."

"Oh-kay," Andrew replies.

I reach up and kiss Michael. "I'm going to shower."

"You sure you feel all right?"

"I feel fine, really. See you in a bit."

He pats my bottom as I head for the stairs. I pause in front of April's door and ever so carefully turn the door knob and peek in on her. She's sprawled out on her bed, which is a complete mess, as usual. In her left hand, there's a tuft of white fur sticking up between her fingers. Smiling, I just as carefully pull her door closed and latch it before continuing on to my own room.

In the midst of drying my hair, Michael enters the bathroom with the house phone in one hand, cupping the mouthpiece with the other. He holds it up to me and frowns. I turn the dryer off and look inquisitively at him.

He mouths almost inaudibly, "It's Brenda. She sounds really upset."

I place the hair dryer on the vanity and take the phone from Michael, who leans against the door frame, arms folded.

"Hello?"

"Faith? It's Brenda." She sounds panicky. "I…I told Scott and…he…he moved out! What am I going to do?" she sobs.

"What? When?"

Michael raises an eyebrow in a wordless question. I shake my head with my finger up, telling him to wait.

"I…I told him this morning and…he…he called me names and…then he packed up his clothes and left. He left me,

391

Faith! I even told him that I broke it off with Nate, but…he didn't listen. He just left!"

"Oh, Brenda. I'm so sorry. Where are you now?" I cover the mouthpiece and quickly mouth to Michael what's happened. He looks pained and shakes his head.

"I'm at home. The girls are all upset, Faith. He hugged them…but then he just left without a word. I…I don't know what to do!"

"I'm so sorry, Brenda."

"I told you I shouldn't have told him, Faith! I knew something like this would happen." She continues to sob.

Is this my fault?

"Brenda, you can come over here if you want. Bring the girls. I can call Lilly and Michelle…"

"No! I don't want anybody else to know about this. It's bad enough that it's happening. I don't want the whole world to know about it!" The panic in her voice ratchets up.

I grip the phone with both hands. "Brenda, listen. We're your friends. We're here to love you and support you and your family, no matter what, okay? That's what friends do."

She continues to sob. "I know, I know. But this is so embarrassing. I mean, who does this?! I…I just don't want anybody else to know. I can't believe that he actually just walked out! He wouldn't even talk to me!"

"Brenda, please. You need the support right now. We're not here to judge you, just to help."

She takes a few minutes to answer, sniffling. "I'll come over with the girls, but please don't call anyone. I just…I can't face them."

I shake my head at Michael and give him thumbs down. He frowns. "Okay, Brenda. I won't call anyone right now. When will you be here?"

"Uh…about an hour or so."

"Okay. We'll be waiting. Do you want us to have breakfast for you guys? Have you eaten?"

She snorts a dark laugh. "As if. I can't eat anything right now. My whole world is falling apart!"

"Have the girls eaten yet?"

She starts sobbing all over again. "Oh, hell. I don't know! God, I don't even know if my kids have eaten! Scott is right! I am a horrible mother!" She's on the verge of hysterics.

"Brenda! Calm down, it's just breakfast. We'll have it ready when you get here. Do me a favor and let Mariah drive. You're in no shape to drive yourself. Promise me."

She sniffs loudly and sighs. "Okay. I will. I'll be there soon."

Before I can even say good bye, she hangs up. I look at the receiver and then look at Michael.

"What's going on?" Michael asks.

I fill him in on the details. When I'm done, he shakes his head. "Wow. That's awful."

"Yeah, she's an absolute wreck. They'll be here in about an hour. Would you mind cooking up something for them? Maybe some pancakes or something would be nice. I'll finish getting dressed."

Lord…as always, help!

****

When I open the door and see Brenda, she's almost unrecognizable. She's still wearing matching designer pieces, but they're disheveled and her hair is pulled back into a knot (she's never, ever worn it in a knot) while her face is completely make up free (also something she's never done before). Her face is so swollen from crying that her features are distorted.

I usher them into the living room. Michael takes one quick look at the brood and immediately takes charge. "Hey, girls!" he says cheerily, addressing Brenda's children. As I survey the children, my heart aches almost out of my chest. They look like deer caught in headlights and Lisa, Brenda's nine-year-old, is wiping her running nose on her sleeve. She's been crying, too.

"Why don't you guys come in here?" Michael herds them into the kitchen. "We've got pancakes and sausage ready for you. I even warmed up the syrup and put it in a cute little pitcher. Are you hungry?" He pats Lisa's little blond head. She sniffs and wipes her nose again, then nods. Michael smiles warily at me and disappears into the kitchen with the girls.

I put my arm around Brenda; she's trembling. I guide her into the farthest corner of the living room so that it will be out of ear shot of the dining room and set her in a chair while I take the chair next to hers.

"Brenda, I'm so sorry."

She looks up at me, fresh tears cascading down her cheeks. "What am I supposed to do now?" She looks so lost and helpless. "He just threw me away, Faith. My own husband threw me away because of one mistake." She pounds her fist on her knee.

I glance furtively toward the dining room. I hope the children can't hear this.

"Why don't we go sit on the back patio to talk? I'll bring some tissues." I grab the box of tissues from the side table near the French door as we head out, clicking the door firmly closed behind me.

Brenda grabs a few tissues from the box, wipes her eyes, and blows her nose noisily. "I can't believe this! I just can't believe this."

"Brenda, he didn't throw you away. He simply left for now. He'll be back. He just needs time to cool down and think."

God, I hope so.

I don't really know Scott that well. He has always worked a lot, so his social interactions with us have been limited. He's gone out with the husbands a couple of times and been to our home a few times as well, but that's all.

"When I went to break things off with Nate, even he told me that he was tired of me. He said he didn't like being with someone who...wasn't available to him all the time. He said he needs someone that isn't tied down. I mean, what does that even mean?! What a selfish jerk."

All I can do is hug her while she cries. I don't know what to say. I wish Julie was here; she'd know what to say.

"Brenda, do you remember Julie, my neighbor? You met her at my house last week."

She nods. "Yes." Sniff. "Of course I remember her. She wore the blouse with the satin sash at the collar, right?" Leave it to Brenda to remember Julie's outfit.

I nod. "Well, she's really got a way of comforting people. I think she'd be a big help to you. Can I call and see if she's home?"

Brenda shakes her head vehemently. "No, absolutely not. I told you I don't want the whole world knowing about this!"

"Brenda, Julie is not the whole world, and she's someone who can truly help you. I wouldn't tell you that if it weren't true. Please let me give her a call. I trust her."

Brenda bites her lower lip and closes her eyes. "Gawd." She throws her hands up, dropping a tissue in the process. "Fine. Go ahead. But she's the only one I want you to call, okay? Promise me!"

I hold my right hand up. "I promise. Now," I bend over and pick up the lost tissue. "I'll be right back. Would you like a cup of coffee?"

She hiccups loudly once and nods, grabbing another tissue from the box.

While I fill her mug, Michael sidles up to me and asks very softly, "How's it going?"

I shake my head and answer just as softly, "She's a wreck. She's going to let me call Julie, at least. But she doesn't want anybody else knowing about this. How are the girls?"

"They're very quiet, but at least they're eating. April woke up a little while ago. I didn't fill her in, but just told her that the girls came for breakfast this morning. She and Mariah disappeared into April's bedroom a few minutes ago. I'm sure April's being filled in as we speak."

"What about Sarah and Andrew?" I ask.

"Oh, they're eating pancakes, too. I'm pretty sure Andrew is oblivious, but Sarah is curious. Good luck." He disappears back into the dining room.

I call Julie and she's home. I explain the situation to her. She's deeply concerned about her newest friend. I barely have time to take Brenda her coffee before the door bell announces Julie's arrival.

"Where is she?" she asks almost as soon as I open the door. Her eyes are wide with concern. I lead her to the back patio where Brenda is still curled up on the chair, looking utterly forlorn.

"Hello, Brenda. It's good to see you again." Julie stoops and envelopes Brenda in a hug which Brenda reluctantly returns. Her guard is up.

Julie pulls a chair up right next to Brenda and places her hand over Brenda's own trembling one. "I'm so sorry for what's happened, Brenda. I really am. Can I pray with you right now?"

Brenda looks at Julie as though her head just spun around, and turns her bewildered gaze on me. "Uh, why? I think the time for any prayers is long since gone."

Julie chuckles. "It's what I always do when big things, both good and bad, happen in my life. Is it okay if I pray with you?"

Brenda wrinkles her nose for a moment, but relents. "Sure. Go ahead."

Julie bows her head and closes her eyes. Brenda stares at her, flabbergasted for a moment before she and I follow Julie's lead.

It's a typical Julie prayer; succinct and heart felt. When she says amen, she opens her eyes and smiles at Brenda. Brenda is unfazed, looking warily at Julie.

Interesting, whenever Julie has prayed with me I always feel a peace inside. Brenda doesn't seem affected at all. If anything, she's pulled a little farther away. If Julie's noticed, she doesn't let on.

"What do you need, Brenda?" Julie asks.

Brenda blinks. "What do I need? I need…" she looks into the distance. "I need this to be gone. I need for it never to have happened. I need…" Her face crumples. "I need my life back."

"I would feel the same way, Brenda. This is so painful," Julie responds softly.

Brenda nods and cries.

Michael's head pops around the corner. "Uh, ladies? I'm sorry to interrupt, but the phone is for you." He gestures toward me.

"Excuse me," I say before following Michael into the house where he quickly closes the door behind me.

"It's Michelle, and she knows what's going on," Michael hurriedly whispers. "She called because she couldn't get hold of Brenda." He hands the phone to me.

I uncover the mouthpiece and address Michelle. "Hello?"

"Faith, Michael tells me Brenda is there? Did you know what happened?"

"Yes, I know what happened. How did you know what happened?"

"Scott called and told me and Richard. I couldn't believe it. There must be some mistake, right? Please tell me this is a mistake."

"No," I sigh. "It's not a mistake. But what exactly did he tell you? And when did he call?"

"He called about an hour ago and said that Brenda's been sleeping around and he's moved out. He wanted to know if he can stay with us for now."

I bristle. "Brenda has not been sleeping around. She made a mistake with one person. She's absolutely destroyed over this. She's already ended the affair, by the way. Are you going to let Scott stay with you?"

"Yes, of course. You know Scott and Richard are friends. Well, we are all friends, so... I can't believe she'd do something like that. What about her kids?"

"Michelle, don't do that." I cast a glance toward the patio. "If you could only see what a wreck she is, you wouldn't judge her."

"Who said anything about judging? I'm just saying that I can't believe she had an affair!"

"Is Scott there now?"

"No, he said he would be here this evening. He said he has some things to take care of first."

"What he needs to do is talk to Brenda. The kids are here, too, and they're scared to death."

"Those poor kids! I can't imagine what they must be thinking."

"It's a mess."

"What's she going to do?"

"I don't have any idea, Michelle. Listen, I better get going. You didn't call Lilly, did you?"

There's a pause. "Well, yes, I did. I tried to call Brenda as soon as I heard, but she's not answering her cell or the house phone. I didn't know what else to do."

Groaning inwardly, I respond. "Yeah, I know. Brenda's just mortified and embarrassed. She didn't want anyone else to know."

Michelle sighs. "Well, it is what it is. Let me know if there's anything we can do."

"I will. Thanks, Michelle. I'll be in touch."

After ending the conversation, I hand the phone back to Michael.

"So Scott's at their house?" he asks.

I shake my head. "No, he said he'll be there this evening, and he's going to stay with them for now. Michelle called Lilly, too, looking for Brenda. Brenda didn't want anyone else to know about this, but it's too late for that."

"There's no way something like this wouldn't get out anyway, Faith."

"Yeah, I guess." I turn and head back out onto the patio where Brenda is sitting back and dabbing at her eyes.

Julie turns toward me and smiles. "Everything okay?"

I cast a quick glance at Brenda. "Yeah, everything is good. How are things out here?"

"Oh, just peachy!" Brenda replies, reaching for another tissue.

"Why don't we go inside and get you something to eat?" Julie asks.

"Yes. There are plenty of pancakes and sausage left. I'll make a fresh pot of coffee," I reply.

Brenda shakes her head. "No, thank you. I'm not hungry."

It takes some convincing, but Brenda finally relents. The kids have dispersed; Michael informs us that Mariah is still upstairs with April while Andrew and Sarah have disappeared into the basement with Jennifer and Lisa.

It takes even further encouragement for Brenda to reluctantly eat a small portion of one pancake and simply roll the sausage around on her plate. Michael makes himself peripheral in the conversation, only helping refill coffee mugs and remove plates and utensils as necessary. I can tell he's listening to the conversation, though.

Eventually, the tears subside and Brenda calms down. After another full pot of decaf coffee, Brenda rolls the empty coffee mug back and forth between her hands.

"Well, for today I'm not going to do anything." She looks up at Julie and smiles wearily. "You said I shouldn't make any big decisions right now, so I'm not going to. I'm going to get my girls and go home."

"Brenda, there's something I need to tell you," I start apprehensively, as she rises from her chair. "Michelle called earlier and...well, Scott called and told her and Richard about this. Scott's going to stay with them for now."

"Oh, my God." Brenda groans. "I can't believe he would tell them! Well, yes I can. He's such a jerk!"

I may as well let her know everything, so I continue. "Michelle was worried about you and she tried to call, but you weren't home and didn't answer your cell. So she called Lilly." I leave the rest unsaid; Brenda can put the pieces together.

She does.

"What?! So everybody knows now? Perfect!" She grinds her teeth and pounds the table with her fist.

"Brenda, you have to know it was going to come out anyway. Scott is not staying at your home. There's no way to keep this a secret," I reply quietly.

Her face screws up. "But did he have to call them just to humiliate me like that?"

"Remember that he's hurting, too. He called them because he needs a place to stay," Julie intervenes. "How would you feel and react if the tables were turned?"

It's harsh, but I can't deny the truth of it. Brenda gawks at Julie for a moment as tears well afresh in her eyes. "You're right, I know. It's all my fault. I totally screwed this up."

"Mom?" Jennifer peeks around the corner, startling us.

Brenda quickly swipes at her eyes and plants an unconvincing smile on her face. "Yes, sweetie?"

Jennifer glances at each of us in turn before continuing. "Uh, can I stay here tonight with Sarah? Please?"

"Why?" Brenda asks.

She shrugs and looks down at her feet. "I...I just want to. Her dad already said it was okay if it's okay with you." She casts a quick glance in my direction.

Brenda looks at me before answering. "Sure. I guess it's okay, as long as Miss Faith says it's okay, too."

"It's fine with me," I reply. "Do you want her to come home with you though, Brenda?" I turn my attention to Jennifer. "Your mom might need you."

Jennifer squirms under the scrutiny. Brenda is quick to respond. "No, it's okay. Sweetie, you can stay here if you want to. I'll go home and pack a bag for you."

Once she collects Mariah and Lisa, she's off. Her demeanor is much improved, but I know there's a long road ahead. What it will lead to, I have no idea.

Closing the door after waving at her departing vehicle, I turn to Julie.

"Now what?" I ask.

She shrugs. "We leave it in God's hands."

I can do that. It's Yours, God.

Chapter Thirty Seven

Lilly graciously took all of the kids to the movies that afternoon; she was glad to help considering everything that was going on. Sarah and Shaun's budding romance (can you call it romance when the ones involved are twelve and thirteen?) turns into almost constant contact through phone calls or texts when they're not at each other's (supervised) homes. Sarah's required to show us all of the texts on her phone. They're harmless.

Scott stays with Richard and Michelle for the next two weeks with no end in sight. He won't accept any calls from Brenda and even took her name off of the bank account; that was one of the things he needed to take care of on the Saturday that he walked out. Brenda lost her job at the boutique because of the company's policy of non-fraternization. One small consolation is that Nate also lost his job; at least it's non-discriminatory.

Any communication that occurs between the couple is filtered through either Michelle or Richard. The strain on the friendships grows.

"This can't continue," Michael says.

"But what can we do?" I ask helplessly. "These are all our friends. We can't choose sides."

"I agree, but something has to be done."

The phone rings, interrupting our conversation. It's Brenda and she's in a full on panic.

"I just got served with divorce papers! He's demanding the house and full custody of the girls! What am I going to do?!" she cries.

I almost drop the phone, but recover it before it hits the floor. "What? He did what?"

Michael comes to my side and tilts his head in close so he can listen; I tilt the phone so he can hear.

"He filed for divorce, Faith! He won't even take my calls and won't talk to me if I go to Michelle's house! I've tried but he just won't listen!"

"Oh, Brenda! This is awful. I don't know what to say." I look pleadingly at Michael. He takes the phone from me.

"Brenda, it's Michael. Listen, calm down. We're going to do what we can. I need to make some calls. If you need to come over, you're welcome to." There's a pause. "Okay, Faith will call you later. Hang in there."

Once he hangs up, he turns to me. "I'm going to call Ben and the other guys and we're going to have a conversation with Scott. He needs to stop and think."

"Is Brenda coming over?"

He shakes his head even as he begins to punch numbers on the phone. "No. She's…" He doesn't continue because the first caller just picked up. Instead he shakes his head.

My stomach knots up and I head for the bathroom out of habit, but fortunately it doesn't require my dropping to my knees.

"Whew. Maybe that's finally done," I murmur to myself.

A nudge in my stomach answers me. The bulge in my belly is growing every day as is the strength and frequency of the nudges. It's hard to believe I'm almost halfway through the pregnancy. My ultrasound is this week.

So is the amniocentesis.

The knot in my stomach twists and I cradle my bulge. Michael and I mulled over the decision of whether to have the procedure or not. We talked over the risks and the benefits with our doctor, but in the end we decided that knowing is better than not. At least we can prepare ourselves.

I just hope we don't need to prepare for anything other than the new arrival.

Your will be done, God.

My stomach responds with a nudge. I smile and rub the spot.

Michael interrupts my moment. "You okay in there, honey?" he asks, peering into the powder room.

I turn to face him and smile. "Yeah, I'm just feeling the baby move."

His gaze drops to my stomach, and he reaches over to place his warm hands on me. He's immediately met with a nudge and he smiles.

"Active little guy, huh?"

"You think it's a little guy? Maybe it's another girl." I smile.

"It's just an expression," he teases.

"So, what's going on?"

Michael called all of the husbands and they're going to stage an intervention of sorts with Scott at Michelle and Richard's house tonight. The ladies are going to gather at Julie's home while it's going on, and the kids will be at our house, the older ones supervising the younger ones. Extra care will be taken to be sure Sarah and Shaun are never alone; April and Mariah volunteered for that duty. They're not going to tell Scott about it, of course. They're just going to show up and do it. Ben is taking the lead.

"I'm so glad Ben is going to be there."

Michael nods. "Yeah, I think it's best if he does it. He's really helped you." His eyes soften. "I wouldn't know where to begin. I don't know if they should get divorced or not, but I do think Scott's making a very hasty decision."

"Yes, and when I see how broken up Brenda is, and how her girls are doing..." I shake my head. "I can't believe he'd leap straight to divorce without even talking to Brenda."

"Well," Michael sighs, "Let's hope we can do something about that tonight."

****

Brenda draws a ragged breath, covering her face with her hands. We've all gathered at Julie's house and, of course, she's laid out a very nice buffet of finger foods. It remains untouched, however. The tension is thick.

"It's going to be okay, Brenda. Try to relax." Lilly encourages her; she's seated next to Brenda and gives her hand a squeeze.

Drawing another deep breath that ends in a sob, Brenda replies. "I can't relax! My whole world has crashed around me and...I did this! Do you know I had to clip coupons when I bought groceries this week? I've never done that before! Ever since he took me off the account, I don't know how to..." She cries in earnest.

Brenda looks downright haggard; she's thinner, has all but stopped applying her always flawless make up and there are no accessories to be seen. Her dark roots are even showing. I didn't even know she had dark roots. Her whole identity is being stripped away. I ache for my friend.

The men are at Brenda's house, trying to convince Scott to re-think his decision to move towards divorce. Gazing upon the shell that is my friend, I sincerely hope it works.

"Have you ever considered this might be a good thing, Brenda?" Michelle asks.

There's a collective gasp around the room.

"What do you mean by good thing?" Lilly asks evenly. "How on earth could this ever be a good thing?"

Michelle continues on confidently. "What I mean is it can provide a fresh start if tonight's little meeting doesn't work. Of course, I hope that he'll agree to counseling or something. But," She looks directly at Brenda and sticks her chin out proudly, "You don't need a man to support you, Brenda. You shouldn't need a man. You are a confident, accomplished woman on your own. You should be a role model for your girls. You have to start believing in yourself. I mean look at you! Learn from your mistakes. Never let a man, any man, put you in this position ever again! You're a wreck and you look like hell."

All of the women gasp again; even Julie blanches. Brenda stares at her, mouth open.

Michelle looks around at us and rolls her eyes before continuing her diatribe. "Come on! Everybody's thinking it. I just had the guts to say it. Now," she leans forward onto her knees and points her finger at Brenda, "you've been moping around for weeks and making a spectacle of yourself. It's time you pulled yourself together and got on with your life."

"Michelle, I really don't think you're being..." I start.

"Helpful?" Michelle finishes for me. "I am the only one being helpful here. I am being helpful because I'm being honest with her."

"I think you're kicking her while she's down, Michelle," Lilly retorts coolly. "How would you know what it's like to be in this situation? You have no idea what you're talking about."

"That's because I would never put myself in this position. I have my own business and my own finances, and that's the way it should be. Always stand on your own two feet, Brenda. Never forget that." Her tone takes on an angry twist.

If I didn't know better, I would think she sounds bitter, too. I've never known Michelle to be bitter about anything.

"Maybe she's right," Brenda sobs.

"She is most certainly not right," Lilly intervenes, her eyes flashing.

"How so?" Michelle challenges her.

Lilly's cheeks pink and her mouth twists. "Because…" She pauses. "Because I grew up in a home like that. A single mom that didn't need any man to take care of her. I can tell you it was sheer hell on me and my sisters. If she would have worked more on her marriage instead of her career, I think everything would've been better."

I'm shocked. I never knew this about Lilly. "What do you mean?" I ask quietly.

Her eyes flash toward me; her tone is icy. "I mean exactly what I said. My father had an affair when I was ten. I remember hearing my parents argue about it. They thought we were asleep, but we heard everything. There was a lot of screaming." Her eyes close and she shudders. "It was awful. He accused her of never having time for him, and she accused him of being a weak, womanizing fool. There was so much name calling and throwing things. Mom was always rather…volatile. I remember my father saying he was sorry and he would never do it again. But my mother wouldn't listen. She just kicked him out."

We're all enraptured by this revelation, even Brenda, who has ceased crying for the moment.

"My sisters and I begged her to talk to him, but she refused. She said he was a no good loser and she never should've gotten tangled up with him." Her eyes drop to her lap. "That made me wonder if she regretted having us, too. Anyway, the divorce went through and we never saw him again. I found out many years later that it wasn't because he didn't try, she just wouldn't let him. He had sent us birthday cards and such, but she tossed them all out without ever even telling us. Her career came first and believe me, we knew that. We were raised by nannies."

Her icy gaze rests on Michelle. "So as you can see, I have a much better perspective on this than you do." She turns her attention to Brenda. "Don't give up, no matter what. You made a mistake, but it doesn't have to be fatal. You should think about your girls."

"I'm sorry for what you experienced, Lilly. And I am thinking about her girls," Michelle replies, defiant. "I stand by my statement that being a strong woman is a good role model."

"Getting divorced doesn't make her a strong woman. A strong woman works through her problems and doesn't give up. What about their father? Shouldn't he be a good role model, too? Breaking up a family is never being a good role model," Lilly retorts quickly.

Michelle starts to respond, but Julie intervenes. "Ladies, please. Let's focus on comforting Brenda, okay? I think we've all experienced pain in our lives." She looks pointedly at me. "None of us has been spared, but hopefully we grow from our pain just as Brenda will grow from her pain. I truly believe it is best if the marriage works out, and I pray that the meeting goes accordingly." Michelle tries to interject, but Julie continues. "Now, let's get something to eat. I tried some new recipes I hope you'll like…"

"That sounds like a great idea! What did you make?" I get up, agreeing with Julie in hopes that Michelle will let this go. Julie, ever thoughtful, has a large bowl of dark chocolate M&Ms at the buffet. I cast a sideways glance at the ladies before sprinkling all of my food with a generous handful of the little rainbow spheres. I've taken to putting them in everything I eat now, even salads.

The scale has not only turned around, but it's begun to spike in the other direction.

Michelle refrains from responding any further, but she and Lilly don't talk to each other as we all get plates of food.

Even Brenda puts a few items on her little plate, but only nibbles at them. I can't help notice her hands are shaking. She looks so fragile.

God, I hope this works.

With the conversation stalled, Julie offers to put a movie on for us to watch. I respond with enthusiasm, but aside from Julie and me, everyone is sullen. I look at Julie and shrug my shoulders helplessly.

Julie smiles and rolls her eyes upward. It takes me a second to realize she's encouraging me to pray, so I do so silently, assuming she's doing the same. She chooses a movie with an uplifting message. Either by chance or design (I err on the side of design; Julie chose the movie after all), the movie is about a couple struggling with their marriage. She wants a divorce; he does not. The message is clear and the couple survives intact.

Once the movie ends, Julie rises to retrieve it and return it to its case. "What did you guys think?" she asks.

Michelle snorts, "I think it sounds very warm and fuzzy, but this is real life."

"This was based on a true story," Julie replies quietly.

A further discussion ensues with Lilly and Michelle on opposite ends of the spectrum while Brenda looks defeated in the center of it all. Julie tries to mediate as best she can; Michelle does concede that some marriages can potentially be saved, but she denies that it happens very often.

"I'm just being realistic," she replies defensively.

"I'm learning things about you guys that I've never known before," I muse.

All eyes focus on me, eyebrows raised in curiosity.

"You've learned that I'm both an idiot, and a fool," Brenda quips.

I shake my head. "No. I've learned that you're like me. Not perfect."

Brenda chuckles darkly. "Well, that's very kind of you." She smiles half heartedly. "Thank you."

"Lilly, I never knew the struggles and pain you went through growing up. I came from a single mom, too. But we didn't have nannies. I'm embarrassed to say that we were dirt poor," I confess.

Lilly is taken aback. "Oh! I'm sorry to hear that. There's no shame in being poor. Having money isn't all it's cracked up to be. I'd have gladly gone without a lot of stuff if only I could've had my father. Or my mother, for that fact." She hastily blinks back a tear.

I reach out, and she squeezes my hand. "We didn't have any stuff to give up, but I would've given anything to have my father, too."

"Having both parents is very important to children," Julie adds. "It's the way a family is designed."

Michelle remains silent. Julie looks at the clock and Brenda notices. The meeting has been going on for over three and a half hours.

"Do you think this is a good sign?" Brenda asks anxiously.

"I think so," Julie replies. "If he weren't open to listening, it probably would've been very short."

Brenda's shoulders slump. She's exhausted. "I hope you're right."

The meeting continues for another hour before Julie's phone rings with news. Brenda trembles, waiting. Lilly and I sit on either side of her while Michelle remains calm and collected in her seat. Upon closer inspection, however, I notice her hands are balled into fists in her lap.

Michelle is just as anxious as the rest of us to know the outcome.

Once Julie finishes the conversation and returns the phone to its cradle, she turns to Brenda and smiles.

"Scott has agreed to put the divorce proceedings on hold for now." There's a collective sigh of relief. "He won't move back home just yet, but at least he is willing to talk to you."

Brenda bursts into tears. She rises and envelopes Julie in a hug, crying into her shoulder. "Thank you so much!"

Michelle rises from her seat and comes to pat Brenda on the shoulder. She also nods toward Julie with a wry smile. "Well, I'm so glad that he listened. I need to get going, ladies."

As everyone collects their things to leave, we rally around Brenda for hugs and words of encouragement. Brenda rode over with Lilly, so she leaves with her, their arms linked together.

Michelle turns toward Julie. "I'm sorry if I came across as crude."

Julie's radiant smile beams toward Michelle, and she brushes it off with her usual grace. "Thank you. You're not crude. You just have a different viewpoint."

Once Michelle departs, Julie turns to me. "I'm glad it went well. So is your amniocentesis still tomorrow morning?"

"Yes. You're still able to make it, right?"

"Of course! I wouldn't miss it for the world. Is Michael able to come?"

I shake my head. "No, he can't get the time off right now. Not with everything that's going on. But he'll be waiting to hear from me."

Julie claps her hands together. "I can hardly wait to see the little guy or gal on the screen! Plus I will need to stop by the lab afterwards, too." She looks expectantly at me.

"You think you might be…?"

Her head bobs up and down. "Yes, I'm almost two weeks late. I waited this long just to be sure."

"Oh!" I grab her in a hug. "I hope so, Julie! That would be wonderful!"

Her eyes are glistening when I pull back. "Yes, it would. But I don't want to get my hopes up too high, you know." A thin veil of sadness descends over her features. "I've been late before and well…"

Please, please, please God. Let her be pregnant this time.

Chapter Thirty Eight

The gel is warm and wet as it hits my abdomen. The ultrasound technician moves the wand around my stomach, and I hold Julie's hand firmly as images appear on the screen. Whereas before there was a definable kidney shaped darkness surrounding a little jumping bean, now there is an easily definable baby moving around inside. The spinal column, arms, legs, and even a tiny little face appear on the screen. Julie gasps as each part comes into focus. Upon the third consecutive gasp, the tech and the doctor both chuckle.

"First baby?" they ask.

"Me? No. This is my fourth child. But my friend has never seen an ultrasound, and she's pretty excited. Will I get lots of pictures to show my husband?"

Assuring me that I will, the tech continues to move the wand around my stomach taking measurements and identifying the baby's body parts.

"Does everything...look okay?" I ask anxiously.

"So far, so good. There aren't any obvious indications of anything wrong. The measurements are exactly where they should be at this point in your pregnancy."

The computer continues to spit out images for me to take home. There are plenty and I'm grateful.

"Can you tell if it's a boy or a girl?" I ask again.

As the tech continues to move the wand around, she starts to frown. "Well, this little bugger doesn't want to show me. I'll keep trying." Finally, she sighs and shakes her head. "I'm afraid we're not going to be able to see the gender right now."

The doctor reassures me that I'll be able to find out the gender with the amniocentesis results and asks if I'm ready to begin.

I look to Julie who squeezes my hand firmly before nodding. "Yes."

The amniocentesis doesn't take very long and isn't painful. If anything, I feel a quick prick as they insert the needle. I prefer to keep my eyes closed and think of my children's faces to keep calm. Julie does remarkably well in controlling her reactions, too, other than to squeeze my hand especially hard a few times.

Once the procedure is done and I'm cleaned up, we make our way to the lab where Julie has her blood drawn. I call Michael to let him know that everything went well and there's nothing to report. He's disappointed we couldn't find out the gender today.

Julie should find out the results of her blood test by tomorrow. I hope with every fiber in my being that it comes back positive this time and if it does, she's able to carry the baby to term.

****

Michael enters the house that evening looking defeated and wary. My heart sinks.

"What happened?" I ask, placing the spoon back into the noodles.

He casts a glance toward the living room and the foyer before asking quietly. "Where are the kids?"

"Andrew and Sarah are watching TV in the living room, and April is upstairs. Why?" I whisper.

He shakes his head, takes my hand, and pulls me through the kitchen and toward the stairs. "We need to talk," he murmurs to me before raising his tone to normal to address Sarah and Andrew in the living room. "Hi, guys! I need to talk to your mother real quick. We'll be right back."

Once we enter our room, he pulls the door closed quietly and turns to me, his expression anxious.

Oh, boy.

"We were informed today that every executive in the company has to take a ten percent pay cut."

I drop onto the bed in shock. "When?" I gasp.

He sighs and places his hands on his hips. "Effective immediately."

I cradle my bulging stomach. "Oh, Michael. How are we…How can we do this? Why so much?"

He shakes his head. "Even though there were a small number of people found legally and personally responsible for this, the company still has to defend itself because they were working for the company when they did what they did. If we don't take the pay cut, the company could go under and we'd all be out of a job, which would mean no paycheck at all. My only hope is that once this is all done and the company's back on its feet, we can go back to our normal rates of pay, too. It was discussed and that's the plan, but they can't give us a timeline for when that will happen."

I shake my head in shock and disbelief. "We'll have to cut back… plus Christmas is coming up…and the baby…"

"I know, I know." He rubs his face before squaring his shoulders. "We'll just look at the budget line by line and see where we can trim. We have a healthy savings account, too."

I nod, but still can't believe it. That's quite a cut to live with.

"Look at it this way, Faith. It could've been worse. It could've been a twenty percent cut."

"Yes, but it's still going to be hard."

Michael breaks the news to the kids after dinner. Their reactions are mixed; Andrew doesn't understand it, Sarah scowls, and April is most vehement in her dislike of it.

"What does that mean?!" she cries.

"It means that mom and I will have to review our household budget and see where we will need to cut back to make this work," Michael replies calmly.

April wails and groans about the unfairness of it all until Michael cuts her off. "April, that's enough. We're all going to have to make sacrifices here, so stop acting like your life is over."

Andrew is concerned after watching his sister's reaction. "Are we going to have to sleep on the streets?"

I can't help but chuckle. Sarah snorts and rolls her eyes.

"No, Andrew. Everything will be fine. We are going to stay in this house. Don't worry," I reply soothingly.

Being mollified for the moment, he casts a glance at April before asking to be excused. Once Andrew leaves, Michael addresses April. "April, please control your reactions. This is just a bump in the road and something we have to deal with, but it's not the end of the world."

She scowls at him and remains silent.

"Like I said, your mother and I are going to go over the household budget line by line and determine what we may need to sacrifice." He looks pointedly at April and Sarah. "That may include some sports for now."

They both groan and April erupts once again. "What?! I may have to give up cheerleading and gymnastics?" she asks, incredulous.

"I only do basketball! Why should I have to give that up? She does more than me!" Sarah cries, jabbing her finger at April who looks aghast at her sister. They're about to engage in verbal warfare when Michael interrupts.

"Whoa, whoa! Calm down you two. I said may. And yes, young ladies, it may mean giving up a sport or two for now."

I wish Michael hadn't said anything until after we look at the budget, but it's too late now.

"Girls, we will see what we can do. We both know how important your sports are to you, and we'll see if we can avoid making cuts there." Michael looks at me questioningly and I shake my head. "We'll at least look, okay?"

He stares at me for a moment before replying, "Your mother is right. Let's just wait and see."

"Fine," April huffs, rising to take her plate to the sink. "I just hope you know that I've worked so hard this year on my cheers, and my gymnastics coach told me I've made such improvements and...and..." Her face crumples and she rushes from the room, crying.

"Good grief," I mutter.

"She's still crazy, Mom," Sarah says, rising calmly. "But I do hope you guys at least let me keep playing basketball. It's a cheap sport, and the season is almost over anyway." She departs.

"I would rather not take their sports away from them, Michael."

"Me, either. But everything in the budget needs to be considered, regardless of how they feel about it."

The mood remains sullen the rest of the evening. Once in bed that night, I turn to Michael.

"Do you think this pay cut will last very long?" I ask.

He shrugs. "I hope not. But I would plan on it lasting for a couple of years, at least."

My eyebrows rise. "That long? Really?"

"Oh, yeah. This isn't going to be cheap."

I groan. "All right. We'll do what we have to do. I just wish we hadn't gotten rid of all the baby stuff years ago. But who knew?"

Michael laughs and draws me close. "God did." He kisses me. "So just let it go. We'll figure out what to do and we'll be fine. I'm just glad it wasn't twenty percent."

Relaxing, I snuggle in closer to his warmth. "You're right. But it's still a lot of money."

Michael squeezes me briefly. "Do you still trust me? I'll take care of this family."

I pat his hand reassuringly. "Yes, Michael. I trust you. You know I do."

He pauses. "Then don't worry about it."

Unable to turn my brain off, I mentally click through the budget and see what can be reduced. The cell phone plans can be pared down, we can turn off lights and conserve electricity, maybe not drive too much to save gas, cut back on the brand names of grocery items, clip coupons… I don't think it'll be enough. Worry creeps in, and my head hurts trying to figure it out, so I force my mind elsewhere. It goes immediately to Brenda.

What occurs to me draws me up short.

I have to cut my budget by a small amount, but her marriage is on the line. Julie is hoping to have a child, while I am unexpectedly having my fourth. What I am dealing with is of little consequence and no comparison to that. I'm stabbed by guilt over my own selfish pettiness in the grand scheme of life. *Sorry, God.*

****

Julie's almost incomprehensible when she calls me the next morning, and my heart sinks into the floor until I'm able to make out a few words.

"...doctor called...positive...so happy...Ben...praise God!"

I blink in surprise. "Julie! Julie! Calm down. Are you saying that you're pregnant?!" I ask incredulously.

"Yes! Yes! I'm pregnant, Faith! I'm pregnant!" She starts screaming into the phone.

"Oh, Julie! I'm so happy for you! This is wonderful!"

Once she calms down enough to have a conversation, she informs me that her first prenatal appointment is set for three weeks from now. She asks if I'd like to come with her, and I tell her that I'd love to, but that she and Ben should share this together instead.

"Are you sure, Faith? You've let me be a part of your pregnancy, and I would love for you to be a part of mine, too."

"Thank you, Julie. I just think you and Ben should share in the appointments together; you've waited so long for this."

"Okay. Thank you. Would you please pray for me? I...I really want to carry this pregnancy to term," her voice drops an octave.

I swallow hard. "Absolutely. I will pray for you every day." I mean it sincerely. I place my hand on my stomach where it's met with a nudge. Hopefully, Julie will experience this soon, too.

Immediately after our conversation ends, I close my eyes and pray God will please let Julie stay pregnant and have a baby this time. She's so excited. If she has to endure another miscarriage, I don't see how she can continue on. It would break me.

The phone rings right after I say amen, startling me.

It's Brenda.

"Hi, Faith! I just wanted to thank you again. Have you heard from Michelle?" she asks. Her usual bubbly personality is peeking through. This is a good sign.

"No, I haven't. Why?"

"Scott has agreed to move back in, at least for now. He said he'll sleep in the guest room, but at least he's coming home."

"Oh, thank God! I'm so happy to hear this, Brenda. I'm sure the girls are happy, too. Is he moving back in today?"

"Yes, he said he would be home tonight. This is a step in the right direction, isn't it?"

"Absolutely. What are you going to do now?"

"We are going to start counseling next week with Pastor Ben. He's at least willing to have a conversation with me now."

I do a little dance before answering her. "Brenda, that's fantastic! Pastor Ben is awesome, and I'm sure he'll be able to help you guys through this."

Brenda gushes her thanks once again before ending our conversation.

The intervention the guys staged obviously had an impact. Michael sure seemed satisfied with the progress they made when he got home that evening. I have high hopes they'll survive this, but I'm bothered by Michelle's behavior at Julie's house. I had no idea how she felt about this sort of thing. I've known these women for years, but what do I really know about any of them?

We've never shared our major challenges with each other. Like my pain over Paul.

You don't know what you don't know.

My mind stops short. Do I really need to share Paul with them?

"Lord," I stare up at the ceiling, "if it will help anyone, I'll share it. But only if you want me to."

Peace.

That's what bubbles inside of me. Peace. Huh. That must be what God's presence feels like.

I like it.

Smiling, I respond very simply and very sincerely. "Thank you."

416

Chapter Thirty Nine

My hand shakes as I return the phone to its cradle and my eyes mist over. I just spoke with the doctor's office, and the doctor wants us to come in tomorrow.

It's been a week and a half; the amniocentesis results are finally in. They won't share the results over the phone. That's never a good sign. Try as I might, I couldn't get anything out of the receptionist.

I cradle my stomach protectively and squeeze my eyes shut. "Please God. Please don't let this be bad news."

Why else would they want me to come in rather than tell me over the phone?

Anxiety creeps in, but I push it back, taking a deep breath.

Michael has to come with me tomorrow. I can't do this alone.

Fortunately, he picks up on the second ring when I call his office and he can come.

"Don't get worked up, Faith. It could very well be something minor or nothing at all. Whatever it is, we'll figure it out together. It'll work out."

Gulping hard, I reply. "Okay. I'll just keep my mind busy and clean house. I've been feeling much better lately."

"Sounds like a plan, but don't overdo it. Take a rest when you need to, honey."

I manage to clean the bathrooms as well as dust and vacuum the living room before my back and hips hurt too much to continue. The kitchen and upstairs will have to wait. Putting the vacuum cleaner away in the hall closet, I spy my running shoes lying against the wall in the back, neglected. It's been eons since I've put them to use.

Smoothing my hands over my hips and backside, I grimace at the rather ample form I've taken on since the last time I wore those shoes. At my age, it may take a miracle to bounce back after this baby's born.

As I stand there for a moment, staring at my shoes, I wonder if I'll start running again once the baby is born. I don't know. Perhaps I'll do it because I enjoy it, rather than use it as an excuse to run away from things.

My past is in the past. The pain I experienced can't hurt me anymore. My sessions with Pastor Ben have become monthly, rather than weekly, appointments. Michael has even joined me in a few sessions and our marriage is stronger than ever since I revealed my past, and my brokenness, to him. In my wildest dreams, I never thought that would happen.

God truly is good.

"I'll see you in a few months," I say to my shoes before quietly closing the door.

Limping over to the sofa while pressing my hands into my lower back, I plop down with a grunt (it happens on the way up and the way down now) and rub my ever-growing stomach. Multiple nudges meet my moving hands. The baby is very active today, probably because of my nervous energy.

"Don't worry, little one. You'll be okay," I murmur. "You have to be."

The door bell rings. Not really wanting to get up, I yell, "Come in!"

The door unlatches and Julie's voice calls out. "Faith? Are you in the kitchen?"

"No!" I yell back. "Just being lazy on the couch!"

She appears around the corner, beaming. "I just threw up, and I hate cake batter!" she cries jubilantly. "It's so slimy! Faith, cake batter is slimy to me! Isn't that wonderful?!"

I frown for a moment before comprehension dawns. "You're feeling sick? You're actually *sick*?" I slowly grunt my way to a standing position and reach out to her. We hug fiercely, smiling and laughing.

Julie bounces up and down before her face suddenly turns a light shade of green, and she bolts for my bathroom where she throws up noisily. Nothing short of my own children's laughter has ever sounded so good.

When she reappears, she looks radiant. It's almost comical: someone looking so radiant and thrilled to be throwing up.

"Did it just start?" I ask.

She bobs her head up and down rapidly. "Yes! I was making a chocolate cake when it hit me. I looked at the batter, felt sick, and had to throw up in the kitchen sink." She grimaces at me and wrinkles her nose. "Sorry."

I wave her off. "Please. I'm just so happy for you!"

"Yes, I've never gotten sick before. With the other pregnancies, I never got sick. I just miscarried early. So maybe this is really good then?" she asks hopefully, placing her hand on her stomach.

"I think so. Let's go with that. See, now that I'm not throwing up anymore, you've just started!" I laugh. "Now, I'm just achy. I cleaned part of my house this morning and now my hips and back are screaming at me."

Her brow furrows. "Oh, that's awful." She looks around my home. "It looks great, though. You must've gotten a lot done."

I groan and lie back against the cushions. "Oh, not as much as I would've liked to. I didn't even touch the kitchen yet. So, is the cake in the oven now?"

She grimaces again. "No. I had to dump it down the drain. I couldn't even look at it. I might have to stop baking. I may try to still make cookies and breads, but we'll see."

"You? Not bake? What on earth are we going to do?" I cry dramatically. "I think the earth has shifted."

I ask her to pray for us regarding the test results. I share my fear about it, and she reassures me in true Julie fashion. I also let her know about Scott and Brenda.

"Oh, Brenda had actually called me already and told me," she informs me. "I'm so happy for them! I think they'll be able to work through this."

"I agree. She said they're going to start counseling with Ben this week. Have they already been in?"

She smiles. "I don't know, Faith. Remember, Ben keeps his patient activity confidential." She looks knowingly at me.

"Oh, sorry. I didn't mean…"

"I know. But we should keep them in our prayers, certainly." She pats my knee and rises to leave. "I better get going. You look exhausted and probably need a nap. I'll keep praying for you. Let me know how it goes tomorrow. Don't worry about it. God's got this!" She pats her stomach and departs.

"I know," I respond in the stillness.

****

Michael and I are ushered into the doctor's office and take our seats across the desk from him. I wipe my sweaty palms across my thighs a few times and Michael clears his throat.

The doctor shuffles some papers around on his desk before placing one specific sheet in front of him. He clasps his hands in front of him and clears his throat.

He begins by telling us about the purpose of the test and that it's supposed to be indicative but not definitive or diagnostic. It is indicated because of my advanced maternal age, etc. Mostly, I don't even hear what he's saying because I really don't care. I just want to know if my baby is all right. He's droning on and on with such mind numbing medical jargon. When he asks if we've understood what he's said, however, I simply smile and nod like I've been listening to every word.

I sure hope Michael was listening.

"First of all, I would like to inform you that you are expecting a boy." He smiles in the thin, superficial way a lot of doctors do.

"Oh!" I clap my hands together and look at Michael, who's beaming. "That's wonderful!"

"I guess Andrew was right. He'll be a big brother!" Michael chuckles as he reaches over and kisses me.

420

The doctor clears his throat. "I also need to inform you that there is a small chance your child may have Down's syndrome."

The air just got sucked out of the room.

"Excuse me?" Michael asks. "How small is 'small'." He makes quotation marks in the air with his fingers.

"Well, Mr. Strauss, I can't tell you a percentage exactly, but the results did come back with it being a possibility. I do want you to know, however, that the ultrasound looked perfectly normal, so we just can't be sure until the baby is born."

I've ceased to listen. My hands creep around my stomach and I look down at my bulging form.

God, would you do this to us? To him?

Michael continues his conversation with the doctor, who hands him some brochures about coping with this (potential) diagnosis. Ice runs through my veins.

Silence. I realize the doctor and Michael have stopped talking and are both looking at me.

"Uh, what? I'm sorry, what?" I ask numbly.

"Honey, the doctor wants to know if you have any questions for him." Michael asks gently.

I draw a deep breath. "I want to know if my baby is going to be okay."

He smiles patiently at me. "Mrs. Strauss, I have practiced medicine for over thirty years in the field of genetics. The one thing I can tell you is that every baby is going to be okay, if the parents are okay. Now as to whether your child has Down's syndrome or not, I can't tell you for sure whether he does or doesn't. I can only share the results of this test with you. I'm sorry."

Searching the doctor's face for some hope or answers yields me nothing.

The ride home is quiet. Michael finally breaks the silence.

"Are you all right, Faith?" he asks, squeezing my hand.

I stare numbly at the blurry images passing by my window. "I'm fine. But is our baby?"

Michael sighs. "We will have to wait and see, Faith. That's all we can do."

When we get home, Michael calls his office to see if he can take the rest of the day off, but he's needed back. Groaning in frustration as he hangs up, he looks apologetically at me.

"I'm sorry, Faith. I..." He's interrupted by the door bell ringing. When he answers, it's Julie.

"Hi, Michael! I'm sorry for intruding, but I saw you guys drive up and I've been praying. So I just stopped by to see how everything went."

"Come in, Julie," he replies quietly and ushers her into the living room where I'm sitting on the sofa.

She takes one look at me and her smile disappears, a frown creasing her brow. She comes over and sits beside me. "What happened?" she asks softly, looking from me to Michael. "What did the doctor say?"

"He said our baby might have Down's syndrome," I reply, biting my lip. "And it's a boy."

"Congratulations! Now you're going to have two boys and two girls." She smiles and hugs my shoulders. "So they don't know for sure?"

Michael rubs his face. "He said it was a small chance. But a chance is a chance, right?"

"When will they know for sure? Is there another test you can do?" she asks.

Michael shakes his head. "No. We just have to wait until the baby is born to find out."

That means I have to wait four more months. That's a long time to wait.

And to worry.

Julie offers her support and comfort, which I so appreciate. Midway through the conversation, she mutters an apology, claps her hand over her mouth and bolts for the bathroom where she throws up noisily just as before.

Michael looks at me, his eyebrows disappearing into his hair line and points toward Julie. "Is she...?" he mouths.

I nod vigorously. "I forgot to tell you! She's pregnant," I whisper gleefully, clapping my hands quietly.

He blinks in shock. "How could you forget to tell me something like that?"

Before I can reply, she returns. "Sorry," she says sheepishly. "It's been happening a lot. Now I know what you mean, Faith. Whew!"

"Congratulations are in order!" Michael smiles. "I'm so happy for you."

Julie grins. "Thank you!" she breathes. "I just hope we're able to go to term." Her eyes darken momentarily as she pats her stomach.

"I'm sure you will," I reply hastily, wanting to offer her the same comfort she offers me. I hope I'm right.

Poor Julie throws up one more time before excusing herself to go home, presumably where she can throw up in private. I can relate.

Michael readies himself to leave shortly after she does, apologizing for having to return to work.

"I'll be home as soon as I can. Don't worry about this, Faith. It won't do any good. It'll work out, you'll see." He envelopes me in a hug.

"I hope so," I whisper back. "I really wish you didn't have to go."

He groans softly and kisses me. "I know. Me, too." He pulls back and pats my bulging belly, smiling crookedly. "I have a family to support, though."

"Yeah and what if…" I start, but he kisses me hard suddenly.

"Faith, don't. Just don't go there," he murmurs. "Whatever comes, we'll be fine."

"I'm so thankful for you."

He chuckles before disappearing into the garage and back to work.

Rather than wallow in my own thoughts, I call Lilly to see if she's busy. Normally, I would call Julie but she's otherwise occupied. Wincing, I send up a quick prayer that she won't suffer at the mercy of the porcelain throne too much.

Fortunately, Lilly is available and invites me over.

Once I arrive, she leads me into her beautifully decorated sitting room; the south facing room gets lots of natural light. The sofa, love seat, and chairs are covered in a rich lemony fabric accented with burgundy throw pillows. There are floor to ceiling windows that frame the view of her back yard and garden perfectly. I imagine the streams of sunlight that engulf the room on sunny days. Unfortunately, it's a typical late autumn day in the Midwest, which means overcast. There are even fresh flowers in an explosion of burgundy and yellow sitting in the center of the glass coffee table.

"Would you like some herbal tea, Faith? It's really good for you," she asks as she settles me onto the love seat with a velvet burgundy throw, tucking it in around me. How sweet. "I was going to make some for myself."

"That sounds wonderful, thank you."

She excuses herself and arrives momentarily with the tea and accessories on a silver tray and begins pouring. Based on what I've learned about her recently, I assume the tray and everything on it are family heirlooms.

Almost as if she read my mind, she says, "These belonged to my mother, of course. Whatever else she was, she was at least tasteful." She smiles and hands me a tea cup on a saucer. The aroma of ginger and honey fills my nostrils. There's a thinly sliced lemon round bobbing up and down in the amber liquid.

One sip and I'm warmed through. "This is delicious, Lilly. Thank you."

She barely shrugs her shoulders in acknowledgement. "So, how's everything? You sounded a little upset on the phone."

I share the test results and the uncertainty of it all, as well as Michael's ten percent pay cut. To my surprise, she takes it all in stride. Not even so much as a frown. Has she had Botox?

"Faith," she begins, placing her empty tea cup on the tray. "It really is going to be okay, no matter what. When I was pregnant with Shaun, the doctors were sure he was going to have a genetic disorder. It was some long scary name." She flutters her fingers in the air. "The blood tests all came back saying that *if* he survived past his first birthday, he was going to have learning disabilities and require corrective surgeries. It was frightening. Sort of like what you're going through now. More tea?" She pauses and lifts the tea pot.

I shake my head, just wanting to hear the rest of her story. She refills her cup and adds sugar before continuing.

424

She takes a sip, sighs, and looks past me, lost in her memories. "Those were scary, scary times," she says quietly. "Tony was beside himself. We both were. It was his family's first grandchild, and they had such high expectations of him. Of us." She shudders. "We had no idea what we were in for. We could have a severely disabled child who could very well not live very long, or if he did, he wouldn't have the kind of life we imagined our child having."

"How did you deal with it?" I ask. "I mean, obviously Shaun is okay. Nothing was wrong with him, was it?"

Lilly smiles and stirs her tea, tapping the spoon twice on the edge of the cup before placing it delicately on her saucer. "Yes, he's fine. He had a very minor form of spina bifida when he was born. It wasn't open like it is for some children born with it. It more or less looked like a furry dimple at the base of his spine. It didn't even require treatment. They just observed him for the first year or so. He developed just fine, and hasn't had any complications whatsoever." She takes another long sip of her tea, then looks pointedly at me. "Faith, those doctors are just human beings. They make mistakes. Your doctor told you there's a small chance your child may have Down's syndrome. That means there is a larger chance he won't. Those are pretty good odds, I would think."

"But what if he does have it? How do we deal with that?"

"How do you think you'll deal with it?" she asks.

"I don't know." I place my cup on the tray and lie back on the cushions. "I don't want to deal with it at all, really. I just want him to be normal and healthy."

"Well, normal and healthy aren't always synonymous, Faith. Just because your child may have some challenges doesn't mean he won't be normal or healthy. I suggest you focus on the larger chance he won't have it."

Mulling over her words, I realize the truth in them. Focusing on the negative causes the positive to be overshadowed.

"Thank you, Lilly. I feel so much better." I reach across and squeeze her hand. "I never knew what you went through with Shaun. After all these years, I never knew."

She smiles, squeezing my hand in return. "Well, it's not your fault, of course. When we introduce ourselves, we don't state our name and then list our problems, do we?"

****

Spending time with Lilly calmed me and gave me some perspective. I have to wait about four more months before I can meet my son. I refuse to spend that time worrying about what may or may not be. I wasted enough of my life worrying and being anxious.

No more.

Michael walks in the door after work that evening, and I greet him with a smile and a hug. His face has become creased with worry and concern lately; there's so much on his shoulders. I reach up and try to smooth the lines on his forehead.

"Are you okay?" he asks, the lines deepening despite my efforts.

I smile wider and kiss him. "I'm fine."

He blinks in surprise. "Okay. Why?"

"Oh, just getting some perspective. Even though there's a small chance of Down's syndrome, there's a larger chance that our son…" I whisper and glance around being sure the children aren't within ear shot. We haven't shared the gender of the baby yet. "…is going to be just fine. I have decided not to waste another moment of my life worrying."

"Just like that?" He snaps his fingers.

"Not just like that, but I can change a bad habit into a good one, right? With practice?"

He shrugs and smiles crookedly. "Absolutely."

Once dinner is done and the dishes have been cleared, we gather the children at the table to share the news with them as well as the budgetary decisions we've made.

April grips the table until her knuckles are white, anticipating end-of-the-world news, I'm sure. Sarah stares at the table sullenly and Andrew simply sits, waiting.

"Well," Michael begins. "Your mother and I did look over the budget, and we heard your concerns about the sports." He looks pointedly first at April, and then at Sarah. "We are

426

going to reduce the cell phone minutes available because a large number of them expire monthly – you'll still have unlimited texts," He cuts April off just as she opens her mouth to protest. "We are going to eliminate our land line because we have cell phones anyway. Andrew doesn't have one, but he's always with someone who does. I am also going to trade in my car for one that's older and less expensive, which will save quite a bit of money. Your mother is going to be more frugal in her grocery shopping and we should be just fine."

Silence.

April is the first one to break it, of course. She blinks a few times, looks around the table and replies wide eyed, "That's it? That's all you're going to do?"

Michael's mouth twitches at the corners. "Plus we're going to cut the electricity off to your rooms, so you'll have to use candles from now on."

I can't help myself; I burst out laughing. By their expressions, the kids look like they believe him for a brief second before they glare at him.

Andrew remains aghast.

"Really, Dad? I have to use candles from now on?" Andrew cries incredulously.

I laugh even harder and gasp for air. "Michael! Stop teasing them."

April rolls her eyes and Sarah snorts a laugh.

"That's so not funny, Dad!" April cries.

Finally, Michael's façade cracks, and he laughs along with me. "No, Andrew, you do not need to use candles. I was just teasing you, buddy!" he chortles.

Andrew looks around before giggling. "I think it would be kind of fun."

"Dad, so we don't have to quit our sports then?" Sarah asks hopefully.

Michael wipes his eyes and shakes his head. "No, you don't have to give up your sports."

April throws her head back and her arms up in the air. "Thank God!"

"We thought that would make you guys happy." I grin. "But we have more news, too. About the baby."

Michael and I agreed to share the gender with the children, but nothing else. Whether the baby has challenges or not doesn't make a difference; he's still our son.

"Do you want to tell them the gender, Faith?" Michael asks.

I nod and smile at each child. "Well, I already know Andrew is hoping for a brother, but what do you two think it is?" I gesture to Sarah and April.

Sarah squints at me for a moment. "I think it's a boy."

"I hope it's a girl!" April blurts. "I want to dress her up."

"Well, the boys have it! You're going to have another brother," I announce.

Andrew can't be contained; he bounces up and down, clapping and whooping. Sarah smiles and April even gives in and smiles broadly.

"Well, I can dress him up anyway while he's still too young to care!" she cries.

Andrew stops whooping long enough to frown at his sister. "You are *not* dressing my little brother up in a dress!"

April grins and sticks her tongue out at him, teasing. Andrew lifts his chin in defiance and continues to frown at her.

"We don't have any little dresses anyway, so that won't be a problem," I reply. "I have to buy everything. April, you can help me shop for things, if you'd like."

Her face is the epitome of joy; I did say shop after all. "Really? I can help you shop for the baby stuff?"

I nod and now it's her turn to bounce up and down and whoop in her seat. Sarah smiles and shakes her head, muttering. "Have fun with that." Sarah abhors shopping.

"When are we going?!" April squeals.

We decided to purchase the baby items from our savings; it's the only option. I promised Michael I would remember the word frugal when making the purchases. I'll keep it simple this time; just the basics. I inform April of this; it doesn't diminish her joy in any way. She loves the thrill of the hunt as much as the purchase itself.

"No problem! I can go on line and start looking for deals…" She leaps from her seat and disappears in a blur, muttering to herself and ticking items off on her fingers.

428

"Good call," Michael murmurs to me.

"I thought she'd enjoy that," I reply.

"Mom, promise me you won't let her put my baby brother in a dress," Andrew asks, his face screwed into a scowl.

"Andrew, I promise I won't let her put a dress on your baby brother."

Convinced, he nods his head once and disappears, as well.

"Sarah, do you want to shop with me, too?" I ask. It never hurts to ask. "I'd love your input."

"No. I hate shopping." She hesitates. "But I would like to decorate the room, if you don't mind."

The nursery is going to be a spare room that we had used for storage at the end of the hall upstairs. It's large enough because it was built to have been a home office, but we used the study on the main floor for that instead.

I had no idea. "Really? What kind of decorating?"

"Well, I like to paint. Maybe I could put some teddy bears or soccer balls or something on the walls."

Michael looks at me and shrugs.

"Sure, Sarah. I think that would be lovely. Do whatever you want, as long as it's not expensive," I warn her.

She grins almost as wide as her sister. "It won't be. Paint is cheap." She rises to leave, turns around on a whim and hugs me, whispering in my ear. "Thanks, Mom. Love you." Releasing me, she punches her father in the arm before leaving.

Michael looks at me, incredulous. "Sarah likes to paint?"

"Who knew?" I shrug.

"This should be interesting," Michael muses.

Interesting, indeed. Thank you, Lord! Thank you for my talented children.

Chapter Forty

"What do you think?" Julie turns to the side, cradling and pushing her protruding belly out even farther. "Pretty cool, huh?" Her ever radiant smile has impossibly increased in wattage. I'm sure it has to do with the fact that she made it through the vomiting stage and well into her second trimester without complications.

Glancing briefly at my own rotund form (I haven't seen my feet in a standing position for quite some time), I can only agree with her because she wants me to. Don't get me wrong; I'm happy for my friend. I am just weary to the bone of being pregnant and don't think of my bulbous form as "pretty cool". Not when every movement for the last month causes a new ache or pain to demand my attention. Even walking makes me groan. My legs have become shapeless tree trunks and I think even my nose has grown larger. I will not discuss my backside; I've refused to acknowledge its enormous presence.

Ah, the joys of pregnancy in my forties.

To Michael's credit, he still tells me I'm beautiful every day. I'm not sure I believe him, but I appreciate the effort.

"You look great!" I enthuse for Julie's sake. "Would you like to come in? It's really cold out, and I need to sit down." I waddle out of the doorway and into the living room, Julie close on my heels.

"You look great, too, Faith. I'm sorry you're so uncomfortable."

Grunting loudly as I dump myself onto the sofa like the giant slug I am, I shrug my shoulders. "It's okay. Only about two months left. Whew, it can't come soon enough."

"Can I get you some water or something else to drink?" she offers.

"No." I gesture to my still full water bottle on the side table. "I'm good. Please help yourself, though. You know where everything is."

When she returns with a glass of iced tea, she sits next to me and rubs her stomach. "Little Ben's been moving a lot lately. It's such a wonderful feeling!"

Julie found out she's also having a boy; I cried with her when she told me. Her joy is infectious.

I pat my own stomach. "Yes, this little guy is active, but he's getting kind of cramped in there. He kicks my ribs and my bladder more than anything else." As if he heard me, he thumps my rib cage from the inside causing me to wince and rub the spot.

Julie winces in sympathy. "I'm sorry, Faith. Is there anything I can do for you? Anything at all? Especially now that you've been told to stay off your feet as much as possible."

Sighing, I shake my head. "No, not really. The doctor told me to just take it easy, but at least I'm not on bed rest. You've all been so great, being a taxi for the kids when they need it and bringing meals."

As soon as Julie found out about my doctor's orders, she organized help from Michelle, Lilly, and even Brenda. She and Scott have continued their counseling with Pastor Ben. All were more than willing to do whatever we needed.

"How was your blood pressure this last time?" Julie asks.

"It's been running high, but I don't have pre-eclampsia. I'm thankful for that." I glance around at my home. "Everyone pitches in and helps clean, but I've had to lower my standards." I remember Andrew's recent attempt at cleaning the bathroom; it caused me to walk in, look around, and walk right back out.

"I know it's difficult for you, Faith. You take such pride in your home." She glances around, her eyes following the same circuit mine just completed. "I think it still looks great."

I chuckle. "Thanks. It will be better once this little guy comes, though."

"Have you guys decided on a name yet? You can't call him a little guy forever, you know."

"Actually, no. We can't seem to agree. Would you believe Andrew wants to name him Amadeus? As he puts it, it sounds noble." We both laugh. "We still have a little more time to decide, thankfully."

The outlandish names Andrew has come up with include Thor and Remulus. Where Remulus came from, I'll never know.

Julie's cell phone beeps and she retrieves it from her purse.

"Hello?"

Silence.

Suddenly, her eyes widen and her mouth forms an "O". "Are you serious?! Where? When? How far along?"

I look inquisitively at her and she waves me off, but grins widely and shakes her head, which puzzles me even more.

"I think it would be wonderful, sweetheart! Let me know when you find out the details!" After ending her conversation, she drops her cell into her purse, bounces gleefully and grabs my hands.

"Faith! You'll never believe this! Ben just got a call from a pastor in California he's known forever. He was Ben's youth pastor at one time. Anyway, there's a girl there in his congregation, a teenager. She's pregnant and wants to put her baby up for adoption. He called to see if we would be interested! He wants to know if we'd like to adopt her baby! Faith, that's amazing! We may have *two* babies instead of just one!"

She leaps up and starts bouncing on her heels.

"Uh, what? You would consider adopting? I thought you weren't sure about that."

She paces the floor.

"Julie, please sit down. You're making me dizzy," I chuckle.

"Oh! Sorry." She joins me on the sofa. "Okay. Ben and I did explore the possibility before we found out we were pregnant. You know, we just put some feelers out there to a few congregations and pastors that we know. We've shared our struggles with them over the years, and they've prayed with us and supported us. We hadn't heard anything from anyone, so we assumed it was a dead end. But now..." She claps her hands together and beams. "Now, we may adopt *and* have a baby, too!"

432

"Oh, Julie! How wonderful! But you don't know if it's going to happen. Maybe you shouldn't jump the gun just yet. Wait until you find out more information."

Please don't disappoint her, God. Please.

Her joy is irrepressible. "I know we don't have much information right now, but the idea is so exciting! God is so good!!" She squeezes her eyes shut and hugs her stomach.

Is it possible for a heart to sink and soar at the same time? Because mine just did.

****

The pregnant teenager turns out to be a runaway who's been taken in by a family in the church in California. She's about seven months along, but has received no prenatal care. Her first appointment isn't actually until next week. From the information gathered from their pastor friend, she's not a drug user or anything; she simply ended up pregnant and was kicked out by her parents because of it. She lived with friends at first and then ended up at the church where she was taken in by a family.

I'm aghast. "How awful!" I exclaim as Julie and I peruse the aisles at the local discount store's baby furniture selection. April and I have shopped for and gotten a few things but haven't purchased the large items like the crib, car seat, or stroller. We've also gotten limited clothing and other essentials. Every time I get close to purchasing anything, April talks me out of it or throws a fit; it's the wrong color, the wrong style, the wrong look. It's getting annoying, and I'm running out of patience and time.

Julie shakes her head as she fingers the fabric on a bouncy seat. "I know. I can't imagine what her parents were thinking to just throw her out like that when she needed them the most. Poor thing."

"Do you think her baby is okay? She hasn't had any prenatal care."

Julie is contemplative. "Oh, I think the baby is going to be okay. She sounds like a healthy young lady. But it really doesn't matter, now does it? We would love to welcome another baby into our home."

My hand reflexively rubs my stomach, thinking about the outcome our child may face. "True. It doesn't really matter."

"As long as we've waited for little Ben," Julie muses as she squeezes the hand brake on a jogging stroller. "I can't possibly imagine turning away any child God would choose to bless us with. However they may arrive in our family."

"Do you have any idea how tired you're going to be? I remember with our first child we were like zombies for weeks. There were two of us and only one of her, but the realities of parenting a newborn are a real shock to the system, to say the least."

Julie's eyes darken. "I've lost a lot of sleep over the years praying for a child. I don't mind losing even more sleep now because I'll have one, or perhaps more than one. As a matter of fact, I'm looking forward to it."

I squeeze her hand. "You're going to be an amazing mother."

Her eyes gleam as she whispers, "Thank you."

"Have you also considered the cost involved? You'll have to buy two of everything if this adoption goes through." I sweep my hands around me. "I mean, look at how much this stuff costs. It's ridiculous! I can't believe how expensive everything has gotten for babies." I bend over to peer at the price on a stroller and immediately regret it. A pain shoots through my left leg, and I reach for the shelf to steady myself as I gasp.

"Are you okay? Faith, let's get you home." Julie reaches in to help support me, but I wave her off.

"No. No, I'm fine. I just can't move like I used to." I grunt as I stand up straight, push my hands into my lower back and stretch upward. "Lord, I'm so pathetic."

Julie chuckles. "You are not pathetic. You're pregnant. In fact, you're *very* pregnant."

I look pointedly at her. If I wore glasses, I'd be looking over the rims at her. "Please! Have you seen my ankles lately? I haven't; they disappeared about a month ago. I can only wear slip on shoes now. This baby can't come soon enough."

Julie doesn't even crack a smile: she just looks concerned. "I think we should get you home. You're not supposed to be out and about too much, you know. Michael made me promise not to keep you out too long."

"We've only been here for thirty minutes. Besides, as you said, I'm very pregnant and we still don't have any of the big things we need like a crib or a car seat. Sarah has the room all painted and ready, but if I don't get these things soon, my poor baby may end up sleeping in a laundry basket."

Sarah did a fantastic job decorating; she painted the walls of the nursery in a very light sky blue and painstakingly added Winnie the Pooh and most of the characters from the series on top of that. She even chose a beautiful fabric to make curtains. I am very impressed. I never knew she had an interest in such a thing, much less a gift.

The budget cuts we made have worked well, but it's still tight. Christmas was scaled back quite a bit. I found I liked that better. It helped us focus on the real meaning of Christmas and the kids enjoyed it, too. Being more involved in church, and everything I've gone through this past year has really allowed it all to sink deeply into my being. My relationship with God continues to grow.

Thankfully, we haven't had to dip into our savings to pay our monthly bills, but once the baby comes all bets are off. Especially if he has any challenges ahead of him. His challenges will become our challenges as a family.

Something flashes across Julie's face before it disappears just as quickly. It looked like she was trying not to smile. "Still, you do look exhausted. Come on, let's go. I could never forgive myself if you or the baby ended up in trouble because I brought you out to shop."

Reluctantly, I follow her out of the store. The brisk late January wind cuts through me like a knife. I suck my breath in and bury my face deeper into my scarf. Julie does the same. Normally, I would jog to my car in this kind of weather, but all I can muster is a quick waddle, and I use the term quick here very, very loosely.

As we bundle into her car, she rubs her hands together after starting the engine and cranking up the heat. "Brrrr!!! I thought pregnant women were supposed to be hot. I'm freezing!"

"I don't think anybody can be warm enough to fight off this kind of cold. That wind just hurts!" I place my hands over the vents in front of my seat to warm them.

When we arrive home, she pulls right up into my driveway. "Julie, you live next door. I can walk that far. You didn't have to pull into my driveway to drop me off."

She grins. "You're welcome!"

Shaking my head as I reach for the door handle, I pause and turn back to her. "Thank you, Julie. You're a fantastic friend. I hope you know that."

"You're a terrific friend yourself! Hey, don't forget that you guys are coming over for dinner tomorrow."

I laugh as I grunt my way out of the seat. "How could I forget? The kids are really excited that you're back to baking again. They're looking forward to dessert more than anything."

Julie laughs heartily, rolling the window down as I close the door to prevent the heat from escaping. "Yes, I know. I promised them something special and I will deliver."

"Are you sure we can't bring anything? It's ridiculous for you to cook everything."

"I'm sure. It's my pleasure. I'll see you tomorrow night! Now go inside and get warm!" she calls as she backs out to drive the few yards to her own garage.

As I waddle through the front door, the earthy aroma of beef stew fills my nostrils and I take a deep, appreciative breath. "Aahhh…"

Michelle peeks around the corner from the kitchen, grinning as she enters the foyer, drying her hands on a dish towel. "I thought I heard the front door. Come in and sit down. I just brought dinner over, and your family is starting without you." The clang of dishes, voices, and laughter spills out of the kitchen.

I embrace Michelle as she approaches me. "Thank you. Thank you so much for taking care of us like this."

Michelle squeezes me hard. "It's my pleasure. That's what friends are for. Now, go sit." She nudges me in the back, and I waddle into the kitchen.

Michael is the first to spy me. "Honey! You're back already? I thought you'd be out a little longer than that. Are you hungry? Michelle made beef stew, rice, salad, and even brownies for dessert."

"Wow, what a spread! You've gone to way too much trouble. How will they ever get used to eating normally after the baby comes with all of you guys feeding us like this?"

As usual, Michelle has her food spread out in a beautiful buffet fashion. Even the containers are disposable so there won't be any clean up afterwards. How thoughtful.

"Eh." She shrugs. "You'd do the same for me. Although, I sincerely hope you never have to." She gestures toward my midsection and laughs.

Michael ushers me to the table, placing my dinner before me. "Oh. Thank you. You didn't have to get my plate, too, Michael."

"Just eat, honey," he replies before disappearing into the kitchen once again, returning quickly with his own plate. Once we're all seated, we say grace and eat.

Michelle declines to eat with us; she and Richard have dinner plans. With much gratitude from us, she beats a hasty retreat.

The food is, of course, delicious. It's always delicious. We've been blessed by the generosity of our friends providing us with meals almost every night for the past several weeks.

Brenda has in typical Brenda fashion eagerly joined the queue of people who've stepped in to help us, in spite of her difficulties. She and Scott continue to go to counseling with Pastor Ben. I don't have to pry; she opens up on her own now that it's all out there, among our friends anyway. It hasn't been easy and they're still not sleeping in the same room together, but they remain under the same roof and things are improving.

She hasn't sought out another job but has gained back some of the weight she had lost initially, and is back to having every hair in place and every piece of her ensemble match. Everything is right in the world when Brenda matches.

After eating less than half of what Michael served me, I push the plate away and lean back.

Michael notices.

"Not hungry?" he asks, shoveling another bite into his mouth.

I grimace. "Not really. It's fantastic, but I just don't have any room left. The baby has taken up all the space I have."

"Can I have your brownie?" April asks, smiling from ear to ear.

"Sure. I'll just eat two of whatever Julie makes tomorrow. Ha!" I reply.

April laughs and rises to retrieve her brownies. Naturally, she's already wolfed down her dinner. I really hope she'll develop table manners at some point; our efforts to teach her have proven fruitless.

She returns with two enormous (I'm not kidding here) frosted brownies with what appear to be glazed pecans on top.

My mouth waters, but my stomach feels like it's in my throat. If I take even one more bite of anything, I'm sure I'll see it again very soon. In an attempt to avoid further temptation, which would include my mostly empty bowl of M&Ms that I still fill too often, I heave myself out of the chair with much grunting and a little help from Michael and plop myself down on the sofa, planting my swollen feet on the coffee table. If I'm being honest, I plant my swollen *legs* on the coffee table.

Michael's face is creased with concern, as usual. "Faith, are you sure you're okay?" he asks quietly, settling a pillow under my feet.

I take a shallow breath (deep breathing is difficult anymore) and relax my head back onto the cushions. "Not really. I'm forty-four and very pregnant. There's nothing really okay about this, physically. But I will be fine once he's born."

The crease in his brow deepens. "I'm sorry you're pregnant, sweetheart. Really I am."

I tilt my head and look up at him. "Michael, what do you mean? Are you sorry about having another child?" My hands creep around my swollen belly.

He sighs and closes his eyes. "No. Not about our child. I'm sorry you have to suffer like this." He places his hand over my own and rubs his thumb back and forth across my wrist. He stares pensively at me in silence.

"Michael, it's going to be fine. This pregnancy is hard on me because I'm not as young as I was with the others. But it's only temporary. I've only got a few more months of this and then we'll be back to normal. And you'll have to get used to eating a regular dinner without dessert every night!"

My attempt at levity hits its mark. Michael chuckles and the crease in his brow smoothes, a rare occurrence lately.

"It's going to be fine, Michael. You'll see." I pucker my lips, and he leans in to kiss me very gently and very sweetly.

What a difference a few months makes. I'm now reassuring Michael that everything will be okay. He's always been my rock. I never thought I'd be strong enough to reassure anyone of anything.

I can do all things through Christ who strengthens me.

The word that Pastor Ben preached this past Sunday bubbles up in my thoughts. I am growing stronger spiritually while my body stretches, aches, and groans its way through to the end of this pregnancy.

Even sleeping is a challenge; I've had to purchase new pillows to prop myself up and Michael has to help me not only get up to go to the bathroom, but also just to turn over. If I lay on one side for too long, the hip and leg I'm laying on go numb.

I have to turn over rather frequently.

Michael has yet to utter one word of complaint.

As far as my nocturnal bathroom habits, it's excruciatingly irritating to go to all the trouble of getting up only to have a few drips to show for the effort. It's the definition of annoying. Even beyond my earlier empty offerings to the porcelain pit.

****

The following day, another attempt at online shopping with April proves futile. She doesn't like any of the items I choose, and finds excuses to not purchase any of them.

My patience is gone, as are my ankles.

"April," I begin, working exceptionally hard at not yelling. "That is enough. I like this crib and I want to get it. If it doesn't work with your vision of the nursery, I'm so sorry. But your baby brother is going to need a place to sleep, and I'm running out of time. I've had it and I'm going to order it."

"Mom, you can't!" she cries, looking desperately at the screen.

It's my turn to roll my eyes. "April, seriously. That's enough! I need to get a crib." I purse my lips and click the order button.

April squirms in her seat. "Mom, just don't. Not yet. Please? We'll…" She appears to be searching for the right word. "We'll find the right one. I promise! You'll regret this purchase. It's…not right! Please!"

This makes no sense, but I'm too tired to care. What's one more day?

Sighing, I close out the window on the screen, my tone becoming irritable. "Fine, April. But this is getting ridiculous. We need to get something for your brother to at least sleep in."

April's shoulders slump, and she huffs out her breath like I just stopped one step short of jumping off a cliff, not making an online purchase. She's so dramatic!

I swivel in my seat to face her. "April, we really need to get things for your brother soon. We are running out of time. Do you understand that? He'll be here in a few months, and we barely have anything for him. Right now, he only has a few things to wear and absolutely nothing to sleep in, be pushed around in, or come home from the hospital in. Will you please relax about what we buy? I may have to just get things without you."

She looks wide eyed at me for a moment before slowly nodding her head up and down.

"Good." I grunt to a standing position and waddle out of the room.

****

"Ready to go? If we don't leave soon, we'll be later than we already are." Michael stands in the foyer with his hands on his hips, semi-scowling at the kids as they put their shoes on. We were supposed to be at Julie's house almost thirty minutes ago. I called to tell her we were running late. She didn't seem to mind. But then again, she is Julie.

Once all shoes have been placed on the proper feet, we make our way next door, me waddling behind everyone else, of course. Michael stays close to my side; the ground is covered in a snowy, icy sheen. It looks beautiful glittering in the moonlight like diamond dust, but it's treacherous for even the sure-footed much less the wobbly, waddling mess that I am.

The kids are anxiously bouncing on Julie's front step when we finally make our way onto it.

"What are you waiting for? Ring the door bell!" I bark, somewhat impatiently. Give me some grace; it's freezing out here and my whole body aches.

The kids look to Michael who nods, grinning.

They ring the doorbell and Julie answers almost immediately, peeking around the door rather than opening it wide, as usual. When she sees us, her grin comes out in full force. She ushers us into the rather dark entry way.

"I'm so glad you could make it! Here, let me take your coat." She helps me out of my coat and then guides me into the living room.

"*Surprise!!!!*"

A crowd of people jump out from behind the furniture and around the corners, all smiling at me.

I gasp and jump back, grabbing my bulbous stomach as I do so, and bump right into Michael.

"Surprise, honey," he whispers into my ear and kisses my cheek.

My eyes flicker from face to face, recognition dawning slowly. All of our friends are here; Lilly and Tony, Michelle and Richard, even Brenda with Scott as well as all of the children, too. Julie and Ben come to hug us first, rapidly followed by everyone else. My children are eagerly jumping up and down and clapping their hands.

"Were you surprised, Mom?!" April squeals.

I can barely acknowledge her; I'm overwhelmed by hugs and well wishes.

Once the tide of people calms down and disperses from my view, I spy the enormous spread of wrapped presents on the table in the corner as well as a crib, car seat, high chair, bouncy seat, and a stroller that are adorned simply with ribbons and bows that line the wall beside the gifts.

"Is this a baby shower?" I ask incredulously.

Laughter rings in my ears. Julie grabs my shoulders and smiles.

"Of course it's your baby shower!" she cries. "Are you surprised?"

I nod mutely and that causes a second round of laughter. "I'm…I'm overwhelmed. Wow."

"Well, come on in. We've been waiting for you! We have food and just a few gifts." She winks at my friends.

I turn to Michael. "You knew about this?"

He smiles broadly and nods. "It was Julie's idea. I just went along with it."

"I helped, Mom! I helped pick out most of the stuff!" April cries, jumping up and down. "Do you like it?" She gestures to the pile.

"April," Michael laughs. "She hasn't opened anything yet!"

April groans and rolls her eyes, still grinning. "So, *open* them!" she cries.

"How about we eat first?" Ben interjects. "I know we're all hungry, and I'm sure Faith is, too."

"Actually, I am," I reply.

"Me, too. My appetite has really picked up!" Julie laughs, rubbing her own burgeoning stomach.

The buffet set up in their kitchen looks like it could feed a group double our size; inquiry determines that Michelle and Julie planned it together, naturally. There are sure to be leftovers. At the center of it all is a humongous bowl of M&Ms. The colorful little spheres are mounded into a beautiful crystal bowl elevated above most of the other food. Upon closer inspection, there appears to be both plain chocolate as well as peanut mixed together.

Ben prays a blessing over the food, and I'm ushered through the line first, followed by Julie (with much prodding). Seeing the mounds of food and tremendous variety offered, it's impossible to make up my mind. I settle for taking a small spoonful of everything in sight.

Once the majority of the food is devoured – more than I thought would be – I plop myself into a chair set up for me to begin the task of opening the mountain of gifts.

As I begin to make a molehill out of the mountain, I soon realize that almost every item I had considered buying when I was shopping with April has been purchased. Even down to the little hooded bath towel beautifully embroidered with Winnie the Pooh. I glance over at April, and she's grinning from ear to ear.

"I remembered everything you wanted, Mom! I took notes and everything! Did I do good?!" she blurts and claps her hands.

Sarah, sitting on the floor next to me dutifully writing down each gift and giver, rolls her eyes, balling up the wrapping paper and stuffing it into a trash bag Julie provided.

"You did it perfectly, sweetheart," Michael replies, kissing April on the top of her head.

The next present Sarah hands me is a small square awkwardly wrapped in silver. The tag says it's from Sarah. I look at her and smile. "Sweetie, you didn't have to get anything."

Her facial expression is almost unreadable, but her cheeks are pink and she's suppressing a smile. "Just open it, Mom."

When I peel back the wrapping paper, there in my hand is Sarah's favorite Little Golden Book from her preschool days. The pages are dog eared and some are scribbled with crayon. Sarah loves her books and has never gotten rid of any of them. I gasp and my eyes fill with tears. The meaning isn't lost on me. I hug the book to my chest and reach for Sarah to engulf her in a hug, too.

"Oh, sweetheart! That means so much to me! Your brother is going to love it," I whisper into her ear.

Sarah nods and draws a ragged breath in. "I know. It's time for me to grow up and pass it on."

"What is it?"

"What did you get?"

Sarah and I pull away, both wiping at our eyes. I hold the much loved book up for everyone to see. Michael, April, and Andrew all gasp in surprise and everyone else looks puzzled.

I explain the significance of it as best I can while wiping my eyes. "This book has been a treasured part of her collection for a very long time." I smile lovingly at Sarah whose cheeks are now crimson and wet.

Once all of the gifts are opened and piled before me, it's overwhelming to realize how very much I am blessed. Gazing around the room at all of my friends and family, those who are most important to me, words are difficult.

"I'm so…very….blessed by all of you. Thank you….isn't enough…for me to…express…" That's as far as I get before I become incomprehensible and Michael takes over.

He comes to stand beside me, placing his hand on my shoulder. "Thank you from the bottom of our hearts. As Faith said, you're such a blessing to us as a family. Life has thrown us some curve balls this year." He squeezes my shoulder briefly. "You've provided us with delicious meals while Faith has had to rest, as well as everything we'll need for the baby and even some things we didn't know we needed!" Laughter interrupts him. "We'll never be able to fully repay you for all that you've done for us. So thank you. Thank you so much." His voice quivers on the last word.

The adults all rise and embrace us in hugs and congratulations.

Julie disappears into the kitchen once more only to return with an enormous three tier cake that looks like it could've come straight from a televised cake competition. Calling it exquisite would be an understatement; it's an amazing work of art. There are sculpted people on every tier that, upon closer inspection, are obvious renditions of Michael, our children, and me culminating in a tiny crib with an even tinier baby nestled in it on top of the cake. All of the sculptures have captured the essence of each person; Andrew is playing with microscopic superhero figurines, Sarah is sitting cross-legged engrossed in a book, and April is in mid-air cheering. Michael is in perpetual motion carrying a briefcase while my miniature replica is reaching out and looking up. Whether I'm looking up at the crib or up to the heavens, I don't know.

"Wow, Julie! Did you make this?" I ask incredulously.

She grins and gestures to Michelle.

"Actually, she and I have worked on it for five days. We went through a *lot* of modeling chocolate, believe me!" she laughs.

"Yeah, we had to make all of you guys at least three times before we got it right." Michelle chuckles, crossing her arms and admiring the handiwork.

Everyone gasps and walks slowly around the cake, which has taken center stage on the table that until recently had held the gifts. Right next to it, Michelle places the slightly less mounded crystal bowl of M&Ms, winking at me.

"I don't even want it to be cut. It's so beautiful," Sarah breathes.

"Can I eat myself?" Andrew asks, causing everyone to laugh. He looks around at the laughing adults, bewildered.

Julie squeezes Andrew and kisses the top of his head. "Of course you can have the piece that has you on it."

"What flavors are in it?" April asks.

"There's carrot, chocolate, and red velvet," Michelle replies.

Once we've all finished admiring the cake and taken plenty of pictures, Julie offers the knife to me. Holding my hands up and shaking my head, I respond, "Oh, no! I am not cutting that up. You do the honors yourself."

Julie grins and shrugs her shoulders. "As you wish."

She and Michelle carefully remove each layer and place them on the table before cutting them into rectangles. I accept a sliver of each of the three flavors.

"These cakes are the most delicious I've ever tasted!" Brenda gushes as she licks the frosting from her fork. "You two should go into business making cakes together. They are absolutely divine."

Murmurs of agreement ripple through those gathered.

"We've actually discussed it," Michelle pipes in, licking her own fork and smiling at Julie.

"Really? You might do that?" I ask, looking from Michelle to Julie.

Michelle shrugs. "Why not? My centers are running themselves right now, and this is something I've always liked to do."

"But what about you?" Lilly asks Julie. "You have a baby on the way, and that's going to take up a lot of your time, you know."

Julie smiles and places her now empty plate on the table before her. "I know and it's just something we talked about. I had so much fun working with you," she addresses Michelle, who smiles and nods. "But we may not be able to do this really soon because…" she looks to Ben, who nods encouragingly. "We are not only going to have this baby, but we are also adopting."

She smiles and casts her glance around the group, her eyes coming to rest on me. She nods before continuing. "We found out earlier today that we are going to adopt from that young lady in California, and she's expecting twins!"

Holy. Lord. I'm…speechless.

Chapter Forty One

Dead silence reigns for about five seconds before cries of amazement mingle with jubilation. April, Brenda, and Michelle have all risen to their feet with identically shocked looks on their faces. Personally, I'm stunned.

Ben and Julie are going to have *three* babies? Three? All at once?

Amid the cries of congratulations and questions, I ask my own. "When are the babies supposed to be born?"

Julie and Ben are fielding the questions as best they can. They both seem relaxed and truly joyful over the whole business.

I would be terrified.

Finally Ben holds up his hands to quell the onslaught. Grinning, he begins. "We literally found out that we'll be adopting twins just this morning. We are over the moon about it. We know that we'll have our hands full, but," he gazes lovingly at Julie and squeezes her hand. "we've waited so long to have children. We are amazed at how God is overwhelmingly blessing us with not one, not two, but three children. The babies are due in about six weeks, but because they're twins they may very well come early. The mother is an unwed teenager and has had no prenatal care. It could be any day now, truthfully."

Julie wipes tears from her cheeks even as she continues to grin. "I can't wait to meet them all!"

"Where...how...how are you going to do this?" Brenda sputters.

"What do you need?" Michelle asks soberly. "I think we'll need to do some more shopping, folks." She glances around the room and heads begin to nod, including my own.

"Absolutely," Tony, Lilly's husband, chimes in. "Whatever you guys need, we'll be here."

"Are you going to move into a bigger house?" Scott asks.

Please don't move. Please.

Ben shakes his head. "No. There are four bedrooms here and that's plenty of space for all of us. Besides, Julie loves this house and the neighborhood. We couldn't leave."

I send up a silent prayer of thanks. I don't want Julie to move, especially not now.

"We don't know anything else, really. We hope to get more details tomorrow. We're going to video chat with the girl for the first time. I'm so excited!" Julies exclaims. "From everything we've heard, she's excited to meet us, too."

"That's wonderful, Julie!" Lilly cries.

"I can help baby sit!" April pipes up. "Sarah and I can team up and take care of the babies." She gestures to her sister who smiles and nods enthusiastically.

"I want to baby sit, too!" Mariah, Brenda's daughter and April's best friend, adds.

April begins to bounce. "We can dress them up soooo cute!" She and Mariah squeal and clap their hands, causing most of the adults to chuckle.

Michael injects a nasty bit of reality. "Don't forget they'll have diapers to change, too."

It barely quells their enthusiasm.

The evening's conversation centers on more food, more cake, and more baby discussion. Ben and Julie's enthusiasm never wanes; I'm not surprised. I know the heartache they've experienced waiting to become parents. Their children are going to be so blessed having them as parents.

"Have you picked out any names? Do you know what the genders are?" Lilly asks.

Julie pats her stomach. "This is Benjamin Thomas Junior, of course. We don't know what the genders are of the other babies yet. But we've picked out Hannah Joy for a girl, and John David for a boy. Hannah is the mother of Samuel in the Old Testament, and she waited a long time to have him. Joy is an obvious choice; we're joyful to have a daughter, if we do. John David means God is gracious and he's our beloved son."

448

"What are you going to do if they're two girls or two boys?" Lilly asks.

Ben and Julie look at each other and shrug. "We'll keep researching and see what we come up with, I suppose," Ben replies.

"I'm just happy to have this as a problem!" Julie laughs exultantly. "I never expected having a problem of too few baby names picked out."

"It's a wonderful problem, indeed," Ben replies thickly.

"How about we all pick names, write them on a piece of paper, and you select them from a bowl?" Audrey, Michelle's seventeen year old daughter, chimes in. "That way we can all have a hand in it and you don't have to research anymore."

"That's a wonderful idea!" Michelle replies, looking expectantly at Ben and Julie, who appear to be having a silent, mental conversation.

"I don't see why not," Ben finally replies.

Once the slips of paper have been passed out and everyone has had a chance to write a boy name on one and a girl name on the other, the folded slips with the boys' names are placed in one bowl and the girls' names are placed in another. The bowls are then placed on the coffee table on either side of the massive M&M bowl, which was brought back out from its place beside the cake.

Kneeling down, Michelle places one hand in each bowl, and stirs them gently to mix them up. "Now," she begins. "Ladies first?" She pushes the bowl toward Julie.

"I'll pick out the girls' names and you pick out the boys' names, okay?" Julie glances at Ben, who nods and smiles.

Julie squeezes her eyes shut for the briefest of moments before looking at the ceiling and plunging her hand into the girls' bowl, swirling it around and pulling out a sheet of paper. She places that on the table and then plunges her hand back into the bowl for the middle name. Gathering both slips into her hand, she opens the first one.

Clearing her throat, she announces, "The first name is going to be Priscilla."

Jennifer, Brenda's twelve-year-old, and Sarah both squeal.

"Did you pick Priscilla, too?!" Sarah asks excitedly, pointing at Jennifer. Jennifer bobs her head enthusiastically. "Cool!"

"Okay, girls. Let her read the next name," Scott chuckles. He's seated next to Brenda. There's space between them.

"The middle name is going to be," Julie pauses, her eyes sweeping the anticipating crowd. "Anne."

"Here, here!" Shane, Lilly's eleven year old, raises his cup in a toast.

"*You* picked that out?" April asks.

Shane's cheeks flame for the briefest of moments before he nods and shrinks ever so slightly.

"Yeah, he's sweet on a girl at school named Anne," Shaun teases his brother, who casts a malevolent look at him.

"That's enough, boys," Lilly warns. "It's a beautiful name."

"On to the boys' names." Ben rubs his hands together eagerly and scoots forward in his seat. He plunges his hand into the bowl, swirls it around and pulls out two slips of paper instead of one. He unfurls them and grins broadly.

"I love it!" he exclaims, looking from one slip to the other. "Honey, look." He leans in toward Julie who looks at the papers, gasps and stares wide eyed at her husband.

"What? Is it Festus or something hideous?" April blurts, which produces a ripple of laughter causing April to glance around, embarrassed. Perhaps someone had chosen that name.

Ben shakes his head and laughs, too. "No, nothing like that. It's…" He glances at Julie one last time and clears his throat. "It's my father's name. Peter Jacob."

Amazing. Simply amazing.

"I still don't know how you guys think you're going to be able to handle three babies! I mean, seriously, I thought I was going to lose my mind at times just having three children that weren't all babies!" Brenda interjects.

"That's because you've always been such a neat freak. Everything always had to be in its place. Even when the kids were still playing, you would walk around and pick up the toys they were playing with," Scott responds.

Brenda glares at him. "Well, it wouldn't have been so bad if you weren't always bringing clients home without telling me ahead of time, so I could've been properly prepared."

I shift uneasily in my seat. Ben intercedes, trying to lighten the mood. Clearly, Scott and Brenda still have a lot of work to do.

"I don't think that's going to be a problem for us," Ben chuckles. "In my line of work, I won't be bringing my clients home, and Julie doesn't mind having some mess. After all, she does live with me!"

His tactic works; the tension releases and conversation centers once again on all of the upcoming babies as well as everything that will follow. Eventually, the kids all tire of our conversation and beg to go to our house to watch a movie, which we allow. The men gravitate toward each other, and the women gather in the dining room and kitchen to clean up. As is usually the case, we end up talking about our labor and birthing experiences.

"Fortunately for me, I never had to experience labor. My pelvis is too small, so I had scheduled C-sections with both Brian and Audrey. I will tell you that the recovery was horrible. It took me quite awhile to get back on my feet afterwards," Michelle says, loading the dishwasher.

Even though it's her home, Julie and I have been forced to sit down with our feet up while Michelle, Brenda, and Lilly clean up. I don't mind so much; the large bowl of M&Ms, which has magically been refilled, is within arms reach. Unfortunately for my backside and me, my arm reaches into it a little too frequently.

"My labors were excruciatingly long, especially with Shane. I felt like he was never coming out. He did finally make his appearance, but only after the doctor used forceps to pull him out," Lilly reports.

"The hardest one for me was April. I think it's because I didn't really know what to expect. You know, you can read all you want and think you're ready, but until those hard labor pains hit, you have no idea what you're in for." I laugh, rubbing my stomach with one hand while grabbing just a few more M&Ms

with the other. "Boy, when they hit, they hit *hard*. I'll just have to wait and see how this one goes, and pray it goes quickly."

"My labor with both Mariah and Jennifer went well, but Lisa about did me in. I was so incredibly uncomfortable with her the last half of my pregnancy. It turns out that she was almost ten pounds, and I ended up with a third-degree laceration. They spent a lot of time sewing me up. I'm glad she was my last, because if she'd been my first, she probably would've been my only one," Brenda adds.

Julie has begun to turn pale and her hands are cradling her stomach.

I reach across and place my hand on her arm. "I'm sorry, Julie. Are we frightening you?" I glance around at the ladies, who've all turned their attention to Julie.

Brenda grimaces. "Oh! I'm so sorry, Julie. We're being insensitive, aren't we? I'm sure you'll be fine. Besides, you only have to go through it once and you end up with three babies!"

Julie shakes her head and attempts a smile. "It's okay, really. I…I just have to admit it does scare me a little."

"That's good. You should be scared," Michelle replies matter of factly, causing us to glare at her. "That means you're sane!" She glares comically back at all of us before returning to the dishes.

Julie isn't reassured at all.

"Julie, everything is going to be fine. There are lots of things they can do to make sure you're comfortable and it goes smoothly," I offer.

Lilly wisely changes the subject, and Julie eventually returns to her normal, bubbly self. I don't know if we really reassured her, but at least she's not thinking about it at the moment.

As the evening winds down, my body begins to ache for the comfort of my own bed with its welcoming stack of pillows.

Grunting to a standing position on the third attempt, I waddle into the living room to retrieve Michael and spy him on the sofa grinning and laughing. Something deep within causes me to pause. I could look through a camera lens and take a snapshot of this moment to savor forever.

Relaxing in the living room, the men are enjoying themselves immensely. Scott throws his head back in laughter at something Richard has said. He and Brenda do have a lot of work ahead of them, but at least they're under the same roof. That counts for something.

Ben wipes his eyes as the laughter dies down. He is not only going to be a new father, but he's going to be a new father to three children. He and Julie have waited so long and now…. Wow.

Michael and I absorbed the ten percent pay cut and haven't missed a beat. If anything, we're more blessed now than we've ever been. My little guy nudges me from the inside to remind me of that fact, and I rub my stomach instinctively in response. After everything that's happened this past year, miraculously our marriage is stronger than ever and so is my relationship with God.

My gaze expands beyond the men to see that sprawled around the living room are the gifts our friends have generously blessed us with. Ben and Julie's house is veritably exploding at the seams with the sheer number of gifts. Everything we need for the baby has been provided, including diaper service for a year. It's more than I could've ever hoped for or dreamed of.

Glancing behind me, the most important women in my life are chatting happily away with each other as Lilly wipes the remaining crumbs off the table. They're such an interesting group of ladies. On the surface, they appear successful and carefree; to an outsider, they look like they've never had a problem or a challenge. But beneath the surface, they've all suffered deeply in some way.

We've all suffered deeply in some way.

Yet, here we all stand, laughing and enjoying life in this moment. Together.

It's time. Go. Share.

Ignoring the weariness in my bones, I turn around and plant my backside on the chair I had just recently vacated.

Sighing, I reach for one more handful of M&Ms before I begin, "Ladies, I would like to tell you about Paul."

Epilogue

GOD, HELP ME!!!!!!

Panting, another wave of searing, white hot pain laps over me. There are no breaks; the epidural didn't take.

"Come on, Faith. Push! You're almost done. He's crowning." The nurse at my side encourages me.

I grind my teeth, grip the bed rails and push as hard as I can even though I'm utterly exhausted. My grip keeps slipping; I'm drenched in sweat. I've been pushing for two hours. My labor began twelve hours before that.

It's been an eternity. An eternity of pain.

"One, two, three…" The nurse counts to ten for the millionth time.

Michael's voice breaks through my concentration. "Come on, Faith! You can do it! I can see the top of his head!" he cries. I feel pressure on my forehead. It barely registers that Michael kissed me.

Unable to keep pushing, I drop my head back on the pillow and quickly try to catch my breath before the next relentless wave of pain overtakes me, causing me to quiver and writhe.

The pain is unbelievably intense. I scream at the enormity of it.

"Don't waste your energy screaming. Push through it!" The doctor directs me. "He's almost here!"

Wanting to tell him to go to hell, instead I follow his direction and push. The pain exponentially increases. There's no end and no break.

Just Pain.

Unable to continue pushing or control myself, my body curls into a tense, fiery ball as I scream with all that I have.

The Pain reaches a zenith.

Suddenly, the baby slides out and I'm empty.

The pain, my energy, my breath. Gone.

There's a flurry of activity around me. I'm too exhausted to care. My chest heaves as I struggle to catch my breath. I can't lift my head off the pillow to look.

My heart is finely tuned, however. I'm intently listening for the sound of a cry.

Nothing.

"He's okay. He's okay," Michael murmurs in my ear as he mops my forehead. "They're wiping him off. He's pink and beautiful."

I open my eyes to look wearily up at my husband. I still can't lift my head. "Is he...?" I can't finish the question.

I don't have to.

Suddenly, there's a loud wail and Michael's face beams. Sighing in relief, I watch Michael's face intently; his eyes are moving about the room, stopping here and there. I'm sure he's following wherever the nurses are taking our son.

He leans in close and whispers in my ear. "They're checking him now, Faith." His gaze turns to me and his cheeks are wet. "You did great, honey. Just great." He kisses me ever so gently. "I'll be right back. The nurse is calling me over." He disappears quickly from my view. I close my eyes.

Please let him be okay, God. Please.

Almost immediately, I'm overwhelmed with peace. Whether our son has challenges ahead of him or not, he's perfect because he's our son. The fact that God has given him to us makes him perfect for us, regardless of any diagnosis.

Smiling weakly, I release my fear once and for all. The space left behind is quickly filled with hope for the future, and a love so intense it takes my breath away.

"Thank you, God," I whisper, waiting to see my baby for the first time.

Michael reappears with our swaddled son cradled carefully, protectively in his arms. Tears stream down Michael's cheeks, and this time it's his chin that quivers as he says, "He's perfect, Faith. Absolutely perfect. There's nothing wrong with him whatsoever." He leans in to kiss my damp cheek as he begins to hand me my newborn son.

Still panting from my labor, I struggle to reach up and embrace the warm bundle.

"Can I sit her up a bit, doc?" asks the nurse.

The doctor glances up briefly from his work, and shakes his head. "Not yet. There's a lot to be done here. Dad, why don't you just hold him for now?" He returns his concentration to the work at hand.

The nurse shows Michael how to angle our son so that I can see him. I marvel at the pinkness of his cheeks and the soft, wispy hair that frames his face beneath the cap on his tiny head. I gently stroke his velvety soft cheek.

"We never did decide on a name," I murmur, my eyes drinking in every part of this new little face.

Michael looks in wonder at our son before turning to me, smiling.

****

The waiting room is filled with everyone that's important to us. They're all waiting anxiously to hear about the latest arrival. As Michael enters the room, all conversations cease, and all eyes are glued on him. He looks slowly around the room, taking in all of the faces before him.

April, Sarah, and Andrew are there, of course. Sarah is sitting next to Shaun; they've become inseparable. Tony and Lilly are there with Shane. He's still pining over the girl named Anne.

Richard and Michelle are there with Brian and Audrey. Audrey has been accepted into Stanford's pre-med program in the fall, and they're over the moon about it. None of us were surprised; Audrey has always been so smart.

Scott and Brenda are there together with their girls Mariah, Jennifer, and Lisa. Jennifer is having some jealousy issues because of Sarah's attention being focused on Shaun. They'll work it out somehow. Scott and Brenda are holding hands; they're doing the hard work necessary and it's paying off.

Brenda has decided to be a stay at home mom right now and focus on her marriage and her children. Brenda can't keep away from her fashion passion, however. She's working on designing a line of children's clothing. Her girls are all over that. The last we heard, she and Scott were no longer in separate bedrooms.

Ben and Julie look rather frazzled. It's no surprise considering she's in her third trimester and they have their month-old twins with them. They were born early, so they're small, but both are healthy. The doctor assures them that they'll catch up eventually.

Julie is walking back and forth in the bouncy way that mommies do with babies; she's holding Hannah Joy. Ben is sitting on the floor with Peter Jacob strapped in his car seat. He's pushing him back and forth and making silly faces at him. Julie has never been so happy or so tired in her life, and these babies are her life. Benjamin Thomas Junior is due in a few short months.

The church not only threw a surprise baby shower for them and provided a list of volunteers to help, but also took up a collection to cover their adoption expenses. Combined with the baby shower our little group gave them, their house really is busting at the seams now.

Paul Michael Strauss entered the world on March 28th at 2:50 p.m. weighing eight pounds four ounces.

He is perfect.

"For I know the plans I have for you,"
declares the LORD, "plans to prosper you and
not to harm you, plans to give you hope and a
future."

Jeremiah 29:11

Recipes

There are delicious recipes shared among the characters throughout the book. Here are some that you've read about. I hope you'll try them while you read the story. So pour a glass of milk, grab a cookie or a bar, and enjoy.

<u>Cherry Chocolate Cookies</u>
Adapted and used with permission from Julia M. Usher's "Cookie Swap: Creative Treats to Share throughout the Year"

1 ¾ cup semi-sweet chocolate chips, divided use
2 Tbsp butter
¼ cup all purpose flour
2 teaspoons unsweetened cocoa powder
¼ tsp baking powder
1/8 tsp salt
2 large eggs, room temperature
1/3 cup granulated sugar
2 Tbsp dark brown sugar
1 tsp vanilla extract
2 cups chopped pecan halves
1 cup dried tart cherries

1. Preheat oven to 350 degrees. Line a cookie sheet with parchment paper and set aside.

2. Melt **1 cup** of chocolate and butter in a double boiler. Stir until melted. Set aside to cool.

3. In a small bowl, combine the flour, cocoa powder, baking powder, and salt. Set aside.

4. In a large bowl, whisk the eggs, sugars, and vanilla together until well combined. Gradually add the cooled chocolate until mixed well.

5. Stir in the flour mixture, followed by the pecans, the tart cherries, and the remaining chocolate chips.

6. Place the cookies on the prepared cookie sheets in heaping tablespoons about 2 inches apart. Bake for 13-16

minutes until done. Cool the cookies on the cookie sheet for about 2 minutes before transferring to a cooling rack to cool completely. This recipe makes about 2 dozen cookies.

Salted Peanut Butter Chocolate Chip Cookies

1 cup butter
½ cup sugar
½ cup brown sugar
1 tsp baking soda
½ tsp fine kosher salt
2 eggs
1 ½ tsp pure vanilla extract
1 cup all-natural peanut butter (ingredient list should say peanuts and salt only)
2 cups all purpose flour
2 cups dark chocolate chunks or semi-sweet chocolate chips
Approximately 2 Tbsp coarsely ground kosher salt

1. Preheat oven to 375 degrees. Line cookie sheets with parchment paper and set aside.

2. In a large mixing bowl, cream butter and sugars on high speed for about a minute. Add baking soda, fine kosher salt, eggs, vanilla, and peanut butter. Beat until well combined. Add flour and combine well. Stir in the chocolate chunks.

3. Scoop the cookies into generous Tablespoon mounds on the prepared cookie sheets. Wet your fingers and press the dough down to flatten it a bit. Sprinkle each mound lightly with the coarsely ground kosher salt.

4. Bake the cookies for about 10 minutes or until golden brown and cooked through. Cool on the cookie sheets for about 2 minutes, and then remove them to a cooling rack to cool completely. (If you can wait that long! I never do....) This recipe makes about 2 dozen cookies, depending on the size of the cookies.

S'mores Bars

Adapted and used with permission from Julia M Usher's "Cookie Swap: Creative Treats to Share throughout the Year"

Graham Cracker Crust

2 ¼ cups graham cracker crumbs (15-17 crackers, finely ground in a food processor)

¼ cup granulated sugar

2 Tbsp firmly packed dark brown sugar

6 Tbsp melted butter

Fudge Brownie Filling

6 ounces unsweetened chocolate, chopped

2 sticks plus 2 Tbsp butter, cut into Tbsp pieces

2 ½ cups granulated sugar

5 large eggs, lightly beaten

2 tsp pure vanilla extract

1 ¾ cup all purpose flour

Topping

1 ½ cups coarsely chopped pecans

2 cups mini marshmallows

1. Preheat oven to 350 degrees. Line a 10x15x2 inch baking dish with foil (sometimes called a roasting pan), leaving a 1 inch overhang around the top edge of the pan. Lightly coat the foil with cooking spray.

2. Prepare the graham cracker crust. Combine the graham cracker crumbs and sugars in a small bowl. Gradually add the melted butter until the crumbs just hold together when squeezed in your palm. Press the mixture into an even layer on the bottom of the prepared pan; it will be about ¼ inch thick. Run a smooth-bottomed measuring cup over the crust to pack and level it.

3. Mix the fudge brownie filling. Combine the chocolate and butter in a large bowl that fits a double boiler. Place the bowl over barely simmering water and stir as needed until the chocolate and butter are melted. Remove from heat and whisk in the sugar, followed by the beaten eggs and vanilla. Stir in the

flour, mixing until smooth. Pour the batter on top of the graham cracker crust and level it with a small off set spatula.

4. Scatter the chopped pecans evenly over the batter. Bake for 30-35 minutes or until a cake tester inserted in the brownie center comes out with dark, damp crumbs on it. Do not over bake. Set the pan on a wire rack and cool completely.

5. Distribute the marshmallows evenly over the top and place the pan under the broiler for about a minute or until the marshmallows are puffy and golden brown. Watch it very carefully and rotate the pan as necessary to brown them evenly and prevent burning. Cool it long enough for the marshmallows to be firm enough to cut.

6. Remove the brownie from the pan in one block by gently pulling up on the foil. Place it directly onto a cutting board. Remove all foil and trim any uneven edges before cutting into 2 inch squares. Enjoy the gooey goodness of a s'more without the fire!

Raspberry Truffle Brownie Bars

Adapted and used with permission from Julia M Usher's "Cookie Swap: Creative Treats to Share throughout the Year"

Don't be scared. There are three separate steps to this recipe, but it's worth it!

Cocoa Shortbread Crust

1 ½ cups plus 3 Tbsp all purpose flour
½ cup granulated sugar
3 Tbsp unsweetened cocoa powder
¼ tsp salt
1 ½ sticks (3/4 cup) softened butter
1 large egg yolk

Raspberry Brownie Filling

6 Tbsp butter, cut into 6 pieces
6 ounces semisweet chocolate chips
3 ounces unsweetened chocolate, chopped
½ cup granulated sugar
3 large eggs, room temperature, lightly beaten
4 ½ Tbsp Chambord or other premium raspberry liqueur (optional)
2 tsp pure vanilla extract
¾ cup all purpose flour
¾ cup seedless red raspberry jam, stirred to loosen

Raspberry Truffle Glaze

8 ounces semisweet chocolate chips
¾ cup heavy cream (cannot substitute milk or ½ and ½)
1 Tbsp light corn syrup
1 Tbsp Chambord or other premium raspberry liqueur

1. Preheat oven to 350 degrees. Line the bottom and sides of a 9x13x2 pan with foil, leaving a 1 inch overhang around the top edge of the pan. Lightly coat the foil with cooking spray.

2. Mix the cocoa shortbread crust. Combine the flour, sugar, cocoa powder, and salt in a medium bowl. Using a fork or your hands, work in the butter and egg yolk until the mixture is

464

uniformly moistened and crumbly. Press the dough into an even layer on the bottom of the greased pan. It should be about ¼ inch deep. Bake the crust 14 to 15 minutes or until dull on top and slightly puffy but still soft. Do not over bake. Transfer the pan and crust to a wire rack while you prepare the filling.

3. Prepare the raspberry brownie filling. Melt the butter, semisweet and unsweetened chocolate in a double boiler. Stir as needed until just smooth and melted. Remove from heat and gently whisk in granulated sugar followed by the eggs, Chambord, and vanilla. Stir in the flour, mixing just until smooth and shiny. Do not over mix or the batter may break. Pour the batter on top of the crust and spread into an even layer. Spoon the jam evenly over the top and spread it into a thin layer that completely covers the brownie filling.

4. Bake the brownies for about 20 minutes. Watch them carefully – don't over bake them. When they're done, they'll be set through to the middle and slightly puffed around the edges. A cake tester inserted into the center will come out with very damp crumbs on it. Transfer to a wire rack and cool completely before glazing.

5. Prepare and apply the raspberry truffle glaze. Place the chocolate chips in a bowl so they form a shallow layer. Pour the cream into a stainless steel saucepan and bring it to just below the boiling point; steam will rise from it, but no bubbles should break on the surface. Pour it over the chocolate chips and let is sit for a few minutes, then whisk until it's completely melted. Stir in the corn syrup and Chambord. Pour the mixture over the brownie. Gently tilt or shake the pan so it completely coats the top.

6. Set the pan in the refrigerator for 1 ½ to 2 hours or until the topping is firm enough to cut cleanly. Conversely, if it's chilled too much it will harden.

7. Remove the brownies from the pan in one block by gently pulling up on the foil overhang and place directly on a cutting board. Remove all foil and trim any uneven edges before cutting the block into 2 inch squares. Serve at room temperature and be sure to lick your fingers.

23376614R00260

Made in the USA
Middletown, DE
23 August 2015